THE DRAGON THE EAGLE AND THE JAGUAR

RODGER CARLYLE

This is a work of fiction. The names, characters, entities, and events are products of the author's imagination and bear no relation to any living person or are used fictitiously.

THE DRAGON, THE EAGLE, AND THE JAGUAR. Copyright © 2024 by Rodger Carlyle. All rights reserved.

Library of Congress Control Number: 2024919701

Published in the United States by Verity Books, an imprint of Comsult, LLC, Anchorage, Alaska. Inquiries may be directed to comsultalaska@gmail.com.

All rights reserved. Except for brief passages quoted in newspaper, magazine, radio, television or online reviews, no portion of this book may be reproduced, distributed, or transmitted in any form or by any means, electronic or mechanical including photocopying, recording, or information storage or retrieval systems without the prior written permission of the author and/or Comsult, LLC.

First published in 2025.

ISBN 978-1-960268-10-5 (paperback)
ISBN 978-1-960268-11-2 (e-book)

Cover design and interior design by Damonza

BOOKS BY RODGER CARLYLE

The Team Walker Series

The Eel And The Angel
The Shadow Game
The Dragon, The Eagle And The Jaguar

The Gritt Family Series

Tempest North
Two Civil Wars
Enemy Patriots
The Opposite Of Trust

Nonfiction

Awake
Still Common Sense

MAJOR CHARACTERS

JUAN AYALA has spent his entire life in Mexico's organized crime and the drug trade. Currently, he is one of three partners working to corner Mexico's fentanyl business. His experience and enforcer mentality make him the perfect front for the new cartel. His only weakness is his daughter, his only living relative.

LUIS CARDENAS is a renowned successful Mexican businessman and a partner in the cartel trying to corner the fentanyl trade with the US. As the business mind behind the cartel, Cardenas' accountants and attorneys have carefully hidden his illegal activities. Driven by greed, he dreams of becoming the puppeteer pulling the strings of Mexican power.

COMMANDER CHAD GRITT is a fast-track Naval Officer with a PhD in electronics who leads a research team at the US Navy's Farragut Technical Analysis Center. The six foot tall, sandy blond hair, blue eyed, Gritt has become a "go to" for the DC intelligence community trying to figure out complex crises. Most comfortable in a lab environment, he is regularly challenged by the kind of field work that can get him killed.

HAO SUN is a colonel in China's PLA-2 human intelligence service. Hao uses his assignment in Mexico to enrich himself through drug and human smuggling. His ultimate dream however is to use the wealth and that of Chinese allies to replace government leadership that he believes is betraying Chinese opportunity for world dominance.

LIEUTENANT DIEGO CERVANTES is an officer in Mexico's Marine Corps who leads a small detachment in the beautiful resort community of Zihuantanejo, Mexico. Incorruptible, and from a wealthy family, the 30-year old officer is determined to help stop the senseless crime and killing surrounding the drug trade on Mexico's west coast.

MAJOR OLGA TVORSHIK is a security specialist assigned to America's most high-risk, high-profile Air Force base. Born in Russia and a naturalized US citizen, Olga's sixth sense of identifying threats has launched her career. Tall, blond and stunning, her professional reputation for toughness keeps the wolves away, leading to a lonely life until she is matched with Chad Gritt on a project. But it's hard to maintain a relationship with another officer stationed hundreds of miles away.

MARIA CASTILLO is the daughter of a drug lord who was murdered after being captured by the DEA. She owns a freight company built from the ashes of her father's empire. To avenge his death, she is coaxed into an alliance with the new cartel. She becomes Mexico's most beloved philanthropist, and the cartel's candidate to replace Mexico's president.

THADIUS "THAD" WALKER is a retired CIA field operator. His extraordinary career and reputation make him one of the few people outside the agency who the CIA director calls when he has especially thorny problems. Walking with a cane, his Gordon Setter always at his side, all Thad wants to do is enjoy hunting and fishing from his small Montana lakeside bungalow. But who can ignore the request for help from the nation's top spy?

SONIA RAMIREZ is Thad's well-to-do neighbor who recently retired after a long and successful undercover career with the DEA. Widowed and alone, she and Thad find that their shared career experiences allow them to understand each other's perspectives and backgrounds. When Thad gets a call to help understand why China would send sophisticated weapons to drug cartels in Mexico, she volunteers her years of experience to help. Warm waters, hot sun, and beautiful beaches entice them.

GINA SANTOS is an attorney and deputy to the attorney general of Mexico. Her specialty is pulling together tiny pieces of information to create profiles that allow the Mexican Government to tackle organized crime. Her frustrations rise as corrupt courts often fail to convict her targets, which makes the offer to work in a clandestine Mexican-American team put together to stop illegal weapons shipments impossible to turn down.

PREFACE

August 12, On the Pacific Ocean halfway between Zihuantanejo and Manzanillo, Mexico

"Steer 315 degrees," ordered Mexican Naval Commander José Alfaro, staring at a faint blip on the radar. The twin Caterpillar diesel engines began to spool up as he increased speed. He was in the third day of searching for a reported drug smuggler running north toward the Baja Peninsula and eventually the coast of the United States. If it was out there at all, the craft would be riding on the sea surface with only a tiny glass enclosed cockpit and cylindrical air intake above the water. Perhaps the so-called vessel sighted from the air had been a whale.

The report had come from a MH-65 Dolphin helicopter operated by the US Coast Guard patrol ship further out in the Pacific, running along the curve of the Mexican coastline. The helicopter had been at its maximum range when it made the report and was unable to verify the sighting or close in on the target. There had been no further sightings.

Mexico's newly elected president had reversed the 'Abrazos, No Balazos,' also known as 'Hugs Not Bullets' drug cartel policy of her predecessor but had quietly ordered the Mexican navy to assist their northern neighbors with drug interdiction again.

The previous president believed that government confrontation of the cartels just fueled more violence in Mexico. His policy seemed to work for the first half of his six-year term but then the violence exploded again, especially west and south of the country and around Mexico City, where the chief executive resides.

The lookouts on the wings of the bridge of the Montezuma, a Tenochtitlan class patrol boat, trained their binoculars directly in front of the racing boat. José ordered the crew to battle stations. Within minutes the twin 12.7mm machine gun mounts were manned. The rest of the nineteen man crew secured watertight hatches and prepared the small jet powered skiff for sending boarders to the target, if it was there at all.

"Captain, there's a disturbance in the sea surface about two miles out," called one of the lookouts. "It's about ten degrees to port."

José moved a couple of feet to the right to give him a clear view. There certainly was something moving out there, leaving a small wake, traveling northwest. He adjusted the course to intercept whatever it was. Within three minutes his blood pressure began to surge as a translucent dome above a dark shape in the water became clear. It was a shape he'd never seen before, manmade, and traveling faster than previous sightings. He ordered a reduction in speed.

"I want both guns to fire in front of that craft," he ordered. "Rip up the surface of the water. Let them know we are here. Be prepared to launch the skiff and board her when she surfaces."

The water in front of the dome erupted as more than a hundred bullets from the machine guns shredded the surface. "She's surfacing," called one of the lookouts, "something obvious to everyone not below deck."

"Engines to idle," ordered José. "Prepare to launch the skiff." He turned to the only other crewman who spoke English. "Radio the American Cutter Mansfield that we are preparing to board the submarine. Ask them to send the helicopter to film the boarding."

As he waited for the Montezuma to lose speed, the submarine continued to surface, revealing a second metal bubble behind the observation dome.

The patrol craft was approaching slowly when the metal bubble opened like a clam shell and a man rose holding a long tube. Seconds later, a flame burst from the tube and some kind of missile began to accelerate toward the Montezuma. There wasn't time to shout a warning before the missile hit the ship only inches to the left of the bow and plowed two thirds of the way through the vessel before detonating in the engine room. The Montezuma rose out of the water as the explosion burst through the hull. The men manning the machine guns as well as the lookouts were tossed like dolls into the sea. On the bridge, men were thrown against the consoles. José slammed the overhead with his shoulder before crashing down on the compass pedestal. His radioman lay in a pool of blood, a jagged hole in his skull. The young ensign at the chart table lay unmoving, as did the radar operator. Only the quartermaster who had somehow stayed glued to the wheel seemed unhurt.

Splashing back into the sea, the ship began to list to port as water poured into the hull. Below decks, those who could, raced for the safety of the open deck, helping the wounded.

Picking himself up, wiping blood from his face, José took only seconds to shake off the shock of what had just happened. The Montezuma was still afloat but listing badly. He pulled himself toward the radios using whatever hand holds he could find, his left leg dragging. *Thank God,* he thought, as he checked the radio frequency; it was still dialed into the American ship's frequency and the lighted dial indicated that there was still power.

"Mansfield, Mansfield, Mansfield. Mayday, mayday, mayday.

This is the Mexican vessel Montezuma. We have been hit by some kind of missile and are taking on water. We have casualties." He stood for what seemed minutes, waiting for an answer.

"Montezuma, Montezuma, this is Captain Paul Thompson. We are on our way. Our helicopter is only ten minutes out. They have a life raft and emergency swimmer on board."

"Captain Thompson, this is Commander José Alfaro. Is the helicopter armed? We'd appreciate it if he would sink that bastard that just attacked my ship. It appears to be a semi-submersible moving north at about fifteen knots." José paused to hear a damage report from his second officer, and then continued. "We're still afloat and will be deploying our skiff if it's undamaged." José looked out to the starboard wing of the bridge where two of his crew were deploying a raft. "Mansfield, we are launching our boat and rafts."

"I'll notify the chopper to be ready to engage."

José and his quartermaster each lifted wounded shipmates, dragging them to a life raft that was already in the water. The effort was excruciating for the Mexican commander, his leg obviously broken. He paused as his crew chief pulled the damaged skiff alongside. "We have four dead for sure," the twenty year veteran called out. "The engine room is fully flooded, and nobody got out. The other raft was destroyed."

José looked in the boat and saw two other men bandaging a crewmate whose left thigh was pumping blood into a mix of saltwater and fuel sloshing back and forth. Three automatic rifles lay in the boat. "If I give you two more men, can you go kill the bastards who attacked us?"

"Probably not, sir. A piece of steel hit the gas tank and it's leaking like a sieve. Besides, we don't dare fire a weapon with all that leaked fuel."

"Then use what fuel you have to find the four men who

were thrown overboard." The boat pulled away just as José heard approaching engines. Moments later, the American helicopter hovered over the Montezuma. A self-inflating raft dropped from the door only feet from where their own raft bobbed with four men aboard.

José slid to an open spot on the deck and pointed north. The tail of the helicopter swished back and forth before the pilot turned, racing toward where José was directing him. He watched it swing to the right to allow his door gunner to fire on the drug craft, now more than a mile away. Suddenly, there was another flash from the submarine. He watched in horror as a missile smashed into the American helicopter which erupted into a fireball and plummeted into the sea.

August 16, Sierra Pinta Mountains on the Arizona border

Sargent Paul Thibs watched three men and a woman cross the border from a quarter mile away. Fifteen minutes earlier, a pickup truck had dropped the four off and then raced back to where it came from. Unlike most of the illegals he'd seen at this crossing, each of the four carried identical backpacks, had multiple water canteens, and no personal luggage. Their leader turned to them and pointed to his cell phone, which Thibs surmised were now turned off, making them impossible to track. Against the reflective surface of the desert, visibility under the light of a full moon was almost as good as daylight.

"I have the targets about four hundred yards in front of my position," he called into his radio. "That tip by phone appears to be legit. Each is carrying a pack. Carlos, you and Moss move toward the border and cut off their escape." Thibs knew that the two agents furthest from his position would close on the border and then move in behind the targets.

"Rayner and Roberts, you are cleared to make the intercept. I see no weapons."

To Thibs' left and right, agents moved quietly from their hides and closed in on the illegal crossers, now only two hundred yards from where he waited. Malcom Roberts to his right stepped from behind a scrub cactus patch and pointed his rifle at the crossers.

"*Alto!* Federal agents. You're under arrest."

The man furthest from Roberts turned to run. He hadn't gone ten yards before Bonnie Rayner, Thibs' youngest agent stepped from behind a rock and threw a shoulder into the runner, knocking him flat. She grabbed the young man, surprised to see an Asian face and pulled him to his feet. She folded his right arm behind him and pushed him back to where her partner had lined the other three up against a rocky desert cliff.

"Roberts and Rayner have the targets in custody," said Thibs. "Close and give them a hand." He slipped from behind the rock pile at the top of a hill and began to jog. He'd only covered twenty yards when he heard the first shot, followed by three more in quick succession. At the bottom of the hill, bodies were slammed against the cliff and then thrown to the ground.

"For God's sake, don't fire!" screamed Thibs, now on a dead run.

"It's not us," he heard Roberts say. "The shots came from across the border. I'm on my stomach moving toward the targets. They're all down and I think Bonnie's hit."

Thibs watched as two motorcycles raced from a saddle in the hills on the Mexican side of the border. Common sense dictated that he follow Roberts' lead and use what cover was available to close in on the targets but hearing that their youngest rookie might be wounded made that impossible. Thibs slid to a stop where Bonnie lay, seeing a hole the size of a golf ball in her chest where a bullet meant for the man she had apprehended, passed through him and then through her bulletproof vest, killing her instantly. The four "mules" had similar gaping wounds.

"My God," screamed Roberts as the last two agents crept into the opening. "What in the hell was that?" The look on Thibs face made it clear that their colleague was beyond help."

"Four shots in less than ten seconds, from more than five hundred yards," said the oldest of the agents, Carlos Ayala. "Probably a Barrett fifty caliber semi-automatic. Whoever was shooting knew what they were doing. Our guys in Iraq were that good. I heard them start their bikes within seconds of the last shot. They'll be miles from here in minutes." He looked down at Bonnie and wiped his eyes. He reached down and tugged a pack from a Chinese looking man, dead at his feet and opened it. Inside were large zip-lock bags of pink pills. "Looks like fentanyl, maybe ten thousand pills. Could be more. There's enough here to poison a small city."

"This is the second time this month we received a phone tip that someone was smuggling fentanyl in this sector," said Thibs. "Last week we found an old Dodge Ram in flames with five bodies inside. We're now part of a war between rival cartels."

"This time they killed one of us," said Roberts.

"With the change in presidents, the Mexican marines have been cracking down on drug shipments moving north. Even the Mexican army with its history of corruption seems to have gotten the message. It appears that the Sinaloa and CJNG cartels were serious about getting out of the fentanyl business. They've been tipping off the Mexican authorities about their competition and now they appear to be doing the same here. They kill them just to prove that they're serious."

As Thibs called for helicopter support, Carlos slipped his camera from his vest and took pictures of the scene and each of the dead couriers. "Two Asians, maybe Chinese, maybe in their early thirties. The other two are probably from Central America, younger, maybe late teens. This is a different set-up from just a few months ago, but whoever is running this op needs to tighten up their security. Whoever tipped off their competition knew exactly where they would cross."

"Maybe," said Thibs as he pulled a jacket from his pack and draped it over Bonnie's face. "Or even better, we need to find a way to share intel with whoever is betraying these people and then give them the weapons to fight it out on their side of the border."

Thibs looked at the faces of his remaining agents before adding, "I don't want that repeated. I didn't mean it."

September 1, Manzanillo, Mexico

The plain white rented Toyota Corolla rolled to a stop just outside a dilapidated chain-link fence surrounding a small metal warehouse. "That truck pulled in here a couple of hours ago," said Maria. "It stayed long enough to unload and then headed back for the highway."

She opened the passenger door and stepped into the dust next to a hole in the fence. Behind her, Angie and Carolyn followed as she crept up to the filthy window on the side of the building. Anna waited in the driver's seat, engine idling.

"I can't believe we followed that truck all the way from Oaxaca. The drivers must have switched off sleeping and driving," said Angie.

"That's what we did," replied Carolyn.

"Silencio," whispered Maria as the three took turns peering through the glass. Moments later they were retracing their footsteps.

"What do you see?" asked Anna. "Are the crates from that truck inside?"

"The place is full of crates. There are two men feeding animals and washing out crates. In the back of the building two more men are loading crates into a big Conex."

"We actually figured out how the smugglers are getting the animals out of the country," added Carolyn, as they quietly closed the doors of the Toyota and pulled away.

"Your own federal government estimates that the illegal exotic species trade here in Mexico might exceed the drug business," said Maria. She turned to the two girls in the back seat. "When we discussed this at school last spring, I didn't think you guys were serious about coming down here to do something about it."

"If the authorities in your country won't do anything, then we have to. I just told my parents that you invited us for a quick tour of your country," said Anna. "I'm glad we came."

Both Carolyn and Angie nodded their heads.

"I don't think it's a good idea for four college girls to just barge in there and demand that they free the animals. Hell, we saw snakes, monkeys, and even cats and birds go on that truck a couple of days ago. If they just open the crates, some of them will eat the others," said Anna.

"We need to get help," said Maria. "The same people who traffic drugs dominate the illegal animal trade in Mexico. Walking into that building might get us all killed."

"So now what?" asked Carolyn.

Maria pulled out her phone and began scrolling. "There is an office of the Policia Federal in town, only a couple of miles from here. We need to tell them what we just saw." She stared at her phone. "There's a station of the local police on the other side of the port, but I don't trust them."

It was after eight when Anna finally pulled into the parking lot of the Policia Federal. "Come on," said Maria, "we all saw this. I want the authorities to believe that we have spent a week tracking the monkeys we first saw in that shop in Oaxaca. I don't want this swept under the rug. With four witnesses, two from notable American families, they won't dare."

"It's your country, Maria. We probably should have developed a plan," said Anna.

"I think we just got caught up in this," said Carolyn. "I personally didn't think we would find anything."

Maria approached the desk while the other girls waited just inside the door. Two minutes later they were all escorted into the office of a sergeant. "Sergeant Gomez believes our story," said Maria, relief showing in her face. I gave him the spelling of our names, but he wants to know our ages, home addresses and where we're staying in Mexico for his report." She handed each of the girls a pad and pen.

"I told him that it looked like they were preparing to ship containers of animals. He agrees that it would be best if he could organize a raid on the warehouse tonight. He's asked us to wait in the lobby in case his lieutenant has any questions."

Thirty minutes later Gomez emerged from his office, a big smile on his face.

"He says he already has two patrol cars watching the warehouse. He wants to know if we would like to observe the raid."

The four University of Arizona students followed Gomez back to the warehouse. They watched one officer jog to the back of the building and then Gomez and one other race through the front door, guns drawn. Inside they heard two shots and a minute later, Gomez walked out in front of the building and waved for them to come in. "You're responsible," he called. "Come see."

The girls followed him inside where five smugglers stood, hands over their head. Gomez pointed toward a stack of animal cages. "He wants to know if those are the cages we saw loaded up in Oaxaca."

As the girls started to move, the smugglers dropped their hands and surrounded them. "What the hell?" screamed Maria.

One of the men, a tall guy with a carefully clipped short beard, ran his hand across Carolyn's cheek and smiled. "You should mind your own business," he said. He turned to Gomez while pulling out a banded roll of bills and peeled off thirteen hundred-dollar bills, handing four to each of the patrolmen and five to Gomez. "Gracias mi amigo," he offered as two of the officers headed for the door.

Carolyn broke out of the circle and raced for the open door. A shout from Gomez caused an officer to spin. He caught her by her long red hair and jerked her off her feet, slamming her to the concrete floor. Pulling her back to her feet he then pushed her toward the other smugglers who were greatly enjoying body searching the girls. They took their cell phones and everything but the clothes they wore and pushed them into an empty crate and slammed the door shut.

All the time, Maria was screaming at the man with the beard. He screamed back. "You wait there while we figure this out."

The girls sat stunned against the padded walls of the pitch black container. Finally, Carolyn spoke. "We are valuable. They will probably hold us for ransom." She looked over toward where she thought Anna was seated. "Don't worry. If your parents can't afford it, my parents will help. I'm sure Angie's parents can help too."

Before her last word sunk in, Maria lifted her head. "I'm not so sure that's what they have in mind. If we get out of here, we can lead the authorities back to this warehouse."

Almost prophetically the door opened. One of the bandits stood aiming some kind of small rifle at the girls. "Move back," he ordered.

The girls stood against the back wall as three men began

stacking boxes, water bottles and piles of blankets and pillows along one wall. They rolled in a barrel, half of a fifty-five gallon drum with a toilet seat attached to the top. Finally, the man with the beard set two electric lanterns and a dozen spare batteries next to the boxes.

"How long are you going to keep us in here?" cried Angie.

"One month," he replied.

"We can't survive in this crate for a month," screamed Anna.

"Crate come from China with eight girls."

"Oh my God," murmured Carolyn.

"One redhead, two blondes, and one feisty Mexican girl, all young and pretty. You will make some rich Chinese businessmen very happy." He paused as he watched the realization sweep their faces. "You're lucky, the ship you go on is fast. Maybe if you please the crew, they let you out once in a while. Our Chinese partners already sold you for five thousand dollars each."

CHAPTER 1

October 2, Zihuatanejo, Mexico

Hao Sun's trip to Mexico City had become routine. But the added link from Mexico's capital to the resort community of Ixtapa-Zihuatanejo added three hours to an already exhausting trip. His Turkish Airlines flight from Beijing arrived late. He'd rushed to his Mexico City hotel booked an afternoon flight on Aeromexico to Zihua using his personal Scotia Bank credit card.

The first leg of the trip was covered by the Chinese government. An operative of 2PLA, the China's military human intelligence agency, with the assignment of developing intelligence assets in Mexico, his official budget was more than adequate. But the abacus army that tracked expenses was very capable of bouncing his expenses for side trips, and worse, reporting unusual activity to his boss, General Ling. As a naval officer with the rank of captain, nothing would upset Hao's career faster than Ling questioning his activities, especially after the face-to-face meeting Ling had ordered only months before.

Since he'd cleared customs in Mexico City, now carrying only a small overnight bag, he was outside Zihua's small airport terminal in ten minutes. There he found a cab driver holding a sign with his name, and soon after, was watching the setting sun flicker through the tops of coconut palms that lined the highway to Zihua. He and the driver hadn't spoken, which was a positive since his Spanish was terrible and he had no idea where his meeting was.

The driver wound his way through the streets of the picturesque village, finally stopping in front of an open-air restaurant with a dozen tables and a patio kitchen. Hao didn't bother to pay the driver as he entered the restaurant, stopping in front of a two-man band playing an electric piano and a guitar. A cover of a Carlos Santana tune was welcome, the rhythm helping to keep his droopy eyes open. To his left, a man in a soft blue linen shirt waved. He was seated with a second man that Hao recognized. It took only seconds to pick out four bodyguards seated at two other tables. Parked across the street was a white Chevy Suburban with two more men Hao assumed were also there to protect that second man.

Both men rose and extended their hand as Hao approached the table. "How was the trip?" Luis Cardenas was at most five feet eight inches tall, and slight of build with greying hair and black framed glasses over eyes that never smiled. He was a businessman with interests in chemicals and transportation, and more recently in natural gas production. The capital for his ventures came from other activities.

"Long, but we needed to meet," answered Hao. He turned to the second man, dressed in jeans and a silver snap up cowboy shirt. This man, Juan Ayala, was taller, older and greying except for a carefully trimmed jet-black mustache and beard. "I'm sorry to interrupt your fishing trip," said Hao as he shook his hand.

The tiny restaurant would have American and Canadian tourists who might understand the only common language of the three men, English. But the corner table they occupied was only feet from the musicians who believed in the adage that if you can't play well, play loud.

The restaurant owner, a big man with a ponytail dressed in a white shirt and black jeans arrived moments later and left with an order for three margaritas and instructions not to hurry dinner, which would be fresh Dorado filets from a fish that Juan had dropped off earlier that evening.

"Your call on Tuesday indicated that you had two things to discuss," said Luis.

"Both may be troublesome," replied Hao and then he paused as the drinks arrived. He waited until the owner left. "When I was here three months ago, we discussed the problems brewing in the Chinese economy."

"I remember you being worried about a huge bubble crisis in the commercial real estate industry," said Luis.

"It's that and more. Our president built his foreign policy on China supplanting the Americans as the dominant economic and political force in the next century. It worked for the three of us. The men I work for have poured hundreds of millions of dollars into weakening America. The products and people you smuggle to the US create turmoil in that society and have led to growing violence, especially in their cities."

Juan finished his first drink and dumped the remaining ice into the one that had just arrived. "We also hep' you get people across the border mi amigo. Some jus' to make more money but I suspect some sent to the states with other missions."

"True," replied Hao. "And you both have helped. Drugs, people, exotic animals, I hope that you have made a lot of money for your efforts."

"And based on what my accountants tell me, you have done fairly well yourself," added Luis. My firm has paid the two shell companies you set up in Mexico more than four million dollars in the past five years."

"All three of us have dealings that our governments should never know about," said Hao.

"All true," replied Luis. "But you didn't just fly across the Pacific Ocean to talk history."

Hao picked up his Margarita and downed it like a soda. "Our economy is much worse off than I originally thought. The Americans have been pulling their manufacturing from China. Foreign investment is drying up. The money borrowed to finance the massive real estate boom that drove our economy is coming due and the buildings that were to be full are empty. There is unrest in cities where thousands are losing their jobs."

Luis rested both elbows on the table and motioned for Hao to continue.

"My country has switched directions. I was told that for the near future, there will be no direct confrontation with America, no actions against the United States that can be traced back to China. The leadership may even postpone the invasion of Taiwan. The authorities in China are moving to stop the illegal shipment of drugs. Our current supplier, who probably makes more on his other manufacturing anyway is shutting down our supply lines. While we will maintain our policy of developing China into the world power we should be, we will do it without directly challenging America. For now," he added.

"You don' seem happy by that," said Juan.

"I'm not, and hundreds of other men who have spent their lives positioning my country for its rightful place in the world are just as pissed. There are a lot of military officers who think the momentary problems in our economy do not justify this change.

Many workers and groups they belong to are angry. There is a faction in my country that believe that substantial change in my government is needed, leadership change. The pronouncements from our current leadership that the only thing that has changed is the timeline rings false."

"In Mexico," started Luis, "the last president embraced the investments that China has made here, especially in the petroleum industry where he has seized much of the power that private companies held over oil and natural gas. Our investment in the new fertilizer plant using the natural gas Chinese companies helped find near our southern border, will start paying in the next couple of months. Our strategy of shipping pills from your supplier through the routes you've set up and sending cash to pay suppliers by burying piles of dollars in containers of fertilizer is ready to go." Luis paused and stared at Hao. "Hell, I never wanted to be in the fertilizer business, there's not enough money in it."

"Don't bitch Luis, my Chinese partners put up all the money through their Bank of Hangzhou."

Luis just laughed. "It's our money. We send you piles of cash. Your country's weak banking laws make it legitimate. You all keep your cut on top of what we pay for product, then bank the balances for us. If there will be any product in the future."

Juan waved to the bartender across the patio, ordering more drinks. His face was ashen. He pointed his finger at Hao's nose before speaking. "I worked four years to build an organization that can quietly compete with the two major cartels. We stay out of most of the products they provide, no meth, no heroin, specializing in safe fentanyl pills you supply us. The profits from fentanyl are ten times that of meth and heroin. We don' need a big organization. We send twenty people across the border every week with backpacks. If half get through, we make ten million dollars. Now you tellin' me we're goin' out of business?"

"Juan, calm down," said Luis. "We got problems too. The Sinaloa and CJNG cartels are both becoming paranoid over fentanyl. The Americans are threatening to send their army into Mexico to stop it. It's almost like the cartels have become agents of the Americans. And we still move people and animals."

Juan shook his head in disbelief. "If they get out of the business, there is just more for us. The other business, you know screaming migrants, stinking animals and human trafficking is just a sideline. The money is in fentanyl." He paused as he made the sign of the cross.

"The cartels bribed one of our men who coordinates the border mules. His wife and children died before I slit his throat. I spent days in church begging forgiveness. And now our supplier tells us that we are done."

"I didn't fly halfway across the world to tell you we are done," replied Hao. "We are just going to have to change some things. One of my allies owns a small chemical company that is willing to supply powdered fentanyl and actinomycin in powdered form to cut it with. I can arrange to ship you pill presses. You will have to mix the two to make your own pills, but other than that nothing changes. Just get the mix right, we don't want to kill our customers. Dead addicts can't raise hell with American governments." He paused to study the faces of his companions.

"The tacit support from my government, from the Chinses military, has ended, but between allies making lots of money and those who are beginning to press for regime change, we have friends."

He sipped from his second drink.

"But we must be very discreet. If my government finds out that we are still in this business, I will be dead, and they will probably inform your government. People who oppose or even disagree with the government of China disappear."

"Speaking of people disappearing, I had to discipline some of our people in Manzanillo a couple of weeks ago. They caught some American girls spying on a shipment of animals to China. They put them in a container and sent them to Shandong." He smiled at Hao. "It appears that some of your partners were willing to pay for new toys." He paused a moment. "They should have killed them and disposed of the bodies. If any of them get picked up by the authorities in China, it could blow our operation wide open. At least they were smart enough to dump their car into the ocean."

"I'll see what I can do to make sure they aren't a risk," said Hao. "Whoever did this was thinking with his dick and not his head. The Chinese government's official position is to end the drug trade."

"That's not much of a worry here. The drug business represents between five and ten percent of the entire economy and puts food on the table for thousands of Mexicans," said Luis. "Between drugs and smuggling, especially exotic animals; the total might be more than that. Our last president wanted no war with the cartels. Hell, he boasted that he could travel anywhere in Mexico in safety."

"They aren't the risk," said Juan. "Last week Sinaloa intercepted another of my shipments. They kill four couriers and left a message that fentanyl to the US need to stop." Juan offered a cigar to each of his tablemates which they refused. Now we have a new president. That woman seems ready to go to war to stop the drug business. We shall see."

"I heard about your new president, but I didn't know about our competitors. They actually killed four of your people?" asked Hao.

"Not my people, two from Guatemala and two Chinese who agreed to be mules in return for cancelling their debt to their smugglers, to your friends. I made sure they weren't the gold star illegals you favor, just a couple of village kids from your country. I've lost a dozen in the last couple of months."

"I appreciate you not sending any of the trained operatives we've discussed. Still, there is a risk that the Chinese government will begin working with the Mexican government," said Hao. "With the unrest, my government is paying attention to immigration and especially to the disappeared here and in the states. They may ask your authorities for help. Your new president was a hard liner on crime in Mexico City, was she not?"

The three men stopped talking as dinner arrived, but both nodded their heads.

"There is a backlash against the new policies in my country," said Hao. "There are a lot of people who want to continue to weaken America. I'm one of them. We have a lot of money available. We got you new, fast, submersibles made in China and shipped in pieces labeled irrigation components. The controls in the Chinese military remain weak. We smuggled you advanced weapons. We have money available for what we need, and I have suppliers in China who want to become rich with foreign bank accounts. In Mexico it has always been possible to manage problems with enough money placed in the right hands."

"I'm not so sure that the woman running Mexico can be bought," said Luis. "I think she wants better relations with the Yankees. I know she considers herself the commander of Mexico, one who will not be ordered around or controlled. I read that she was furious that one of our transport submersibles wrecked a Mexican navy patrol boat and shot down an American helicopter. Our new President Martinez even appointed an American as a close policy advisor."

"Maybe we need a new president then," said Juan.

"I'm not sure that there is anyone waiting in the wings who would be any better for us," said Luis.

"In China, my friends, there are people who have begun grooming a successor for our current leader," said Hao. "Mexico is smaller, with fewer factions, and it has a population that understands and accepts money for favors. That same plan to groom and elect a leader who will favor the people and Mexico's friends rather than the Yankees could work here."

CHAPTER 2

October 3, Washington DC

Lieutenant Mike Stephens sat nervously in the small conference room adjacent to the office of the Director of the CIA. He'd heard that Mathew Chang tended to be overly brief, even gruff at times, especially when he thought someone was wasting his time. As a relatively low-level staff officer of the Farragut Center's Kennedy Maritime Analysis Group, a division of the Naval Office of Intelligence, ONI, he had been warned to be brief and concise by his boss, a full captain who wanted little to do with Chang.

The Kennedy Analysis Center was the ONI group tasked with adversary activities analysis, including foreign influence on maritime issues. That included counternarcotics. They also were tasked with planning actionable activities in the event of a crises. They offered analytics to the Navy, and to allied decision makers. It was in this capacity that Stephens was sitting nervously in Chang's meeting room.

The door opened and a graying man of medium height and

weight with a military style haircut dressed in a simple blue suit with a red power tie entered the room. The man offered a quick smile at Stephens, his face glowing for only a moment before he took a seat so quickly that Stephens couldn't rise to shake the hand the CIA director offered.

"Be at ease, Lieutenant," said Chang. "Over the last couple of years, I've had several briefings from ONI people and not one of them has been a waste of time."

"That's good to hear, sir," said Stephens. "Let me get right into it. Four days ago, I received a phone call from a Commander José Alfaro of the Mexican navy. He was calling from Puerto de Lazaro Cardenas on Mexico's Pacific coast. I'm not sure how he got our number. Alfaro was the captain of the Mexican patrol ship that was damaged the same day someone shot down a US Coast Guard helicopter. He spent several days in the hospital after the attack that killed five of his crew and all four men aboard the helicopter. He had just arrived at the small port where his wrecked ship had been beached after the American Cutter towed it to shore."

Stephens halted to give Chang, who was taking notes, a moment to catch up. "He was ordered there to see if he could offer any help to the Mexican authorities who had spent weeks pouring through the wrecked vessel trying to ascertain what kind of missile hit his ship and where it came from. In a nutshell, sir, after more than a month of analysis, they failed to nail it down." He paused again.

"I'm here to ask if the CIA could assist in the analysis. It's becoming critical since a second missile fired at an American Coast Guard ship hit its five-inch gun mount yesterday, killing four Coast Guardsmen. The semi-submersible they were tracking turned out to be capable of submerging, at least for a period. The commander of the Coast Guard ship ordered his helicopter to monitor the vessel from a distance since the aircraft has no defense against a surface to air missile. After the craft that fired the missile at his ship submerged, the helicopter closed and watched it for several minutes. It appeared to be under power and submerged slowly turning away from its original course. The water was clear. They submerged far enough to disappear."

Chang dropped his pen on the pad in front of him. "Lieutenant, what do you think we can do that the navy can't?"

Stephens wasn't quite ready for the question, so he paused a moment before answering. "Sir, a man you know well, Commander Chad Gritt with the Farragut Center, is planning to make a trip to the site. He said your group has more experience with forensic analysis. As you know, the Farragut Center is tasked with analysis of military hardware and those risks. They like to get their hands-on foreign weapons and analyze their potential. They have little experience in investigative forensics. He thought you might have someone who could help. He said that if we ran this up the flagpole some analysis group under your command might already be investigating how some pissant drug group in Mexico has acquired shoulder fired missiles capable of destroying a small ship."

"Did Gritt also tell you that I've been trying to recruit him for a couple of years now?" offered Chang with a laugh.

"No, sir, he just thought this might be the kind of threat that you needed to be aware of and probably fit your mission better than ours. He's not tasked with the kind of analysis the CIA specializes in, but he did mention that while the Mexican navy has by and large been beyond reproach, there is a lot of the Mexican government including some of their military that could be corrupt. Your people would know more about who to trust. This is not like someone selling them AK-47 rifles. They now have surface to surface missiles and surface to air missiles."

"Lieutenant, there is a small war going on in Mexico, one that appears to be between the bad drug dealers and the good drug dealers. Now there's an oxymoron. Gritt's right, someone appears to have the horsepower to source weapons that are almost impossible to find on the black market. That's all that I got in the five-minute brief before our meeting. The same people traffic humans, drugs and other contraband including exotic animals. They operate worldwide. We aren't the right agency to do damage assessment analysis, but I can task someone to go kick some cans on what our intelligence sources may be able to find on who has that horsepower." Chang started to rise.

"We're already talking to Mexico about trafficking. President Martinez has an advisor who used to be one of ours, although he didn't leave on the best of terms. Still, she has asked him to work with us on the trafficking issue. A cohesive illegal smuggling conglomerate with sophisticated weapons already exists in the Golden Triangle of Asia. We don't need another on our border. I'll have someone contact you by tomorrow with any ideas we have on the technical analysis. I'll also make sure that any direct intelligence on the weapons sourcing we come up with gets to you."

Chang rose, picking up his pad and turned toward the door to his office. "Tell Gritt to take a couple of days off while he's down there and enjoy some sun and the beach. That guy works all the time."

⁕

The next day Stephens met Gritt for lunch. "That Chang guy isn't so bad. He couldn't offer more than tasking those under his command to do some research. But he did have a Jana somebody call me this morning with a suggestion that the Bureau of Alcohol, Tobacco and Firearms would be a source for a scientist to help you on the Mexico trip. She said they don't have much on military weapons, but if they can get enough on the propellants or the explosives on the missile, they can probably figure out where they were manufactured."

"That woman, Jana, runs the agency's field operations. I'm sure she talked to the guy who runs the technical division before she called. You are getting whatever help Chang can arrange from their top people. I'm kind of surprised that the Kennedy Analysis Center doesn't have the kind of scientific staff we need."

"Kind of like your group, we're focused on the before, not the after. You still going to Mexico?"

"Yeah, but I've got a bunch to do this week. I'll be flying to San Diego on Saturday. With the attack on the Coast Guard cutter, this is becoming a big issue. The Navy is flying me directly to Mexico from there. I love that part of Mexico. Many of the cities on Mexico's Pacific Coast now look like San Diego, with everything focused on tourists. They've lost their cultural charm. Not the small places like Zihua. They pushed the high rises out ten miles from the village."

"Tough duty my friend," said Stephens. "What about finding someone from ATF to help?"

"I'll have my boss make that call," said Chad. "You know that director to director might get the bureaucracy moving faster than I can."

"I promised this José Alfaro that I would call him back," said Stephens. "What should I tell him?"

"I don't know Alfaro," said Gritt. "Tell him I'm looking forward to meeting him and that I should be in the area by Tuesday morning." Gritt paused as Stephens finished his sandwich. "A couple of years ago in San Diego, I met a guy at a meeting between the American and Mexican navy and marines. He was a hot-shit young marine captain who was stationed somewhere in the area. The guy was whip smart and more importantly he invited me to do some deep-sea fishing if I ever got down there. I think I'll give him a call. I have more leave coming than I'll ever use."

"Your old friend Chang recommended you go find a beach for a couple of days."

CHAPTER 3

October 6, Manzanillo, Mexico

Maria Castillo was still angry over how the invitation to the hotel in Manzanillo had been delivered. A woman who she'd never met followed her into the spa she visited every Wednesday and handed her a note from someone in her past, someone she never expected to hear from again, someone her father had relied on, but didn't trust. That would have been all right with Maria, but the note demanded that she leave that afternoon without notifying anyone, even her aging mother.

The note invited her to travel to Manzanillo from her home outside of Mexico City. It included a first-class air ticket, a reservation at one of Manzanillo's nicest hotels, and one thousand dollars US. The note simply read, Please join me for a meeting that will give you the revenge you seek and that will change your life forever. It had been signed by Juan Ayala, a former enforcer for the drug enterprise of her late father, an enterprise that had paid for her education at the University of Southern California and amazing lifestyle at the family home north of Manzanillo.

It was an enterprise that the Mexican government with the help of the American Drug Enforcement Agency had destroyed seven years before. Her father had been arrested and jailed in Mexico City where he was then murdered by someone from a rival gang. The authorities never figured out how the killer ended up in the prison, since there was no record of him ever being arrested.

The killer escaped from custody on his way to trial, the same day that Maria and her mother were informed by a corrupt police chief that their business had been 'sold' to a rival gang. They were 'allowed' to keep the legitimate transportation company that she now ran, but the drug business that provided most of their contracts was gone. They were advised to leave Manzanillo and that they could keep whatever they had in the bank, and the proceeds from the sale of their house. They were also given a bank book that showed that the three million dollars of proceeds from the sale of the business had been deposited into an account of a Canadian bank that operated throughout Mexico. It had been a classic Mexican offer of *plata o plomo* – silver or lead. Take it, shut up, or die.

She sipped on champagne found in the small refrigerator in the luxurious fantasy suite at the Las Hadas-Brisas hotel. It was a beautiful room, with an ocean view, but nothing like what her room had been like while growing up. While knowing that she was there for a reason, she was still startled by a knock at the door. Opening it, Ayala brushed past her carrying another bottle of champagne.

"Close the damn door and only speak English," he said.

"Juan, you do not boss me. You tried after papa died but failed. I am nobody's pawn."

"An' you still that spoiled brat," replied Ayala. "But you here Maria, and I know why you come. You cannot ignore the opportunity to avenge your father's death. An' I was right, you curious about changing your life. It must be hard to go from getting everything you want to havin' to earn a livin' like normal people."

"What do you want, Juan?"

"I want you to be president of Mexico and the most loved woman in the country."

Maria wasn't sure why she had been summoned, but Ayala shocked her. She carried her champagne to the bed and curled up on the pillows, her back pressed against the backboard. Even in shock, she was careful to tug her short skirt down as she sat.

Ayala's eyes never left her, even as he drained the champagne split, she had started into a second glass and moved to the overstuffed chair near the window. "You still drip sexy," he said. "Not beautiful like my Eugenia. Your father always worried that you attract wrong kind of man. Probably why you still not married in your thirties."

"I don't remember ever caring what you thought," replied Maria. "Now what is this all about, and why are we speaking English?"

"We are speaking English because I know that you will probably not believe what I'm going to discuss with you. So, after we meet, I'll send you down to Zihua to meet another man, a man from China who will verify my message, and while he don' speak Spanish, he also went to a fancy US school, and he speak English. After that there will be two parts to your life, and in the one you will discuss with me and my associates, we will only speak English to make sure that there is no mistrust."

"Your right, Juan, it's funny that I would trust you to defend my life, but not to plan it. Now quit talking in riddles."

"I dunno this word, riddle."

"Puzzles, codes, games. Anyway, what is this all about?"

"There are powerful forces here and in other countries that want Mexico to be truly independent, with political leaders who want poor Mexicans to be rich and don' give damn what the gringos think. In fact, those forces would like to see the US pushed into chaos like they do to us when they destroy people like your father."

"Juan, the Americans are always pushing their anti-drug efforts. Our last president offered them only tacit help. He refused to use his government to destroy people like my father."

"That was the last president. The new one, Lupita Martinez, is again helping the Americans. She is afraid that their threats to use their army are real. Even the big cartels are making war on the small suppliers, people only trying to help their villages, demanding they stop sending the most profitable drugs north."

"Maria finished her champagne and set the glass on the nightstand. "My father always said that we were just merchants, supplying products that the Americans demanded. I agree with that. As long as the Americans can't solve their addiction problems, someone will supply them and if that helps Mexicans live better, I'm all in favor of that."

"But our new president does not seem to share your feelings," said Juan, rising from his chair and opening the second bottle of champagne. He filled his own glass and then Maria's. "My friends and I want you to become the woman who all of Mexico dreams of as a generous mother. We want you to be the face of an effort to use enormous financial resources to make the lives of the people better. Over a relatively short period, we want you to be the people's choice to lead our country."

"Juan, you don't have the money to do something like this. In America there are huge groups of philanthropists dedicated to making lives better for people. They've been accumulating money for decades. They have more money than God. Here, our tradition of philanthropy is different. Much of our giving means people doing good deeds for others, not financial."

"I don' know that word you use, Maria. But in Mexico you can do for a dime what costs a dollar in the states. My friends have the money to fund the beginning of what we plan. Once we prove what we are doin' the big cartels will help. Your only job will be to do good for the people and do it very publicly. Once we make you president, you will refuse to help the Americans kill the goose laying the golden eggs. You will publicly announce just what you told me earlier. America can stop their addiction problems themselves."

Let's assume that I think this idea might work," replied Maria. "How will this help you and your friends and how can it help the cartels? Our newly elected president still has years to run on her term in office."

"That may not be true, Maria. The public part of this plan, the part that will be spoken of in Spanish might just change how Mexicans feel about their government and its leaders."

"And the English part of the plan, the accumulation of money and groups to manage and disperse it, won't there be a trail and large group of people who can figure out what we are doing? What if this leaks out? We will all be in prison."

"You need to discuss those concerns with my friend Hao Sun. You are a smart girl Maria, your father say you smartest in the family. Hao Sun is very smart, and he has many rich and powerful friends. When we succeed, maybe China will be Mexico's best friend."

"I think you are crazy," said Maria. "This whole thing seems crazy."

"Maria, the money come from rich Mexicans and rich Chinese. Part of the money will come from what we sell to the gringos. Eventually all of it from the gringos. We take it from them and use it to help Mexicans." He paused as he refilled their glasses, noticing that Maria's words did not match the look on her face.

"I have a small plane reserved that will fly you down to Zihua tomorrow morning. One of my partners will pick you up and take you to lunch with Hao. After lunch you will fly back here and tell me whether you are part of our plan or not. You need to know that Hao sees this as only a part of a larger plan and that if you ever disclose any of this, he will have you killed."

Maria began to laugh. "Even as a small child, I remember my father making similar statements when he was negotiating deals out by the pool. You do not frighten me, Juan."

CHAPTER 4

October 7, Zihuatanejo, Mexico

Luis Cardenas extended his hand to Maria as his chauffer opened the door to his black Mercedes. He had an aversion to airplanes and when possible, used his own car for relatively short trips. From his home in the capital the drive was less than eight hours. He and his driver had remained in Zihua after Juan flew off to Mexico City. The driver headed straight for Cardenas' luxurious penthouse suite in a five-story building he'd built years before.

"I am one of Juan's partners," he explained as they drove. "Years ago, I was one of the suppliers your father used for inert materials needed in his labs. Even then the man you are lunching with, Hao Sun, helped with supply. All of us knew and respected your father. We were all sorry about what happened to him and the business. We still owe him a debt for not disclosing our relationships."

Maria rode, deep in thought. A half hour later Luis's driver slid from his seat and opened the door for her. "Walk straight through the lobby to the elevator." He took out his cell phone and made a quick call. "Someone will meet you at the elevator and escort you to lunch with Hao Sun." He turned to face Maria. "You need to know that beyond working with us, coordinating supply and support, he is also an intelligence officer of his country. Anything more, you will have to discuss with him. Ask my butler to call when you are ready to fly back."

"You aren't having lunch with us?" asked Maria.

"No, better to leave you two alone. I have a shipment to coordinate." Luis hoped that was the right decision as he watched the striking woman cross the lobby.

"I guess I was expecting someone different," said Hao as Maria was escorted into a formal dining room overlooking the bay.

"I'm not quite sure how to respond to that."

"Someone more Mexican, maybe," he replied, "not a stunning five-foot eight blonde who looks like she is on her way to a photo shoot."

"Juan commented that I drip sexy," she offered. "I hate that description."

"He's wrong," said Hao as he lifted Maria's hand and kissed her fingers. "You are beautiful, sensual, which is kind of like sexy, but it includes confidence and intelligence and will last forever. Anyway, thank you for coming."

They shared only small talk until a lunch of shrimp sautéed in a mix of fruit and vegetables over white rice was placed in front of them by a maid who disappeared after serving.

"I am sure you have a lot of questions," started Hao. "Let me begin with how we make you rich with the resources to make you famous."

"Before we go there, tell me what the end game is. What is in it for you, your country, Mexico, and me?"

"Simple," a smiling Hao answered. "For me and our group, we will grow wealthier, but that isn't the important thing. On the world stage, Mexico and China will be stronger and America weaker. My country will take its rightful place of leadership in Asia. Mexico will no longer have to make policy based on what the Americans want. In both countries there will be leadership change. In Mexico, you will expand your economy with our help, including exporting to the United States. But you will do it as an equal."

Hao took a minute to organize his thoughts. "I tasked one of the students studying at your Universidad Nacional Autonoma de Mexico with preparing a little history. From the early 1500s through 1860 Mexico was basically ruled by Spain through the church. After the revolution in 1861 when the state nationalized most of the church's holdings, and a second revolution in 1920, the state became the dominant power. Mexico became paternalistic, the people dependent. Since 1960 a third period in your history has emerged. This one characterized by more citizen involvement, groups emerged to take on societal issues. This period shows promise, but suffers from one major weakness, the nation remains poor and over twenty percent of the population remains desperately poor."

"I never thought of our history in those terms," replied Maria, picking at her lunch. Inside she wondered how many of the thousands of Chinese students studying in Mexico were only students.

"You will lead Mexico into its fourth period. A strong leader will take away the Yankee influenced limits on the people. You will lead Mexico to manufacturing dominance, with our help, but at the same time eliminate the police controls over products that generate enormous profits. There will be new jobs and more importantly, capital accumulation that will transform Mexico.

The true democracy will be within the ruling party where people with a similar vision will compete to make a better life for the people."

"And in China, what will happen?" asked Maria.

"Our periods look different in that we have such a long history," said Hao. "But when this is done, our system will look almost identical to yours. Instead of one man's rule of our party, there will be a competition of ideas. But those ideas will transform a nation that a hundred years ago could be carved up by foreign powers, into one that no other nation dare influence."

"An interesting vision," replied Maria. "I'm not sure that I'm prepared to be the leader you are looking for. My story does not lend itself to the history books."

"Nonsense," replied Hao. "In this country few could have a better launching point. You are beautiful in a nation where women still prize that, and men respect it. You are educated. You are the daughter of a historic bandit who was crushed by the state and the Americans. You will be the center of attention as you accumulate great wealth and then use it to make lives better. People will sit in awe of one so generous. Soon you will pronounce a political philosophy that stresses economic growth creating true independence."

Hao rose from the table and strode to the windows. "Come, look with me. This is a fairly wealthy city, yet in the hills and outlying neighborhoods people struggle to eat. On the beach this morning I saw young mothers, babies on their backs, selling trinkets to put food on the table. There are hundreds of beautiful hotel rooms and condominiums and houses around the bay, almost all owned or for use by rich Americans and Canadians. This isn't right, and you can make it better."

Maria stood gazing over Zihuatanejo Bay. Finally, she turned. "How will this all work?"

"Chinese companies, losing business because of the short-sighted policies of our leaders will open factories here. We already are, and most of the Chinese executives running those firms are political allies. Many Chinese economic and political policies seemed good in the beginning. But when they began to fail, one man's stubborn mindset assured they were not corrected." Hao motioned for Maria to move to the deck overlooking the beach.

"Your transportation company will 'negotiate' lucrative contracts with the new enterprises. Your firm will have no-bid contracts to handle Mexican transport of products like nitrogen fertilizer from our new factory in the south to ports where they will be loaded on Chinese ships. New opportunities will present themselves to you quickly, which will be financed by Chinese banks. I have people in Mexico already looking for opportunities. My job description includes economic research. All of this will happen after you announce that you can no longer live your comfortable life while so many are suffering."

"Mr. Sun, Mexico already has four political parties. And I am not part of any of them."

Hao smiled. "That is the kind of response I hoped for. It is why you are the right choice. You are already thinking of how to make this work. Remember the party that your president belongs to didn't exist until her predecessor, a man with his own vision, but without friends with deep pockets started it. When the time comes you will have the best political advisors available. People will already be talking about you. You will be a folk hero. All you need to do is convert that to a political movement."

"And what of our current president?" asked Maria.

"There are several possible scenarios," replied Hao. "Any discussion would be conjecture."

CHAPTER 5

October 9, Lázaro Cárdenas, Mexico

THE US NAVY T-44A touched down at the airport, literally only a few feet above the tideline in the Mexican city of about 160,000 people. Offering help to the Mexican authorities try to figure out what had turned a well-designed small warship into junk with a single strike did not warrant traveling by jet directly from DC. Instead, Gritt flew commercial to San Diego where he was joined by Peter Balsak a chemical analysis expert from Alcohol Tobacco and Firearms and a second ATF employee, Lorenzo Mado. Lorenzo was a structural engineer who could assess the actual damage from the missile penetration on the Mexican warship and from the blast. He also spoke fluent Spanish. The T-44, the Navy's version of the Beechcraft King Air, had taken more than six hours with a refueling stop at the southern tip of the Baja Peninsula to reach Lazaro Cardenas. The flight had given them plenty of time to talk.

Waiting in the eighty-eight-degree heat was the man that Gritt had been corresponding with, Mexican Commander José

Alfaro. The men shook hands. "You must be tired," offered Alfaro. "The navy has no facilities here, so I booked you into a hotel only a few hundred yards from where my ship is beached."

"If it's all right with you, commander, we'd like to start work right away, said Gritt. Mr. Balsak here is an expert on explosives and propellants and Mr. Mado who was born in Mexico is a structural engineer who specializes in blast analysis. They will only be here for a day. Both were already slammed with work when I asked to borrow them from ATF. Our two pilots could use some help getting refueling started, a ride to the hotel, and I would appreciate a guard on the airplane overnight."

Alfaro motioned for a couple of seamen in the van to take their bags and spoke briefly to an older navy chief standing next to a khaki green Ford. "Have them work with Chief Gonzales here. He doesn't speak much English, but he understands what you need."

After a short conversation with the two pilots, Gritt slid into the passenger seat of the van and loosened the collar of his shirt.

"You are not returning with these men?" asked Alfaro.

"No, I was invited by another of your officer brothers to do some fishing down in Zihua months ago so I'm going down there to take him up on his offer."

"Who is the officer, if you don't mind me asking?"

"Marine Lieutenant Diego Cervantes. I met him at a joint forces conference. Seemed like he had his shit together. Spoke better English than me. I kind of figured he was from a well to do family, the kind of guy that could do anything with his life but chose to serve."

"You nailed Diego. I have known him for years. Your description fits him perfectly. Based on my intel commander, that's your story too." They pulled up to an old dock, next to where the Montezuma lay beached where bulldozers had dragged her above the tide line. Gritt looked over at Alfaro and watched him wipe a tear from his face.

"Whatever hit this ship was designed to pierce armor," said Mado as they walked up to the ship. He stopped to further examine the hole punched neatly through the bow. "There is no evidence of expansion or detonation where it hit. I did a couple of tours in Iraq and Afghanistan back before I decided the Army wasn't my future. This hole looks like what you would find when a tank or some other fighting vehicle was hit with an anti-armor rocket or shell."

Alfaro pointed to a ladder propped up halfway to the stern. "You'll find a similar hole through every bulkhead back to where it entered the engine room. Every bulkhead below the deck is steel. Our technicians couldn't figure out why it didn't detonate earlier. It might have done a lot of damage, probably not destroyed the ship."

Gritt stopped at the top of the ladder. The ship looked like someone had literally blown it up like a balloon just aft of center; everything was pushed out. "Commander, I am mostly an analysis kind of guy, but just keeping this thing afloat appears to have required incredible seamanship. You and your crew must have done outstanding work."

Alfaro stopped at the open hatch leading to the lower decks. "Thanks for that. We just got lucky. We buttoned up the ship only moments before we were hit. She had just enough buoyancy for your cutter to drag her one hundred fifty kilometers. Before we pulled her up on the beach, only the top fifteen feet of superstructure was showing."

Below deck, the team was met by four Mexican investigators. Within minutes, the American and Mexican technicians were sharing information. While Balsak and two of the Mexican investigators made their way to the engine room, Mado and the others began to work their way back toward the bow, measuring every hole and taking pictures.

Gritt and Alfaro made their way to the bridge where Chad began a very loose interview of the Mexican officer trying hard not to act as an inquisitor. "When you debriefed your crew, did you happen to record the conversations?" he asked.

"It never occurred to us to do that," answered Alfaro. "Why?"

"Sometimes what you hear in a recording can focus on one word or one difference from interview to interview. I was involved in the investigation over the atomic detonations in the US and that conflict with China out in the Aleutian Islands," answered Gritt. "In the Aleutians we recorded interviews of some Chinese detainees. One of them made a comment that led to a line of questions that helped us understand the entire case. In the bombing case, one guy who remembered which direction someone drove after buying his truck helped solve the case."

Gritt paused working out his follow up. "Here, anyone who actually saw the man launch the missile might remember one clue that fills in a blank for your people or Balsak and Mado."

"My crew are all on leave except for two still in the hospital," said Alfaro. "I will get you transcripts of their statements tomorrow. They will be in Spanish, so you will have to use your own translator. Look at them. If you think a second recorded interview will help, we will get it done."

The darkness of a moonless night ended the day's work. Gritt, who had only slept four of the last thirty-six hours ran up to his room for a shower. Too keyed up to sleep, he wandered down to the patio bar for a beer while the others grabbed a nap. Chinese businessmen sat at the only two other occupied tables. Two were in suits and the other two were dressed in jeans and T-shirts. There was a clear view of the wrecked Mexican ship from where they sat.

That night over dinner in a private room of a Mexican seafood restaurant, the two groups began comparing notes. "First thing," offered Mado, "the missile was designed to take out heavy armor. It penetrated eleven metal bulkheads before it hit anything solid enough to detonate. The strike looks more like what an American depleted uranium tank round does to a vehicle than a missile hit." He turned to Gritt. "I'll send my measurements to your office. I'll bet that that alone will refine our search to no more than five or six countries of origin, and maybe only a handful of missile types." He translated his statement into Spanish.

"Because of the engine room being submerged for hours on end, techs from neither country were able to get positive samples on swabs taken in the blast area," added Balsak. "But this afternoon, we found some melted plastic and remnants of two manuals that were almost incinerated in the blast. I have samples of each. I'll bet we will get a signature of the blast when we do an atom level spectrum analysis."

"We had the same problems," added Mado, indicating the two Mexican techs he was working with. There is nothing left after the saltwater bath. Without a traditional ion spectrum analysis, we aren't going to be able to identify the propellant."

"Which gets us to where we are," said Gritt. He turned to Balsak. "Make sure you get copies of all the work that was done prior to our arrival before you leave. We can have it translated back in the states. Leave a copy of your notes for your Mexican colleagues. I want to get a complete package of your work to both the FBI and the DEA. Let's see if what you come up with fits any of the profiles they are already working on."

He turned to Alfaro. "Commander, our technical work may just fit like a key in a lock with work already underway. We know that whoever killed the men in your crew are engaged in the transport of illegal drugs. This investigation must be multi-dimensional."

Alfaro smiled for the first time that day. "Most of the small arms that the cartels use come from the US. Some are American, but the AKs and some of the machine guns are from Russia and its allies. The rocket propelled grenades are all Russian design. But recently a couple of weapons made in China have turned up. Are you thinking what I am, that the weapon might have come directly from China, supplied to protect their allies in the drug trade?" Alfaro repeated his comments in Spanish.

"There were several Chinese businessmen at our hotel this afternoon," said Gritt.

"In the last two years, they seem to be everywhere," replied Alfaro. "They are pumping a lot of money into Mexico. We know that they supply a lot of the drugs coming through our country, but under our last president, the security community wasn't allowed to press investigations."

"We will get to the bottom of this," said Gritt. "Another team is doing a similar analysis on the Coast Guard cutter that was hit." He paused, then raised his Pacifico. "A toast to the memory of the shipmates you have lost. And to those on the American cutter."

CHAPTER 6

October 10, Zihuatanejo, Mexico

THE TWO OFFICERS were standing on the tarmac at Cardenas Airport as the copilot of the T-44 aircraft did his preflight before departing for San Diego. They watched as Balsak and Mado shook hands with their Mexican counterparts and boarded the plane. Five minutes later the plane was airborne.

Gritt turned to his new friend. "My lucky day. Thank you for the ride down to Zihua."

"We have to stop there anyway," said Alfaro. "Zihua has a small marine detachment. The four marines you saw guarding the Montezuma are from there. Two of the men are due for rotation, so we'll be dropping them off."

The Ford van was followed by a double cab pickup truck as it pulled onto the highway for the drive south. Besides the driver, Gritt and Alfaro, two of the techs rode in the van. They were on the road for about thirty minutes when Alfaro's phone rang. The brief conversation ended with the officer leaning over the front seat to talk quietly with his driver. A moment later the driver passed a small aluminum box over the seat.

"The truck behind us thinks we are being followed. A white Ford Excursion that was at the hotel is following but being careful to keep a couple of vehicles between them and us."

Alfaro opened the box and lifted three Barretta 9mm pistols with clip on holsters from the box. He turned to the two techs behind them and handed one to each, repeating what he had just told Gritt in Spanish. He then wiggled around in his seat to clip the last one on his own belt. "My driver is already armed."

"Why in the hell would anyone want to follow us?" asked Gritt. His body tensed like a tiger ready to leap. Only seconds later Gritt showed no concern at all.

"It's probably just some family on their way south," said José. "But robberies are not rare along the coast highway, and we have been looking into some group trying to sink a navy ship. I don't think anyone would be foolish enough to take on nine-armed men, but I never thought someone would launch a missile at my ship and destroy one of your helicopters."

The rest of the drive was quiet. Just over an hour and a half later they passed the bustling resort area of Ixtapa, where the Mexican government had dedicated miles of beach to building a modern bright lights high-rise resort area only miles from Zihuantanejo. The resorts provided employment for the region and had somehow managed to allow the city of Zihua to maintain its original small-town charm.

The driver took the first exit from the highway and started into the picturesque city. "I'm going to assume that you have hotel reservations somewhere," said Alfaro. "If not, it's still early in the season and there are rooms available. Where do you want to be dropped?"

Alfaro's phone rang again. He talked for only seconds and then hung up. "That white Ford followed us into town but turned off a few blocks back."

He looked over at Gritt, trying to figure out how this tall, muscular man with light hair and blue eyes could appear so calm one moment and a few seconds later seemed ready to take on the world. His own nerves had been on edge for days. "Before we part," he said, "if you ever would like someone to show you and your wife around Acapulco, my wife and I would love to host you."

"I'm not married," replied Chad, "but my girlfriend loves a beach, so when we get this under control, I'd love to take you up on your offer."

Chad was surprised that you couldn't drive right to the tiny marine compound in Zihua. Instead, the van and truck parked in a small lot next to where the community pier jutted into a beautiful oval shaped bay. Escorted by Alfaro, Gritt walked past the pier, noting the sport fisherman on their way back from fishing trips, and Mexican families carrying lunches and beach supplies heading out onto the concrete pier. A water taxi could be seen shuttling people around the bay. Alfaro's driver followed, packing Gritts small duffel bag. From where they parked it was only a three-minute walk to a series of small white buildings surrounded by a cement wall on the beach, in the center of town. They stopped at a steel gate next to a pole with the Mexican flag flapping in the late morning breeze. Alfaro and a sentry standing guard chatted for a moment. Moments later they were escorted into the small office of the compound commander.

Alfaro had a short conversation with the desk sergeant and then turned to Gritt. "Lieutenant Cervantes is out working some of the newer men. He didn't expect you until later. If you would like to look," Alfaro followed the sergeant to windows overlooking the bay, "you can see them swimming from Las Gatas, a day resort across the bay, back to the compound. Looks like maybe three kilometers."

He turned to Gritt. "It's been a pleasure working with you,

commander. Please keep me informed on what you and your group find out. I want to be part of destroying whoever it was that killed my men." He extended his hand. "We've still got a long drive, so we need to get on the road." He turned for the door, before offering, "you can catch a cab to your hotel from where we are parked. The sergeant here will call for you."

Gritt had just changed into a swimsuit after checking into the boutique Del Mar hotel on the beach when his cell rang. Cervantes was offering dinner invitation at a restaurant only steps away from his office. 'From your hotel, take the beach walk into town. David's Restaurant will be on your right before you get to the plaza. My good friends there will set up a table on the beach across from the restaurant for us." The two agreed to meet at seven-thirty.

Ten minutes later, Gritt walked down two flights of steps, past a beautiful swimming pool and then another flight of steps to the beach. Four or five couples rested on chairs and beach lounges, all middle aged and already tan. A younger crowd partied noisily at a beach bar next door. He threw a beach towel from his room over a chair and waded out into the small surf. Moments later he was swimming hard out into the bay. He swam for a half hour before heading back. Only half of the lounges and chairs at the resort were full as he spread out his towel and plopped down in the bright sun. The Mexican marine officer had been exercising his men with what had to be a two-hour swim. Gritt's thirty minutes had exhausted him. Marines everywhere were tough.

He had fallen asleep when a voice woke him. "You look like you just got here," said a woman's voice with a Canadian accent. "Better watch how much sun you get at first. This place will cook you." Gritt looked up as a middle-aged couple, both with bronze tans headed for the water.

"Thanks for the heads up," he called. He moved his lounge under the shade of an umbrella.

He dug out his phone. He almost felt guilty as he told Air Force Major Olga Tvorshik where he was.

"I'm on duty right now," she commented, "sitting in my office watching an early snowstorm sweep through the Dakotas. If you'd given me a heads up, I have a lot of leave coming and the beach in Mexico sounds a lot nicer."

"I didn't know I was coming. I came down here to investigate that missile attack that really tore up a Mexican Naval ship. I'll be here two more days and then stop in California where two of the scientists who came with me should have some findings on who was responsible."

"Was that the same incident where our Coast Guard lost a helicopter?" asked Olga.

"Yup, and we are probably chasing the same bad guys who hit that cutter with a missile last week."

"Chad, that doesn't seem to fit with your job description. Isn't this some kind of a drug thing?"

"Maybe," he answered. "But whatever hit that ship was advanced enough to turn it into scrap iron. The Farragut Center got a request for help, and I was available."

"We'll color me jealous," said Olga. "The beach sounds nice right now. I just seem to gravitate to the opposite environment. First Alaska for years and now North Dakota in a blizzard."

"Take heart, love, for we have a standing invitation to spend our first vacation together with new friends from Acapulco. I called to let you know that I'm putting in for some leave the first February. I thought you might do the same."

"Count me in," said Olga. "Now I've got to get back to work. Some of my people are starting a security sweep exercise out by the flight line in an hour. It's snowing sideways out there, and I need to find my hat and gloves. Love ya'."

Gritt hung up and checked his watch. Just time for one beer before he had to shower for dinner. He waved at a woman carrying empty bottles on a tray and ordered a Pacifico.

Mexican marine Lieutenant Diego Cervantes was still in his khaki uniform when Gritt approached the table. The two men were almost identical in stature, six feet, one hundred eighty some pounds and toned. Gritt's light complexion, now slightly pink from a little sunburn, contrasted with Cervantes' dark eyes and black hair.

"I wasn't sure that I would recognize you again," said Diego. "We only had an hour together last fall."

Gritt smiled and extended his hand. "I cheated. I took a minute to look at some pictures I took at the conference. But even without that, there can't be many marine corps officers on the waterfront here."

Gritt was probably three or four years older than Diego. The two had hit it off, not because of their backgrounds, but because both were somewhat obsessed with fishing. Gritt, raised in Alaska where his family owned a remote fly-in fishing camp had invited Diego to join him sometime. Diego had reciprocated with an invitation for deep sea fishing in Mexico.

"When you called to say you were coming, I reserved a couple of days with my favorite guide," said Diego. "We have big diesel-powered sport fishing boats here, but I prefer fishing out of an open panga."

"I can't tell you how happy I am to be here," replied Chad. "I have no idea what a panga is, but I'll take you at your word that it will be a blast."

The two men ordered one of the restaurant's famous surf and turf dinners, a small New York steak matched with two small rock lobster tails. The palm frond-covered dining area on the beach had only five tables. Diego explained that during peak season there would be twenty tables, and all would be packed. The owner placed their table away from the others at Diego's request.

"Were you able to nail down what hit the Montezuma?" asked Diego after the waiter delivered a margarita to Gritt, and a second Coke to Diego.

"Not yet," replied Chad. "I had a couple of engineers with me. They took a lot of measurements and chemical samples. The men working with Commander Alfaro also sent a box of fragments back to the states with my colleagues."

"Only five years ago," replied Diego, "the drug gangs were only lightly armed. In the last year or two they are killing each other with weapons you might find in a major war."

"Is that happening in Zihua?" asked Gritt.

"Not right here," replied Diego. "We have a national guard base nearby, and the commander has managed to keep his people from being compromised. But the Pacific Coast, from Manzanillo to Acapulco has been the center of the drug problem. Right here, the local government combined with the national guard keep the bad guys out. The reputation of the marines also helps. Nobody messes with us."

"Your navy department has asked ours for help. Alfaro's ship was hit while working closely with an American Coast Guard ship trying to stop a shipment of drugs from the south of Mexico. An educated guess is that the weapons came from China. I'm told by our drug enforcement people that as much as ninety-five percent of all the drugs creating problems in our two countries originate in China, including fentanyl, the most damaging drug both here and in the states. The Chinese authorities claim to be cracking down, but either they aren't making much of an effort yet, or they do not have much control over their industry and their border. Some of our investigators believe that these drugs are part of a plot to undermine American society."

"The Chinese have their fingers in lots of pots in Mexico," said Diego. "My family has interest in the telecom industry as well as electronics manufacturing. Most of our partners are American, but my father claims that he gets at least monthly visits from Chinese businessmen offering financial support. He's mentioned a couple of times that the visits are so regular and so canned that he thinks the effort may be tied to a Chinese intelligence network that we know is operating in Mexico."

"Is there an official concern here about Chinese influence?" asked Chad.

"Not under our last president. He welcomed almost every offer from the Chinese. Their money could transform Mexico. It really worried many of us in the security services."

The conversation finally shifted to fishing with the arrival of dinner. "Diego pointed toward the municipal pier that Gritt had passed earlier in the day. "From your hotel it's about a twenty-minute walk to the pier. I'll meet you outside the harbor-masters office at seven tomorrow morning. Don't worry about breakfast or lunch, there will be tables set up by the women in town where you can pick up meals to go. You will need pesos. If you don't have any, your hotel will have a currency exchange. There will also be a store open by the pier where you can buy drinks, although I will have beer and bottled water with me."

Diego looked at his watch. "I must go now. With four of my men up in Lazaro Cardenas guarding what is left of the Montezuma, we're shorthanded. I'm taking a communications watch shift until midnight."

"I'm already tired from the last few days," said Gritt. "That won't give you much rest before we meet for fishing."

"I'll sleep in my office tonight. I don't know about you, but there have been a lot of days when I went fishing with no sleep."

Gritt laughed as the men rose from the table. Gritt reached for his credit card, but Diego stopped him. "You are here to help us, and my guest. Except for your hotel room and a breakfast burrito, your money is no good here."

After settling the check, they stepped onto the beautiful brick paved waterfront walk. Diego nodded at four people setting up lawn chairs in a darkened section of the beach just past the next waterfront restaurant. "They are going to guard the nest of a sea turtle until the mother makes her way back to the ocean. Some of our people consider the eggs a delicacy so unless they are collected and sent to the turtle sanctuary for incubation, they will be gone by morning."

Gritt turned to look. It wasn't the people in lawn chairs that he noticed. Sitting at a table watching him and Cervantes were the same Chinese men who had been at the restaurant in Cardenas the previous evening.

The walkway back to the hotel was well lit, with numerous tourists wandering along, entranced by the glistening lights of the waterfront community. Here and there, young local couples sat holding hands or leaning on each other. Even with all those people, Gritt stopped several times to quietly see if he was being followed.

⚜

The panga was a twenty-foot-long open boat with a small cabin over the middle third of the craft. A 150 horsepower Yamaha outboard pushed the well-designed hull through the ocean swells and wind driven chop from at a steady twenty knots."

"I've fished with Enzo Martinez on the Porpoise since I was stationed here," said Diego. He's the best guide in the harbor.

My parents keep a home over on the Cabo San Lucas side. My dad has a thirty-eight-foot Mediterranean Sport Fisherman. It's big and comfortable with a nice, air-conditioned cabin, a real head and kitchen, but I like this better. On a panga you are almost part of the ocean, not riding on it."

They ran straight out from the harbor, just about an hour before Enzo throttled back and set out five lines at a fast troll. "This time of year, there are mostly sailfish and dorado out here. We're fishing the continental shelf drop off where the currents push a lot of bait fish."

On the run out, Diego learned about Gritt's family ownership of mineral mines and commercial fishing interests in Alaska as well as majority ownership in a hundred-year-old marine transportation company.

Diego's family owned the second largest cell phone company in Mexico as well as a manufacturing business park only miles south of San Diego, California. It was clear to each of the men that the other had chosen a military career to serve even though they both could have pursued cushy corporate jobs in the family business.

They caught four sailfish and four dorado that afternoon, releasing all but one small dorado, which they kept for dinner. "Meet me in front of your hotel at seven," said Diego. "Tonight, we will dine at one of our more extravagant restaurants. It's just a mile or two drive. I'll drop off the fish on my way home. I live across the bay in a townhome in what we call La Ropa, the cloth. It's named after the beach where local native tribal members once gathered a small fortune in clothing and other things, including silk from the wreck of a Spanish galleon."

The restaurant sat high on a bluff overlooking the harbor. Off duty, Diego joined Gritt in a margarita and ordered wine with an appetizer of shrimp and spices in a steamed squash.

"I was thinking about your comments this afternoon," said Diego, "about Chinese involvement. We have no real manufacturing here, and no major port facilities, but over the hill in Ixtapa, the Chinese are financing a new high-rise hotel. We marines have been the most trusted authority to conduct operations against the cartels. Every place we found fentanyl, we found documentation of Chinese supply. We've had some drug issues in the area, mostly security conflicts when dueling drug honchos are here."

He paused as a platter of steamed vegetables and grilled dorado filets smothered in a spicy tomato sauce arrived at the table. As Diego used a large flat wooden spatula to divide the meal onto two plates, he continued. "On the hillside behind us there is an abandoned palatial home that was built by a corrupt police chief from Mexico City. He obviously double-crossed someone because when the police arrested him, they found boxes of incriminating records inside his home. Nobody would have been stupid enough to keep such records in a property they owned."

"Or maybe someone thought he was being paid too much," said Gritt.

Out in the bay, the last of the water taxis ran across the flat calm water, returning workers from the small Las Gatas day beach back to town. With the extraordinary cuisine in front of them, all was quiet as the two enjoyed their meal.

"In the states," said Gritt finally, "only the dumb drug people flaunt their wealth. Usually, they wait until they accumulate a lot of money and then invest it in legitimate businesses. Only then do they buy their mansions."

"I sat in on a briefing only a month ago," replied Diego. "A couple of investigators from the federales who had been sidelined by our past president were talking about growing evidence of huge amounts of drug money going into legitimate business here as well. Many of those investments seem to be tied to Chinese banks."

The two men finished dinner with Café Diablos, a mix of citrus, sugar and liquors served flaming. "I've got a couple of men down with some bug," offered Diego as they made their way to his mint 1965 Mustang convertible. "I've got to work tomorrow. Spend your day enjoying Zihua. We've got a great museum right downtown. But if you meet me on the pier at six tomorrow evening, Enzo has offered to take us night fishing for Barracuda. It's a blast, all fast trolling. You can't see the baits, so the sound of the fish hitting them right on top of the water is a rush. They fight hard and the shoreline at night is beautiful."

As Diego backed out of his parking spot, Chad noticed a white Chevy Suburban parked just across the road. Four men, two probably local and two who were obviously Asian sat watching them leave.

"I don't know if it means anything," said Chad, "but we were followed by a similar white Suburban all the way down from Cardenas the other day. I noticed a couple of Chinese businessmen at the restaurant where my tech and yours were comparing notes the night before we left for Zihua. The same two Chinese men were sitting where they could observe us last night."

"I'll make a call tomorrow. Maybe some of my local associates know something about that vehicle or about overt Mexican-Chinese problems in the area. If it is the bad guys, they are probably just keeping an eye on you. You look like you're DEA. There aren't a lot of younger single American men here this time of year."

Diego was right, Chad had no trouble using an extra day. Between the beach, the colorful central open-air market, the museum and finding small local restaurants for a late breakfast and an early dinner, Gritt found himself jogging to meet Diego for night fishing.

Night fishing was as much fun as Diego described it. The afternoon breezes had calmed. They were only a few miles out when four rods were baited with strips of bait fish and run out behind the boat.

"Barracuda fishing is best on a night like this," said Enzo, pointing to an almost full moon overhead. They trolled past a dozen boats anchored with lights near the rocky lighthouse just off the harbor.

"Those are local fishermen, jigging for snapper and other bottom fish," offered Diego. "They will fish all night and then bring their catch to sell in an open market early tomorrow. When you walked to the pier you had to notice the dozens of open fishing boats pulled up on the sand right in front of the central plaza and basketball court. Each morning the restaurants, markets, and mothers of Zihua come there to buy fresh fish."

Minutes later, the men heard the splash of a strike and the scream of a reel as a barracuda took one of their baits. Enzo trolled south, past several huge rock islands where several more night fishermen were anchored. By midnight they had hooked more than a dozen fish, releasing all of them. As the men popped the caps off the last of the iced Modelo beers, they surrendered to the inevitable. Enzo placed the rods in rod holders and turned back toward the harbor.

"Is that another beacon?" asked Chad as they ran. He pointed out to sea almost directly off from the lighthouse at the mouth of the bay. "I saw a green light blink three times and then a few minutes later the same again."

"Probably just a light off from a passing ship, or commercial fishing boat. The blinking might just be the boat rising and falling on the ocean swell."

Both men continued to stare out to sea as Enzo turned the speeding boat into the bay. "I saw it too," offered Diego finally. Both men turned toward the lights of the town spread out along the hillsides around the bay. A moment later there were three distinct flashes of green light from the window of an apartment near Gritt's hotel. "That's a little odd," commented Diego.

Halfway across the bay, nursing the last of their beers, the men stood in the back of the boat consuming the beauty of the moonlight on the ocean. "That's odd too," said Diego pointing. "I just saw three or four pangas take off from Las Gatas. Usually by midnight only the night watchman is still over there." He motioned toward the point on the south side of the bay.

"I count four boats," said Gritt, "all racing without running lights and headed out to sea, not back to the harbor."

"I talked to a police sergeant this afternoon," replied Diego as Enzo began to slow the boat. "I asked about any local reports of Mexican-Chinese drug activity in the area. He indicated that there had been a couple of tips, but after investigating there was nothing to worry about."

As Enzo slid the boat up to the cement steps of the pier, Diego held the boat in place and Gritt stepped to the landing. Gritt held the top of the tiny cabin to steady the boat for his friend. Then Gritt handed his guide a hundred-dollar tip. "Thanks for a great time. I'll be back."

Enzo handed the bill back. My friend Diego says your money no good here." The men shook hands.

As Gritt and Diego walked down the pier, both were deep in thought. Finally, Gritt said what both were thinking. "The strange blinking lights, a blinking light in town, boats heading out from where there should be no boats, running without lights is suspicious."

"It is," replied Diego, "I'll call my friend at the police station in the morning. Maybe it will be important to him."

They reached the end of the pier. "You need a ride? I'm going right by your hotel. "How 'bout a ride to the airport tomorrow?"

"I think I'd prefer just walking," said Gritt. "And tomorrow I'm on the Alaska Airlines flight in the afternoon. I'll just take a cab."

"Keep me informed on what you find my friend. The Mexican navy only has a handful of ships. We can't afford to lose many and still have a navy."

The men shook hands. Gritt headed down the mile and a half lighted beach walk, soaking in one final evening along the bay. As he walked his cell phone chirped. He looked down at a message. It was from Peter Balsak at ATF. Change of plans. Meet Lorenzo and me in Los Angeles. We sent several of the fragments we gathered from the Montezuma to a lab in Los Angeles. One of the metallurgists asked us to meet him there tomorrow. I made you a reservation at the Holiday Inn LAX. Take the shuttle to the hotel. Will pick you up on the morning of the fifteenth at 8:00.

CHAPTER 7

October 15, Los Angeles, California

THE LAB AT USC was primarily dedicated to doing structural failure analysis and materials testing for engineering purposes. But with an insane amount of federal grant money flowing through the university's bank accounts, the Director of the Structures and Materials Research Lab, Dr. Daniela Gromonov, picked up the phone almost any time a federal official called.

She welcomed Balsak, Mado and Gritt in front of the building and escorted them to the lab that she nicknamed the dungeon. "Several fragments that you sent appeared to be aluminum with a ceramic coating," she offered as she led the men into the lab. Several students were busy at other tables as she led them to a computer screen above a counter where a wooden vice held a fragment with some form of box above it.

She switched on the screen which brought up an image of the edge of a fragment. Dr. Gromonov tapped the keyboard several times, each of which expanded the image on the screen.

"What you sent me is a tiny piece of aircraft grade aluminum that has been bathed in a chemical bath under precise voltages. The material is not coated, rather the treatment turned the surface of the aluminum into a ceramic. It makes it very hard, while still allowing some flexibility, strength, and puncture resistance. It also makes it much more resistant to high temperatures and when coupled next to other metals, corrosion resistant."

Balsak and Mado stood enraptured by the new information, while Gritt couldn't figure out how that description helped figure out who destroyed a Mexican ship.

"This process was originally developed by the Russians because they struggled to make several types of aluminum that the west was using for combat aircraft. This piece, however, began with aluminum originally designed in South Korea. The Chinese hacked the Koreans some time ago and have been manufacturing this material for about a decade. They used the Russian process to convert the surface of aluminum to ceramic, high grade treated aluminum. With about ninety percent confidence I can tell you that this piece came from the Chinese aviation and armaments industry."

"That matches what I found," offered Mado. "The holes made by the missile were almost identical from where it penetrated the bow until where it exploded. There was little deformation and the scrapings of the holes we took showed an odd ceramic that we'd never seen before."

The three men thanked Dr. Gromonov and headed out to find a quick spot for lunch near the airport so they could drop off Gritt for his late afternoon flight back to DC.

꧂

"Commander, this issue is greater than a simple missile attack on an allied warship," said Balsak. "At a conference that I attended a couple of years back, a number of people were warning of America falling behind in energetics."

"I've heard the term at work," replied Gritt, "but I don't know what it means."

"It's the study of advanced chemicals used for propellants and explosives. In the states, we still use DDX and HMX, explosives developed more than seventy years ago. In the 1980s American scientists developed an explosive that was more than forty percent powerful than HMX. It was called CL-20, but the US did nothing with it."

He stopped talking to finish his burger while Chad and Lorenzo discussed how the treated aluminum would make a very strong missile without the weight of steel. "On the way to pick you up this morning, Peter and I were talking about traces that look like CL-20 he found in the plastic and charred binders he brought back. Chinese spies stole the design for CL-20 years ago and have been perfecting it. We have nothing like it."

"Worse," added Balsak finishing his sandwich, "the Chinese take energetics seriously. They are rumored to have propellants that require smaller amounts to accelerate a missile to higher speeds, quicker than anything we have. What is left of those propellants, when a missile hits, adds to the explosive power of the warhead."

"I've heard discussions of the need to advance our missile technology at the Farragut Center," replied Gritt. "I never understood much of it. My specialty is electronics and lasers."

"Advanced energetics allows you to pack more punch into an explosion and to accelerate a missile to higher speeds more quickly," said Balsak. "You can do it in a smaller package. Your people will take the data we have put together and do a better job of identifying exactly what type of missile was used. Our data-based guess is that it is an updated version of a handheld

Chinese anti-tank weapon built by Norinco. The original weighs only about fifty pounds, which would make it really viable on a small vessel. The original never caught on as an export product because of its cost. But if the bad guys of the world figure out that this newer version can tear up a ship, these things are going to be a real threat."

"Scarier to me," said Gritt, "is that the Chinese appear to be willing to make it available to their drug partners to protect shipments. I can't imagine the Chinese government doing that, but they are." He handed a waiter his credit card.

"It would be pure speculation," added Mado as they made their way to his car, "but if the rocket we are studying is Chinese, then the anti-aircraft rocket that hit the helicopter is probably Chinese as well. Based on our database, it may be a Chinese Hongjian-12. It's also built by Norinco and uses a soft launch system designed to be fired even inside a building. It would be perfect for use in a drug runner's submersible. Let us know what you find."

Two hours later, Gritt was at thirty thousand feet headed for DC.

CHAPTER 8

November 1, Mexico City, Mexico

THE GRAN HOTEL Ciudad de Mexico was the perfect venue for the launch of Maria Castillo's new persona. It was a mix of traditional and modern Mexico with its elegant colonial architecture housing luxurious rooms and multiple richly appointed conference halls. Hao Sun, in his official role of business development director for the Shandong Commerce Committee, moved to the podium. He waited until the guests donned the translation headsets in front of them, since he would deliver his remarks in English.

In the invitation only audience for this lavish luncheon were all six of the anchors for Mexico's nationwide news outlets and the business editors for more than a dozen regional newspapers. They were mixing with the governors of five Mexican states, more than thirty national legislators, and two advisors to President Lupita Martinez. Filling the remaining one hundred-fifty seats were business leaders from across the nation. The invitation had come with prepaid airfare to out of town guests, and a room in one of the city's most desirable hotels.

"Thank you all for attending today's celebration," started Hao. "As noted in your invitation, the Chinese Government, and especially my friends in the Shandong Region, welcome you to this milestone event. This year, private sector Chinese business groups will complete more than five hundred million dollars in new project development here in Mexico."

The announcement was met with polite applause.

"These projects include helping with developing new natural gas reserves. My friends at Shandong Energy are proud to assist your own Pemex with this discovery that will reduce your dependence on foreign supplied gas. Your expenditures for energy will now create Mexican jobs." He paused and smiled. "The taxes and royalties from this development will provide a substantial boost to both local and national government budgets." He paused again. "That is, if those governments decide to keep it all. Perhaps they might just reduce your taxes. What do you think?"

Laughter swept the room.

"We are helping Mexican communities and companies improve your ports on both the Pacific Coast and in the Gulf of Mexico. These improvements will allow the revolution in Mexican manufacturing to access markets in Asia, including my own country, as well as across the Americas and in Europe. By the end of this year, Mexican ports will accommodate the world's largest container ships. Chinese shipping companies will be among the first to contract for docking privileges."

"Speaking of the manufacturing revolution, let me see a show of hands of communities and companies that are opening new manufacturing facilities for high tech products including computer and telecom assembly plants. I'm especially looking to see how many of you have taken advantage of the development financing that Chinese banks are offering."

He waited as more than fifty hands were raised followed by a full minute of applause.

"You all have heard that Chinese technology companies are partnering with Mexican firms to manufacture export products that you will sell here in the Americas and abroad." He paused for effect. "Some of these products will compete with products made in China. But my partners have targeted products that you can sell easier than we can, as well as products where demand is outstripping our own manufacturing ability." The crowd knew that many of those products faced enormous tariffs when imported into the US from China. Hao knew that they didn't care if Mexico benefitted from the change in origin.

"Not long ago, your government agencies granted fishing privileges to Chinse fishing fleets. You still accommodate some of that, but we have figured out that much of the catch from your waters should be processed here. I know that at least six of the communities represented here today are building seafood processing plants, using Chinese Banking capital and Chinese technology. When they come online, my country will be a major customer. But even more important, these facilities will be better for the environment as the seafood waste that our at-sea processors just dump back in the ocean will now go to new fertilizer plants. They will combine nitrogen fertilizer from plants made possible by new natural gas, and seafood waste. It will make Mexican agriculture more efficient and more importantly to me, the export of these new products will help China grow more of the food we need."

"I want to keep this short so that we can enjoy a fusion meal of Chinese and Mexican flavors developed just for this meeting. Later, I am looking forward to meeting as many of you as possible. I want to emphasize that we are interested in participating in any area of commerce that can be successful. We have capital resources available for direct investment and for financing."

Hao paused to let the applause subside.

"Let me close with the next phase in our plans to become a good partner of Mexico. This is the surprise promised in your invitations. Today I am introducing a new initiative. Companies that we invest in will emphasize contracting with Mexican firms for services. We are looking for well-run firms where our capital help can change lives. Today I want to introduce you to the first company selected under this initiative." Hao paused and nodded to Maria sitting at the first table. "Maria would you please introduce yourself and share your plans."

Maria started from her seat. "Ladies and gentlemen, I am Maria Castillo of Castillo Transportation."

Maria, whose small regional freight company was little known swept to the podium and began to arrange her notes. Murmurs around the room included references to her looks, and questions about whether she and Hao were lovers among others.

"Thank you," she started, turning to Hao.

"Let me introduce myself. I am Maria Castillo, daughter of Frederick Castillo, who at one time earned his living producing and transporting drugs to the United States. Before there were big name cartels, my father built a small empire. Those illegal activities attracted too much attention from the DEA and our own security services. The business was disbanded several years ago, and my father was murdered while in jail. Most of the family wealth came from drugs, and we lost everything, even our home."

Maria could tell she had everyone's attention.

"While the family had the resources of that enterprise, I was sent to the US for an education. Over seven years I received my MBA from the University of Southern California. I watched my father's business lead to his death. So, when I had the chance, I resurrected one tiny piece of that enterprise and built a legitimate small transportation company that emphasizes service and efficiencies. With the help of Mr. Hao Sun and his associates, we have committed to a major expansion of the business. I've extended the management team and with their help will be serving not only the three areas we've worked in the past but have a plan to expand that footprint tenfold. My family name will no longer be tainted."

Maria's eyes swept the crowd, trying to read the response. It was positive, especially since the invitation only event excluded any other transportation company.

"More importantly, I believe that this opportunity is a blessing, one that will lead to substantially greater profitability. And here is my pledge to you. I will commit half of that increase to you, the people of Mexico. With that said, I announce the creation of the Castillo Foundation. It will be the first of what I hope will be many. The Castillo Foundation will reach out across Mexico and find worthy students from families that cannot afford higher education. We will provide our youth with an opportunity to learn so that they can become managers, executives and leaders of your firms; perhaps even someday sit in a room like this. We will also teach them to be proud Mexican citizens, dedicated to our economic and political independence, with a commitment to create jobs that will lift families." Again, she surveyed the room, which was silently mesmerized. "Thank you and I am looking forward to earning your business," she finished.

As applause swept the room, many standing to cheer, Maria returned to her seat. As the room quieted, Hao again moved to the microphone.

"This is the kind of company we will be looking for in our contracting initiative. And to show how serious we are, I want to announce that my partners of the Shandong business community are providing the Castillo Foundation with twenty million pesos, more than one million US dollars as a gift so that they can staff up this worthwhile effort and start making kids' lives better."

Over dinner that evening, Hao and Maria were joined by Luis Cardenas. "That was better than we ever could have imagined," he said. "I've had people monitoring all the news outlets. They're all talking about Mexico and China as partners, but for every word about that, they are gushing over Maria's speech. You are the like Joaquin Murrieta, the female Poncho Villa. You are the new Mexican Robin Hood. They loved your passion for making Mexico more independent of our northern neighbor."

"I know," said Maria, sipping her favorite drink, Sangria. "My phone is ringing off the hook with requests for interviews."

CHAPTER 9

November 15, Washington DC

"I can't believe that we still do not have a formal report," said Lieutenant Mike Stephens. "After your trip to Mexico, you thought we had this pretty much figured out."

Stephens and Gritt sat in the almost empty Oasis Bar not far from the Farragut Center in DC. Gritt was trying to keep the young officer from a minor meltdown over America's commitment to help Mexico nail down how their ship had been so badly damaged. "I promised Commander Alfaro our best effort almost six weeks ago," said Stephens.

Both men did something almost impossible for those at the Farragut Center, they had slipped away late in the afternoon for a beer, leaving hours of work piled on their desks. "Talk to Alfaro, he's a really good guy who is driven to avenge those killed on his watch," said Gritt. "Give him verbally what we have."

"I tried that," said Stephens as he ordered a second Blue Moon. "Without a written report, his boss, a Captain Diego Acuna, is not willing to press for any formal government to government confrontation with the Chinese."

"Mike, you know how bureaucratic the navy can be sometimes. It appears that our friends at the DEA and ATF are even worse. The guys who went to Mexico with me, Balsak and Mado, had their part virtually done before I left Los Angeles. Their boss wanted to cross check their findings with any intelligence from the DEA. My friends at the CIA laugh about what happens when you try to make a stew with help from the alphabet agencies. Everyone wants to be the chef, nobody wants to be wrong, until someone finally says screw it, take what we have. That hasn't happened yet." Gritt took a swig of his beer.

"The US and China are finally at least talking rationally with one another. I talked to an analyst that I trust at the CIA yesterday. China has some internal problems, both with their economy and within the Communist Party itself. Interestingly, the more internal issues they face, the easier it has been for our two countries to work together. Nobody wants a confrontation with China over supplying advanced weapons to a Mexican Drug Cartel until we are one-hundred percent confident. It is especially sensitive since both American and Mexican servicemembers were killed."

"So, what do I tell Commander Alfaro?" asked Stephens.

"Tell him that Peter Balsak, who he met, has promised us a final report in the next ten days. Don't promise what it will say. Tell him that the China connection is sensitive to us right now."

Gritt took a moment to devour a handful of French fries. "Look, Mike, this doesn't pass the smell test with me. If we are right about the weapons, especially the missile that hit the Montezuma, it doesn't track that the Chinese government would give or sell them to a Mexican crime group. They refused to send advanced weapons to the Russians in Ukraine. I think we are right about the origin of the missiles, but how and why they got to Mexico needs a little sorting out."

"Okay, I get it, and I will try to keep José Alfaro just unhappy and not militant."

"Tell him what I said about this not tracking. "I'm leaving tomorrow night to go do some pheasant hunting in Montana. It's late there for pheasants, but I have a friend who is an expert on hunting and fishing there. He is also a former spook with a lot of experience dealing with China issues. Since I still don't have formal authority to do any more, maybe a little off the record research might help us." He paused almost a full minute. "My boss is telling me that this isn't a Farragut type problem. She wants it handed back to the DEA. Maybe my Montana friend can offer more perspective."

"Anything might help," said Stephens. "Do you think that the DEA dragging their feet has anything to do with the murder of one of their agents up around Puerto Peñasco a couple of weeks ago?"

"Maybe," said Gritt. "My contact at the CIA mentioned it. Apparently, there have been several shootouts among rival gangs right along the Arizona border. Someone on the Mexican side of the border is killing drug mules. While the DEA and FBI will work with anyone trying to halt the drug trade, especially stopping a group leaving piles of bodies including a woman border agent, they trust the Mexican navy more than anyone else from that government. The report on the DEA agent's death state that he was driving with a Mexican naval intelligence officer when they were ambushed. Someone hit their truck with a type of rocket on a remote road near the border. Blew it all to hell. They removed the bodies in pieces from the wreck. We were never given access to the vehicle. Local police refused to release it to either their federal authorities or to anyone on our side of the border."

CHAPTER 10

November 16, Flathead Lake, Montana

"WHY IS IT that every time I come to visit you, you have a new truck?" asked Chad, as he leaned in the window of a Toyota Tundra that hadn't lost its new car smell. The driver, Thadius Walker still looked fit for someone in his seventies, his graying hair cut short, his well-developed shoulders and arms displayed under his maroon pocket T-shirt. "You just have to show off your hard man points," continued Gritt. "Short sleeves on a day when the temperature won't hit thirty."

"You come all this way to go hunting or be a smart ass?" asked Walker. "Throw your pack in the back of the truck and slide your gun case behind the front seats. Be careful opening the back door. Winchester has been cooped up in the truck for a couple of hours and he probably needs to pee. We'll stop when we get out of Missoula."

Gritt slid into the passenger seat, welcomed by a nuzzle and sloppy lick on the back of his neck. "Nice to see you too

Winchester," he said. He turned and watched Walker's Gordon Setter sniff the gun case and then begin to dance on the back seat.

"Your dog knows we're going hunting," said Gritt as he extended his hand to his older friend and mentor.

Walker started the truck and headed for Highway 93 and Flathead Lake. "You don't usually call and ask to come hunting without notice," he said.

"I wanted to see you and do some hunting, but I also admit that I need a little old bull advice on a problem that my new boss doesn't think is my problem."

"Wouldn't happen to involve that rush trip to Mexico, would it?" asked Walker.

"For a guy that retired from the agency a decade ago," started Gritt, "you somehow have remained more informed than a lot of the current agency people I know."

"Only because Mat Chang and I go back so far," said Thad. "His people are a bit confused over the Chinese weapons issue, can't quite figure it out. He called me. Wondered what I thought. Mentioned your trip."

They waited until passing French Town to find a place to pull over and let Winchester out. "Stay off of the road," ordered Walker pointing at his dog. Gritt seated himself at a roadside table as Thad used his cane to follow the dog making a beeline toward a clump of willows along an open pasture. Moments later the dog locked up in a point.

Thad walked up next to the dog before ordering, "flush."

With a lunge, the dog darted into the willows which exploded with four pheasants. "Had a good hatch last spring, and a dry summer," called Thad as he patted the dog on the head. "A lot of birds this year." The dog took his place next to Walker's left leg as the two made their way to where Gritt sat.

"About the Chinese weapons thing," said Walker, "that discussion can wait until tomorrow evening. I have some ideas but I'm not ready to share. Besides we have a dinner invitation this evening. For tomorrow, I called in a couple of favors, and we have an invitation to hunt the far side of the Flathead reservation. Its all private land and probably hasn't seen a hunter this year."

"Okay with me," replied Gritt. "Where are we having dinner?"

"I have a new neighbor. Well kind of a neighbor. She lives about a mile from my place, toward Polson. Her residence is on the lake, but I guess she's always traveling, I just met her a few months ago. We've kind of been seeing each other for several months."

"Woah," said Chad as the two walked back to the truck. "The most confirmed bachelor I know has a girlfriend."

"You know kid, I often think of you like the son I never had," replied Walker. "I got you when you were already grown, but I still have to expect, like any kid, that you are going to be a little shit sometimes."

Chad stopped. "I didn't mean to piss you off."

Walker started to laugh. "You didn't. But I'm not a confirmed bachelor because that was my life's plan. The first woman in my life wasn't comfortable with what I did for a living. The second disappeared into a place where I couldn't go look. After that, I guess that I've never been ready for a serious third strike."

The air was crisp, but not brutal as Gritt followed his mentor to their favorite place to solve problems, a patched up old dock jutting into the crystal waters of Flathead Lake. Winchester sat near the front door of Walker's bungalow house staring at the truck. "Your dog thinks we should be out beating the bushes for pheasants," said Gritt. He turned back to Walker just as the man draped his cane over the arm of a folding chair and plopped into it. "And I approve of what you have done to the place. No more sitting on the dock and dangling our feet in the water."

"The chairs are more comfortable and easier on my worn body," replied Thad, "but feel free to use the dock and to dangle your feet. I personally find the November water a bit chilly compared to August or whenever you were here last."

Gritt slid into a chair just as the dog gave up his 'let's go hunting vigil' and trotted to the dock, jumping into the old wooden boat tethered to a piling. "He expects his daily boat ride," said Gritt.

"We row almost every day. Keeps me in shape; solitude for my head and the exercise for everything else," replied Walker. "It's good to disappoint Winchester once in a while, otherwise he might start taking all this for granted."

"Is that the same reason we didn't grab a couple of cold beers from the fridge before we came down here? You don't want me to take your hospitality for granted?"

"You know kid, you can be a bit of a pain. No, I would enjoy a beer, but in a couple of hours you are going to meet Sonia Ramirez. She was married to a guy who made a lot of money designing fishing lures. That's where they got the money to build a home on the lake. She spent thirty years with the DEA. That's the only thing that kept them married. He was a drunk and she was always away on assignment. She isn't a teetotaler, but she only drinks on special occasions, like champagne for a celebration or a margarita on the beach."

"I assume they are no longer married," observed Gritt.

"No, he died almost a year ago from liver cancer. His liver was so damaged that there was nothing they could do. The only good thing was that he quit drinking for the last year. She was his hospice nurse. Took a lot out of her."

"Not a lot of women would stay in that situation, I suspect," said Chad.

"More than you would guess. There was a third woman in

my life for a year or two. She turned out to be an alcoholic. By the time I got out of that, I was sicker than she was, totally co-dependent. No matter what I did, it didn't help. A lot of people can't let go."

"But you did," observed Chad.

"Not really. One evening after I pressed a little too hard, she just looked at me and said, 'Go, I'm a drunk and I like being a drunk, and all I want in my life is someone who will join me or at least get me home alive.'" Thad paused a moment. "I took her at her word."

"Being with a drunk or an addict has to be brutal," said Gritt. I know we're going to discuss the China thing tomorrow, but the thread running through the whole problem is the drug trade down there."

"In thirty years with the agency, I knew a lot of people who developed drinking problems. The job can create a lot of stress. Almost all of them recovered with help. I also worked with a handful of people who got hooked on drugs, mostly heroin. I knew a couple who kicked the stuff, but they never got over the craving."

The men watched as Winchester finally gave up on a boat ride and leaped to the dock, curling up next to Walker's chair.

"How are you and Major Tvorshik getting on?" asked Thad.

"Incredible," replied Chad, "but it would be nice if we were a little closer. It's more than thirteen hundred miles and twenty-four hours driving time."

"You know," said Walker with a laugh, "relationships between military officers are always difficult, even if they're in the same service. If you guys are going to build on what you've started, one of you is probably going to have to change careers."

Chad needed to change the conversation. He and Olga had discussed it, but without any commitment. "What's the drive like for tomorrow? I don't know the Flathead Reservation at all."

"From the house, less than an hour." Walker looked at his watch. "Time to feed Win and then put on a clean wool shirt for dinner."

~

They parked the pickup next to what Chad estimated was a five-thousand square foot home on a bluff just above the lake. The home was surrounded by decks above landscaped lawns dotted with pine trees. Massive windows offered a three-hundred sixty-degree view. Below was a boathouse with a concrete ramp extending into the lake.

Sonia Ramirez was technically still Sonia Ramirez Thompson, but she'd never used her married name, initially as a layer of separation from her DEA duties, and later as a bit of a barrier to her anger. Gritt estimated she was maybe sixty. At five foot four with smart short black hair, her brown eyes darted up and down as she studied him. She wore a white wool fisherman's sweater and form fitting jeans that confirmed Thad's earlier description of someone who ran distances for fun. She smiled as the two men climbed the stairs to where she waited. Burgundy lipstick added a little color to her deeply tanned face.

"Welcome Commander Chad Gritt," she said after kissing Walker on the cheek. "I hope you like wild game." She paused. "That was silly, you're here to do some hunting. Anyway, we're having a venison rump roast with vegetables."

"Sounds wonderful," replied Gritt. "I've been so busy the last few years that the only hunting I do is here with Thad and one trip in the Dakotas with my girlfriend."

"This is the last of my venison," she continued. "My late husband hunted deer every year, but I never was bitten by the bug. Maybe I can get Thad to harvest a deer for me before the season closes."

Gritt knew that wasn't going to happen. After a terrible incident when he was ten, Walker could never point a rifle at any living thing and pull the trigger, with the exception of critters with feathers. Even the Marine Corps had to find another way to use a man with extraordinary language skills, decisive judgment, and endless energy, because he wasn't going to be an infantry leader. Just taking up bird hunting had required years of soul searching for Walker. He rationalized it. He would shoot in front of the bird, and the pheasant would fly into the shot.

"We're hunting birds on the reservation," replied Walker. "We stopped in Poulson for licenses and permits this afternoon. There is no big game hunting for non-tribal members."

"Damn," replied Sonia with a smile. "I guess I'm going to have to take up hunting myself." She turned to the oversized carved door behind her and opened it. Please join me. I have some Dr Pepper cold and homemade lemonade or tea and coffee. The roast will be done in an hour."

Sonia took drink orders and pointed to several overstuffed leather chairs near a freestanding glass and soapstone fireplace in the middle of a living room that was larger than Thad's house. Outside was clear, except for a small grey squall that spit tiny flakes of snow over the center of the lake. Moments after they seated themselves, Sonia was back with two lemonades and a Dr. Pepper for herself.

"Thad told me that you were just in Mexico," she said as she used her free hand to drop another piece of split pine onto the fire. "I spent years with the government, many undercover in Mexico and later working with their government on anti-drug issues."

"After what I learned in my short trip, that sounds like dangerous work," said Chad.

"It was, but it needs to be done," replied Sonia. "It's not just the drugs, it's that those in the drug business are responsible for almost all the violent crime in the country. The murder rate is just crazy and kidnapping for money and to supply the sex trade makes it dangerous. I personally think that those four college girls who the authorities said drowned when their car went off a cliff north of Manzanillo were abducted. I would bet that they are being pimped somewhere."

The three enjoyed an evening of dining and conversation on a night when the sky cleared so completely you could see the reflection of stars in the lake. About ten, Sonia strode over to the southeast facing windows. "I'm putting the house up for sale in the next year. It was never my idea of a home, too damned big and impersonal. There aren't enough good memories here." She turned to Chad. "I mention it because Thad mentioned that you have a serious lady friend who likes the outdoors and that you love Montana. When my husband and I bought the land, the previous owners had planned an even more elaborate home here, and they carved out a half-acre lot down on the water to build housing for domestic staff. They wanted a full-time watchman and groundskeeper. I mention it because I'd be happy to make you a deal on that lot. Maybe before you leave you might want to look at it."

"That is a wonderful offer," replied Chad. "I don't know if we are going to be a couple, I mean all the time couple yet, but I'd love to own a little piece of this place." He turned toward Walker who beat him to the punch.

"Tomorrow, we hunt. You aren't flying out until late the following day, and we have some things to talk about. If the weather holds, you, I and Winchester can row down here that morning and take a look."

Walker had been right about the small ranch along the mountains they were hunting. The tribe and Montana Fish and

Wildlife had jointly managed much of the reservation for years, supporting good hunting and generating revenue for the tribe. The land they hunted hadn't been part of the generally accessible property. From the time they gave Winchester a direction, working a brush line between two pastures, they were on birds. They shot one limit before breaking for lunch.

Sitting on the tailgate of the truck, they took turns slicing chunks of summer sausage from a huge roll and coupling it with slices of cheddar and Swiss cheese. Between them, a huge bag of corn chips slowly disappeared. Winchester lay below their dangling feet, waiting for the occasional reward for finding every bird that they hit.

"I was thinking about the weapons from China issue," offered Walker as he refilled his mug from a hot thermos. "I kind of have an unwritten agreement with them."

"I remember you mentioning that when we were working on the EEL AND THE ANGEL project."

"That lost love I mentioned, the one who disappeared, her name was Tan," started Thad, "she was kidnapped by a Vietnamese General she'd had a baby with. It was while the Americans and Chinese were going through a real thaw in our relations. The Chinese invaded Vietnam for a few weeks and allowed me to go along with their army. Tan was supposedly living near the border. I was 'loaned' to the Chinese to coach them on the American weapons we had abandoned in Vietnam, and they agreed to help me find Tan. We missed her by only minutes."

Thad pointed to two whitetail deer moving at the far edge of the pasture. "We had a couple of other incidents together," continued Thad. "A couple of them were off the record, even to government leadership. I agreed never to participate in anything that might lead to conflict between the countries, and they agreed to lose my files. That was years ago. The people I worked with over there are probably mostly all dead by now, but maybe not all of them."

"Where are you headed with the history lesson my friend?" asked Chad.

"Just that while the Chinese talk a lot about the doctrine of the CCP, the Chinese Communist Party, it's been my experience that they remain primarily guided by the teaching of Confucius. They are focused on order above everything else. Disorder among the various ethnicities of China or among rival groups could spin out of control quickly."

"Makes sense to me," replied Gritt after draining his Moose Drool, slipping the empty back into the ice chest that sat behind them.

"They are not above medaling in other country's affairs," continued Walker. "But selling premium, current generation weapons to drug dealers where they might stir up trouble that can come back and bite the Chinse government's ass seems out of character."

"So, your thought is that the weapons might not be moving across the Pacific with the full agreement of the government," said Gritt.

"The current leader thought he had almost total control over the country. But my sources tell me that is not the case. There are cracks in the wall. I might still have some contacts in the Chinese military. There may be more to the problem than we see."

"I laid the groundwork to stay in touch with that Chinese intelligence operative from Project Eel," said Gritt. "Maybe it's time to make contact to discuss what we are seeing."

"And I can see if any of my old contacts are still in play," said Walker. "But we don't want to pull the trigger on this until we have more to share. If we even cast a shadow over any person or group before we have hard data, it might get people killed and destroy any credibility our contacts might have. If there are powerful people operating outside the official playbook, they may take out our friends before we can make a case."

The two men filled out the second limit of pheasants within an hour of finishing lunch. That evening they retired to the lawn chairs on the dock after a dinner of pheasant cooked in Apfelwein and sliced fruit. "It might be a bit chilly rowing the two miles to look at that land tomorrow morning," said Chad. He poured another glass of the apple wine from a jug that came from Walker's wine cellar dug into a bank below the house.

"Maybe cold for you," said Thad, "but I'll be rowing. You need to spend more time outside, and I don't mean on the beach in Mexico."

"I'll try," said Chad, pulling a stocking cap down over his ears. "Speaking of Mexico, Olga and I are headed down there for vacation in February. She's taking a crash course in Spanish."

"Sonia's parents are originally from central Mexico," said Walker. "Her parents came across the border in the forties and met in California several years later. In those days the US was offering work permits to anyone willing to pick up the slack for our guys fighting in the war. Sonia was born in the US and is a citizen, but she loves Mexico."

"You two are getting pretty close then?" inquired Chad.

"We've both given our lives to service. Both of us have more to give, but we agree that we've earned a life of our own. I hadn't heard about her selling the big house until she told you," added Thad. "But she sat in the chair you are in and sketched out how to expand my bedroom. She says when I dream, I sometimes thrash around, and a king-sized bed might be helpful."

Chad smiled at his friend and mentor and offered no comment.

Twelve hours later he was winging his way back to DC, thinking about his conversations with Thad and about a beautiful pine covered lot right on Flathead Lake.

CHAPTER 11

January 15, Washington DC

The International Advisors in Philanthropy Conference at the Intercontinental attracted professionals and activists from across the world for their three-day event. The meetings emphasized the need for private foundations and offered workshops from fundraising strategies and grantmaking to investment strategies, law and finance. Lunch on each of the conference days included recognition of both groups and individuals, with most of those honored names from American families and European aristocracy. The honoree on the last day did not fit that model.

"It is with great pleasure that I introduce a new global powerhouse in philanthropy," said the IAP's vice president, former US Senator Amy Dickson. "I've only gotten to know Maria Castillo for a few days, but I can see why she is one of our guests of honor. Ladies and gentlemen, the woman the press calls the Mexican Robin Hood, Maria Castillo."

Maria didn't walk to the podium, more like flowed, her floor length black linen skirt swishing around her ankles, her embroidered bright red puffed sleeve cotton blouse, out of place on a blustery Washington day that spit snow. "For those women in the audience who believe that bright red and blond hair do not go together," started Maria, "if you could read the small black lettering on my left shoulder, you would understand that for me, it is the only color that I could wear today."

She pointed to two lines on her shoulder. "The first line I stole from one of America's great social foundations. It reads, A Mind Is A Terrible Thing To Waste, and the second line simply says, The Castillo Foundation." She paused for effect before adding, "of course, it is in Spanish."

The laughter interrupted her for almost a minute. "The blouse is issued to every volunteer of the foundation, which in my country so far are all women. In just a few months, we have raised more than three million dollars for scholarships for bright Mexican youth who come from families that could never dream of their kids doing anything but tending the fields, sweeping floors, or selling trinkets from too early an age. Our goal is to reach one thousand kids this first year and double that every year for a decade."

"Our program has been so successful that next month we will begin work on a second foundation, this one dedicated to modernizing small family farms in Mexico so that those hardworking families can grow more than what they need to survive. Improving productivity of these farms, allowing cash crops as well as subsistence will lift thousands of peasants out of poverty."

Maria's speech continued for a few more minutes before she politely asked for help from any in the room already running foundations dedicated to similar goals. As she returned to her seat, there was another round of applause. Senator Dickson, the moderator, returned to the podium.

"My new friend Maria is far too modest," she said. "What she didn't tell you is that she came from a family torn apart by the drug business in Mexico, and while launching her efforts on behalf of the Mexican people, she is also the CEO of a transportation company that is one of the fastest growing companies in the Americas. You should also know that her own company contributes most of its profitability to her foundations. Her generosity is so well documented in Mexico that national lawmakers are pressing to modify national tax laws to encourage her kind of giving. Now that's what we mean when we emphasize what all of you do can change a whole country or the world. Maria, would you please stand again for a well-deserved round of applause?"

A dozen media photographers rushed toward her table to catch the moment. By that evening, Maria's picture and the story of her international recognition was the lead headline on every media outlet throughout Mexico.

That same evening, Chad caught a short story about Maria on the evening news. Since his return from Mexico, he'd devoured news about Mexico. His new boss, a Navy Captain, pressed him to turn one hundred percent of his focus back to using his engineering background to the development of conceptual tools that made the navy and marine corps safer from the autonomous drones being deployed by the world's nations. She was due to get her first star in the next few months. She had rocketed up the career ladder, developing a reputation for personal discipline and a 'do one thing to perfection' management philosophy. She'd made it clear to Gritt that Mexico was not his problem. But somehow it still was.

His friend Mike Stephens kept him apprised of the Office of Naval Intelligence efforts to help the Mexican government. Earlier that month, a Mexican navy surveillance plane had been fired on by a submersible. This time whoever fired the surface to air missile had failed because the plane was out of range.

A vehicle stopped by some local police, resulting in a shootout, was found to have very sophisticated frequency hopping radio equipment, communications impervious to Mexican government intercepts. Mike also mentioned that José Alfaro was growing concerned over cartel violence in Acapulco, including direct threats against personnel of the navy's pacific command, located there.

People in Chad's own division of ONI's Farragut Center were trying to figure out how a small submersible could evade the listening devices and active navy submarine sweeps in the San Diego area. The Navy had been recruited by the DEA and Coast Guard. Drugs were flooding across the border.

Some group had changed the drug dealer's traditional strategy of adding fentanyl to other drugs to make them more powerful. Now they were selling what they called 'safe' fentanyl pills on the streets of American cities. These were supposedly guaranteed to get you high without the risk of overdose. The drug came stamped 'SF' for safe fentanyl on the face of the lime green tablets. They might not kill you, but the 'safe' pills were pulling thousands more people into addiction. The assumption was that Mexican submersibles were moving the drugs north of the border where small boats were shuttling them to shore. None of that was officially Chad's problem, and that had been made clear.

Chad opened the refrigerator and popped the lid off a Modelo and then searched through the vegetable bin for something to make a salad for dinner. Seconds later, a head of brown lettuce, wilted green onions and squishy cucumber went into the trash and out came a package of beef hotdogs, and the last two stale buns in a bag. He reached into the cupboard for a can of Hormel Chile. He put the hot dogs in the microwave and set the pan of Chile on the stove and took his beer into the living room of his Georgetown home. His briefcase sat on the coffee table. Inside were files created by his staff, all evaluating possible contractors to build prototypes of his most promising drone defense idea.

He'd just opened the briefcase when his phone rang. "Hey, lover, it's me," said Olga when he answered. "Did I catch you before you start your late-night work?"

"Yup," he replied. "If you were here, I'd get nothing done."

"Same with me," she said. "Sounds nice, doesn't it?"

"Yup," he said again.

"I was just checking in, love, and confirming your exact vacation days for February."

"I've got from February fifth through the fifteenth off," replied Gritt. "I thought this was all set, or is it?"

"Nothing has changed, I guess I'm just excited. Sun, someone else cooking, not worrying if your troops are around if you have one too many drinks at the bar, the beach and of course you."

"A buddy of mine who's still in the loop on the Mexico problems told me that Commander Alfaro is worried about the cartel violence in Acapulco," he said.

"Yea, I got a bit of the same vibe from one of my people. Her name is Francesca Mateo, and she is originally from that area. She was wondering if I knew of any way to get her little sister legally across the border. There is a long lead time for visas and it's dangerous where she lives. She'd like her sister to follow her into the military."

"You'll have to contact an immigration attorney, I guess. I know that once you have legal status you can enlist and after at least a year of service you can apply for citizenship," said Chad.

"That's what Francesca did. She enlisted in the Army for four years, and after two got her citizenship. She transferred into the Air Force. She's about thirty and as committed to her job as anyone in the unit. I've recommended her for officers' school."

"Damn," replied Chad as he headed for the kitchen and a pan of Chile that was within seconds of igniting. "What did Francesca say about Acapulco?" he asked, lifting the pan from the stove.

"She said that there had been several nasty shootouts down there. One was right on the beach with hundreds of tourists around. It's why she wants to get her sister out."

"I'm not so sure we want to go there," said Chad. "I know it's a little late to book somewhere else, but it might be a good idea. It wouldn't be the first time either of us has had to dodge bullets, but that was for work."

"We've still got a couple of weeks," replied Olga. "Call your friend José. See what he thinks."

The two hung up and Chad wolfed down his dinner of microwave hot dogs on stale buns smothered in beans with a slightly smoky flavor. Then he dialed José.

An hour later he was back on the phone with Olga. "He sent his wife and daughter back to her home in Zihuantanejo. She's living in an apartment at her parent's small hotel. I told you I love Zihua. I'll call my friend Diego and see what he recommends."

CHAPTER 12

February 1, Mexico City, Mexico

Luis Cardenas hadn't seen Juan Ayala for more than a month. They made it a point not to be seen together very often, but Juan had demanded the meeting without discussing why.

"I know that you talk to our friend Hao," said Juan. We need to increase the deliveries of product to our distributors in all four hubs."

"We agreed that the fastest way to get caught was to get greedy, my friend," said Luis.

"The demand is going through the roof. Protecting our distribution channels is becoming very expensive," added Juan. "Our man in Yakima, Washington tells me that the other cartels are distributing counterfeit pills that look like ours. But they kill people. That's bad for business. Our customers trust our dealers, but if we can't supply, they are going to go elsewhere."

"It's not just making more pills," said Luis. "We then must get them to the Arizona border and that means more submarines. It means you will need to beef up security from the northern end of the Sea of Cortez to the border and then from Arizona to LA, Yakima, Denver, and Amarillo. We need to build up our transportation in the states."

"We only distribute in the western states now. Hao wants us nationwide. He can find the money," replied Juan.

"Remember, a lot of the profits are going to prop up Maria Castillo," said Luis. "That plan is working. In months she has become the most popular woman in Mexico."

"I was the one who recruited her, remember. That spoiled brat is living the good life while we take all the risks."

"That's what the plan was all about, my friend. Our new president has asked the Americans for more help. The more we expand, the more worried our competitors are becoming. They are fighting us and the government. Their leaders have allies in the army, but so far, the army is unwilling to directly challenge her. The president seems determined to crush us all. That's why it's important that she not remain president and that she be replaced by someone who will help us. Getting Maria all the funding she needs is important."

"Hao will understand what I am requesting," said Juan. "He will find the money. He will make sure his contacts in China send you more raw product. Your labs will press more pills. Hao will get us more weapons. When the time comes, we will make an offer to the army, to help them with modern weapons and money and they will help us."

"I thought you were only interested in the money," my friend. "Now you sound like you have higher plans."

Juan smiled as he lit a cigar. "I do not mind Maria Castillo becoming the president, if she remembers who is boss. She may need to slow her plans, if we need the funds."

Luis laughed. "Do you not understand that we are all now working for Hao?"

"I do, and I also know that he has infiltrated trained operatives into the US with our help, and probably Mexico as well. But one word from you or I could ruin everything he is working towards. Just talk to him. Get his help. Now I need to get going. One of the men I bribe in Sinaloa tells me that they are moving one of their attack groups up to the border to block our mules from crossing. That will need to be dealt with. It will give us an opportunity to test the new armed drones that Hao supplied."

Across town, Castillo Transportation was moving into a five-story glass and steel office building that the government had confiscated from a banker who had been caught laundering drug money. The company management team had grown from five to twenty in months and accounting and logistics personnel now numbered more than a hundred. Maria's office was on the top floor overlooking a park. Most of that floor was dedicated to the two foundations she now ran. Maria still struggled with delegating, but her VP of operations had the move under control. She checked her watch, refusing to be late for the most important appointment she had each week.

Only two miles away, in her still modest home, she now employed both a maid and a caretaker for her aging mother. The woman's dementia was taking away the woman who had kept Maria grounded during the loss of her father and his wealth. Once each week, the caretaker helped Angelina dress as she had when life was good, and then take her to meet Maria for a leisurely lunch at a favorite restaurant that played Tejano music. The music brought life to Angelina's eyes, and by the end of the meal, she would be singing the songs she and her poor but ambitious new husband had danced to in their tiny home across the border in Texas long ago.

The restaurant owner led Maria to a table in the back where her mother and caretaker were waiting. With Maria's newfound fame, the owner removed several tables around theirs when they were coming and blocked anyone with a camera while they dined.

"Maria, it is good to see you. You must visit your mother more often. I miss you."

A tear slipped from Maria's eye as she tried to come up with an appropriate answer. She and her mother had breakfast that morning and Maria sat and read the paper to her on the patio before work. "I promise I will, mama."

The regular lunch of rice, squash and chicken had just arrived when Maria's phone rang. It was a facetime call from Juan Ayala. She reluctantly clicked on the call, knowing that he would redial her until she picked up."

"Juan, please speak in English," she said as she answered.

"I wanna' tell you that Luis is pressing Hao to ramp up our business. It must be done. The challenges to the company are becoming expensive to deal with. We need to grow revenue. If Hao struggles to find the money, we may need to reduce our contributions to your charity work."

"Juan, we have a plan. Luis and I just increased the foundation budget. Our partners think the window for change must be opened more quickly."

"I tell you that will still happen with new funds from Hao. But maybe not. Anyway, now you are informed. Do not challenge me, Maria. We must expand or die."

Maria laid her phone on the table as she waited for Juan to figure out how to disconnect the call. He always fumbled with that."

She looked up to see her mother staring at the phone. "That man used to come to the house. I never trusted him." Angelina leaned back in her chair. "Or maybe it was a different man."

CHAPTER 13

February 5, Zihuantanejo, Mexico

CHAD AND OLGA arrived within minutes of each other. Her Aeromexico shuttle from Mexico City allowed her to clear the Zihua airport quickly since she'd already cleared customs. Chad's American flight from Phoenix left him in a long line at immigration. Fifty minutes after landing, he finally carried his one bag out of the airport where he found Olga attracting substantial attention sitting on her bag near the cab stand, a smaller bag at her side.

"God, this is better than Minot, North Dakota in the middle of winter," she said as he approached. Before he could wrap his arms around her, he heard his name called.

"If you had informed me to be looking for a tall stunning blonde, I might have spared this woman from the leering of these sharks," said Diego Cervantes, still in uniform. He extended his hand to Chad. "Welcome back, Commander."

Chad resisted sweeping Olga into his arms and instead settled for a kiss on the cheek, which he returned. "Olga Tvorshik this is my friend Lieutenant Diego Cervantes. Diego, she may not look like it right now, but Olga is a US Air Force officer, and she outranks you."

Diego began to laugh. "My father always coached me to recognize when I was out of my league. I am pleased to meet you Olga Tvorshik, had I connected you with my friend Chad here, you wouldn't have had to sit here like a common tourist."

Olga smiled as she extended her hand to Diego. "You knew someone was joining Chad. What did you expect?"

Diego picked up both of Olga's bags and turned to the parking lot where his Mustang was parked. "I just assumed that Chad had been raised a lot like me, to know when he was a minor leaguer playing in the majors."

The three piled into Diego's convertible and moments later were racing into town. "Do all handsome military officers drive old convertibles?" asked Olga, not waiting for an answer before throwing her arms up in the air and screaming with joy.

A half hour later Diego pulled up to the lobby of the Del Mar, the same hotel that Gritt had stayed in earlier. The front desk seemed pleased to see him again. "Thank you for finding us a room at this late date," said Chad.

"It's not really a room," said the clerk as she reached into a refrigerator under the counter and handed Olga and Chad a cold Pacifico. "I assume, Diego", she said, "that you do not drink in uniform. Perhaps a cold Coke instead." She pointed at a small terrace overlooking the bay. "You will be in the penthouse apartment just up the stairs. The maids are finishing there now, so if you wouldn't mind a short wait on the terrace, I'll have someone deliver your bags and then come get you when they are done."

"Wow, the penthouse apartment," said Olga. "I thought we had agreed to split the costs for this trip. I don't know if I can afford the penthouse."

"I loved this place when I was here in October. The penthouse was the only room available after we backed out of the hotel in Acapulco. Olga, I can afford it, my treat."

"You would have probably been okay in Acapulco," said Diego. "But I talked to José Alfaro just yesterday, and there are gun battles in the residential areas almost every day. Gangs fighting gangs, some over drugs, some over prostitution, some over other things. It was a little nasty in that city before the hurricane a couple of years ago, but the tourist business still hasn't recovered, so things are tight. Even here, don't walk the unlighted roads away from the waterfront at night. We've had a few robberies, and the local police think the bandits are Acapulco men just trying to feed their families."

The three leaned on the railing overlooking the hotel spaced out along the hillside below and the ocean beyond. "It is as beautiful as you described," said Olga. She turned her face up toward the sun. "And the warmth is divine." She turned to Diego who was just finishing his Coke. "As a kid I grew up in Russia before my mother married an American and we moved to the states. I'm comfortable in cold climates. In the states, we lived in Arizona, and I admit I like it hot."

"I wondered where you were originally from," said Diego, "I couldn't place the slight accent. Anyway, welcome. I made dinner reservations for you two at David's. It's not the best restaurant in town, but they will have a candlelight table for you at eight, right on the beach." He started to leave but stopped. "I don't know if you heard, but one of our patrol boats disappeared last night just south of Cabo San Lucas. They had reported something low in the water traveling north. So far, they have found no wreckage. Anyway, I'll call tomorrow. My girlfriend wants to meet you and we would like to show you around maybe the day after tomorrow. For tomorrow I recommend nothing but the beach."

Chad walked back to the lobby talking with Diego and watched him pull away. Moments later a white Suburban pulled away from the curb just downhill from the hotel and followed. *There must be more than one Suburban*, he thought while walking back into the open-air lobby. Still, it bothered him. Olga had disappeared from the terrace.

The clerk pointed at a set of stairs. "She followed Carlos up to your room. She has both keys."

Chad passed a fifty something aged man with a huge smile on his face coming down the stairs. "Close the door," said Olga. "This is a full suite with two bedrooms, a kitchen, and a beautiful open-air living space," she said, her face peeking around a doorway. "It's beautiful and come here and look at this huge, tiled bathroom and shower."

Chad tossed the jacket he was carrying on the couch and followed her voice. She stood naked adjusting the water in a shower larger than most bathrooms. "I need a shower and I thought you might like to join me. Then how 'bout a swim and a rest before dinner?"

Olga's modest one-piece bathing suit did nothing to hide her curves. Like on his October trip, most hotel guests were older, but not all. There were even two couples with children at the pool as they passed on their way down six garden flanked flights of stairs to the beach.

"That water slide looks like fun," offered Olga. "I haven't been on one since I was a kid in Arizona."

They found two lounge chairs under a palm thatched umbrella only feet from where a small surf broke onto the white sandy beach. "Do you want some sunscreen before we swim?" he asked.

"No, it's afternoon sun and we need to get started on a tan or we will end up burned."

They waded into the small waves before diving through a

larger one and swimming. Chad was surprised by how Olga powered through the water. He worked to catch up, as she headed down the beach toward a point along the pedestrian walk to town where several young men were fishing. He began to tread water where she had stopped.

"I don't want to interfere with their fishing," she said.

"You swim really well for someone stationed in North Dakota," he offered.

"And you for someone in DC. Once we decided we were heading for the beach, I tried to swim laps every day. Let's head back and find a place to soak up some sun."

"I'm in," he replied. "Maybe a margarita to celebrate being here and a little ceviche."

The two dragged their heavy wooden lounges into the sun and a waiter appeared with drinks and a snack. "No more than an hour of direct sun for me, "she said. "I burn easily. By the way you didn't tell me that you were ordering raw fish. I usually don't like sushi, but this is delicious."

"Ceviche is not really raw. The acids in the marinade cook it but leave the texture firm. Chopped onions and peppers add a little bite."

Olga smiled as she loaded another corn chip with ceviche. "Without staring, do you know the two men in slacks and knit shirts sitting in chairs under the furthest umbrella at the bar next door?"

Chad casually glanced up the beach, stopping his gaze at several people walking, finally taking in those in the bar area. He picked out the two dark complexion men he thought she was referring to. "No, Why?"

"They came down the stairs from the hotel next to ours as we headed out to swim. Since we came back in, they appear to be watching us."

"Damn, Olga, any guy over the age of ten is probably watching you. If they are watching me, maybe they are thinking what Diego said, that I'm out of my league. Probably trying to figure out why you don't get rid of me and give someone else a chance."

She rolled off her lounge, sitting on the edge of Chad's before leaning down and smothering his face with kisses. Stretching out on her back moments later, she offered, "if I didn't want you around, I would have let that terrorist shoot you a second time last year."

That evening as the two finished up a candlelight dinner on the beach, Olga poured the last of a great local white wine into their glasses. Chad handed his credit card to the waiter who came to clear their table. The lights of the small village reflected on the black water all around the horseshoe bay. Small water taxis continued to shuttle around the bay, while out by the lighthouse the twinkling lights of the night fishermen reminded Chad of his great night of fishing only months before. "I'm going to see if Diego can set us up with his fishing guide. Have you done any deep-sea fishing?"

"Only for salmon and halibut when I was stationed in Alaska," she replied as she finished her wine. "Can we go for a walk? There seems to be quite a commotion along the walkway right in the middle of town."

"That's the village gathering place," said Chad as he worked to slide his chair back in the soft sand. "There's a basketball court there with games almost every night."

The two walked into the bright lights of a small plaza. Instead of a basketball game on the court, a stage had been set up and the speakers were blaring Tejano music. Banners hung above the stage and four women in red blouses circulated through a crowded seating area handing out brochures. Chad and Olga found a seat on the cement bleachers just as a stunning blonde woman wearing a red blouse left the stage.

A man followed her to the microphone and the music stopped. "For those of you from the US and Canada here tonight, the Castillo Foundations are Mexico's largest public benefit foundations. I am not the public speaker that Maria is, but her speech tonight was to inform parents with bright children that they could apply for higher education scholarships from her foundation. For the subsistence farmers, her foundation has economic development grants that might change their lives. If you would like to help, we would appreciate a donation. Just take an envelope and brochure from one of the volunteers. If you would like information on how to become a major donor and what that might mean to the people of Mexico, please let a volunteer know, and we'll be delighted to meet with you."

The man turned toward Maria Castillo, who was with two bodyguards and a gentleman in a tan cotton suit at the side of the stage. "Thank you, Maria, for taking time from your busy schedule to be with us in person tonight." Turning back to the crowd, he offered a few more comments in Spanish before translating. "Maria is the guest tonight of one of the strongest donors to her charity, Luis Cardenas." A short round of applause for someone who has committed to donate more than one hundred thousand dollars a month for the next two years."

"I saw that woman on the news back home," said Chad as they accepted a brochure from one of the volunteers. She was being honored by some group in DC."

The brochure was printed in Spanish on one side and English on the other. "She seems to be quite a remarkable woman," said Olga as she read, "brains, beauty, passion."

"I'll have my family foundation look into her. Maybe we

can help," said Chad. "As to the brains, beauty and passion, in a contest you would win."

Two days later, Diego and his girlfriend, Elena picked them up just after noon. An hour later after a boat shuttle from Ixtapa, they found themselves snorkeling in a small sanctuary along an island just off the coast. The area had been so well protected that dozens of species of brightly colored fish swam, sometimes only inches from where they used swim fins to kick slowly along the surface, their mask covered faces taking in what Chad and Olga had only seen on television nature shows.

Elena and Olga had hit it off especially when they discovered that both were learning Spanish. Elena's family had immigrated to Mexico from Italy six years before, but she'd stayed on to finish at the university, studying medicine. She joined her parents in Guadalajara where they ran a very successful Italian restaurant. The two women were about the same age difference as Chad and Diego, about five years.

The meeting between Elena and Diego had been a fluke. Her flight from Rome had been late arriving in Mexico City and Elena had missed her connecting flight. Struggling with her Spanish-Italian dictionary she was having trouble getting on another flight until Diego noticed that she carried a novel in English. He acted as a translator for her, helping get her on a flight after only a two hour wait. They had used the time to have lunch, and stayed in touch, and Diego used every excuse he could to visit. Elena accepted a part time job at a clinic in Zihua, while she studied to become licensed in Mexico.

"It must be exciting to be a security officer in your air force," said Elena, as the two women waited at a snack bar.

"It must be rewarding to be a doctor in a new country," answered Olga.

"Most of the time," said Elena. "Sometimes, it seems more than one should have to deal with."

"At least when it gets like that for you," replied Olga, "you are probably trying to save a life. In my line of work, I've had to draw my weapon and do the opposite."

"Only a couple of weeks ago, I went with Diego to Manzanilla. His troops were wrapping up guarding that damaged navy ship, providing security for the salvage crew who were loading it on a barge. The night they finished we all went out to dinner." Elena wiped at tears in her eyes.

"A young Asian looking girl stopped on the sidewalk just feet from our table. She'd been running. She wore ripped pajamas and was haggard and bleeding. Moments later a man ran up and began dragging her. Diego and his four men rushed to follow as the girl was dragged into an alley. They arrived just as the man began beating her. Diego ordered him to stop, and the man pulled out a gun. Diego's sergeant shot him dead."

"That's a terrible story. But it's probably good that he is dead."

Elena turned to watch the two men talking on the beach, still wiping tears from her face. "Dead, dead, he's not dead enough. I rushed to give that poor girl first aid. I don't speak Chinese and that girl tried to talk. She was so thin, with sores all over her body and she had been beaten so badly. She died before we could get her to a hospital."

"Not dead enough. That must be hard for a doctor to say," said Olga, handing Elena a handful of bar napkins.

"I already love Mexico," said Elena finally smiling again. "But there are things going on here that remind me of what the Mafioso do in Italy. Brutal, inhumane things. Like back home, much of Mexico's legal system is corrupt. I worry about Diego. The navy and marines are about the only group in this country who seem completely committed to the law and justice. The new president is counting on them more and more. I worry that it is putting a target on his back."

"Chad is one of those officers who is rocketing up the ladder in our navy. He has an amazing sense of people and is one of the most analytical people I know. He has great respect for Diego. I think he will be okay." Olga turned to watch the two men talking. Diego was sitting in the sun and Chad was under the shade of a huge tree.

Their evening finished later after an Italian dinner cooked at Diego's condominium and served on his terrace overlooking the bay. Diego offered to drive them to their hotel, but Chad insisted on calling a cab. "Diego told me about that girl while we were discussing how they finally got the Montezuma out of Manzanillo. One of his guys got it all on his cell phone. The girl was Chinese, and she was begging Elena to find the other seven girls that had been in the shipping container. She ran the moment they opened the door."

"Was anybody arrested? Did they find the others?

"They found a shipping container filled with clothing and sleeping pads on the dock, but not the other girls. The local police didn't seem too worried. They didn't even take statements from Diego, Elena or his troops."

Olga slid closer to Chad as the cab started down a hill into town, turning left toward their hotel. He could feel her shiver. Moments later he handed the drive a hundred peso note and helped her from the car. She stood in the open lobby of the hotel for several minutes before pointing at the terrace bar. "How about a drink? I could use a brandy."

"The bar's closed. But if you run up to the room, there is a small bodega store only three minutes from here. I'll go buy us a bottle."

Olga had composed herself by the time Chad got back. She was sitting in an overstuffed chair in the open-air living room with two brandy snifters in front of her. "I hate stories like that," she said as he poured brandy into the glasses. "When I'm done being an air force cop, maybe working on problems like that will be my next career. We had one of our young airmen get into drugs a few months ago. Couldn't afford her habit so she ended up being pimped in her off-duty time. Before anyone could help, she overdosed"

She looked up at Chad. "Is this place safe? All of the sudden, I feel naked without my Barretta."

"It's safe for people like us if we are careful. There are thousands of tourists here and no one is bothering them. The locals we've been around all seem okay. I wouldn't have brought you here if I didn't think it was safe."

"But it is not safe for people unlike us," she said.

"The ship attacks, violence on the border, the drug trade, human trafficking, and the corruption is all part of the problem that I came down to help with." He put his hand on Olga's knee and squeezed. "It's a Mexican problem, and it's getting worse. But people like their new president seem determined to fix it. People like Diego and Commander Alfaro who I worked with last fall are part of the solution. That woman we saw the other night, that Castillo woman seems committed to make a difference."

Olga leaned over and kissed Chad on the ear. "Elena told me that Diego doesn't trust her. Nobody is asking where all her money is coming from. He says that at least part of it is from China. And it's more and more an American problem."

She finished her brandy. "Thanks for the drink. I'd like to go to bed now. I just want to be held."

Eight days later, Diego and Chad talked in the front seat

of the Mustang while Elena and Olga shared cell phone information in the back seat. The couple shared a flight to Phoenix where Olga was to catch a flight to Minneapolis and then Minot and Chad a flight straight to DC. As they waited for their connecting flights, they shared pictures of deep-sea fishing, touring ancient native ruins and walks on the beach. "We're going back next year," said Olga. "We will book it earlier. I don't need a big fancy suite. Hell, we didn't spend any time there except to sleep. But the big bed was nice." She blushed.

The great memories of the trip and of a woman that he was falling head over heels in love with occupied the first hour of the four-hour flight to Reagan International Airport. He was a bit angry when the thoughts of the Montezuma and the discussions he and Diego had shared about problems crept into his mind. The story of the Chinese girl, and worse of little effort to solve the case, troubled him. Even Diego's update on the strange lights they had seen while night fishing and the darkened boats heading out to sea was troubling. The local police had politely suggested that they had investigated and found nothing. His close friend on the force had bluntly told Diego to drop it. Chad knew that his friend wouldn't.

CHAPTER 14

February 20, Arizona-Mexico Border

Sergeant Paul Thibs hadn't been to that section of the border in six months. The tip that led to his last deployment had been legitimate. There was a major drug smuggling effort that night, but it had cost the life of an officer. This tip was different. The call had come directly to him from a burner phone in Mexico. The caller suggested that he might be interested in how Mexicans are cleaning up their own mess, and how committed they are to stopping fentanyl from crossing the border. The caller gave him the specific coordinates to watch and recommended that he bring a camera capable of filming in low light.

Thibs and another officer used ATVs to cross part of the air force target range on the American side of the border and sometime before midnight set up a camera on a hill overlooking the same spot where bad guys had killed bad guys before.

The full moon that night illuminated the terrain, and with the night vision equipment, they could see for miles. Shortly before 1 a.m., a Dodge super cab pickup rolled into view from the east. It stopped almost exactly where the same truck had stopped the last time. Thibs watched as six people stepped out of the truck and five of them began to adjust the straps on huge backpacks. So far, the only thought in Thib's mind was that he didn't have enough people along to stop that many smugglers.

He watched the truck driver direct the five mules into a circle and just like last time, they turned their phones off. Before they could move, a Ford pickup raced out of a wash only a few hundred yards in front of the group. Moments later, a second Ford truck appeared out of a narrow valley behind the Dodge. Four men jumped out of each truck pointing guns at the drug runners who then dropped to the ground.

Men from both directions began walking toward the Dodge. The lead man in each group fired shots that skipped on the ground only inches from the drug runners. Through night vision binoculars, Thibs watched the shooters point and laugh, taunting those they were about to kill. Seconds later, a loud buzzing sound came from across the border. From behind a ridge a quarter of a mile away, a large aircraft with an eight-foot wingspan popped into view. Before he could shift the camera, the craft launched two rockets at the men walking in front of the Dodge. The ground around them erupted and all four were tossed like dolls into the air. Thibs watched in shock, but luckily his partner picked up the camera and began tracking the aircraft.

The people in front of the Dodge didn't move. Behind them, the four from the second Ford truck scrambled back into the cab and the driver spun the truck and gunned it toward the same track that the Dodge had arrived on.

The aircraft or drone or whatever it was circled out over where Thibs and his partner hid and then turned toward the racing Ford truck. Two more rockets reduced that truck to shredded metal exploding through a fireball.

The two agents sat, stunned, observing what was now obviously a drone begin a sweeping turn back toward the border. They watched as the craft wiggled its wings while flying directly toward them. From directly above, another rocket flashed, tracking to where their two ATVs were parked and blasted them.

Below, the driver of the Dodge lifted a large box from the truck bed and set it on the ground before the five mules piled into the bed of the Dodge truck and headed west. He drove around the smoldering bodies of the four men who only minutes before were about to kill them. He stopped next to the remaining Ford truck, halting just long enough to toss something under the truck which exploded in a fireball as he drove west.

Thibs watched through night vision binoculars as the truck stopped only a mile further west and the drug mules piled out and headed toward the border.

"We won't catch them on foot," said his partner, "not with a head start and a ridge between us and them."

Thibs slipped his radio from his belt and lifted it to call. The instant he keyed the transmit button a loud screech sounded through the speaker. His partner tried his with the same result. Somehow their radios were being jammed. The same thing happened when they tried their cell phones. It would be a two hour walk to the road where they had left their truck and ATV trailer. Thibs knew that if he didn't check in within an hour help would be on the way, but it would be several hours. He also knew the packages the mules carried were so valuable that someone was already waiting to rush them out of the desert.

"Whatever that is sitting on the ground just across the border is blocking our communications," offered Thib's partner. "I can run down there and smash it."

"You stay put," replied Thibs. "The last time I was here there was a sniper across the border. Bonnie died."

An hour later, the Dodge truck passed the wreckage below them and then stopped and picked up the box it had left earlier. The driver waved to the two agents and then drove past the second wrecked truck and disappeared.

Thibs was not surprised when his radio and cell phone began working again. Whoever had orchestrated the evening was sending a message. The game had changed.

CHAPTER 15

March 1, Governors Point, Virginia

"Mat, thank you for meeting with me," said David Lopez. "I assume that we are meeting at Sportsman's Grill because I am still not welcome at the agency?"

Mat Chang waited until his two bodyguards were in place before extending his hand to David. He took a minute to study an old colleague dressed in a grey business suit, white shirt and a tie emblazoned with the image of a Native American brave seated on a horse in a snowstorm. "David, I wouldn't say, not welcome. More like there are still some people who think you should have been shot instead of retired."

"Just sour grapes. I always thought my job was analysis and threat assessment. I was never very good about parroting the party line." Lopez had been the head of the Latin America Desk at the CIA, leaving when his counsel on how ignoring that region was damaging America's relationships with young impressionable liberal leaders of several countries. America was obsessed with the Middle East, and it showed. Lopez had his PhD in international affairs. His mother was from Nebraska and his father Mexican. Carrying either a Mexican or American passport helped him in his job until it didn't. He was a progressive in a cauldron of conservative thought. He and Chang met in college when both were working on advanced degrees.

"That description might be a little self-serving," said Mathew Chang. "But I'm assuming that your request for a meeting wasn't to reminisce on old times."

David sipped the beer he'd ordered before Chang arrived. "I think you might already know why I called. In my job, I advise the new president of Mexico on issues of international relations. She asked me a question that I couldn't answer. 'Why would China supply sophisticated weapons to Mexican criminal gangs?'"

Chang waved at a waiter and ordered a Coke in the mostly empty restaurant. "I'd join you in a beer, David, but I have a dinner meeting with a couple of people on the Senate Intelligence Committee. Part of that discussion will be about why Mexico would allow China so much access to their economy and media when they were supplying weapons to the bad guys."

"Two sides of the same coin," replied Lopez. "You know that I disagree with American foreign policy in Latin America. After I left the agency, I taught in a couple of colleges in the states and then in Mexico. The more time I spent there, the more it felt like home. I renounced my American citizenship three years ago and now carry only a Mexican passport."

"With the Mexican passion for fierce independence, I'll bet having a former American in Lupita Martinez's cabinet has raised a ruckus in Mexico."

"I'm not in the cabinet. I have an office down the hall from the president, and my official duty is coaching young Mexican diplomatic staff. That's worked as a cover for being her primary counselor on international relations, especially with the US."

"Okay," replied Chang as a plate of popcorn fried shrimp arrived at the table. "What do your internal intelligence people think is happening?"

"My colleagues at the CNI, our intelligence agency have no answers. The Secretaria de Relaciones Exteriores, our equivalent of the State Department has pressed China on this and in every meeting the Chinese swear they are not the source," said Lopez.

Both men watched as a young couple entered the restaurant and approached their corner window table before one of Chang's men motioned for the waiter to seat them further away.

Chang felt a little used by an old friend. "A guy I trust was part of the group we loaned to your navy to determine the origin of the rocket that crushed one of your small ships. His team determined that both that rocket and the missile that downed one of our Coast Guard helicopters were products of China's Norinco Group. That drone incident on the Arizona border was also a Chinese manufactured weapon. The CH-92A drone is available for export, but the export model only has wing hard points for two missiles and a center point for a larger rocket." Chang watched his old colleague slide his appetizer to the center of the table.

"Sorry about eating your shrimp, I didn't have time for lunch." Chang popped a couple more into his mouth. "You remember Pete Wilson, he's now running our tech group. His people watched the video of that drone and are confident it was a CH-92 from China, but a version built for their own military, with six hard points on the wings plus one center point."

"Mat, I believe you. I'm here because we know that Chinese weapons are being supplied," said Lopez. "The cartels use them to kill each other and against the government. Which gets me back to President Martinez's question, why? We need your help on this. Your navy is already helping our navy. Can you work with our CNI? Together we might at least develop a thesis on why the Chinese are supplying weapons and what the long game is."

"The short answer to your question about the CIA working directly with your CNI is: not now." Chang knew that wasn't the answer that his old friend was looking for. "David, under President Martinez's predecessor, our efforts to stop the drugs flowing over our border, especially fentanyl were met with half efforts or none. He facilitated much of the illegal human smuggling at our border. His position that addiction was an American problem was probably mostly accurate, but it wasn't a position that our political establishment accepted. I'm a political appointee. I'm close to the president. For right now, his official position is that the turmoil in Mexico is a Mexican problem."

Lopez popped a couple of tiny fried shrimp into his mouth and chewed them as he thought through a response, finally offering, "I get it. If what goes around comes around is good enough for American concerns, then it is good enough for Mexican concerns. The problem is our side was wrong before and your side is wrong now. Fentanyl is killing Americans and Chinese weapons are killing Mexicans. The source of both is mostly China and neither seem to be in the best interest of the Chinese government."

Chang laughed. "It must have been a bitch being a progressive in the agency. Fighting for attention for a region where nobody was shooting at us or our allies. Working the Latin America desk had to be frustrating. You know as well as I do that being right in an environment where nobody cares accomplishes little." Chang finished his Coke and motioned to his guards that he was ready to leave.

"David, I personally think you are mostly right in your analysis. But remember, you are asking me to embrace that analysis from someone who my predecessor lost confidence in, someone who later walked away from his American citizenship. I'm not able to formally offer any direct support. If it hadn't been for a US Coast Guard helicopter being shot down, killing four crew, I doubt that the Mexican Navy would have gotten as much help as they did on the loss of your ship."

Lopez began to smile. "That's why we are meeting in the middle of the afternoon in a restaurant isn't it? President Martinez cannot be seen asking for your help. It would be perceived as unpatriotic and might get her killed. But I heard what you said just now. That leaves me with one question. Can you tell me what you have in mind for indirect support?"

"No," answered Chang. "But someone will be in contact in the next few weeks. They will not be tied directly to me. Perhaps you and they can work out a plan. I will tell you that what the Chinese are doing right now worries people who work for me."

The men shook hands before Chang headed for his limo, followed by his two guards and then the waiter who tossed his apron across the bar as he followed. Moments later the bartender arrived at the table with a bill for three Cokes, his beer, and the shrimp.

Chang was almost to his dinner at the Shanghai Lounge in Georgetown when he finally got Chad Gritt to answer his phone.

"Director, how may I help you?"

"Commander," I am on my way to dinner in Georgetown," replied Chang. "Will you be home about nine this evening?"

Gritt looked at the four folders on his desk. Each contained test results of anti-drone technologies, and he had an appointment to brief his boss on each the next morning. Still when the director of the CIA wanted to meet, it was probably something important. "I can take what I'm working on home," he offered. "I can order dinner, and have it delivered, so yes, I can meet you at nine."

"Order whatever you want from the Shanghai Lounge. I'll have my advance man drop it by," said Chang. "And thanks."

A man in a black Chevy Tahoe was waiting in front of Gritt's townhome. He carried a large white bag as he jogged to catch up to Chad opening the door. "Just go ahead and eat," he said as he handed Gritt the bag. "I'll need a few minutes to do a security sweep of your house and then I'll be out of your hair."

Chad grabbed a bath towel and then carried his dinner and briefcase into the living room. He seldom had time to go to his favorite Chinese restaurant and it was a treat to have the advance security agent for the director of the CIA hand deliver vegetable spring rolls, Szechuan beef and an order of fried dry green beans and bacon. Spreading the towel like a tablecloth he opened three wax containers and ripped some chopsticks from their plastic wrap. He thought as he stared at his briefcase. There was plenty of room on the coffee table for him to start work while he ate, but the files he needed to review were top secret, and off limits even to a security officer of the CIA.

At precisely nine, his cell displayed a text that Mat Chang was five minutes out. He packed his files back into his briefcase, thankful that Chang's security man had quickly retreated to his car, giving Chad over an hour to work. "You know, Director, I would have made time to drive over to your building tomorrow," he offered as he opened the door for Chang.

"Better this conversation take place away from the office," replied Mat as Gritt ushered him into a living room that reeked of garlic. "How's work?"

"If you are asking if I am slammed, no, but I'm glad that I'm able to work twelve hours a day. I am on a project that is going to take another year, but my boss is pressing to speed it up. But you know technology challenges, sir. You run hard until you need to stop and evaluate."

"And how is Olga? I understand she joined you for your second trip to Mexico a few weeks ago."

"Do you have someone tracking everyone in the country? asked Gritt with a laugh.

"No, but Jana passed on your report on the first Mexico trip and the results of your study. One of her people was talking to Lieutenant Stephens and he mentioned that you were taking a few days off."

"I did, and Olga loved it. I've made a couple of friends down there. I'd bet that both will someday make admiral. One, the young marine officer who commands the tiny base in Zihuantanejo showed us around, swimming, fishing, exploring ruins, but mostly just eating well and soaking up sun." Chad looked over at Chang, trying to figure out why he was there.

Chang almost never showed any emotion, which made him difficult to read. "While you were there, especially after the first trip, did you develop any strong impressions of how widespread the troubles are in Mexico?"

"Director, you have experts to give you a far better briefing than I can offer. One call and it will be in your office before I even get out of bed tomorrow."

"But I wouldn't find what I am looking for." Chang paused long enough to open a picture on his phone, extending it to Chad. "The man in the picture is David Lopez. He is a PhD who not long ago ran the Latin desk at the agency. Now he is a citizen of Mexico and a close confidant of Lupita Martinez. I met him earlier today at his request. David, President Martinez and now I can't figure out the Chinese play in Mexico. China's diplomats seem to be trying to mend fences with us, while building economic and political ties with Mexico. At the same time, they are the source of most of the fentanyl coming across our border.

According to your report and others I've seen, they are supplying military grade weapons to the cartels."

"The Mexican officers I work with have the same questions," replied Gritt. "Almost every piece of illegal activity in Mexico is orchestrated by cartels. But the two major players seem to have at least one new competitor fielding technology beyond what the Mexican military has. Hell, the vessel that killed the Montezuma and our helicopter can submerge and disappear. The damned thing is an actual submarine."

"Do those same officers have any ideas on who is fielding the new sophisticated weapons or supplying them?"

"I didn't even hear any speculation on who the new power broker is, but it's clear to them that the weapons are from China." Gritt paused a moment. "While I was there the first time, a couple of oriental men seemed to be following me. On my trip with Olga, some Mexican men were shadowing us. The marine officer mentioned that there were a lot more Chinese businessmen all up and down the west coast. His sergeant had to shoot a man beating a young Chinese woman who had been transported across the Pacific in a shipping container. The whole time Olga and I were in Zihua, someone was shadowing Diego."

Chang put his phone away. "David unofficially asked for our help to figure out the Chinese link. I officially declined. With strained relations between Mexico and the US over the last few years, some people in our government think the problems Mexico is experiencing are their own problem. I met with a couple of them this evening."

"But," said Chad, "those problems are more and more becoming our problem as well."

"I agree, but unofficially. You already have a little experience with this. I'd like for you to give some thought to how we might get David an answer for President Martinez and maybe for ourselves."

Chad smiled at the older man who had somehow been involved in his life over the last few years. "You know that I already talked to your old friend Thad Walker about some of this."

"Yup, I talked to Thad the afternoon that David first contacted me. His take was that unless we got lucky with one contact who had the whole story, it might take a lot of digging both in Mexico and in China."

"You know from the EEL project that the Chinese field agent, Ma, and I agreed to keep the doors open to future discussions, should that be important to both countries."

"As I recall, his full name is Ma Mingze Li, and I think he has moved up a bit. He's kind of an odd duck over there in that he still isn't military. He went from an errand boy who always got the ugly jobs to more like a consultant whose job is to keep the zealots over there from blowing things up while at the same time keeping an eye on American technology."

Chang rose, slipping his tan raincoat over his blue suit. "You know, I still think you should consider working for us." He held up his hand as Chad started to object. "However, it might be even better to have you outside our bubble. Give some thought to our conversation this evening. Make a call to Walker and anyone else you can think of. The agency is not officially going to take on answering Mexico's problem. But I know the president is anxious to keep rebuilding our relationship with China and he would give his left nut to figure out how to stop illegal drugs crossing our border." Chang extended his hand to Chad. "Finding the funds for an off the record run at figuring out China's play in Mexico would be reasonably easy. It wouldn't be the first time that we found the money for Walker or his associates."

"Director, I know I said that I wasn't slammed right now, but that's because I work all the damned time anyhow. My boss wants to push my research."

"But unless I miss my guess, the thing in Mexico and getting to the bottom of why so many are dying is also damned important. It's the kind of thing that keeps you awake."

Chad nodded his head.

"If you and Walker can come up with a plan, let me or the president deal with your boss."

CHAPTER 16

April 1, Shandong, China

Hao Sun sat sipping tea. He'd been home for more than two weeks, just long enough to assure that his wife was well, and his son and daughter were channeling their frustrations into productive work. Like so many young Chinese who had watched the explosive economy wither, they each struggled with jobs that seemed dead end and dreams that were constantly downgraded. His son was an officer in the army. His daughter had followed his lead and studied in the US, returning to China with an MBA in finance from UCLA.

With most of the scaled down defense budget going into expanding the navy, promotion in the army had almost stopped. His daughter's dream job with a massive real estate developer had soured as the company struggled to fill vacant housing they'd built. Most of her time was now spent with lawyers and politicians trying desperately to find some way to keep the company from being crushed by massive debt and past due loans so vast that they had stopped making even interest only payments.

The paradox in his own mind was not lost on Hao. He was

still a passionate believer in China's future as the dominant world power. That demanded America's slide as much as China's rise. At the same time, he understood that a militant foreign policy especially with neighbors, pushed potential partners away. Revisions in business laws that protected Chinese theft of foreign technology while at the same time criminalizing any foreigner who even did due diligence on a company promoting Chinese technology were destroying the economic miracle that had come with partnerships with western companies.

He and the small group he represented all believed that problems arose because the Chinese Communist Party had abandoned its first founding principal, collective leadership through internal party democracy. No one man had all the answers. China had more engineers, more scientists, more teachers and even more skilled finance experts than their rival. But the centralization of power in the party excluded almost everyone who thought differently than the party chairman. Even the politburo, the cabinet around the general secretary, had been purged of dissenting views. So, when things started to unravel, his only solution was to do more of what wasn't working. China was wasting its opportunity for world dominance.

Hao had driven to Baotu Spring, one of China's most beautiful parks, built around an artesian spring that poets and musicians had honored for centuries. He was meeting two of the ten men who made up what they laughingly referred to as the gang of ten. They were all CCP members, all patriots, and all committed to a five-year plan to resurrect the Chinese economy at the moment that economic collapse would create open unrest. If their plan worked, China's rebirth would come at the exact moment America's internal crises would become overwhelming, leaving China at the top of the world without anyone even recognizing it until years later.

Horan Wu was a banker, the head of the Shandong Foreign Investment Bank and a member of the politburo. Admiral Muchan Gao was the youngest three-star admiral in the Peoples Liberation Army naval division, and an architect of the country's naval expansion. Other members included three industrialists including Yichen Liu' whose factories produced the fentanyl ingredients that supplied Gao's Mexican partners, the head of a ship building consortium where the submersibles used in Mexico were built, and the head of the shipping company that moved products, including contraband, back and forth to Mexico. The head of one of China's largest domestic banks, the number three person in China's foreign ministry and an Army General made up the other members.

Hao rose as Horan Wu and Admiral Gao entered the private pavilion on the banks of Baotu Spring hours before it was open to the public. The three spent a few minutes making small talk before Admiral Muchen Gao took a seat forcing the others to do the same. "You called this meeting, Hao Sun, you must have something positive to report."

"I can report that our strategy in Mexico is working. We are quietly crushing the two major cartels forcing them into distribution of less profitable drugs. Our new transportation system of using submersibles has cut our Mexican transport losses to almost nothing. Our competitors and the Mexican government, who were attacking our mules carrying product into the US, now run away. The Mexican navy remains the real threat to the drug business, but they have been forced to back away by the weapons we supply."

He was encouraged by Wu and Gao nodding their heads. He continued.

"We are using a portion of our profits to invest in legitimate Mexican ventures, always with a focus on partnerships with their most powerful companies." He again waited for the nodding heads to stop.

"On a political note, the last time we met I discussed how our Mexican partners were grooming a possible replacement for the new Mexican president. I am happy to report that the woman chosen is well on her way to building the notoriety that will allow that to happen. Our goal of having her in place within two years is within reach. Once in place she will prohibit Mexican security forces from interfering with any group creating good paying jobs in Mexico allowing our drug operations more freedom. She will encourage Chinese-Mexican joint venture companies, especially those who supply products to the US, to build business ties. After the economic ties are so strong that American business really needs Mexico, she will openly strengthen diplomatic ties with China and authorize Chinese military training bases in Mexico."

"All of that is good," offered Wu, a balding man dressed in the only suit at the meeting. While all the men were at risk, his position close to the party chairman would be considered treason. "But most importantly the capital we are accumulating from your efforts is well above what was projected. Within five years we will be able to leverage it internationally. Out of nowhere we will have the capital to step in and save our most important industries who by then will be capital starved. The workers will praise their salvation. The party will be forced to listen." Wu was the politician of the group and had a way of clarifying a strategy.

"That will be done only after we announce an alternative strategy to dominance. China will succeed and the United States will slide, and no one will notice." He paused again. "We will build on understanding how existing policy and economics have failed. We will soften our foreign policies and make our economic policies more realistic. We will appear to be responsive to complaints, but other than the occasional sacrificial lamb, none of the legal cases will proceed in court. Laws that threaten foreign companies for basic business research must go away. Instead, we will slowly increase taxation on foreign companies and control them that way."

Hao began to laugh. "By then the Americans will be so compromised with massive immigration and drug induced unrest in their cities that they will not even see what we are doing."

Admiral Gao turned to Hao. "And in five years, you will have infiltrated more than twenty thousand trained agents into that country. And they will have recruited at least that many more young men from other countries who will be willing to risk their lives for the money we will send to their families. I hope we will not need this hidden army, but if it becomes necessary to create further disruption in America, we will have the tools to do it. Thanks to you and our Mexican partners, not one of our trained operatives has been deported by the Americans."

"With our plan in operation, I see only one weakness," offered Wu, "our share of the profits from the drug trade will only yield a little more than fifty billion dollars in that period. Even leveraged, that represents only about four hundred billion dollars. Remittances from prostitution will add about five billion more; leveraged another forty billion," He paused before clarifying, "remittances from the hard-working women running massage parlors. My banker friends have not yet been able to calculate revenues from our legitimate business ventures. Maybe a total of five hundred billion from all three."

"Is that not enough," said Hao. "Our original calculations show the Chinese economy shrinking within two years. My daughter who studied finance tells me that organizations with money will have outsized influence in a down economy."

"Your daughter is right," said Wu, "but for our plan to work we will need almost two trillion US dollars at our fingertips."

"How much money are we laundering for our Mexican partners?" asked Hao.

"It will grow to perhaps another forty billion in that period. That is in addition to the money we are already 'loaning' them for investment in legitimate business and what they take for themselves." Wu was speaking from one page of notes. "We are going to need every dime of the money we hold for your Mexican partners, and they must be encouraged to do more, a lot more."

Hao turned to the admiral and politburo member. "This is why it is so important to continue to provide sophisticated arms to our Mexican partners. It will help them crush their competitors. We will cement the reputation of our weapons."

"Hao and I have discussed this," said Wu, turning to Admiral Gao. "In China, the army is loyal to the party, not the country. We will do the same in Mexico. Beginning in three years the new Mexican president will negotiate an agreement with us to rearm the Mexican army using our weapons. A portion will be offered as a gift and the rest at bargain prices. When the time comes, we and their new president must have the Army's unconditional loyalty."

"What if this new president does not honor her commitments to us?" asked Gao.

"We have placed accountants in her business and her non-profit ventures," said Hao. "We are tracking every dollar. We will wait until she takes office and then make it clear that the release of that information would destroy her, but we will do it in a way that only threatens her a little."

"I am but a humble sailor, or perhaps I missed a meeting, so will someone connect the dots for me?" said Gao.

"In five years, maybe sooner, we will simply wipe the funds

of our Mexican partners from the ledgers of the bank. The money will be ours to use to fulfill our plans here at home," answered Hao.

"Will that not lead to conflict with our Mexican partners?" asked the admiral.

"They already recognize they have nothing without us. Their new president will simply announce that she is seizing the 'drug' money that was never taxed and order the army to crush any opposition. By then Army loyalty to her will be complete. Ten percent of the funds we hold will be turned over to the Mexican government as a gesture of good faith when we 'discover' that we have been handling illegal funds. There will be no record of the balances. If we need more, we can sell part or all our legitimate business holdings to our Mexican partners."

"Captain Hao," started the admiral, "we are both navy officers. We understand how to manage subordinates. How do you intend to manage the handful of close Mexican partners who are helping us when we take much of what they have worked so hard for?"

"We only have two partners. All the other players work for them. By the time we move, each will be able to retire comfortably, although with only a portion of what they expect. Retired, they will be happy relaxed men. On the other hand, they may become angry men, and angry older men often die of heart failure or do stupid things that lead to accidents."

Horan Wu smiled at his partners. "Until we are ready to execute our plan at home, we are all at great risk. We must be very careful of who we bring into our small circle. We must be strategic about recruiting. Still, it is obvious that we will need a much larger group to control the chaos we expect in China. For centuries Chinese leaders have understood that unrest in China can lead to an uncontrolled explosion, and who knows where that might end."

Wu stood and extended his hand to Hao. "I will keep the Mexican pill factories supplied with product. Admiral Gao will continue to ship weapons. Speaking for the Gang of Ten, we congratulate you on the success of your efforts, but I do have one final question. The current Mexican president still has almost six years left on her term in office. I assume that you have a plan for succession."

Hao smiled. "Mexico is past due for a revolution."

CHAPTER 17

April 10, Mexico City, Mexico

Maria Castillo sat quietly watching the Puerto Escondido News. The relatively small earthquake only a few miles offshore had done little damage to major buildings and industry in the area. Several of the villages were not so lucky. Homes had collapsed, schools were damaged, and a quick hitting tsunami had smashed more than a hundred small fishing boats. Fewer than thirty had died, according to the initial report. Television cameras showed the devastation. Especially heart wrenching were the images of poor fishermen just staring out to sea, wondering how they were going to feed their families.

She picked up her phone and dialed Luis Cardenas. "Can you call our friend Hao? I have already directed my foundation director to send food and supplies from Acapulco to the quake area. I would like to offer low interest loans to the fishermen to buy or repair their boats, and want the Castillo Foundation to coordinate them, probably about a half million dollars total, with interest only payments for the first year."

"Help me understand your plan, Maria," said Luis.

"I would like to fly down there tomorrow and make the offer. The place is alive with news crews, so we'll get good coverage. I want to be able to promise that within a year, I will work to raise the money to help pay off the loans. Then in a year, we'll hold another press conference and announce that the foundation will pay the entire bill."

"That's good Maria. First, we help the kids with an education. Then we help small farmers grow more. Now we reach out to fishermen. All of that in just a few months. I'll try to reach Hao. He's back in China, but if it's only a half million and for now all loans, I think he will agree, but until he does, I'm good for the money. Go get yourself on a plane."

"You seem a little extra anxious, Luis," she said. "I didn't expect the money from you."

"I'm just responding to the news reports over the last few days. The papers are reporting that David Lopez who is on Lupita Martinez's staff has been traveling in the states. Hao told me that he used to be a high-ranking intelligence officer for the US, before finding his Mexican roots. I'm assuming he was trying to get them to help counter our efforts. We may have to move up our plans, so anything that makes you an alternative to the president is a good idea."

"Okay Luis, I'll be on a plane this afternoon. I have Red Blouse volunteers in Acapulco. I'll ride down to the quake area on one of the food trucks." She paused a moment. "You know Luis, doing this work feels really good."

"Just imagine Maria, how good it will feel to direct the entire Mexican government to do this kind of work."

Maria's volunteers now numbered in the hundreds. Gloria, her coordinator in Acapulco was closest to the quake area and had already established a disaster services office in a damaged school only a few miles from the quake's epicenter. She'd never met Maria and was excited when the head of the foundation asked her to set up a press conference for the next day.

Maria was a big draw for the press and her instincts allowed her to maximize the timing. Staring from the cab of a large box truck loaded with food and water, she saw at least ten camera crews and more than a hundred others standing around a makeshift stage on the school's basketball court. The truck pulled to a stop and Maria made her entrance wearing a pair of jeans and a canvas work shirt. "You will excuse us for a few minutes," she announced, "while we get the supplies off of this truck and on the way to those who need them." For five minutes she helped unload the truck until several men in the crowd stepped in to help.

Stepping up on stage, she tapped the microphone and began to speak. "When I set up the first Castillo Foundation, my goal was to help disadvantaged kids get a better education. Then we set up a second foundation with a focus on how to make small farms stronger. Both of those were strategies for making long term change in Mexico. Providing disaster relief was never part of the plan, but we have the resources to help, so here we are."

Maria brushed loose strands of long blond hair from her face before continuing. "On the drive down here, I began to think of how we might help out on a permanent basis just as we are doing for education and farming. Here's what I came up with. My foundation will make small loans to the fishermen who have lost their boats, and their livelihoods. We will provide low interest loans of up to ninety-thousand pesos to repair or replace boats damaged by this disaster, and you will only pay the interest for the first year. One of my accountants will be here within five days to start the process. I don't know if the half million US dollars I will personally borrow from banks will help everyone or provide everything needed, but I know we can make a difference."

The crowd that had gathered to see Maria, mostly to pick up something to feed their families sat silently for more than a minute before bursting into cheers.

"I have a few minutes for questions before I need to get back to the distribution of aid," she said. Maria fielded questions until one reporter finally asked the one she was waiting for.

"Señora Castillo, many of these people barely earn enough to feed and clothe their children. What happens if they cannot make the payments to repay the loans? Will their boats be seized?"

"That's a great question, one that indicates your personal concerns for our citizens matches my own. In the last six months I have been surprised by the generosity of individuals and companies when given the opportunity to fund well managed and worthwhile projects. I will commit today to try to raise the money to turn these loans into grants before the first payments are due. To you fishermen in the crowd, go fix your boats and catch fish. Taking away your boats next year defeats everything I am working for. I will not let that happen."

It was after dark when Maria finished her tour of the quake damaged area. She and Gloria stepped out of the car of one of the local volunteers and watched it drive away. Gloria rummaged through her oversized purse for the keys to her Chevy Impala. "I think that went as well as possible," said Maria.

"I am so proud to be part of what you are building," said Gloria as she unlocked her car. "Where is the government? You are the only one offering money and resources."

They were interrupted by two men on a motorbike screeching to a stop. The driver pointed a gun at them as the other man leaped off the back of the bike showing a pistol and looking directly at Maria. "You!" he shouted. "The one with all the money. Give me your purse." The man snatched it from Maria's hands and began to rifle through it. He found her wallet, stripped the cash out and stuffed it in his pocket just as Gloria confronted him.

"Do you know who this is?" she screamed. "This woman is here to help! You can't do this!"

She never saw the pistol before it hit her in the side of the head, dropping her to the ground. She rolled side to side, her hands covering a bleeding wound. "You are lucky that I don't take your money too," snarled the man. "But the rich bitch can afford it." Moments later, the men disappeared, and Maria helped Gloria to her feet.

Within minutes, the village priest helped Maria bandage Gloria's wound. "She will be just fine," he offered. "The wound will heal in a few days."

"Why would someone rob a woman who has come all this way to help us?" asked Gloria.

"There are desperate people all across Mexico," said the priest. He turned to Maria. "You, Señora, are rich and too well known. You have a target on your back."

"I'm not married, Father," answered Maria, "but I understand your warning."

Maria and Gloria spent the night at a small fishing lodge halfway back to Acapulco. Maria didn't know why, but Luis had insisted she stop there. The room was simple but well-appointed so that it wouldn't disappoint the loyal gringo sport fishermen who kept the place alive. In a small cove next to the dock was a new metal warehouse which opened to cement pavement extending into the ocean. She assumed that the warehouse was used to repair the lodge's small fleet of fishing pangas.

Gloria was packing the car, and Maria was finishing morning

coffee on a small terrace overlooking the Pacific when two black Ford Excursions and two army Humvees pulled into the parking lot. Several casually dressed men and soldiers fanned out around the lodge. One spoke into a microphone clipped to his collar and only seconds later a third black Excursion pulled in. Before the driver could open the back door, President Lupita Martinez, dressed in a white business suit, stepped out and made a beeline directly for where Maria sat.

"Maria Castillo, I saw your remarks on television last night and had my staff track you down. I'm just starting a tour of the damaged area. I wanted to personally thank you for all you are doing for Mexico and especially for what you are doing to help with this crisis."

"Madam President, thank you for your kind comments. Would you join me for coffee?"

"I am on a tight schedule, so I will have to decline your offer. I am trying to show my staff how cutting through our own red tape can expedite assistance to suffering people. We should be embarrassed that you mobilized even faster than our government, but I, personally, am not. Instead, I will use your performance to demand we do better." President Martinez handed Maria a card. "This is my direct number. If you would take a few minutes in the next couple of weeks to call me, I would love to host you for lunch."

Maria noted the security around Martinez, shuddering over what had happened only hours before.

CHAPTER 18

April 15, Washington DC

THAD WALKER HAD grumbled when Chad called the week before. It was springtime in Montana and trout season always opened about the middle of April. He had flatly refused to travel east until Gritt sweetened the deal. "I'll rent an old New England beach house in Deale, Maryland and arrange for a couple of early season striped bass fishing trips." Gritt recommended that his old mentor invite his new love interest and made note that the place he had rented was dog friendly.

Gritt borrowed a Jeep Cherokee from another officer at work, as cramming Walker, Sonia Ramirez, Winchester and himself into his 1960 Corvette was a stretch. The rented house, right on Chesapeake Bay, was a perfect place to privately discuss the Mexico problems. Having Thad's half century of intelligence experience and Sonia's three decades of counter narcotics knowledge seemed like a good place to start answering the question that Mat Chang had posed. It somehow didn't surprise Chad that, as the largest stockholder in her late husband's fishing lure company, she still had access to their Cessna Citation corporate jet. What he didn't know was that she was the pilot.

They took their time driving from Hyde Field to the beach house, stopping for a late lunch and to let Winchester do his thing and once more at a dog park where Chad threw a tennis ball for Winchester for over an hour.

Their conversation while driving reinforced the reason Gritt had arranged the meeting. Those discussions continued as the three settled onto the lawn overlooking the Bay. Thad opened a bottle of German Riesling while Chad struggled to open a small pile of oysters they'd picked up in town. Winchester wandered down to the beach and began poking through rocks.

"I made a couple of calls before I left," said Walker. "A couple of operators I know, one Korean and one Aussie, pay a lot more attention to China than I have since the EEL project." He poured some light white wine into a glass and handed it to Sonia and then another to Chad. Filling his own glass, he settled into a large wooden lawn chair. "Neither of them was paying any attention to what was going on in Mexico. Both are as puzzled as we are. The most recent CCP party congress seemed to be focused on improving their international relations and cutting through red tape to make foreign investment more welcome in China. Both believe that China is serious about reigning in the drug trade. Stirring up trouble in Mexico and further antagonizing America, especially right on our own border, doesn't add up for them."

"That echoes what Mat Chang is hearing from his China desk," said Chad. "Sonia, your thoughts? Much of your professional career has centered on Mexico."

"I know almost nothing about China," she started, "but I've been battling the drug trade in Mexico for much of my life. Some estimate that the revenues now exceed fifty billion a year, maybe even twice that. Those supplying the Mexicans are making more in a day than my husband's company made in a year. I doubt that the Chinese have the kind of control to stop that. Fentanyl is a combination of only a few ingredients, and it is dirt cheap to make. Because it takes so little to induce a high, the shipping volume for raw materials to Mexico is low and the amount of transport to get it across the US border is minimal compared to marijuana or cocaine or even meth. My point is that there is a lot of money changing hands."

Chad sprinkled a little Tabasco on an oyster and slipped it into his mouth, savoring it before chewing for a few seconds and swallowing. "Okay, so there is a lot of money in this. But both big-name cartels are unofficially on record as trying to stop fentanyl shipments to the US. They've heard more than one senator and even a couple of army generals talk openly of sending the US Army over the border to crush them."

Sonia picked up an oyster and starred at it. "I've never eaten one of these raw."

Thad smiled as he dropped an empty shell into a bucket they'd found in a shed. "Don't think about it, just try it. If you don't like them, I can light the gas grill on the deck and broil a couple for you."

Sonia continued to stare at the oyster. "You must take any pronouncement from the cartels with a grain of salt. Maybe one or both are pressing to stop fentanyl, but more likely they are just running a PR campaign and pointing at the competition."

"I don't know," said Thad, "Mat had one of his people send me copies of a couple of border reports from both DEA and border protection. Someone has been tipping them off on cross border fentanyl transport and at the same time someone on the Mexican side is killing drug mules. Only a few weeks ago they got a tip and while they were watching the border, someone used a Chinese made armed drone to blow up a group trying to kill some mules." He paused and took a deep breath. "My God, what a quagmire."

"I agree," said Sonia. "It's been a mess for a long time, but one that made sense if you just focus on the money. But it's changing. Hell, think about how much money we are discussing. We are talking about tens of billions of dollars. Who needs that kind of money? You can live like a king in Mexico for a few million." She brought the oyster to her lips and then into her mouth. "Palatable," she said, "but the next one will be bathed in Tabasco."

"You know," said Thad, as he finished his wine and reached for the bottle to refill his glass, "what Sonia just said resonates. If people on the Mexican side were putting that kind of money into circulation it would show in their economy. On the Chinese side, with suspect banking laws, you could hide it. But even there, that level of spending on personal gratification would be noticed by someone who still believes in the old definition of communism."

"Okay," offered Chad, finishing another oyster. "What we have is enormous amounts of money, much of it at least starting as cash, being stockpiled or used somewhere nobody is looking. So, the task is to figure out who and why."

"That's part of it," replied Thad. "The other part is finding out who has access to these advanced Chinese military weapons. They are either making a ton more money selling them to Mexican drug groups or more likely helping Mexican partners protect their business. Compared to the enormous inventories of Chinse arms, we aren't talking about a flood of weapons, more like just enough to help a partner. It doesn't seem to be raising a red flag in China."

Sonia flooded a second oyster with hot sauce and popped it

into her mouth while waving a finger in front of her. She swallowed and smiled. "But let's get back to the ungodly amount of money already changing hands. If you are already making billions, making a few million selling arms doesn't make much sense."

Both Chad and Thad looked over at her. Finally, Chad offered, "so the weapons are probably for protecting the business, not about making a more money."

"One other thing," said Sonia, "just before I retired, a new grade of fentanyl was hitting the marker. It was addictive as hell, but the pills we intercepted were dosed so that it gave someone a hell of a high, but not deadly when taken individually. That kind of quality control is new. In the past the cartels didn't seem to care if they killed their clients. Now they seem content to just hook millions of customers."

"Sounds like good marketing to me," said Thad. He looked up as Winchester got up from a nap after his walk along the bay and plopped down near an empty food bowl next to the door.

"Maybe," said Sonia, "but the nature of the dragon is that for most addicts, the buzz becomes harder to find the more they use. The pills we saw came in different doses. One color was a beginner dose and then there were two other colors, each a little stronger. By the time you hit the heaviest dose, you were really screwed up. Any beyond that and you were dead. In a way I guess that's better than filling a six-foot-deep hole after taking one bad pill."

Chad opened the laptop he'd set beside his chair and began typing. "I have a short list of questions starting with who and why. My contacts in Mexico told me that the drug trade had splintered in the last few years. The big two were still dominant, but smaller players had come into the market. We need to know who needs this much money, which for now is being cached, and why. It's way more money than any one or small group can spend on a lifestyle. We're talking money that could buy a small country."

Thad extended the oyster tray to Sonia, offering her the last one. He looked up at Chad. "You're right, and it is also the kind of money that can be used to fund a revolution or major disruption in a larger country." He paused. "Maybe even here, but more likely in some place like Mexico where there is a history of revolution."

"Or even in China if things turn really bad," said Chad. "Who in China can handle this windfall without being noticed? Who in China can access very advanced weapons and move them across the Pacific without attracting attention? Who in Mexico is sophisticated enough to operate a small fleet of submersibles and from where to where? Where did they come from? Who built them? Any boatyard can build the semi-submersibles they once used, but this is a whole different ballgame."

Sonia began to laugh. "It doesn't feel like we are getting any closer to answering your friend Mat's question. We are just adding more. It reminds me of a lot of meetings while I was working." She stared out over the bay. "Beyond the big question, we are discussing people's lives. Thousands more are being sucked into the drug life every month. Our cities are scrambling with impossible budget issues to offer any remedies to those who want out, which leaves only one solution for too many, and that is to die."

As promised, Chad kept business to a minimum for the next two days as the three spent several hours fishing out on the bay, catching six striped bass, one of which went on the grill for dinner the last night. It must have been the daily rowing trips on Flathead Lake, but Winchester took to the boat like he'd spent his entire life on saltwater, barking wildly each time someone hooked a fish. The weather turned rainy on the third day which was okay with Winchester, who spent hours in front of a crackling fire as Thad, Sonia and Chad talked.

They were in the Jeep on their way back to the airport when Thad voiced what he and Chad had been thinking. "It's going to take a specialized group to begin tying the pieces we see together. This isn't like chasing nuclear weapons, but it is important. Sonia is right, for everyone killed in those two blasts we worked the last time we put a Team Walker together, a thousand Americans are dying from the poison flooding our country."

Thad looked over at Chad. "Assuming I can get Mat Chang to sanction and pay for this, do you have any ideas on who we need on Team Walker?"

"You and I have contacts in China, so we'll need to chase that end. A lot of this is going to be just pouring through data to find the patterns, so maybe Pinky Swanson and her buddy Winston Wang who helped us last time. It will help that Winston reads and writes Mandarin. One of Olga's security crew is from Mexico, and she has a sister who she is trying to get into the states. Maybe they can help. Beyond that, your friend David Lopez needs to be part of this effort, and I'd like my Mexican marine buddy from Zihua to be in too. If we're going to pull this off, we're going to need help in China and in Mexico. This will have to be off the record. Neither Mexico nor China will acknowledge our efforts." Chad turned into the airport where the Cessna Citation waited for a return a trip to Montana.

Thad extended his hand to his young partner. "I'll call Mat early next week and tell him what we are thinking. Sonia and I are going to spend the first two days after we get home fly fishing." Thad looked over the seat at Sonia and smiled. "And no more oysters for a while. My aging body can just barely keep up with this younger woman without them."

Chad's Friday morning was interrupted by a call from his boss. Captain Donna Church did not greet him warmly as he was ushered into her office. "I need to remember," she started, "just how much pull you have the next time the Farragut Center needs something. Maybe we are using you all wrong. Perhaps you should be our chief lobbyist."

There was no correct response to that.

"How is it that a Navy commander, one of my people, who is tasked with an important technical challenge, conjures up a phone call from the secretary of the Navy? He politely asked me to cut you some slack from your current assignment. He said you were needed on some other work critical to the health of the nation, diplomatic intelligence work with no direct ties to the State Department or the Intelligence Services."

She handed Gritt a memo. "Since this is all off the record, this is the only authorization I can come up with."

Chad stared at the single paragraph. "Commander Gritt, you are hereby authorized to participate in a multi-disciplinary convening as requested by the secretary of the Navy. Please advise my office if this convening will exceed ninety days as soon as practical. In the interim, I expect that you will assign progress on your existing project to staff and make yourself available to them for consultation from time to time." Captain Church had signed and dated the memo, which Chad noted had been typed on plain paper without any logos or headers.

"Captain, this is news to me," said Chad. "I was asked to discuss my findings from the Mexico trip with a couple of people, but…"

Captain Church cut him off. "Just do whatever it is that only you seem capable of doing and get back to your job. We will discuss it then." She handed Chad a tiny slip of yellow paper with a phone number. "You are to call this number tonight at six. That is all."

The rest of the day was spent coordinating continued work on the drone interception project. He closed the door to his office at six and dialed the number.

"Commander Gritt, my name is Paul Frost, and I work directly for the president's chief of staff. I want to thank you for taking on the challenge of Chinese drugs and arms flowing into Mexico. I will need a budget for this work within five days. If it is within reason, it will be approved but you should probably work with your buddy Mat Chang since this will flow through his agency, but it is not part of his official mission. You will need to include a budget for travel since, unlike your last two projects with Chang, you do not have access to official government transportation. If you need anything, give me a call and good luck."

Chad sat for several minutes digesting what he'd just heard. "He was it. It was all up to him. And, he thought, I'm just a damned electrical engineer."

Those thoughts were interrupted by his cell phone buzzing. "Chad are you ready for a quick trip?" asked Thad. "Sonia and I are on our way to Mexico City. Can you be in New Orleans tomorrow by noon? We can pick you up at the naval air station in New Orleans."

CHAPTER 19

April 25, Mexico City, Mexico

David Lopez met the Citation at a contract air service company near Toluca Airport, an hour out of Mexico City. Two customs agents were parked next to him, waiting to clear the plane and its occupants. In under fifteen minutes, David was driving the group into Mexico City, where they had reservations at the historical Gran Hotel Ciudad De Mexico. It is harder to eavesdrop in old concrete buildings, and not letting David know in advance of where they were staying, hopefully kept the trip from interested ears. This time Sonia was paying for the jet and a crew. With the Citation pilots along, the conversations into the city centered on the weather, baseball and what sounded good for dinner. They dropped the pilots off at the Sheraton.

Walker and Sonia checked into a corner room on the fourth floor with Chad's room adjoining. They and Lopez finally got some alone time as they settled into the elegant sitting area of the corner room. "President Martinez got a call from your president's chief of staff asking that I personally escort you," said Lopez. "I know nothing more."

"Mat Chang said you should expect us," said Walker.

"He said that someone would show up, hopefully ready to help me answer a question."

"Maybe, why would China supply sophisticated weapons to Mexican gangs?" asked Chad.

"That's the question," answered Lopez. "I asked that about a month ago. Any answers?"

Thad Walker smiled. "David, I was a senior field agent while you were on the Latin desk. Now I'm retired but from time to time, Mat Chang asks for a favor. Those of us north of the border are as concerned about this as you are and after weeks of discussions, we have absolutely no answer."

He pointed at Chad. "This is the guy who worked with your navy to study the damage to your ship and the loss of one of our helicopters. Sonia here just happens to live next to me in Montana. She spent years with the DEA here in Mexico. Neither of them has an answer for you, but we do have a plan."

Lopez opened a notebook he had carried into the hotel and clicked a pen. "Okay."

"Chad and I worked on the US-Iran nuclear crisis a year ago," said Walker, "and before that a stickler with China. This is different, but it's going to take the same level of effort. We will need to dig into who in China benefits from smuggling people and drugs through Mexico and find the connection to who has access to the weapons. We will need to find out who in Mexico is benefitting from the relationship. We need to know the shipping routes between Mexico and China, especially routes and carriers who would risk everything to carry contraband. But we three are most interested in tracking the money. The fentanyl trade alone probably generates fifty billion plus. That much capital flowing through your economy would show up like a sore thumb. Other smuggling down here might generate just as much money. Someone in China is profiting and probably laundering a ton of money for Mexican partners. It's profitable enough to justify sending the weapons you are concerned about to Mexico."

Sonia leaned forward. "We don't think the Mexican side is paying for the weapons. We think that the Chinese side is supplying them to protect their business interests."

"With all due respect to you three, we've figured all but that last part out," said David.

"Here's the critical question, the one that might unlock all the other answers if we can figure it out," said Chad. "This ungodly amount of money is vanishing. It is being stockpiled. For what and where? Who in Mexico is benefitting? Who would benefit in China? What is their plan, and if it is already being implemented using this massive cash flow, what are they doing today toward a longer-term plan? It's just too damned much money for a simple criminal enterprise."

Lopez sat quietly for several seconds. "If the agency cannot figure this out, how are you going to do it?"

"It will take you and us, with people from both sides of the border working as one team, along with our contacts in China," said Chad. "It will have to be off the record since our government and your government still have their differences. On the China side it will take someone outside their official bureaucracy. This is a problem for three countries, none of which will want to acknowledge the other's problem or role in figuring this out."

Sonia leaned forward in her chair, staring at Lopez. "In decades of working the drug problems between Mexico and the US, every time I saw us closing in on the major players, someone would tip them off and blow up the case. For us to get to the answers we are looking for, the team we create must be small, competent, and committed without any hard connection to any outside agency that could compromise us. I'm willing to help, as is Thad here, but only if we do this right."

"On our side," started David, "we will need President Martinez's support."

"That will work, but other than her helping free up a handful of team members to work with us, she cannot include any other people," said Walker. "You, the president, and a few handpicked team members. We'll need to keep you close to President Martinez, since once we start pulling threads, some will probably try to stop us. No one else can know we even exist. On our side, we will recruit members with contacts in our agencies, but they will be people who understand that those agencies cannot know about us. Any formal questions that might be traced to us will go through Mat Chang. Again, to protect our existence."

David leaned back in his chair. "I spent years digging for answers to questions and solving problems that seemed unsolvable. I get it. "The amount of money involved means that the other side can beg, borrow, or steal their way into any group. The only protection is a firewall. They can't compromise what they don't know about."

He stood and folded his notebook. "I'll talk to the president tomorrow. How long are you here for?"

"Just long enough to get your answer. If it is yes, we have a couple of people in Mexico that we would like to recruit, and we will get you profiles of several more that you will have to recruit," said Chad. "To make this workable, we need to keep the total at about ten."

ॐ

David waited for President Martinez to finish her breakfast meeting and get back to her office.

"Give me a minute to jot down some thoughts from my meeting with Maria Castillo," said Martinez. "Growing a tradition of philanthropy has been difficult in Mexico. Our people are generous with giving their time and labor. But Maria has somehow charmed the entire country into supporting her and she is doing a lot of good. I want to figure out how to help her." She smiled at Lopez, "look into that when you have time."

Martinez took about five more minutes to jot down notes before turning back to Lopez. "Now, you asked for this meeting. You said this was urgent."

"We have been offered help to answer your question about China arming the cartels. It will be different than we anticipated and will take your approval." Lopez spent the next few minutes sharing the details with Mexico's president.

"You know David, leaving out the leaders of our military, intelligence and foreign service is going to create problems down the road," she said.

"Madam President, I believe that this is the best chance we have to resolve the problem without armed conflict. The people I met with are volunteering. We're both Mexican, we know how susceptible many in our country are to the temptation of a lot of money. The offer is that only you and I know of this team, and a few handpicked people who become part of it. The three people I met with last night have no dog in this fight except to help us. Two are retired. One was probably the best field officer ever in their CIA. They didn't say so, but I think this is a 'take it or leave it' offer."

"And you think we should take it?"

"Madam President, someone with a lot of horsepower north of the border pulled these people together. They are helping themselves by helping us. I think that there is a very real possibility of finding American military patrolling our streets if we don't reign in the drug trade. I'm not so sure that, at least part of our own military wouldn't help them. Nothing makes a military commander feel more worthless than seeing their troops die and not knowing how to stop it. My answer is yes."

Lupita paused for several seconds. "In my morning with Maria Castillo, she indicated that she refused offers of funding from American companies. She doesn't trust them. She takes money from other countries, but not from the US."

"Madam President, I don't know Miss Castillo, but I remember her first press conference. Her dad died in prison, and his arrest was made by our police working with the American DEA. She's probably just bitter. But how she feels has nothing to do with our problem."

"You're right, David. Let's do it. But you must be my eyes and ears. If you even think that we cannot trust this small group, we must end this."

CHAPTER 20

April 30, Los Angeles, California

THE SIGN NEXT to the door, Border Consulting Group, was the only indication that the newly formed LLC existed. Four private offices surrounded three open bays, two of which had four desks and the third a conference table. Walker, Gritt, Sonia, and Mexican Naval Captain Ramón Acuna, deputy commander of Mexican Naval Intelligence, occupied the offices. Acuna, thirty-eight, balding, medium height and weight, had been recommended by Diego Cervantes when Gritt recruited him to what was becoming Team Walker III. Acuna's father had died in a shootout with a drug cartel while his son was still at the Mexican Naval Academy.

Pinky Swanson and Winston Wang were borrowed from the CIA. Both specialized in data mining. Joining them was Ashley Cortez, borrowed from the DEA, a computer guru who at one time had been a world class hacker before being given a lifestyle choice by the American court system. The five-foot-four, wiry built Pinky, with pink hair, now streaked with blue, was the boss.

Winston was her opposite, with short hair and a button down suit, and was a bit of a disappointment to his Chinese American parents who had hoped for a doctor in the family. Ashley was a bookworm. A little overweight with plain brown hair and thick black glasses, and few friends other than her online community. Together, they made up the data team.

The second open bay, the Mexican Bay, so far had only two residents. Diego Cervantes had flown in from Zihua that afternoon. The second member of the, Sergeant Francesca Mateo had arrived from North Dakota that morning. Olga recommended her and had signed off on a leave of absence until a formal 'sabbatical' release came from the Air Force.

A third person from the Mexican attorney general's FGR department, had not yet been released. She would be the liaison with David Lopez and had been requested by President Martinez. The AG was furious about one of his best and most trusted investigators being loaned to Lopez, especially since the request had come without any explanation. Hopefully a private dinner between the attorney general and the president that evening would have Gina Santos on a plane the next morning. "Fifty, with styled graying hair and a trim build, Gina had been targeted twice for assassination by cartels. She'd been part of the drug war even when the government wasn't serious about it and had the scars to prove it.

Gritt had chosen Los Angeles as Team Walker III headquarters for three reasons: It was close to an airport with flights to almost anywhere in the world, the DEA, ATF, and FBI had major offices there (including a group from the FBI who had installed a secure phone system and twelve computers operating through a server running the FBI's proprietary security software), and finally, the location was only five minutes from the Holiday Inn LAX, where staff and any 'visitors' would not draw attention.

The rooms were clean and functional, and fit an incredibly tight budget approved by Mat Chang.

The four offices were empty, as the occupants joined five other team members in the conference area. "I discussed what we are working on with each of you when I called to see if you would like to be part of this," said Chad. You all know the challenge. But just to make sure, there are three rules. First, none of you can talk to any outside agency without clearing it with Thad Walker, Captain Acuna or me. Second, none of you will travel anywhere alone until this team is disbanded. Finally, if any of you even get an inkling that someone is tracking you or digging into what we do here, you will immediately take your concern to Sonia. Any Questions?"

With no response, Chad turned the meeting over to Walker. "Here is how we are going to attack this problem. First, Chad and I will be working some contacts in China to see if we can get a simple answer to how sophisticated weapons are being sent to Mexico. I suspect that we will have little success until we can give those contacts hard proof on the weapons. While we will begin kicking tires right now, I think we will have a lot more success if we can go to China armed with answers.

Sonia will take the point on the most challenging question. There are literally billions of dollars being earned by the drug trade, most of it now from fentanyl. It isn't being spent, so where is it going?

Ramón, your job will be to nail down whether we are battling all the cartels, not just on drug sales, but on the use of the new weapons, or if there is one specific group we need to target.

Chad will take the lead on transportation. How are the ingredients for drugs getting from China to Mexico? Are the same routes being used for arm's shipments? How are the finished drugs being moved to the border? How are they being moved over the border?"

I suspect that, like any investigation we will find one thread, so nothing is too insignificant to report. Hopefully when we pull that thread, it should all become clear. Are there any questions?"

Winston Chang tugged at his tie but said nothing.

"Winston, I know that look," said Chad. "Spit it out."

"Why, if the primary question is about supplying weapons from China, do we not have a specific China group?"

"Good Question," said Walker. "The Chinese will not be very forthcoming on any part of this investigation. They hate dirty laundry. Any thread that we uncover in China must wait until we have hard evidence and until we can convince China that it is in their best interest to help. What we don't want is to point the Chinese government in a direction where all the people who can answer our questions simply disappear."

"You do understand," said Acuna, "that the same thing is true with the cartels. They have no compunction about killing anyone they think might be a risk."

"Agreed," offered Sonia. "But what is different, is that with the cartels it's all about money. So, if we lose a good lead, within days or at most weeks, that person will be replaced. We just keep our eyes open. That isn't possible in China."

"So, where do we start?" said Pinky. "I'd like to wrap this up quickly so that I can get a little time on the beach before I go back to a rainy Maryland."

Chad waited for an answer, but hearing none, he offered, "let's go after the big stuff first. We know there is smuggling between China and Mexico. Some of it is big stuff. The Mexicans are not building their own submarines. So, let's figure out how and who is handling the shipping. That's going to start with Winston, since what we may be looking for may be in Mandarin or one of the other Chinese languages. If you can identify a logical target, then we can unleash Ashley on them, see if we can get inside their networks."

"Pinky, while he digs there, let's look at the national data on fentanyl seizures. If we can track where the new sophisticated pills are being sold, we might be able to backtrack one step at a time. While the local police and DEA can only cajole the people they pick up, we can reward them."

"Diego, hopefully Gina Santos will be here tomorrow. There must be a pattern on the use of the weapons that can tie them to some one group. You two help Ramón."

He turned to Francesca. "Let's have a conversation about your home country and about your sister. I suspect that once we find a thread, we're going to have to put boots on the ground to pull it. An angry former US Air Force sergeant passed over for promotion who returns to Mexico, one with both security and intelligence training might be too attractive for some groups down there to pass up. I don't know your sister, or her situation, and she may be able to help, but it would have to be in a way that cannot compromise the team."

Within seconds, Thad, Sonia, and Chad's phones went off with wildly different ring tones. All began to thumb through a message. Finally, Thad looked up at the others. "Somebody just shot down a border patrol helicopter in Arizona and killed three crewmembers. They reported seeing a missile fired but couldn't evade it."

"That's six Americans killed by sophisticated weapons in six months," said Chad.

"In the same period, thousands have died from fentanyl in the US and dozens in shootouts in Mexico," commented Sonia.

Chad looked a bit startled. "You're right, this problem is killing a lot of people."

He turned to Pinky and Winston. "To nail down the shipping issue, where do we start?"

Winston began walking toward his desk in the next bay.

"I don't know about Mexico, but the Chinese corporations I've investigated keep meticulous records. They're good at hiding things they don't want to advertise, but the nuts and bolts stuff is usually all there."

"So, you assume there is no reason for a shipping company to hide the fact that their ships are making trips from China to Mexico and back?" observed Pinky, sitting on the edge of her desk.

"That's it," replied Winston. "Maybe we will get a quick pattern for one or more ships."

Ramón Acuna had followed them. "There are dozens of ports in China. But you might be able to narrow down your search by focusing on the harbormaster reports in Mexico. The ships carrying small weapons and drug ingredients could offload anywhere along the coast, but it makes more sense to me that what we are looking for is containerized. Only five ports in the Pacific handle containers. The harbormasters generate all the revenues to run their operations through port fees, so they keep tight records. I'll be your translator."

"Is there a central place that keeps those records?" asked Chad.

"No," replied Acuna. "Each port keeps separate records. I'll have one of my people make the request for the last 12 months. Everyone thinks I am doing a harbor inspection trip before taking some vacation."

Pinky smiled as she plucked a bag of Skittles from her pack and ripped off the end. She sprinkled a few in her hand and then passed the bag on. "I can work with you on Mexican records." She turned to Winston. "And my partner here can begin downloading the same from the Chinese container ports. Director Chang can request those files from his people and then forward them to us. We hack Chinese systems every day. We can use the

Agency's supercomputer to merge Chinese and Mexican records and see what pops out."

Chad left them and headed for Walker's office. He dropped into a chair across from Thad's desk. "I have Diego Cervantes outlining a lead he and I came up with. There were some strange small boat activities while I was in Zihua. He and I both questioned them, but when he made inquiries with the local police, he was 'encouraged' to let it go since they had already done some digging and found nothing."

"And what more can he do from LA?" asked Thad. Walker paused to pack his pipe. "Just what was it that you thought might be happening?"

"Maybe shuttling drugs out to a waiting sub or shuttling money in. Zihua is a quiet little tourist town. It's not the kind of place that the authorities would be watching."

"We have access to some tools they don't have down there," continued Chad. "I asked him for a plan that might nail down the pattern better. Maybe we can arrange some satellite surveillance at specific times on certain days."

"I think we can get almost anything we ask for," replied Thad. "Let's assume we see something, what can Diego do, other than maybe close down the shuttle?"

"He trusts his marines totally. While there is a major cartel presence in the state of Guerrero, there isn't much overt activity in Zihua. Anyone involved in running out to a waiting submarine is probably just a local fisherman trying to put a new roof on their house. If we can confirm that there is a submersible out there, his guys can identify one or more people running the small boats. He knows most of them, maybe someone who will point up the ladder. Worst case, we can begin watching them and get a picture of the transport."

"You're technically running this ship," said Walker. "But I

can probably get through to Mat Chung faster than you. Just let me know what you need, and I'll make the call." He held a lighter to his pipe and puffed on it until the room smelled like the inside of an apple cider factory. "Good thinking from both Diego and you. We may only need one string."

Chad smiled. "Are you going to call David Lopez in Mexico City, or should I?"

"We need David," replied Thad, "so go ahead and let him know that we are operational. But keep in mind that David left the agency because his beliefs weren't aligning with the agency's needs. He has no compunction about acting on his personal values. Until we know just where this is taking us and how we are going to get there, keep it vague with David."

"Are you saying you don't trust him?" asked Chad.

"I trust him explicitly, to do what he thinks is right in the right way. Let's wait to see how that fits where we are heading before we accidently give him something that pisses him off."

CHAPTER 21

May 5, Mexico City, Mexico

THE MEETING WAS in the conference room of Luis Cardeña's chemical company headquarters. Luis had insisted on a second meeting after a 'substantially unproductive' one with Juan Ayala. Ayala had diverted a delivery of finished fentanyl pills to the port of Vera Cruz and rerouted them to another of the Castillo family's old hands now living in Spain. The pills had been a hit, and the contact was pressing Ayala for scheduled shipments.

Cardenas, Hao Sun and Maria Castillo all sat sipping coffee as Ayala delivered a pitch to broaden their European market. "Our delivery issues have settled down to the point where my assistants have nothing to do some days. We can handle the expansion."

"Just how much money will you need to retire when the time comes?" asked Hao, remembering his conversation only weeks before in China. "I don't keep track of how much my friends in China are scrubbing for you, but by now you must have twenty or thirty million dollars stashed away."

"By my count, it better be ten or twenty times that," replied Juan. "But it isn't the money that's important. I think we can become bigger, much bigger. Why stop at controlling what happens here and helping you and your friends with your plans in China? We can do the same all over the world. We can become like an international government. Then we would never have to worry about anyone challenging us. Look how easy it has been for Maria to position herself to run Mexico."

"And someday, she will," answered Hao. He struggled to fight off his growing anger at Ayala's betrayal of their plan. China will become the dominant world power, and it won't be by drugging the rest of the world. The drugging strategy is for destabilizing the United States. But once that is accomplished, China's one-party democracy and its economic power combined with the dominant military will be enough to assure its dominance. "Juan," he finally continued, "your idea may have merit. But it will be much safer and easier once we have Maria in office. Until then and until the Americans are so ravaged by their inability to control what is happening in their own country, we must stay focused. Let's vanquish one foe at a time."

Both Maria and Luis nodded their heads. Juan scowled at his companions. "I know that I cannot do this myself," he said. "To expand we'll need raw materials from China and Luis will need to expand production. It will be easier to ship to Europe if we can use the same Chinese shipping company we use now. After the demise of President Martinez, the revenues we funnel into Mexico's treasury will turn Maria into a God."

"As I said," repeated Hao, "the idea has merit. But not now. Can you not wait two or three years to run the world, Juan?"

Defeated, Juan settled deeper into his heavy leather chair. "You three are political. Perhaps you are right. I am but a simple drug dealer."

"No, my friend," said Hao with a smile on his face, "you are a very great drug dealer and one who will someday retire wealthy. Maybe even buy some little country and run it. Now we should get on to other business."

"Luis, you mentioned that the increased demand from Juan's partners north of the border require more supply from us. I discussed it with Yichen Liu' and he assures me that his factory can double the supply to you starting with the next shipment. Right now, you receive a shipment about every ten weeks. That is because we use only one ship, and it takes about ten weeks to make a round trip. It would be safer to simply double the order for each of those shipments than run the risk of using a second ship, with a crew that is not already part of our effort."

"Maria," asked Luis, "will it be a problem for your trucking company to handle a larger shipment?" He paused before adding, "I agree with Hao that we reduce our risks by continuing to use the one ship."

Setting her coffee cup on the table, Maria began tapping on her phone. "Our company operations are all computerized. My VP of operations should be able to get me an answer to your question in a few minutes." She looked over at Luis. "Correct me if I'm wrong, but we're only talking of increasing from four containers to eight, are we not?"

Luis nodded his head. "And I suspect that the movement of finished pills to the two locations where we load the submersibles will not be a problem?"

"No," replied Maria. "The vans we run to the coast are only half full now. We must be cautious. Our wholesaler supporting the merchants in Zihua and Lazaro Cardenas can only handle so much merchandise. We don't need to advertise by making too many trips to their warehouses. We have room on the vans to hide twice as much product."

"But we do not have enough capacity on the two submersibles we run," said Juan, finally getting over his anger about Europe. "Unless we open a new route to the northern border, we will need one more submarine."

"With two already under their belt, our partner in the ship building business should be able to supply another sub without much trouble," said Hao.

"The subs require a couple of days of maintenance every three trips," said Juan. "I swap out crews every trip. Being cooped up in that tin coffin days on end takes a toll. I'll need to recruit two new crews and a couple of more replacement workers." He looked up at Hao, now pacing as usual next to the windows. "You'll need to send a trainer when we're ready to put the new boat online. And we'll need to arm it. So far, we have only used two of the anti-ship rockets, but between the subs and the group who sends product across the border, we've used four of the anti-aircraft missiles and half of the rockets you supplied with the drone."

"All doable," said Hao. "Now how are we doing on replacing your president?"

"We are ahead of plan, I think," offered Maria. "I now have a full-time public relations person working for the foundations. We are in the news about every three or four days. The effort we made after the earthquake was covered by every major Mexican news agency and even several foreign ones. It even got me breakfast with Lupita Martinez. The president offered to help publicize our efforts. I like her."

"That might make it a little hard on you when the time comes to take her out," said Juan.

Hao watched Maria go rigid. "What Juan means," he started, "is that the campaign to discredit her will be hard on her and her reputation. I have a couple of our university students planning out what that might look like. With artificial intelligence, we can put words into her critic's mouths. I am told that we can create visuals of her doing things and saying things that will destroy her." He turned to Juan. "There is no need for her to die. In fact, when things go all to hell for her, it will be very helpful if she endorses Maria's candidacy. I am told that there is no formal succession plan in your constitution."

⁂

David Lopez waited at the door for the Lupita to finish a phone call. He walked in and closed the door. "I just wanted to let you know that the team we discussed, the one trying to figure out the Chinese weapons problem, have started their work. The only one missing is the woman from the attorney general's office. He is holding up her release for some reason."

"He promised her release when we had dinner. I'll make a call," said Lupita.

CHAPTER 22

May 7, Zihuantanejo, Mexico

Diego Cervantes and Francesca Mateo strode together from the terminal at the Zihua airport. Across the parking lot, Elena waved from Diego's Mustang convertible. "I wish you could tell me what you are working on," said Elena. "First you take off with only little notice and then you expect me to leave the clinic early to pick you up at the airport." She looked over her shoulder at Francesca in the back seat. "And when I go to pick you up, I find that you are traveling with a pretty redhead."

"All I can say is that our friend Gritt and I are trying to figure out how to stop the kind of smuggling that killed that Chinese girl you tried to save."

Elena adjusted her glasses and visor to block some of the glare from the setting sun and took off towards town. "That does not explain the redhead."

"You remember Chad's girlfriend Olga," started Diego. "Well, Francesca was working for her, in the American Air Force.

Olga tried to get her promoted, but instead, her superiors in Washington DC decided that she wasn't needed. First, she was passed over for a promotion and when she objected, they pushed her out. She's damned bitter."

"So, she gets on a plane and follows you down here," said Elena, slowing as she merged into traffic, passing an old flatbed farm truck loaded with coconuts broken down beside the road.

"Francesca grew up near Acapulco. She went to the states for college about ten years ago. Olga found out that I was coming down here to see you and to check in with my troops. She asked if I would escort Francesca. Her only family left in Acapulco is a sister who is living with friends." Diego slipped his hand onto Elena's knee. "Francesca has just about had it with America. Even with an American green card, she's considering moving back here."

"So, you are looking for a job?" said Elena loud enough to be heard in the back seat.

"No, well maybe," replied Francesca. "For now, I'm just taking a couple of weeks' vacation. I've been gone so long that I wanted to spend some time in the country of my birth before I make up my mind. I reserved a room at the Pescador Hotel on the northwest side of the bay. My sister is coming up by bus tomorrow. Both of us find ourselves searching for a new life."

Elena felt Diego squeeze her hand and looked over as he mouthed a kiss. "I promised Francesca that we would get her and her sister out on the water before I have to leave again."

"And just when is that?" replied Elena.

"I'll only be home three days and then I need to fly to Mexico City to meet someone who might be able to help Chad and I on our project. That woman will be flying back north with me." He paused a moment before adding, "don't worry, she is old enough to be my mother."

Elena began to laugh. "I love to needle you, my love. I'm not worried or jealous. I've felt how perfectly you curl up around me in bed. It's a perfect fit. God made us for each other. Now, I'm assuming we are taking your new friend to her hotel."

The Pescador was the only hotel on the northwest side of Zihua bay. Elena and Diego helped Francesca carry her bags to her room. Dropping them inside, all three walked onto the veranda. Diego pointed towards town. "That four story building, the tan one high above the beach is right next to where Olga and Chad stayed when they were here." He shifted his gaze across the bay. "And that is Las Gatas beach, the swimming and snorkeling beach they told you about. Boat shuttles run hourly from the pier to Las Gatas.

"What is Francesca really doing here?" asked Elena as the two headed back to the city center where Diego needed to check in at the Marine post.

"Elena, I told you when I left that the less you know about what I am doing, the better. Knowing anything might put both of us in danger."

"I remember you and Gritt talking about the strange lights in the city and out on the ocean. Now a woman shows up and the only orientation you give her seems to track where the light in the city came from and where the darkened boats departed from. You didn't have to send somebody here to watch for that. I could have done it," said Elena.

"Please Elena, forget about those lights. Treat Francesca like a new friend and nothing else. You follow the news enough to know how dangerous Mexico can be," he replied.

Two nights later Elena and Diego met Francesca and her sister, Mary, at the city pier after a beachfront dinner. Diego and Elena arrived with thermos bottles of spiked Mexican coffee and ceramic mugs for a moonlight boat ride. It had taken a little persuading by Diego to get Enzo to take three women out on the Porpoise. He'd pleaded that he was a fishing guide, not a tour operator, but in the end taking care of one of his best customers and a hundred-dollar bill had sealed the deal.

"Your sister is younger than you," observed Elena, nodding at a petite dark-haired girl dressed in shorts and a long sleeve puffy blouse.

"She'll be nineteen in a couple of months," replied Francesca. She was a surprise to my older parents. Mary was waiting tables down in Acapulco, but evidently the restaurant was serving the wrong crowd. The owner suddenly closed it and left town about six months ago. Since then, she has been working as a maid. She has two years of college, but no professional experience."

The spiked coffee slowly disappeared and over the next few hours, Diego found excuses for Enzo to cross the mouth of the bay several times. With each pass, he and Francesca seemed to focus on town for a few minutes and then gaze out to sea. Finally, a little before midnight Enzo, who had an early morning fishing charter lined up, convinced Diego to call it a night.

Both couples walked to the beach area in front of town where you can catch a cab in a few seconds. "It was nice meeting you Mary," said Diego. Turning to Francesca, he added, "I'm out of here tomorrow morning. If you need anything, or just someone to show you around, give Elena a call. If it's something that might take a man's help, you can call Jorge, my first sergeant. He's the guy your sister seemed so taken with when he joined us for dinner the other night. He's a good man. You can count on him. But with your 'situation' it would probably be best to use your sister as a go between."

The cab ride to Diego's townhome took them high on the hill at the south side of the bay before dropping down toward la Ropa beach. Elena slid close to him and leaned up to whisper in his ear. "Too bad there were no lights to show Francesca. And you seemed determined to keep her away from your marines."

Diego reached down and squeezed her knee until it almost hurt. "Elena, forget about the lights, please," he whispered back. "I just think Francesca, with her education and former employment could be trouble for some hot-blooded marine."

"I only commented because of that," replied Elena, pointing at a faint red light flashing several miles past the lighthouse at the mouth of the bay.

Diego looked at the cab driver, who seemed to be paying no attention to them. He reached down for his cell phone but stopped. You never know. He slipped his phone back into his pocket. "Damn," he said.

∞

The American Airlines flight from Mexico City to LA departed right on time. Diego thought he'd picked out Gina Santos in the waiting area but wasn't sure until he looked down at seat 1B and saw the middle-aged professional woman next to his aisle seat. He wasn't sure how someone on Team Walker had arranged for their first-class seats in the front of the Boeing where they could talk without being overheard.

Diego introduced himself as did Gina and the two spent the four hour flight quietly discussing what was going on in Mexico without ever discussing what they themselves were doing. After the awful walk through the bowels of the Los Angeles airport through customs and border security, Diego, who had made the same trip only a week before, led Gina to a waiting hotel shuttle.

An hour later the two sat at a tiny table in the corner of Gina's room. "The third member of the Mexican team," said Diego, "is in Zihua. I just got back from there myself. Francesca is following up on a lead we developed. She's observing some strange lights and small boat activity out in the bay. She's just doing the tourist thing for now as a cover, but we've started laying the groundwork for her to relocate back to Mexico undercover. She grew up there."

"I'm the new person," said Gina. "I wish I'd had an opportunity to talk to her before her trip. There are several parts to all the cartels. Some of them are more deadly than others." She watched Diego inhale a burger as she talked and then waited for him to finish a Coke. When he said nothing, she continued.

"The production phase is mostly run like any business. The transportation phase is more cautious and paranoid. The security operations are downright nuts. The transportation and security usually have the same leadership. The one's I've followed all see themselves as modern Pancho Villa's leading glamorous revolutionary armies. Our third partner needs to be very careful."

"For now, she's just observing. Her sister is with her. Depending on what she sees, she should be back here in a couple of weeks. You will get a security briefing tomorrow, but one of our rules is that we do not travel alone, so when she is ready to come back, I'll probably go to meet her."

"That's an odd rule," said Gina. "I mean she's all by herself right now. What's different about traveling?"

"Only you and I are authorized to carry a weapon in Mexico. Francesca is a dual citizen, but lives in the states for now, and we don't want to point anyone in her direction by applying for a weapons permit. The three people running the show just think that two sets of eyes is safer than one," replied Diego.

"Or," started Gina, "If any one of us sees someone doing something or meeting someone who is suspicious, they hope that we'll mention it. By traveling in pairs, there is always a minder close by."

"Seems a little paranoid if you're right," said Diego.

"But a good idea," she said. "I've been compromised twice, and one of those times was by someone I absolutely trusted. It turned out there were plenty of clues, but nobody saw them."

CHAPTER 23

May 12, Los Angeles, California

THE MORNING MEETING began with the introduction of Gina Santos and then turned all business as Winston handed a copy of his report to each person. "Two Chinese shipping companies operate most of the container transport between China and Mexico. While we cannot ignore either, one small company, Shandong Limited, operates three ships that make stops on Mexico's west coast. That by itself means little, but one ship the *MV Jai Mew* operates almost like one of those paddle and ball toys, bouncing from Shandong and the port of Lazaro Cardenas or Manzanillo. The *Jai Mew* makes the trip every sixty days. That ship is way underutilized. Most container ships are at sea ninety eight percent of the time."

"This is important for three reasons," offered Pinky as Winston paused. First, it is a small company, not one where risk management is a high priority. Second, Shandong is one of the centers of chemical and pharmaceutical manufacturing in China. Third, from discussions with Sonia, the DEA has suspected that much of the final manufacturing of illicit drugs in Mexico is done under the cover of legitimate firms. They probably operate production runs like for any other product which means that having a hard schedule for the delivery of ingredients, especially when mixing and pressing fentanyl pills, would be critical."

"If you're right," said Chad, "then virtually every time the Jai Mew arrives in port, it is carrying drugs or the materials to make drugs."

"One other supposition makes this ship interesting. With a schedule like that, the crew never changes. Regular crew changes risk someone who doesn't like something they see, blowing the whistle," observed Winston.

Sonia and Ashley Cortez glanced at each other. Finally, Sonia added, "Assuming that's right, as a former DEA agent, I can tell you that you can pack enough materials to supply the fentanyl trade in the US into two containers every couple of months. If the ingredients are hidden with other goods, maybe ten containers. There are hundreds of containers on each ship. Even in Mexico you would need to get a search warrant and have probable cause, a description of the containers to be searched and of what you're looking for, and a magistrate's signature. I doubt that you could get a warrant to search every container without hard evidence. And getting a Mexican magistrate to sign it off, especially in an area with strong criminal control would be difficult. That could get them killed."

Ashley, the other DEA member on the team nodded her head. "It's a place to start. Maybe the owners of the shipping company are also in the chemical business. Maybe they have ties to the Chinese military. On the Mexican side, perhaps we can set up a trace on where the containers go after they leave the ship. The DEA identified the probable routing of the drug ingredients into Mexico years ago, but never with enough evidence to legally stop it."

Winston nodded his head. "We aren't calling this the thread you are looking for, just a place to start. I'll dig into Shandong Ltd. There must be a shipping manifest that identifies who is consigning each container to the Jai Mew."

Gina Santos set her coffee on top of a file cabinet next to Winston's desk. "I was 'loaned' to David Lopez by the attorney general, to assist our new president with developing an anti-crime policy. I have access to our database, even from here. I'll start digging in to see if we have any suspect Mexican chemical or pharmaceutical companies under surveillance now. Most of our work is on the cartels themselves, but there might be something."

"Pinky, we need a list of the chemical and pharmaceutical companies in Shandong Province," said Gritt. "We can cross reference those company names with the manifests that Winston is researching."

"Commander, I'm not criticizing your computer or analytical skills, but Winston and I have a plan. You work your side, we'll work data. Any suspicious companies will go over to Ashley and Gina to see if they can trace a connection in Mexico," said Pinky.

Chad smiled as he noted that Pinky had changed the color of her hair, but not her scrappy demeanor. Her hair was now almost a florescent pink. She wore a matching tank top and shorts. So much for remaining 'anonymous' he thought.

He found Walker and Sonia huddled in front of a computer in Walker's office. Walker waved him in as he pressed his finger over his lips asking for quiet. He motioned for Chad to take a seat across from them. Thad pointed at his ear and then at Chad.

"I don't know how the bad guys got my cell number," came from the computer. "It happened months ago. Since then, I've received six calls, what you would call tips, on narcotics mules crossing the border in the Arizona segment. Each specified how many carriers and gave me almost exact locations where the mules would cross. We only had manpower to respond to four of them."

"We read your report on the mission where you watched somebody in Mexico shoot other cartel's mules. Your report on the incident where a drone was used was concise. We'd like to help, in fact we already are," said Sonia.

"The pictures you got of that drone and the missile fragments you picked up confirm that both are military grade Chinese weapons," said Thad. "We two old, retired people have taken it upon ourselves to see if we can help. I did some time in intelligence and my friend here was with DEA."

"We can use the help. I had operational control over the last intercept. I might have written the location wrong because the border crossing was almost five miles from our hide. We watched the same truck we'd seen before cross the dirt track on the other side of the border. It stopped and deployed that same jamming box, but it kept going. I thought I had this figured out, with the drone and all, so this time my backup was a National Guard helicopter, carrying three guardsmen and one of my agents sweeping inland ten miles on our side of the border. Again, our radios and cell phones failed, but we fired a flare in the direction the truck was traveling. We didn't know that the helicopter had been shot down until the same truck stopped to pick up the jamming device. We tried for an hour to reach the chopper and then jumped on the ATV's and headed cross country. We saw the smoke from the crash when we crossed the next ridgeline. There was one survivor. That's how we knew it was hit by a shoulder fired missile." He paused and you could hear a change in his voice when he started again. "The twenty-year-old kid who survived, managed to get a tourniquet on what was left of his left leg before he cut the last of the flesh pinning him into the wreckage. He crawled away only seconds before the wreck started to burn."

"We would love to have access to any missile fragments. It would help us trace their origin," said Thad. "I know that's not your responsibility, but you sound like the kind of guy that will find a way outside the rules."

"Fragments, any other details, will help us," added Sonia. "An old friend at DEA gave us your number. Before we go, do you have some final thoughts?"

"It just pisses me off that the only help we seem to get on the other side of the border are other bad guys trying to take out their rivals. If we can get some serious help on the Mexican side, we might be able to stop more of this."

"Tell me, Sergeant Thibs, "how much lead time are you getting when you get those calls?" asked Thad.

"Two or three days. Until the last time, when I think we got played, the location, date and time estimates have been fairly accurate," said Thibs.

"You have to remember that we are just a couple of doddering old has-beens," replied Thad, "but over the years we've developed friends on both sides of the border." Walker stopped while he plucked a second cell phone from his desk drawer. "I don't know if I can gin up any uncompromised help from old friends in Mexico but let me give you a cell number. If you will call it immediately when you get another tip, I can try." Thad read the number on the back of the phone.

"Like I said, any help is appreciated. "I'm tired of funerals." Thibs dropped off the video call.

Walker looked at Chad. "That was Sergeant Paul Thibs of the US Border Patrol down in southern Arizona," said Walker. "We got no fragments from the loss of the helicopter over the water in Mexico. We were just hoping he had some from the loss in Arizona."

"The FBI and National Guard are doing the investigation," said Thad. "So far, they have nothing, but what we are looking for might be buried in their formal report. That might take months unless your Border Patrol friend can kick something loose. Sometimes those guys find evidence that can't be used in court."

"Still, the call may be helpful," said Chad. "I assume your thoughts on giving him the alert number is to give us enough time for Diego or Ramón to set up a reception party on the Mexican side of the border."

"I see why you two work so well together," said Sonia. "If we can get our hands on an actual missile before it's fired, we might be able to trace it when we reach out to China."

"And," said Chad, "If we can get a missile and the man carrying it, we might be able to start backtracking to whoever provided it in Mexico."

"Pulling threads from each end would speed up the investigation," said Sonia. "Now, if you two will excuse me, Gina Santos asked for a few minutes to explain her last project for the Mexican AG."

"Does it fit our mission?" asked Chad.

"She said that they were using Mexico's strict foreign deposit laws to try to track drug money in Mexican banks."

Thad smiled at the woman who was changing his life. Eighty percent of his adult life had been spent in service to his country. The rest was all spent on wilderness and rivers and lakes, all things that helped him leave the other behind. It was fun to see Sonia's professional side even though the attraction for both had been leaving their pasts behind. The two feelings were incongruent, but then, so was most of his life.

"Sonia," he said as she headed for the door. "Don't tell Gina this, but the CIA has a backdoor into every bank in Mexico and they found only a handful of transactions where unexplained cash was deposited. Mostly small stuff. One thing occurred to me the other day. If we assume that the mountain of cash from drugs is not being banked in Mexico and that same mountain is creating only minor ripples in their economy, then one of two things is happening. Either someone is stockpiling it in a warehouse somewhere, or more likely, it's leaving Mexico and being laundered somewhere else."

"Probably right," replied Sonia.

"Some group is paying China for a lot of raw materials and for protection," offered Chad, jotting notes in his folder. "Containers of drug ingredients and arms into Mexico could also be used to carry cash out. Maybe we should be looking for banks with connections to China, especially ones making overly large loans to Mexican entities. Transactions that looked overly risky or rushed might be laundered funds flowing back, disguised as loans. The transactions in China would be almost impossible to track, but finding laundered money coming back into Mexico might be possible."

CHAPTER 24

May 21, Zihuantanejo, Mexico

Diego's Alaska Airlines flight from LA was met by Sergeant Jorge Cano, the twenty-three-year-old noncommissioned officer who was commanding the small detachment of marines while his officer was on the 'inspection' tour. In a small city where anyone of note knew everyone else of note, Diego, even in civilian dress was pestered with good natured questions as he made his way out of the terminal.

"Are you headed to the office or home?" asked Jorge.

"The compound," replied Diego. "Elena is picking me up after her shift at the clinic. I'd like you to join us for a late dinner at my place. We'll have two other guests."

"If one of them is that cute sister of your friend staying at The Pescador, I'd love to come," said Jorge. "She's different, quiet, and serious. Not hunting for a husband. We've been out twice since you left."

Elena had all the ingredients for chicken parmesan, a favorite recipe of her family's restaurant. While she and Mary finished preparing dinner, Francesca, Jorge and Diego carried their wine glasses out on the veranda and slid the door shut.

"Francesca, tell Jorge what you've been watching and what help you need," said Diego.

"Is this cleared with our friends up north?" she asked.

"The Americans deferred to Ramón Acuna. He signed off on bringing Jorge in."

"Okay," replied Francesca. She turned to Jorge. "I'm seriously thinking about moving back to Mexico, but on the way, I was asked to see if my former security experience might help figure out who blew up the Montezuma and why. Diego had observed some odd occurrences before he left and asked me to keep an eye peeled for the same while my sister and I vacation."

"It wouldn't be the strange lights at night and odd pangas running out of the harbor with their light off?" asked Jorge. He watched Francesca turn pale. "I only know because Diego casually discussed it with me when it first happened. He told me that the local police assured him it was nothing, but I could tell he wasn't satisfied with the answer."

Diego nodded. "It's okay."

"I'm just uncomfortable with others knowing what I might be doing. My sister and I have noticed several men, including two Asians, who might be shadowing us. My sister is just a kid. She wouldn't know how to defend herself. Hell, I can't carry a weapon here, so I'm a little defenseless myself."

Francesca paused as she watched one of the last water taxis cross the bay in the moonlight. "Anyway, what is done is done. I have confirmed that what you saw. Every seven days there are blinking red lights from the ocean, followed by the occasional flash of lights from town. About fifteen minutes later three small boats leave Las Gatas and head out to sea. When they come back about two hours later, they anchor off from the pier and a smaller skiff runs out from the inner harbor and ferries men from each boat."

"Suspicious, but so far nothing illegal," said Diego. "Tell Jorge about what happened when you followed up."

"The last time we saw the boat go out, Mary and I waited an hour and then called a cab. We were going to play a couple of slightly inebriated sisters out trying to walk off too much tequila. We had the cab drop us off a couple of blocks from the parking lot entrance at the inner harbor. When we walked there, we were met by three men who told us that the parking lot was closed. They reminded us that it was dangerous for two women to be wandering around at two in the morning and forcefully suggested we walk back to town. All of them were wearing jackets on a muggy night, and I'd bet the bulges under their clothes were handguns."

"That was a dangerous thing to do," replied Jorge. "I suspected that you and Lieutenant Cervantes might be more associates than new friends, but I never suspected that your sister was involved. I thought she was just your super cute sister visiting while you were in Mexico."

Francesca began to laugh. "She isn't involved, I told her that I was just trying to see if Mexico was as dangerous as advertised. She refused to let me go alone. Oh, and she thinks you're cute too." She thought for a minute. "I get a blow by blow on every one of your dates. I think she's a little frustrated that you haven't tried to kiss her yet."

"What Francesca was trying to do is get a look at what was coming back into the harbor after the boats went out," said Diego, moving the conversation back to business.

"I suspect that drugs are going out to meet a submersible and piles of cash might be coming in," said Francesca. "We need to see what's going out through Las Gatas and what they're bringing back. Cash coming in would probably be easy to transport in duffel bags. There would be no reason for night fishermen to carry duffel bags in their boats."

"They could just be night fishermen like when we go out with Enzo on the Porpoise," said Diego. "But I don't believe that, so can you think of any way to get a look in those boats Jorge?"

"If they're moving drugs, they must have paid off the night watchman at Las Gatas," replied Jorge. "It makes sense to leave from there. Three boats leaving the harbor late would eventually draw attention. If I show up at Las Gatas hours after the vendors have gone home, it will tip them off. I'll have to think that through."

Jorge stared out over the bay, sweeping his gaze from Las Gatas on his left to the pier directly across the harbor. "We could raid the inner harbor when they return, but if we get the timing wrong, they will just go somewhere else." He turned to Francesca, "can you identify which boats are being used?"

"Not by name," she replied, "but I can take a picture of the harbor and circle where each boat is moored. If we question any of the boat operators now, it might tip off the people further up the ladder. Suspicions are not evidence, not even here in Mexico."

"Especially here," replied Diego, "but I have an idea. The half-dozen sightings of the submersible all indicate that it prefers to stay on the surface. It's probably running on either a gas or diesel engine most of the time and charging batteries for when it needs to submerge. At twelve to fifteen knots, the trip to the upper end of the Sea of Cortez and back would take about seven days. A sighting every seven days means there are two subs. If this is the southern terminus, then the boats we see going out are probably carrying hundreds of pounds of pills and enough fuel for a round trip."

"So, the boats from Las Gatas, are buying and hauling a lot of fuel each week," said Francesca. "We need to set up surveillance. If we're right, we're a little closer to probable cause."

"If they're smart," said Diego, "they are buying only part of the fuel here in the harbor, and the rest around town. They have seven days to accumulate what they need without drawing suspicion. Every fishing panga and every water taxi carries plastic jugs of fuel. The jugs are the same as farmers or construction workers, so they would draw no attention at filling stations in town."

"That might even be easier to monitor," said Jorge. "If we watch each panga and the shuttle that is used to ferry people to the anchored boats, we can watch for extra jugs of fuel being loaded. Any more than 20 liters for a three or four hour trip would be excessive."

"How long will it take to plan out surveillance?" asked Francesca.

"A couple of days," replied Jorge.

"The boats run every Wednesday," she said. "Mary and I are making a trip to Acapulco starting tomorrow. My sister wants to pick up her stuff from the apartment she shares. Her roommate seems to have a new job. She's making a lot more money and wants to live alone."

Jorge opened the door and walked over to where Elena and Mary were just setting dinner on the table. He leaned down and kissed Mary on the cheek. "Smells really good," he said.

Diego and Francesca laughed as they watched the young woman turn beet red.

"The confrontation with an American diplomat we discussed is set up for the third day you're down there," said Diego. "The military attaché from the American Embassy will be there making a goodwill visit. I'll get you the information on his hotel. He won't know it is coming, so whatever you do should create quite a stir."

"We shall see where it lands me," replied Francesca as she started to open the door.

"This is risky. All to get preferential treatment for your sister to move to the states," offered Diego. "With Jorge around, she may not leave, you know?"

"I'm serious about helping," said Francesca. "She and I haven't figured out where we will eventually settle. Here or there, it doesn't make any difference. You would be shocked by the number of young kids, even young military people who are ruining their lives because of drugs in the states. It's only a matter of time until it creates a crisis here too."

∽

Col. Markus Johnson stood at the head of a long table in the dining room of the Ritz Acapulco. The commander of the Mexican Navy's Pacific fleet warmly welcomed him with all the appropriate words for an ally. Five other Mexican officers and their wives at the table smiled. Others in the dining room, both gringo and Mexican had politely applauded as the Mexican admiral introduced the American officer.

Johnson was halfway through his short remarks when an attractive woman with red hair leaped to her feet. "You should be ashamed of yourself," she shouted. "Talking nonsense. You have no place lecturing Mexicans on a professional military. I spent six years after college in your American military. I was a highly trained security and intelligence member of your Air Force. I even became an American Citizen. But when it came time to promote this Mexican woman, your military instead threw me out. You, your military, and your country are all prejudiced liars."

As hotel employees and military security escorted the woman and her friend from the room, the redhead screamed, "Don't believe a word this liar says! I denounce you and the military you serve."

CHAPTER 25

May 21, Mexico City, Mexico

"You knew that I was mugged on my last trip," said Maria Castillo. "Just the other day, some men tried to stop my car only a few miles from here. I rammed the shitty little pickup truck they were driving with my Mercedes and just kept going. Both times I was scared to death."

Luis Cardenas smiled at the woman they were grooming to be president. "There is a downside to your newfound notoriety," he said. "The public knows you are doing good things for the people, but they also now know you are rich." He looked over at a bodyguard sitting across the room from where he and Maria were having lunch. "I find that a showing of a little security is all that it takes to keep the riffraff from targeting me."

"Where did you get your man over there?" asked Maria tilting her wine glass in the direction of a bodyguard."

"He was one of Juan Ayala's enforcers. I keep him on a short leash. He has few of what you might call interpersonal skills," replied Luis. "More than once I had to stop him from roughing up someone who wasn't really a threat."

Luis waited while a waiter in a white jacket refilled Maria's wine glass. "With the increase in donations from our friend Hao, you're going to be even more in the public eye. Your monthly travel to places where your foundation is helping may double or even triple. The plan is working; you are becoming the talk of the nation. You will be President."

"It will do you or Hao no good if I end up dead or so injured that I cannot do the job."

"You need someone who can protect you," said Luis.

"Not one of Juan's thugs," she replied. "Can you imagine how much damage to my image one 'over the top' response might cause? My mother doesn't trust Juan."

"Your mother suffers from dementia. Juan is critical to our business." He paused.

"Perhaps there is someone," said Luis. "Did you read the accounts of that woman who disrupted dinner with the military attaché from the American embassy in Acapulco? She was born here but spent years in the American military doing security work. If you can take her at her word, she is very bitter about her treatment in the US Air Force."

"I read about that in the newspaper a couple of days ago," replied Maria, "but without vetting her, she seems a little risky."

"Perhaps," said Luis, "but two of Juan's top associates were former American military people. He's asked his distributor in the Midwest to check out this woman's story. He thinks it might be helpful to have a woman on the team, someone who might be overlooked by our enemies."

"Luis, you know I don't like Juan. My mother often remembers old things as if they were yesterday." Maria sipped her wine. "It's what happened yesterday that she struggles with. She remembers every song from her past but can't remember if she ate breakfast. If this woman works for Juan, I'm not interested.

But having female security would make traveling with a guard easier."

"Let's not get ahead of ourselves, Maria," said Luis. "Apparently, this woman's last post is in the north-central United States, an important base where most of the American nuclear bombers are stationed. It's also close to several American Indian Reservations. Those places have the highest percentage of customers for the pills we ship north. Our American distribution partners have people in North Dakota already checking out the woman's story. Their findings indicate that she is telling the truth. She's highly trained, and she was pushed out of her job by her superiors."

"Still, I don't want one of Juan's people looking over my shoulder all day long," replied Maria.

"My own people tell me that when this woman came back to Mexico, she was befriended by a young officer in our marine corps. We're working to figure out if they are connected by anything but friendship. She seems to respect the military and if that's correct, she'll never work for Juan. I'll ask Juan to keep me posted on what his people north of the border report. If she checks out, I'll tell Juan that you want to talk to her before he does."

"I appreciate your efforts," said Maria. "I'm just getting my footing in my philanthropy role. I love what I'm doing. I would just like to feel safe doing it." Maria took a minute to finish the excellent seafood stew in front of her. Then she continued.

"I have a second meeting with President Martinez in about a week. My new public relations person is setting up press coverage for after the meeting. I'm already on record as wondering why government is so ponderous in helping the people. It will give me an opportunity to emphasize my belief that cutting through the red tape to take care of people is an important goal for a president."

"Maria, I am increasing production of product every month. Your companies are increasing transport. Juan is increasing Yankee distribution. Hao has lived up to every commitment he has made to us. Contrasting yourself with Lupita Martinez without criticizing her directly is exactly what you need to do to complete our plans."

"And what should I do about my personal security?" she asked.

"The woman we have been discussing, seems to be serious about moving back to Mexico. I am told that she and her sister have moved out of the hotel they were staying in and rented an apartment in Zihua. If she checks out, I'll facilitate a meeting. We should have Juan's report in a week or so. In the interim, he has people keeping an eye on her."

CHAPTER 26

June 1, Victoria British Columbia, Canada

CHAD RENTED A small two-bedroom apartment overlooking the picturesque harbor of the island capital of British Columbia. The man he was there to meet, Ma Mingze, was staying at the historic Fairmont Hotel on the waterfront, a five-minute walk away. Both men agreed during their clandestine phone conversation that the extra leg from Vancouver for Ma and from Seattle for Chad offered an opportunity to make sure that neither were followed. That step was followed up over the next day by each taking turns watching the other with no obvious meeting, except for a few seconds where Chad passed a burner phone to his Chinese contact.

On the second morning at 10 o'clock, Ma walked to the entrance of Chad's apartment building. He dialed a number on the burner phone and seconds later a click unlocked the security door. Ma took the elevator to the fourth floor where Chad waited in the hall.

The two men shook hands but said nothing until Chad ushered Ma into the apartment and closed the door.

"This is much more pleasant than the last time we met," said Ma as he seated himself on a plush leather sofa.

Chad took a minute to turn on the television across from where Ma sat. He turned up the volume and then took a seat in the chair next to his guest. "Let's see," he started, "in the middle of the Aleutian Islands, in a place where our two countries almost started World War III, without even a cold beer in the worst weather in the world… yup, this is more pleasant."

The two men kept their voices low. Without any prior indication of their meeting place, they were confident that there were no listening devices inside the apartment, but the huge windows could transmit harmonic vibrations which might be listened to. The television noise assured them further that any listener would not be able to hear their conversation.

"I appreciate your understanding that our meeting might be misunderstood by my government," said Ma. "Renting an apartment with security that keeps anyone from following me out of the building was a good idea."

"If you're concerned about security, why did you agree to meet with me?" asked Chad.

"We agreed to keep a back door open in case either of us found a threat that we thought the other should know about," said Ma. "Your call indicated that what you wanted to talk about might be more important to me than even to you."

"I meant that," said Chad, "so let me spell it out. I've been involved in trying to figure out how a drug smuggling submersible in Mexico destroyed a small Mexican navy ship and one of our coastguard helicopters. We both know that most of the fentanyl-related substances flowing into Mexico for the illegal drug trade is coming from China. What has changed is that someone in China is now supplying their drug partners with weapons that our intelligence says are used exclusively by your military."

"Commander Gritt," started Ma. "Oh, and congratulations on your promotion, my country will never admit the origin of the drug shipments we are now trying to stop."

Chad laughed. "I understood exactly what you just told me."

"And," continued Ma, "After our very short phone call, I did some checking. There are no military drones missing from our inventories. All are accounted for."

Chad opened his laptop and brought up the video of the drone attacking targets along the Arizona border. "While you're here, I can give you a copy of this video. It will take you only a few minutes to see the differences between the export version and the one that was used in Mexico. Fragments from the rocket didn't even have their Chinese part numbers removed."

Gritt waited for the entire video to run before continuing. "Two American helicopters were shot down by surface-to-air missiles in the last few months, one over water where we couldn't gather fragments and the second over land. The report on those fragments is not yet finished, but I'm confident they will prove Chinese origin as well."

"I'm aware of the Mexican government asking my government about such weapons. We know of nothing like that."

Chad tapped a few keys on his laptop, this time bringing up the report on the Montezuma incident. "I personally headed up the American support for the Mexican government's investigation of the damage caused to their ship. We proved that it was an armor piercing rocket built by your Norinco corporation. Again, there is no export version of that rocket. I have a sanitized version of this report that you can take home, one that one of your North American operatives might logically have uncovered themselves."

"Beyond the weapons issues, let me assure you, Ma, that in spite of your government's stated goals of reducing or eliminating illegal drug shipments to North America, they are in fact increasing," finished Gritt.

Ma sat for some time before commenting. "You wouldn't happen to have a beer?"

It took Chad less than a minute to return from the kitchen. He twisted the cap off from a Molson and handed it to Ma and then opened one for himself. Ma had been educated in the US. His CIA file indicated that he favored Canadian lager style beer.

Ma chugged about half the beer before turning to Gritt. "I'm sure that your own intelligence is telling you that China is going through some difficulties right now. I'm not officially part of the government, but I hear enough to tell you that is an accurate reading. We have some challenges in our economy. Our working population is shrinking. Those problems have led our leadership to rethink some policies, at least for now."

"Now it's my turn to congratulate you on your promotion," said Chad. "I understand that you have graduated from a 'go to' guy for field operations to a 'go to' guy for interpretation of intelligence. From what you told me while we were trying to figure out a solution to the EEL crisis, you have never actually been part of the military. But you are on the inside of the intelligence apparatus."

"All true," said Ma. "In fact, I actually have direct conversations with General Ling from time to time."

"That would be the same General Ling who is the commander of the People's Liberation Army's human intelligence operations?" asked Chad.

"I prefer to leave it at an occasional conversation with a General Ling," said Ma. "We recently discussed the internal conflicts within the party. Not everyone is happy with the new direction set out by the general secretary."

"If the official announcements of the CCP's change in

direction can be taken at face value," said Chad, "then what I am showing you conflicts with the secretary's directives. Only your government knows for sure whether what you call a 'new direction' is real or not, but on the assumption that it is, I felt that I should pass on the information I just shared with you. Someone or some group may be sabotaging the official policies and whoever is doing that is accumulating massive amounts of money. Our side believes that it is way more money than any person or small group could ever use for their personal lives. We're potentially talking hundreds of billions of dollars. Enough to buy a lot of influence under the right conditions."

Ma smiled at Gritt as he took another pull on his Molson. "Defiance, off the record arms, and a pile of money would be my goals if I was trying to take over a small country."

"The Mexican government has some concerns," said Chad. "But the same formula could also be destabilizing for a large county going through some tough times. What is happening is already running up some red flags in the states, and some in our government are worried enough to be less than completely rational."

"Now it's my turn to say that I understand what you just said," offered Ma.

"But to me," offered Gritt, "and the handful of people I've discussed this with, the other possibility is that all of this could create long term challenges for any government having problems, especially in a country where any breakdown in social order could spin out of control quickly."

Ma finished his beer. He stood, looking down at Chad who was closing his laptop. He reached into the pocket of his jacket for a pad and pen, and then jotted down an email address. "When you figure out how to get me the sanitized material you discussed, send it to this address. Use an account that cannot be traced to you or your government. It would be best if that happened in the next three days before I fly back to Beijing, since that address is no good in China."

Chad rose and began walking Ma toward the door. He too pulled a folded sheet from his pocket and handed it to Ma. "I doubt that you're being followed, at least I saw nothing that worried me yesterday," he said. "But this sheet is a full workup on both leasing and purchasing a unit in this building. For a guy who may not retire in China, a city like Victoria with thousands of immigrants from Hong Kong, many who speak Mandarin, might be a place that you would consider retiring. At least it's a good explanation for this past hour with me."

Ma turned back to Gritt and extended his hand. "I must be very careful with what we are discussing. If your suspicions are right, there might be someone close to leadership who would need to stop my inquiry before it gets going."

"I agree, but those at the very top need to know. I can't help you decide how to raise these concerns. I just hope that you do. I don't leave until tomorrow, so if you need a follow up meeting, just call. Be safe and thanks. Keep me posted," said Gritt.

Ma turned to go. "Give me a couple of weeks after you get those materials to me. I'll call you."

Chad checked his personal phone for an update on his scheduled flights back to LA. There was no practical way to change them for an earlier departure. He wished Olga was with him in Victoria, his favorite city on the west coast. At dusk, he would wander down to the harbor to enjoy the lights of British Columbia's Parliament buildings across the bay before walking to Chinatown for dinner. But for now, he needed to get some work done, beginning with a call to Pinky. She would know the best way to get information to Ma without leaving an audit trail.

CHAPTER 27

June 3, Zihuantanejo, Mexico

FRANCESCA AND HER sister had moved to an apartment on the hill above the hotel that offered a view of the entire bay.

Mary had been shocked by her sister's behavior in one of Acapulco's best restaurants, and even more surprised when her former roommate explained her newfound wealth and then tried to recruit her. The job entailed caring for exotic birds, monkeys, and reptiles at a warehouse on the city's outskirts. Every two months, the job included preparing travel crates that would be hidden in legitimate freight shipments to Manzanillo where others would ship them out of the country.

Mary and her friend were at odds when they parted company. Mary was concerned about the loss of wildlife in Mexico and her roommate demanded that Mary not disrupt what her roommate saw as her first big break in life. It took a lot of willpower for Mary to live up to her commitment to an old friend, but she had a plan to improve her life as well, so she promised not to tell anyone, even her sister.

The night after they moved, Francesca and her sister sat quietly in the moonlight, each sipping wine as they watched the city below fall asleep. "How much longer can you afford to live without getting a job?" asked Mary. "I can go back to doing maid work. The manager of the Pescador offered me a job. He thought it might be useful to have a maid who spoke English, especially with VIP guests."

"If I was in the states, maybe three months," answered Francesca, "but down here, six months, and if we're careful with our money, maybe more. You don't need to look for work yet. We have a plan for you."

"Tell me, Sis,' how is you moving to Mexico helping me to move to the states?" asked Mary. "I'm not sure I want to move north if you aren't there."

"Jorge is a very handsome young man," observed Francesca, trying to change the subject. "You may choose to stay here too."

"Not if you move back," said her sister. "I have a dream to go to an American university like father arranged for you before he died. I told Jorge my plans, and so far, he seems okay with them. He tells me that his commander, Diego, thinks that the Mexican navy and US Navy will be working closely together. In two more years, even without a university education, he'll be eligible to apply for officer's candidate school. Then he too, could go to school in the states."

"I'll figure it out in the next few months," said Francesca. "Life here is slower. I thought security work was my future. Now, I'm just enjoying not having to worry about life for a while. If we go back, I'll find a way to legally get you into the states. You will get a crack at your dreams. But if something pops here, we might have to go through all the hoops to get you a traditional student visa. That is, if whatever I end up doing pays enough for me to help you."

Francesca poured more wine as her sister headed inside the apartment for bed. She checked her watch. Unless the schedule had changed, the lights from the ocean should start within an hour. Forty minutes later, beyond the lighthouse and the handful of night fishermen anchored near it, a red light flashed three times. A minute later it flashed again.

She turned her attention toward town just as a blue light flashed from the top floor of the tan apartment building. She picked up her phone and hand dialed a number she had memorized. At the other end, a voice answered, "Si."

"Luz roja, luz azul," she said. Then she hung up.

Ten miles away, near what the locals call Bird Rocks, two fishermen trolling for nighttime barracuda reeled in their lines and turned their borrowed panga back toward Zihua. Jorge sat in the front of the boat with a pair of night vision binoculars glued to his eyes. He braced himself as the young Marine corporal, who had grown up on the water, firewalled the throttle. Jorge described their outing as a simple recon of some unidentified boat activity. For the corporal, it was an opportunity to get closer to his sergeant. In seconds the sixty horse Yamaha outboard had the panga dancing across the wave tops.

Ten minutes later, Jorge called out. "I see them! Three boats leaving the bay with no running lights. Slow it down a little. The waves from our bow will show in this moonlight."

The two marines followed the three boats, about a mile in trail, for twenty minutes. "Slow down," called Jorge, "they appear to be stopping. If they see us, I don't want to be within rifle range. Leave the motor running in case we have to run."

"Why are we really here?" asked the corporal.

"Remember when we were pulling guard duty for the wreck of the Montezuma? I think these boats might have something to do with it."

As Jorge watched, a red glow appeared in between the boats. He opened a waterproof case, extracting a digital camera with a long lens, propping it up on the gunnel. He began snapping pictures. "I don't think there's enough light, but maybe we can capture enough for some computer nerd to enhance this." He snapped pictures for another couple of minutes before switching back to the nighttime binoculars. "It appears that a door on top of a low-lying craft has opened. Right now, they are taking bundles out of the boat."

He continued watching, offering a play by play to the corporal. "Now they're loading things into the pangas." He watched as a man emerged from the low-lying craft and slid into one of the pangas. Moments later, two men from the pangas crossed over to what had to be the rumored submersible. Working with a third man they continued loading what might be fuel containers into the sub. "A second man just moved from the sub to the pangas." Jorge picked up the camera and snapped several more pictures. "They must be changing crews on the subs as well as loading and unloading."

He placed the camera back in the case, snapping it shut and picked up the binoculars again. "Christ! One of the men in the sub is staring right at us with binoculars. Let's get the hell out of here."

The corporal slammed the boat into gear and spun the wheel toward the harbor.

Where three pangas surrounded the submersible, there was panic. The man with the binoculars swung them, watching Jorge and the corporal flee.

"I knew better than to let you guys talk me into coming out here," said Juan Ayala. "Damn, damn, damn. Someone has been watching us." He looked down through the open clamshell doors of the sub. "Close up and get the hell out of here," he yelled. "We'll try to catch them before they get to shore."

"I have a better solution," said one of Ayala's submarine crew, holding a short rifle type weapon and sighting it. "I have a buzz. The weapon is tracking the heat from their motor." A second later, a flash sent a tiny rocket, no more than two inches in diameter and just over a foot-long, headed for Jorge's boat.

"Shit, I think they just fired a rocket at us!" screamed Jorge. "Change directions. Zigzag. We're a mile away. Let's lose that thing."

He watched as the missile changed direction. "Left, open it up. Right again," he screamed. The tiny missile missed the back of the boat by less than twenty meters. Jorge was just about to breathe again when the missile began to turn. There was no time to shout a warning before the heat-seeking warhead detonated against the Yamaha, blowing the stern of the boat apart and showering the two marines with fragments. Both were dead in seconds. The boat tipped on its side but continued to float.

The man who fired the rocket looked up at Juan. "Your Chinese friend has given us three new weapons in the last few months. I didn't think we needed what he called his GN-202. I thought it was too small to do much damage. I was wrong. It came with a pack of six missiles. We still have five left."

Ayala smiled down at the sub crewman. "Our Chinese friend said that rocket was effective out to two kilometers." He reached into his pocket and pulled out a roll of hundred-dollar bills. He stripped off five and handed them to the man now reloading the launcher.

"You earned a bonus today, Gustavo. I'd forgotten about the third weapon you now carry."

Ayala leaned over the opening to the sub. "Finish storing the load and then head north," he called.

Then, to the man running the motor of his panga he ordered," get me over to that wreck. We need to make sure that it and any bodies sink with the boat. We want no record of what happened tonight."

Anyone looking fifteen miles out to see could not have missed the fire as the wreck, soaked in fifteen gallons of gas erupted. Ayala watched it burn as they ran toward the harbor. Then the fire went out almost instantly as the wreck sunk. No one was watching.

Francesca had agreed to stay up until Jorge returned from his surveillance. When he hadn't called by 3 in the morning, her worry turned to fear. She glanced down at her phone, ready to call the local police or at least the ready desk at the marine compound in town. Swearing at her phone, she stood and headed for the bedroom. Any call from her would give away her mission. The same person who might have betrayed Jorge's surveillance effort might answer the phone or at least hear who called in the tip.

She was lying awake when her sister came into her room in tears. "Sis,' wake up! The whole harbor is mobilizing. They say that Jorge never returned from his night fishing trip!"

Francesca slipped on a robe and stumbled into the kitchen. "Get dressed, Mary. Call a cab and head down to his base and then call me when you know something for sure. I'll call Diego and see if he can mobilize more help to find Jorge."

Her call fifteen minutes later did nothing but make her feel useful. She discussed Jorge's planned night surveillance with Thad Walker since Diego was at LAX picking up Chad. Both agreed that any knee jerk response other than getting Diego on a plane back to Zihua could blow the whole mission. Thad committed to get Diego on the way. "You have to back away for a few days," advised Thad. "Other than helping your sister with her grief, you can't show concern beyond what any local will show. Let's see what a normal search and investigation tells us. In the interim, you are our only contact on the ground down there."

Francesca and Mary were having a late dinner after spending the entire day at the harbor, monitoring the search along with hundreds of townspeople. A man dressed in an impeccably tailored white cotton suit and open collared linen shirt approached their table. "This is one of my favorite restaurants for traditional foods as well," he said in English. "The chefs here take great care never to give in to the tourists' Tex-Mex tastes."

"You're right," replied Francesca. "I lived in the states for years. What they call Mexican food isn't Mexican food—too many spices."

"We agree. Miss Mateo, my name is Luis Cardenas. I am a businessman with factories near the capital where I am told you and your sister grew up. I also own a getaway at the top of one of the beachfront buildings here." He watched both women stop eating to stare."

"Do not be concerned by me knowing a little about you. After the commotion you caused down in Acapulco, I wanted to meet you. More importantly, I have a friend, one of Mexico's most revered women who wants to meet you."

"I must apologize for my outburst down in Acapulco. I was out of line, just a bit bitter. I am not normally that type of person," said Francesca. "I embarrassed my sister here."

"Do not apologize," said Luis. "Without that outburst, I would have not asked some of my people to research you a little. I passed on what they found to my friend who would like you to join her for lunch tomorrow." He handed Francesca a folded note. "I will be hosting you and her. I will ask my chef to prepare a traditional meal since I now know that you both enjoy the best our country has to offer." He turned to leave but stopped. "Shall we say noon? That will give me time to pick my friend up at the airport. The note has the address."

He turned to Mary almost as an afterthought. "I am told

that you know one of the men who went missing last night. I have a friend with an airplane. If you would like to accompany me to the airport tomorrow morning, I can arrange for him to take you up to search for the missing boat while your sister has lunch. Her new friend will need to be back at the airport for another trip by three in the afternoon, but that would give you four hours to look for him. It might make you feel better instead of just waiting."

"That's very nice of you. Where shall I meet you?"

"I often have coffee at the cafe across from where the fishermen bring in their catch," he said. "I'll be there tomorrow morning between 9 and 10. That gives me time to get to the airport and back without keeping your sister waiting."

Mary didn't hesitate. "I know the place. I'll be there, and thanks."

CHAPTER 28

June 4, Zihuantanejo, Mexico

Francesca's cab wound its way down the hillside and through town, finally stopping behind a condominium project in the middle of the waterfront. Upon entering the building, a maid was waiting in the lobby to usher her into an elevator, using a key to select the top floor. Luis met her in a sunroom that might have been an exhibit of pre-contact artifacts.

"I've heard of you," said Francesca after Luis introduced Maria Castillo. "You're the woman who some are calling the Mexican Robin Hood. Francesca wondered why they were speaking English, but it didn't matter.

"It's a newfound calling," replied Maria as Luis ushered them to a table set on the huge terrace overlooking the bay. "A year ago, I was just a small-time businesswoman from a checkered family. Then Luis and some friends introduced me to some of his business associates. My company began to grow rapidly. I'd always thought about what I could do to help Mexico if I had the money. Finally, I have the opportunity."

"Your company must have hit a gold mine," replied Francesca as the slid into the leather chair next to a heavy table on the deck."

"It is only partially my money," said Maria. "Once I began helping, others have come forward offering financial help. I now run the company and two fast growing foundations, the biggest in Mexico."

Luis placed a finger over his lips. Conversation stopped as a lunch of cheese stuffed Poblano peppers and a green salad arrived at the table. The three watched the young woman who served them retreat into the massive apartment and close the doors.

"My friend Maria here," started Luis, "is becoming famous. That is both a blessing and a curse. It has attracted some of the wrong type of attention."

Francesca popped a bite of pepper into her mouth, delighted by the mild spiciness mixed with creamy mild cheese. She watched Luis look over at Maria as if it were her turn to talk.

"I was mugged while I was helping the victims of that earthquake. Two men put a gun in my face and robbed me. And only days ago, some men tried to run me off the road only minutes from my home. It happened where there have been several carjackings and robberies this year.

Luis now has a full-time security person. He suggested I do the same. The problem is, all the managers in my foundations are women, as are most of the officers in my company. I am more comfortable with women and there are few women in your former profession in Mexico. After learning a bit about your background, I asked Luis to introduce us."

Francesca smiled at Maria. "Don't you think that two relatively young, attractive women traveling together might attract even more attention?"

"That's the kind of thinking I am looking for," said Maria.

"Perhaps, but when we announce that you are joining me and then explain your background, it might even make that the type of attention just we are looking for. You know, admirers of two professionals. Not the kind of scum that will only attack defenseless people."

"I'm intrigued," replied Francesca. "Just what would I be doing and how often would I be doing it?"

"You would need to accompany me only when I travel. For the first few weeks I would want you with me all the time, but when you are ready, you could help me recruit an armed driver. And, of course, I would want you near whenever I hold important meetings with important people. Then you would need to coordinate with their security people."

Francesca stared down at her plate. "For example?"

"Oh, when Luis and I meet, or other customers and business associates. Occasionally, even the president. You would have to work with her people. I'm sure she wouldn't want me bringing an armed guard to our meetings unless her people approve."

"I don't have a gun, not even a permit," said Francesca.

"We can take care of that," offered Luis as he finished his lunch. "You do shoot, don't you?"

"I was an expert marksman with a 9mm Barretta while I was in the US Air Force. I never had to use it, but yes, I can shoot."

"Assuming Francesca accepts your offer, we should hold a press conference somewhere where she could demonstrate her skill with a firearm," said Luis. "That alone might keep anyone from challenging you, Maria."

"I didn't hear any offer," said Francesca. "It would need to be enough to cover my expenses, my personal needs and to help my sister. She is working menial jobs. She is considering an offer to become a hotel maid. In the next couple of years, she wants to finish her education."

"My sources tell me that a person doing what you were doing in the American military earns about fifty thousand US dollars per year. Since I can't offer you benefits, I was thinking of a salary of twice that amount."

"Before you make that offer," said Luis, "I have one question. How do you know Diego Cervantes?"

Francesca paused.

"I ask only because, should you need help from time to time, someone with his experience might be helpful," said Luis. "Like most marines he is probably not corrupt."

"We met at the airport in Los Angeles. Both of us have military backgrounds. We were ordering coffee and somehow it came up. There are a lot of differences between the US and Mexican military, but far more things in common."

"For example?" asked Maria.

"Both are dedicated to protecting their country. Both require an oath of allegiance. Both train the physical person and their mind. Loyalty is mandatory." Francesca paused for several seconds, "but that may be where the two militaries differ most. In the states the loyalty only ran one way. A soldier is required to be loyal to the corps, the command structure, the country, and the mission. But my personal experience is that in the states the country, the command structure and the corps can choose when and to whom they owe their loyalty. My outburst in Acapulco was my first opportunity to voice my anger at America's betrayal. I gave them my commitment and they betrayed me. Diego tells me that at least for the Mexican marines, loyalty runs strongly both ways."

"Are you and Cervantes close?" asked Luis.

"Just casual friends. His girlfriend, Elena has helped me make the adjustment back to life here. But Diego is a little to gung-ho for me."

"I do not understand that term, gung-ho," said Luis.

"Diego is still filled with the military spirit. It is his life. My military spirit is over. Now I just want a meaningful life, without all the bullshit rules. I'm not ready to settle down and start having babies, but someday I might like that."

Maria reached across the table for Francesca's hand. "I do not have your betrayal experience. But your description of what you want in your life is like my dream. I would be pleased if you would accept an offer to become my head of security."

"I think yes," replied Francesca, "but I would like to discuss it with my sister. May I call you in the morning with my answer?"

Maria nodded. Rising, she picked up her purse from a table near the elevator and plucked ten bills from her purse, handing them to Francesca. "If the answer is yes, I will ask you to come to the capital to plan out your work. Ten-thousand pesos will buy you a one-way first-class ticket. If you turn me down, use the money to do something fun with your sister."

Minutes later the three rode the elevator to the lobby. "May I offer you a ride back to your apartment?" asked Luis.

"Thank you, but no," replied Francesca. "I find that a good walk helps me figure things out."

Maria extended her hand. "Have a lovely walk then. I hope to hear from you tomorrow."

"And I'll have your sister back to your apartment in a couple of hours," added Luis.

Francesca headed down the steep steps next to the building. Moments later she stepped onto the waterfront walk that extended all along the beach. She turned and stared up at the condominium building that she'd just left for several seconds before heading from Playa la Madera beach into town.

She stared down at her phone, noticing a missed call from a

number she didn't recognize. Tapping recall as she walked, she was surprised when Diego answered.

"Gritt and Walker felt that I needed a separate phone to contact you," he said. "We should get together. So far, the effort to find Jorge is a failure. Only some partially burned material and a couple of life jackets have been recovered."

"I don't think it's a very good idea for us to meet right now," answered Francesca. "I just left a lunch where I was offered a hell of a job."

"Will it help us answer the questions that brought us together?"

"Perhaps," answered Francesca. "It was at a private luxurious apartment. The same one that puts on a light show every Wednesday."

"Perhaps it's time for a couple more of the team to come down here," said Diego. "We're going to need someone to act as a go-between."

"You have the unregistered phone," said Francesca. "You make the LA call and then let me know. If I see this number come in, I will answer. If you miss me, and I have a missed call notice, I will only call at five minutes past the hour. Any call from my phone at any other time means someone else is tracking my calls. Now I need to head home and wait for Mary. The same people who just offered me a job arranged for her to spend a couple of hours with a pilot looking for Jorge."

"One moment, before you go," said Diego, "Pinky and Winston think they've identified the Chinese ship and shipping company we discussed. Chad met his Chinese contact a few days ago. That end is coming together. Your lunch might be the break we need."

CHAPTER 29

June 5, Los Angeles, California

THE MORNING MEETING began without either Thad or Sonia. They were shopping for the kind of clothes that would be appropriate for a Midwest couple leaving for an unplanned summer vacation in Mexico. Diego's call to Chad the previous evening, noting Francesca's possible breakthrough and documenting the loss of two of Diego's marines had started wheels rolling.

The handful of Team Walker members still in LA met early the next morning. "Before we start, let me update you on a call from Diego last night." Chad waited until he had their attention. "First, it appears that both of Diego's marines have disappeared working with Francesca, surveilling the turnaround on a submersible. He suspects they might have been killed. Diego now has no doubt that Zihua is one of the hubs for the submersibles running drugs to the US border. He thinks it was chosen because it's a tourist town with no major industry or port facility. Kind of out of an out of sight, out of mind location."

Chad looked down at his notes. "The missing men were assisting Francesca in observing some suspicious activity. It included light signals coming from a building in Zihua. Out of the blue yesterday, Francesca was invited to lunch in that same building and offered a job. Either the bad guys are on to her, or hopefully her cover story of anger at the US combined with her security training has opened a door for us."

Chad waited a moment, his concerns about Francesca mirroring those on the faces around him. "Diego will be totally occupied with his marine corps duties until they reconcile his missing troops. More importantly, if Francesca really is being engaged by the bad guys, she must reduce her contacts with Diego. Thad and Sonia will be leaving for a vacation in Zihua tomorrow morning. They will become Francesca's primary contacts and move information between her and Diego." He glanced at his notes again. "The problem is that Francesca's new job will put her in Mexico City much of the time. I don't like her operating with no one else in the area. Think about what we might do. We'll come back to that problem later." He watched the other team members. None were leaping out of their seats with a solution. The remaining LA team members were all researchers, not field people.

"Okay," said Chad. "What's the latest on the investigation of Shandong Ltd and the Jai Mew?"

"Only a bit more than yesterday," said Pinky. "On the Chinese side, the Jai Mew manifest includes shipments from more than a hundred companies. But one stands out because they place exactly three containers on the Jai Mew every shipment and possibly receive three containers back on every ship."

"What do you mean, possibly?" asked Chad.

Winston began typing on his laptop. "The return manifest shows three containers of nitrogen fertilizer from a new company in the south of Mexico on every ship. But, let me stay with the China to Mexico leg. Liu' Chemical Company Limited. is a small chemical and pharmaceutical company in the Chinese province of Shandong. They have a minimal online presence. Their available information advertises chemical production primarily used in the medical field. They also produce acetaminophen for companies who market store brand headache medicines."

The DEA data analyst on the team, Ashley Cortes, interrupted. "The extremely high-quality fentanyl pills we have been discussing all include acetaminophen. The three levels of potency are managed by adjusting the percentage of acetaminophen and fentanyl in each pill. Having one vendor supplying both would make it a lot easier to assure quality control."

"Now let me get to your question," started Winston. "The three containers that supposedly contain nitrogen fertilizer are as regular as the three containers that Liu' Ltd ships to Mexico. The problem is that the 'ship to' name on the manifest does not match any known company in the Shandong area. The company name translates to Farm Supply Ltd. The address, according to area street maps, shows a large warehouse near a couple of seafood processing plants, but without access to local records, we don't know who owns the building. But here is the critical part we can document, the container numbers leaving China from Liu' Ltd often match the containers used to ship the fertilizer."

"Three containers of acetaminophen and fentanyl would produce how many illegal pills?" asked Chad.

"Perhaps as much as half the fentanyl flowing into the US, maybe more," said Ashley. "It might match exactly the high-quality pills we've been discussing."

"One more thing, boss," said Pinky. "The Jai Mew is loading in China right now. The latest manifest includes a fourth container from Liu' Ltd, and the same ship has a container from that

Farm Supply Ltd which supposedly contains irrigation equipment. It is the first Farm Supply container leaving China.

Chad turned to the woman on loan from Mexico's attorney general's office. "Gina, is this enough to get a search warrant in Mexico?"

"We could ask, but I don't think we will be successful. I have an idea though." Gina looked up some data on her phone. "A ship the size of the Jai Mew can carry about 6,000 TCU's."

"Stop, said Chad. "What is a TCU?"

"One TCU is the equivalent of one twenty-foot container unit. Each ship can carry twenty or forty-foot containers, usually a mix. Most Chinese trade is in forty-foot containers, so the Jai Mew, fully loaded might carry 3,000 forty-foot containers. A ship into central Mexico generally would not be fully loaded, so let's estimate that the Jai Mew might arrive with 2,500 containers. It would be impossible to track the movement of every container. But we have container numbers. If we could set up a surveillance in Manzanillo using cameras and AI, we might be able to identify one or more of the containers consigned by Liu' Ltd and then plant trackers on them. We in Mexico couldn't track them, but I bet you Americans would know how to do it."

She turned to Winston. "It might also be interesting to track the oddball container coming from that Farm Supply firm. I've learned to trust my nose and the instincts of my colleagues on these."

Gina turned to Ramón. "I'm thinking about Francesca in the capital. Maybe you or I should go back to our regular duties. It would at least put someone in the same city."

"That leaves this office pretty thin, and if we both go, nobody who could cut through Mexican red tape. Besides, any activities outside of our normal duties will be obvious. I'd like to think we can trust our colleagues, but it's a risk."

"Let's move on for now," said Chad. "I love Gina's idea for surveillance and tracking from Manzanillo. If the Jai Mew leaves China in the next day or two, that gives us two weeks to figure out what is needed and get it in place."

Thad, Sonia and Chad wrapped up dinner a little before eight that evening. Minutes later, Chad tapped on Thad and Sonia's hotel door. "I wanted to touch base again on my meeting with Ma."

"Come in. We're just packing for tomorrow," said Sonia. She motioned to a chair in the corner.

"At this morning's meeting, Pinky and Winston came up with some solid leads in China. We're putting together a plan to track several containers coming into Manzanillo. But on the China end, Winston has a lead that we can't trace from here." Chad explained the odd warehouse and the containers to Thad and Sonia. "I don't think Ma has the horsepower right now to go into Shandong and identify this mystery company. I don't think he officially works for anyone. But it would be very helpful if we knew this warehouse and if Farm Supply is part of the problem or just a distraction."

Thad began to smile. "My God you have a memory."

"I thought I remembered that at one time you had contact with Ma's boss, General Ling."

"He was PLA Army Major Ling then," said Thad. "He was my minder when I accompanied the Chinese army on their invasion of Vietnam four decades ago. His boss, General Yang Dezhi eventually became the PLA army commander. I made Dezhi a promise that I would never participate in any activity that might seriously hurt China. In return, he helped me look for Tan when she went missing from her hotel in Thailand. Dezhi commanded the short war between Vietnam and China."

Thad turned to Sonia. "Tan was one of only two women that

I ever loved. That was a long time ago." Sonia's smile reminded Thad of his mother when her suspicions paid off. It was odd that he remembered that, since she had been murdered when he was only ten.

He turned to Chad. "I will get ahold of Mat Chang's office before we leave in the morning. I'm sure the CIA will have a phone number for General Ling. I'll call him from Mexico. I'll remind him of our past adventures and my commitment to his former boss. And then I'll ask him to talk to Ma. Ma's documentation is solid; perhaps Ling can offer some help."

"How are you going to explain knowing what Ma knows?" asked Chad."

"I'll just explain that I'm on vacation with a beautiful woman who just happens to have contacts with Mexican intelligence. I'm sure that the PLA has files on me and maybe on Sonia. I'll tell him that Mexican intelligence is working the Chinese weapons problem and had some concerns about what was happening in China. I'll tell them that one of their paid contacts is reported to also be connected to Ma."

"That's good. One final thought," said Chad. "We may need your help on the surveillance thing we talked about. I have no idea what that might look like, but it may come up."

Thad nodded.

Chad headed to the door. "Let me know how that call goes." He stopped and looked at his greying mentor and the first woman he'd ever seen Thad show interest in. "Have fun down there. Remember your cover for now is that you're on vacation. Don't do anything I wouldn't do."

Thad shook his head. "I'm too damned old to do most of what you might do, but that doesn't mean that I won't try."

CHAPTER 30

June 10, Mexico City, Mexico

FRANCESCA HAD EXPECTED to stay in a hotel. Instead, Maria picked her up in a bright red Mercedes with a crumpled front fender and drove straight to her home. The two women talked into the night, interrupted several times by the nurse caring for Maria's mother. They fixed a late dinner together. The next day was spent at Maria's offices, her time split between her business and the foundation. By the third day, Francesca began to question whether her new job and the woman she worked for had anything to do with drugs or Chinese weapons. She had been an observer to every conversation and none of them seemed out of line. Maria seemed a lonely woman, bright and committed to her work. Francesca liked her.

The press conference the morning of the fourth day was held at the training facility for the Secretariat of Citizen Security, the Mexico City uniformed police. And as usual, when Maria Castillo held a press conference, it drew a crowd.

"Thank you all for coming," started Maria. "You all know

how my foundations are making a difference in education, farming, and even in helping fishermen recover from the disaster along our southern Pacific Coast. I am very proud of every one of those efforts. I recognize that asking you to this facility must seem incongruent. But you are here for two reasons."

She glanced back at Francesca, standing behind her in a lime green cotton business suit and smiled.

"First, I want to announce the latest initiative of the Castillo Foundations, an initiative made possible by a donation from three of my freight company's largest customers. They choose to remain anonymous for now, but all are owned by Asian businesspeople, people who share one of Mexico's most important cultural values: family."

She waited until the buzz from that statement died down before continuing. "We all know that too often families in our country are torn by domestic violence, usually when the man of the house is confronted with work problems or other stresses. They bring these stresses home and, especially when combined with too much drink, the family suffers. They simply do not know how to handle the problems and worse, often actually resent their wives trying to help. If the crisis escalates, people like the police are called and men end up in prison, which just makes things worse. Some of these men, especially if they are financially strained, target women to rob. You can't justify pointing a gun at a defenseless woman and robbing her, but you can empathize with the man's desperation. Being mugged creates a fear that stays with you."

Every eye was on her. "Today I want to announce a new program. Beginning next month, counselors will be holding classes for men arrested for abusing their families. The sessions will be designed to offer new ways of coping with stress and with making it clear that the 'beer or tequila' remedy does more harm than good. Instead of just housing offenders, their jail time will include classes to help assure that families are not harmed, and men do not make their lives worse by sitting in jail. The coursework will teach stress management skills as well as help with employment ideas and personal responsibility. Mexican women should not be afraid of Mexican men."

"What do you think? Can we make a difference?" she asked.

The question was answered by a sea of nodding heads.

"The pilot program for this initiative will begin in four local jails around our city, and we will take what we learn and begin expanding the program across Mexico next year."

Reporters were checking their notes. The announcement hadn't created the uproar that previous press conferences had. But Maria hadn't yet played the card that she hoped would move the crowd.

"The second thing, I want to announce is that I, myself, was the victim of the type of crime we are discussing today. Only weeks ago, two men stuck a gun in my face and demanded money. I escaped a second robbery attempt only days ago, only by pure luck. I am not married, although that is still a possibility, if I ever stop working long enough. I don't worry about a drunk, stressed husband taking out his frustrations on me or children, but my assessment of the men who mugged me was that they believed they were helping their families."

"My fears are the same as too many women in Mexico. I have unintentionally put a target on my back by disclosing my wealth and giving it away. Now, I have chosen to protect myself. Allow me to introduce my new traveling companion, Francesca Mateo. Some of you may have heard of her. She was trained in security by the American military but has chosen to return to the land of her birth. Ladies and gentlemen, my friend and protector, Francesca."

Francesca stepped forward, prepared with a short speech

handed to her by Maria that morning. "I have agreed to be part of Maria's new initiative as well as to offer her more security. I believe that no woman should fear for her life, especially one who devotes her life to doing good."

There was polite applause as Francesca stepped back and Maria moved to the microphone. "And now I have a bit of a surprise for my new friend, Francesca."

A tall greying man in a policeman's uniform stepped onto the stage and introduced himself as the Undersecretary of Public Participation for the police force. "Francesca, thank you for offering security to one of Mexico's treasures, Maria Castillo. We have expedited your permits and I take pride in presenting you your firearms permit and a newly registered Barretta M-9 pistol. It is the same weapon you carried while in the military."

He smiled at the crowd. "Perhaps, in order to send a message to anyone who might try to harm Maria, you would demonstrate your proficiency with the weapon for the cameras."

This had not been part of Francesca's script from Maria, but it was clear that it was part of the show. "I haven't had an opportunity to sight in this weapon," she said.

"One of my marksmen assures me that the sights are right on," said the officer.

He led the crowd to the open-air firing range behind the stage where two human silhouette targets were displayed: the first at ten yards and the second at thirty. The police commander handed Francesca two clips of ammunition. Moments later Francesca moved into a double-hand stance and fired eight rounds at the closest target. When the weapon locked open, she laid it on a bench while an attendant retrieved the target. "Five through the heart circle and three in the head," announced the officer. "Do not challenge Maria or this woman up close," he added with a laugh.

Francesca popped a second clip into the pistol and began

methodically shooting at the other target. Again, the weapon locked open after eight rounds. "Five in the chest, all kill shots, and two in the head," announced the officer. He turned to Francesca. "You missed one shot."

"I wanted to see how accurate the sights were at the longer range," said Francesca. "If you look up at the big O in TARGET OFFICIAL, I think you will find the hole from my first shot."

The man looked stunned. "Perhaps, if you tire of traveling with my friend Maria, and in helping with her new domestic violence initiative, you will come here to teach our patrol officers how to shoot," offered the officer to Francesca before turning to the crowd. "To all who see this on the evening news or in the newspapers, I would leave my friend Maria alone." He handed Francesca the remainder of the box of ammunition he carried and extended his hand.

"I have a lunch with two of my associates," said Maria as the two drove away from the police facility. "You have already met Luis. I need to chat with him and another man who helps him out from time to time. You may choose to dine alone, or I am sure both men will have their security people with them, so it might be an opportunity to pick their brains about what might be different here in Mexico." She paused as she waited for the bus in front of her to make a left turn. "It is possible that a third man, one who raises money for the foundations will be with Luis and the other fellow."

Maria and Francesca parked behind a small Italian restaurant not far from the famed Mexican National Museum. They entered through a back door where the owner led them to a small private room off from the main dining room.

"Francesca, you already know Luis here," said Maria. She turned to a less polished, bearded man dressed in jeans and a denim shirt. "This is his associate, Juan Ayala."

"Juan, this is the woman that you and Luis vetted for me.

We just finished with the press conference announcing the violence initiative and where Francesca put on quite a shooting exhibition."

Juan didn't offer his hand but smiled. "Two beautiful redheads. One becoming a saint and the other a viper." He turned back to Maria. "We need to get started. We have some problems brewing up north that will require my attention."

Maria pointed to a table where two tough looking men sat sipping minestrone soup. "Francesca, you can go introduce yourself to Juan and Luis's security men, or, if you prefer, the owner has saved the other table that overlooks this room for you." Turning back to Luis she asked, "is Hao joining us?"

"He hopes to, but called and said that he might be a little late," said Luis.

Francesca walked over to the table where the security men were eating and introduced herself. She didn't like how each of them undressed her with their eyes, before inviting her to join them. Neither seemed friendly, but both agreed that it was good for Maria to have her own security. Strangely, most of the conversation as they ate was about American baseball.

The slow pace of lunch made it clear that they had accompanied their employers to similar lunches in the past. Francesca figured that they knew a lot about the group, but it was way too early to ask any pointed questions. She had just been served a plate of ravioli when an Asian man, medium height and weight wearing a suit and tie burst through the front door and made a beeline for the private room.

She started to rise when one of her lunch companions placed his hand over hers and mumbled "todo está bien."

The next three days were spent shadowing Maria as she went about her work of building a successful transport company and saving Mexico. The only interruption to her time with Maria was when Francesca met with the same police executive who had handed her the Barretta she now concealed in a clip-on holster behind her right hip. He'd recommended Paco, a retired cop for the job of being Maria's chauffer around the city. Paco was in his fifties but had married well which allowed him to retire early. He'd lost his wife to cancer and desperately needed something to do. At Francesca's urging, Maria hired the man, who drove a Cadillac that once belonged to his late wife.

The day before Francesca returned to Zihua she rented a nicely furnished apartment only a couple of blocks from Maria's home. That evening, she and Maria spent an evening shopping for clothes appropriate for travel, including three light jackets that hid Francesca's Barretta.

Over dinner, they discussed Maria's upcoming travel schedule and Francesca's return to visit her sister for a few days. "I want to thank you for taking the job," said Maria as Paco drove them home. "I love having someone with a different perspective to bounce ideas off of and I'm sleeping better already. You make me feel safe. I wish you weren't leaving."

"Maria, I took the job based on what we talked about. I am still adjusting to life in Mexico and becoming close to a younger sister who I should have known better for years. You are safe with Paco in your city. Everyone around you is protective of you. The only people I've met who I didn't really like were Luis' bodyguard and your friend Juan Ayala and his guard. Those men give me the creeps, but you know and trust them."

"My mother doesn't like Ayala, but he is indispensable to some of the business and political ventures I'm involved in. Both he and Luis prefer security that screams 'I'm a tough guy,' You're a better choice for me."

"Paco will drop me at the airport tomorrow before picking you up. I'll be back on the Aeromexico flight next Monday morning ready to visit five cities over seven days. Is there any homework I can do on your itinerary? I hear that Ciudad Juarez can be a little rough."

"If we are going to sell my education initiative, then we have to go to where it can do the most good," said Maria. "If you weren't along, I would never set foot on the soils of our enemies. Anyway, I'll have Paco pick you up when you get back, we're leaving the next morning."

Francesca noted the word 'enemies' but said nothing.

The flight back to Zihua was only an hour, barely enough time for Francesca to organize her thoughts. She had either nothing or everything in ten days. One of Maria's 'partners' was obviously a thug, and another was probably Chinese. Both the Ayala guy and Luis needed badass security, which, at least for Luis, seemed overkill. Maria was involved not only in business ventures, but also in non-profits, and she'd even mentioned political aspirations, although there hadn't been further discussion of that. Francesca allowed herself one daily call to her sister and two calls to the off the record phone at Team Walker. She'd learned that Thad and Sonia were now in Zihua. Maybe they could help figure out if any of it was important. She was supposed to meet them accidentally that night at a beachfront restaurant only steps away from their hotel.

Part of her conversation with Ramón Acuna in LA intrigued her. With the Mexican navy technically in charge of port security, Team Walker had created an American Mexican joint business venture to expand the use of security cameras, starting with Manzanillo. She'd been out of the loop. Did that mean that the team was closing in on answers? She kind of hoped not. She liked her new job.

"Wow," started Sonia, "I'm intrigued by a former Air Force cop now providing security for one of Mexico's most famous women." The meeting between Francesca, her sister and Sonia and Thad worked out better than planned. The older couple had reserved a table near the walkway that fronted the Zihua hotels. The beachfront popup restaurant had grown so popular that every table was filled when Mary and Francesca stopped to study the menu. "Would you two care to join us?" called Sonia as the women discussed how long it would be before a table was available."

Over grilled seafood dinners and a bottle of Chilean wine, the four carried on the kind of conversation that any newcomers might have with locals. The two hour dinner had given Thad plenty of time to survey the other diners, people on the beach as well as on the decks of rooms overlooking the open-air restaurant. He'd seen no indication that Francesca was being watched.

"Our trip was kind of a spur of the moment thing," said Thad. "The only room available at the hotel was a suite. We're celebrating our first trip together. Leaving LA for the trip, Sonia splurged on a bottle of Dom Perignon champagne in the duty-free shop. We've been too busy to open it."

"It's more than we can drink at our age," offered Sonia, "and you cannot recork champagne. Would you two like to join us for a nightcap?"

"What do you think?" Francesca asked her sister.

"I told you that Diego and Elena invited us to join them at BANDITOS for a nightcap. They called while you were on the plane. The Navy is giving up on its search for Jorge and his friend. The marines are getting together to have a drink in their honor, and I was invited."

"You should go then," said Francesca. "You were really close to Jorge. Please apologize for my absence, but these new friends are from Montana, right next to where I used to serve. I'd like to join them if you don't mind."

Thad handed the waiter his credit card as they began slipping on the sandals they'd shed to bury their feet in the cool sand while they ate. "Our treat," he said.

The six flights of stairs were a challenge for a man who used a cane, but the elegant suite where Chad and Olga had stayed only months before made it worthwhile. Sonia and Francesca moved out onto the extensive deck overlooking the harbor and walked along the railing, looking for anyone observing them as they talked. Thad brought champagne and glasses from the kitchen.

He popped the cork and poured three flutes of bubbly as they settled into chairs around a small glass table.

"You first," said Francesca. "Bring me up to speed on the team."

Thad and Sonia took turns, each discussing different aspects uncovered by the data miners. "The most important thing," said Thad, "is the tracking of several containers coming in from China next week. The ship Jai Mew appears to be connected to all of this, and she is on the way. Mexico's former president put the navy in charge of port security. Ramón Acuna tells us that the operational Pacific Command for the Mexican Navy is in Manzanillo, so he has contacts there. As we speak there are cameras being installed on each gantry of the five container wharfs. Another five are being installed where containers are loaded on trucks. All download data to a central data center that will be operational next week. We're using AI software to look for the five needles in a haystack of probably twenty-five hundred containers. The program is designed to bring up an alert when any of the targeted containers is loaded on a truck."

Sonia picked up the conversation. "If it all works correctly, that alarm will trigger a short shutdown of the port for a truck safety inspection. We will trigger a couple of trial runs before the Jai Mew arrives to make the procedure routine."

"When the Jai Mew is in port, Diego will take two of his

people up there to do the inspections. He will plant a tracker on as many of the containers as he can. We can track them using satellites all the way to their destination," added Thad. "We still won't have evidence to conduct a legal search, but at least we'll have some idea of the players here in Mexico."

"If there is already a Mexican navy base there, why is Diego needed?" asked Francesca.

"Because the less people who know our mission, the safer it is for all of us," answered Thad.

"There is more, but before we waste your time with any of it, tell us about your new job," said Sonia.

Francesca sipped her champagne as she talked casually about the job and Maria. "Nothing seems out of line," she offered. "But I did accompany Maria to a lunch where she met with some interesting men." She pulled out her phone and opened the pictures. She sorted through them and then paused. "The first is a man named Luis Cardenas. He owns manufacturing companies both in Mexico City and in the south." She sent the photo to Sonia's phone.

"The second guy's name is Juan Ayala. I have no idea what he does, except that Maria indicated that he had a role in vetting me. I didn't like him. Maria seemed to know him from her past. She said that her mom, who by the way has dementia, doesn't like him either." She transferred that photo.

"This third guy came in late. It's the best picture I could get of him without being obvious. I didn't meet him, but the two other security people I was seated with said he was a regular. I'd bet he's Chinese."

"This last picture is of the two-security people traveling with Cardenas and Ayala. Both were carrying holstered pistols and the one on the right had a second pistol in an ankle holster.

That's a lot of firepower to watch over simple businessmen." She transferred the last two photos.

Sonia leaned across the table, almost spilling her wine. "Most of the drug groups I've studied have a producer and a distributor who also coordinates security. That might fit Cardenas and Ayala. The group we are looking for also has a Chinese connection. That third picture fits. The last picture, the one of the muscles, could be any two men from a Mexican gang. But they may be what they said they were, security for paranoid people in a country where a lot of people won't drive the roads alone at night because they're afraid of being robbed or kidnapped."

She paused for a minute. "Remember, we are talking about enterprises generating hundreds of millions, even billions of dollars, so the organizations are also huge. With that said, what you saw is important. If these people aren't at the top, and if they are dirty, they will lead us to the top. I'll send the photos and names to LA tonight."

"My question is," said Thad, "what's Maria Castillo's role in all this? Could she be the brains behind the whole thing? That is if there really is a thing. If she's not running it, then what's she doing?"

"I shadowed her for days. Other than this meeting, there was nothing that didn't fit a woman buried in a successful company while trying to save the world," said Francesca.

"Okay, how do you want to play this?" asked Sonia.

"I think we need to study the people I took pictures of," replied Francesca, "and I need to get back. Maria will be touring several cities next week. I'll be with her every minute that she isn't behind the walls of a hotel room."

"I'm sure you have the critical phone numbers committed to memory, so that anyone handling your phone couldn't compromise you," said Sonia. She jotted down Thad's and her phone number on a sheet from a hotel notepad. "Memorize these as well. When you left LA, we set up an emergency protocol. As I recall, any conversation that includes 'I'm worried about my sister,' means that you need help. While you sister was with us this evening, I cloned her cell number. If you need help, I'll respond using that number to avoid suspicion."

Francesca looked a little shocked. "You can actually take over her phone?"

"Not her phone, but I can call you and the number that will come up on your phone will be hers."

"Francesca," said Thad, "We don't know how sophisticated these people are. We know they have enough money to buy almost any technology they need. They are buying weapons that aren't even for sale. They can jam radios and cell phones. We need to assume that they have defensive layers around them that are comparable to our own. Our edge is experience.

∽

Chad finally got out of the office a little after eight that same evening. He carried a burger and fries from McDonalds to his room and dropped them on the table in the corner as he fished a cold Modelo from the mini refrigerator. He'd just started his burger when the emergency phone next to his own rang.

"Yes," he answered, not recognizing the number.

"This is Paul Thibs from the border patrol, who am I talking to?"

"Paul, it's Chad Gritt. I was in the room when you talked to Thad and Sonia."

"Mr. Gritt, I just got one of the phone calls I mentioned to your friends. Someone just called to tip us off on a trans-border shipment of fentanyl. I'll text the date and the location after this call. Your guy Walker indicated that he might be able to rustle up some help on the Mexican side if we have lead time. According to the caller, we have three days."

The morning meeting in LA was short and intense. Gina Santos was working on tracking the men in the pictures that Francesca had taken. Ramón Acuna and Chad began putting together a team to monitor the Mexican side of the border that Paul Thibs called about. The rest of the team remained focused on the shipments to and from Mexico, including tracking a call from China. The warehouse in Shandong was reportedly empty, a repossessed building once owned by a company that had failed the year before, and now owned by an investment bank. General Ling, after his conversation with Thad, had contacted the mayor's office in Shandong for help. Someone from the city records office had called with the information, but with so many small company failures, no one had inspected the building. There was no need because the building was now the bank's problem. General Ling had seemed to enjoy reconnecting with Thad and listened carefully when Thad discussed the Mexican government's concerns about weapons shipments. He'd called Thad only a day later with what he'd learned. He and Ma were meeting that afternoon.

CHAPTER 31

June 20, Zihuantanejo, Mexico

Sonia had a message on her phone when they got back to their room after an early morning swim. They showered and ordered fruit and pastries with a pot of coffee from room service before returning the call. It was from the Mexican investigator, Gina Santos. The LA team had identified both Ayala and Cardenas. Both might be critical components of a Mexican drug gang, at least their profiles fit. Francesca needed to be informed.

Francesca recognized that it wasn't her sister the moment she heard the voice over the phone. "There are people around." she said. "What have you got? Quickly. Quietly."

"First, your new friend Luis Cardenas owns two chemical companies. The one near Mexico City specializes in over the counter drugs. It would be a perfect cover for pressing fentanyl pills. His second company is using natural gas from the new field in southern Mexico to manufacture nitrogen fertilizer. We didn't discuss it while you were here, but containers supposedly moving fertilizer to China are somehow tied to the containers we think might be bringing fentanyl materials to Mexico."

"So, this might be a what Americans call a two-fer?" said Francesca.

"Yes, and Ayala has deep ties to Maria Castillo. Her dad was in the drug business. He died in prison. Ayala was always suspected of being his top enforcer. In my experience, the enforcers and the people who manage drug distribution are often the same."

Sonia heard someone calling Francesca in the background. "My new friend Maria is meeting with President Martinez soon. We need to discuss the meeting, so Sis, you'll just have to figure out whether to take the new job or not on your own. I've got to run."

While Sonia updated Francesca, Thad was on the phone with Diego.

"We discussed the inbound containers from Liu' Chemical," he started. "We also discussed the possible connection to outbound shipments of fertilizer. Francesca gave us a name, Luis Cardenas. He's somehow connected to Maria Castillo. It turns out that this Cardenas guy owns a company that would be a perfect cover for drugs. He's also involved in the fertilizer business. I'm sending you the company names. "I'd bet that the containers from Liu' Chemical will end up on trucks headed for his company in Mexico City. I have no idea yet of how the fertilizer thing fits in, but I think it does somehow. We still have no idea how Maria Castillo might be involved, but her father died in prison after being convicted of drug smuggling. One of his enforcers met with Maria and Cardenas while Francesca was there."

"Thad, we've only been here for one day," replied Diego. "The Jai Mew is still anchored waiting to unload, but at least ten percent of the trucks leaving the port has Castillo Transportation on the side. Maybe she's running a simple freight company, but it would also be a perfect cover for moving drugs, and everything else we are looking for," said Diego.

Thad paused a minute to sip his coffee. "Do you have enough markers to tag every Castillo truck?"

"Not even close," said Diego, "but the preferred routing for trucking between Manzanillo and the capital would be south on the coast highway and then east on Highway 134. It connects just outside of Zihua." He paused a moment before adding, "this is coming together, but we still have nothing that justifies a warrant. My sleepy, touristy, hometown might have some pretty deep secrets."

"I agree," said Thad. "But maybe someone will screw up and give us something. Have you talked to Captain Acuna in the last day or two?"

"No, why?" asked Diego.

"We have a tip on a drug shipment over the border. The US border patrol asked if we could help arrange some support on the Mexican side. Ramón tried to put something together, but everyone he talked to asked questions that would compromise us, so that's not going to happen." He waited for a response which didn't come. "Don't ask me how Gritt arranged it, because you officially do not want to know, but there will be a high-altitude surveillance drone over the area when this is supposed to go down. Maybe it will give us some pictures or descriptions that we can chase."

"So the US Government is going to be flying a surveillance mission over Mexican air space?" asked Diego.

"Like I said," replied Thad, "you don't want to know."

"No, I don't. But I don't need to. The Jai Mew will begin unloading in a couple of hours. From the time the first container comes off from a ship, it usually takes forty-eight hours before the first truck leaves the yard. We're going to be busy getting trackers on the target containers. But if something looks promising up north and we can help, let me know. We're not really wanted here; Acuna kind of imposed us on the local command as a training mission. We should be done in the next four or five days. My troops would relish pay back for the loss of Jorge and Ro."

CHAPTER 32

June 21, Arizona-Mexico Border

Paul Thibs was disappointed by the inability to arrange for a Mexican counterpart to his surveillance. This time the crossing site was more remote, ninety miles west of Cactus Pipe Monument. He led three other officers across the Air Force bombing range at night on Polaris ATVs, reaching the border just before dawn. Most drug movement through the desert happened at night, and it seemed strange to him that every tip he had received was for a daytime shipment. He knew the two largest cartels never did daytime desert crossings which reinforced his suspicions that one of those cartels was trying to prove to the Americans that they were serious about stopping fentanyl.

Dividing into two groups, the border patrol agents climbed peaks on the southern end of the Copper Mountains and set up cameras. This time they carried satellite phones, hoping that the jammers used in the past would not work on them. Helicopter support would be waiting at the Yuma airport. The National

Guard didn't want to put another aircrew at risk without knowing what they were up against.

They had been in place more than an hour when the same truck they'd seen before made its way along the track on the other side of the border. Just like last time, it stopped and deployed a large box. Thibs guessed it was a jammer. He checked his cellphone and field radio which offered nothing but noise. His sat phone worked.

Minutes later, five men strapped on packs and began walking toward the border. They hadn't traveled a hundred yards when four ATVs burst from a draw a quarter mile away. Three raced toward the men while the other turned toward the truck which was just turning around. At almost the same moment, one of Thibs' officers pointed to a small dot in the sky south of the border. "Probably the same drone we saw blast those trucks after the last tip," said Thibs to the man next to him.

Before the drone could get there, automatic rifle fire from men on the ATV's cut down all five of the mules. The fourth ATV began spraying bullets into the cab of the truck, which lurched to the left and smashed into an embankment on the US side of the border.

Thibs called to his team on the next ridge. "Get down there and secure any evidence you can," he ordered, "but don't cross the border." He watched as the shooters stripped the packs from three of the dead mules. They started toward the other two before one of them began gesturing wildly at the approaching drone. Mounting the ATVs, they raced toward the draw they'd emerged from only a minute before.

The fourth ATV driver looked over at Thibs people heading toward the wrecked truck and also turned toward the draw. A rocket launched from the drone exploded well behind the zigzagging ATV. Thibs looked up, surprised that the drone had closed so quickly. He looked back down just in time to watch the racing ATV disintegrate as a second rocket landed only feet away. Then in horror, he watched the drone swing to its right and launch two rockets, this time targeting the wrecked truck just as his two agents arrived. The truck, ATV, and men were blown to pieces.

The drone turned back and launched its final missile at what Thibs guessed were the ATVs hidden in a deep draw across the border. The missile hit the bank and exploded. Thibs had no idea whether it also hit any of the men who had just cut down the mules and taken their packs, but it really didn't matter. He watched as the drone made another circle over the destruction and then turned south.

He and the man next to him waited to make sure the drone was actually leaving before he picked up the sat phone lying in the dust at his feet and made a call to the helicopter, then he and his remaining deputy started toward a sight that neither had ever hoped to see.

※

Three hundred miles away, at Navy Air Station Point Magu California, Commander Chad Gritt, Mexican Captain Ramón Acuna and two other American officers crowded around a young Navy tech staring into the screen of a guidance system for a Navy MQ-4C Triton high altitude surveillance drone above where Thibs was making his way down the hill. The men had watched the entire event as if it was on television.

It was deathly quiet in the room. The view displayed from the drone was so clear that you could count the body parts. "Five, maybe six or seven dead from one cartel and at least two from another," said Acuna. He looked up to see Chad chewing the end of his pencil. "And, at least two of your people as well."

"Can you tighten up the view of that drone?" asked Chad.

The tech made an adjustment which left the drone filling the screen in front of the men.

"It's the same Chinese manufactured drone that the border patrol got video of weeks ago," said Chad.

"The guy who took the earlier video may be dead down by that truck," said a young Navy lieutenant standing next to Chad.

"Just stay on that drone," said Chad, not wanting to think of Thibs, or any of the other men they had watched die. "I want to know where it lands."

Twenty minutes later they watched the drone touchdown on a packed dirt runway near a small village just north from Puerto Peñasco on the northern end of the Gulf of California. They watched the drone taxi to a small warehouse where four men met it and then pushed it inside. Several other buildings made up a small compound.

"Let's just watch that building for a while," suggested Acuna. "There are nine cars parked nearby."

A few minutes later, two men walked from the building, one talking on a phone and gesturing wildly. They stopped next to a white Chevy Suburban. The taller man finished his call, placing his hand and phone into a pocket in the jacket he wore. It was clear that the taller man was screaming at the other. His hand emerged with a pistol. Without warning, he placed it against the shorter man's head, which jerked before he dropped into the dust.

"Obviously, there was some security leak in their organization," mumbled Acuna. "Even if that didn't plug it, the message was loud and clear."

The shooter slid into the back seat of the Suburban. The drone followed the vehicle to the Puerto Peñasco airport where the man in the back seat walked to a waiting older Lear Jet and climbed aboard.

"We can't track the jet," said the tech, "It's too fast for the Triton."

"Okay, Max, let's bring the bird home," said the lieutenant.

Five minutes later, Gritt and Acuna stood outside the building, thanking the lieutenant for his help.

"I don't know if we got you what you were looking for," said the lieutenant. I'll log the flight as a training exercise. My people will sanitize the video and get rid of any markers that could identify the location before I get you a copy. You should have it tomorrow. Take a look and let me know of any specific shots you want. I can get you enhanced images of any frame. You should be able to read the tags on the shirt collars from what I send you."

The drive back to LA started off quiet. "If we hadn't lost any good guys, I'd call this a success," said Acuna. "Maybe ten bad guys dead. No drugs crossed the border. And most importantly, we now have an idea where the northern base is for the smuggling submarines."

"I've seen close ups from the Triton," said Chad. "If the guy who boarded the jet looked up, we should be able to identify him. Even if we can't, we can track the plane by its tail number and find out who was on it. Maybe your people can raid that location and seize the drone."

"Maybe," said Acuna, "but with the number of cars and buildings in that compound, we'll need a lot of people. The cartels never give up a site without a fight. Did you see the sandbagged security posts around the compound? Even taking that facility won't tell us who is running this group."

"Then for now, let's concentrate on the guy we saw. We can start looking for that jet," added Gritt. He pulled his phone out of his pocket as the traffic on Highway 101 slowed. "Pinky, I have a Mexican aircraft XA tail number that I need you to track for me. I need to know the owner and where it is based."

"Piece of cake," replied Pinky. "Anything else?"

"It's airborne now. I don't know if you can figure out where it lands, but that might be useful."

"That might be tough," she replied, "I'll have to see what I can find for tracking outside of American airspace." By the way, a Paul Thibs just left a message for you on the secure phone. He didn't sound very happy."

"He wouldn't be," replied Chad. "We just watched two of his men killed."

"How, I mean what… where are you?" she asked.

"Just calling in a favor from a man I helped promote a year ago. Acuna and I will be in the office in an hour or so." Chad hung up as traffic slowed to a crawl.

CHAPTER 33

June 23, Los Angeles, California

CHAD FINISHED HIS morning call updating Thad and Sonia. The pictures from Point Magu were due within an hour, but Chad suspected that they would just confirm what Pinky had given him earlier. The plane was registered to a small company in Mexico City called MEXAIR. The company had three planes, and strangely they had managed to stay in business for three years. Strange because their Mexican tax records showed barely enough revenue to buy fuel. The company had been created by a legal firm that the Mexican attorney general's office knew well. While they had never been able to make a case, it was suspected that most of their clients were criminal organizations. You never knew if the owner names that firm used when creating a company were accurate or not, but in this case the sole owner listed was Juan Ayala.

The team started off looking for a string to pull. Now they had several, and most of them somehow involved Ayala.

Chad's computer beeped as the pictures from Magu came

in. He and Acuna had scrubbed the video the previous evening and asked for six shots. Chad clicked on the first picture, which was a clear image of the Chinese attack drone. The second was of the compound where the drone was housed, including the men pushing the drone into a hanger. The third was a shot of the man next to the white Suburban with a gun at another man's head. The last three were all taken as the man in the Suburban made his way to the waiting Lear Jet. Chad studied each. All showed the plane and Suburban with the man walking. Finally, the last frame caught the man staring up at another plane circling to land. "Got you, you bastard," echoed out into the room.

Everyone descended on Chad's desk. "That has to be the Juan Ayala guy that Francesca got a picture of," said Acuna. "At least it looks like him."

"Here, let me drive a minute," offered Pinky.

She slid into the chair that Chad vacated and called up both Francesca's picture and the one from the Triton drone. She dropped both into a facial recognition program which mapped out both photos. It took less than ten seconds to confirm that both were of the same man. "'Got you, you bastard,' seems to be appropriate," she said.

"We can't forget that our mission is to figure out who is shipping Chinese military hardware to Mexico and why," said Chad. "We've got this guy cold for murder and we can show him around where illegal drug activity is occurring. But we have no murder victim. And we can only tie him to a drone that killed some people who killed drug mules."

Both Gina Santos and Ramón Acuna looked at each other for a moment before Gina leaned across the table to stare at Chad. "Commander Gritt, we have a picture of this man pushing the Chinese drone into a hiding place. He's tied to the drone which means he's tied to the supplier."

"Okay," said Chad. "We can also tie the drone to the murder of two American Border Patrol Agents. That may be enough to pick him up and sweat him."

"Except," said Acuna, "the evidence we have is from a drone that never entered Mexican airspace. It won't fly in Mexican courts or in the states."

"So," said Gritt, "our task now is to begin filling in details. Let's see if we can tie him to any other illegal activity. Let's bear down on the link between Liu' Chemical and this Luis Cardenas guy. Diego called this morning and told me that the containers from the Jai Mew will be moving out of the port."

He had just finished the sentence when his phone rang. "Diego, we were just talking about you and your project," said Chad. "Here let me put you on speakerphone."

"Evidently someone didn't like me and my guys poking around the Jai Mew. The trucks are lined up to take on the containers from that ship. One of my guys was in the control building monitoring the AI reading of the container numbers when the power to the entire port failed. We've got nothing. They are using forklifts to load the containers and trucks are leaving."

"No sweat," said Ashley Cortes, tapping Gritt on the shoulder. "When I helped set this up, we made sure that the cameras are all solar powered. They should still be transmitting to the server in the control room and those computers are all backed up with battery power."

"That's how it's supposed to be," said Diego, "but nothing in the control room is working."

Gina Santos smiled at Ashley who smiled back. "This kind of interference is expected in my country," added Gina. "I can't tell you how many set ups I've done from the attorney general's office where power failures or transportation snafus ruined a plan. Ashley told me that in her work with your DEA, similar things occur when dealing with the cartels. The port is under the protection of the Mexican navy, but outside the chain link fence, the cartels run that place."

Chad looked at both women, trying to figure out how that was helpful. Gina's smile just got bigger as she watched him. "The cameras themselves are solar powered. When we helped design the surveillance system, we specked redundant feed capabilities from each camera. One feed uses a local area network to tie them into the server in Manzanillo. But the actual AI analysis is being done at a DEA facility here in LA and then looped back to your server."

The group around Chad's desk just stared at her. "And?" offered Chad.

"If Diego can tell us which camera or cameras are monitoring the loading, we can activate the second feed using cellular telephone protocols. That feed goes directly to the AI computer here in LA and we can monitor the results here." Before she finished the sentence, Ashley was on her way back to the computer on her desk.

"Both cameras five and six cover the loading area," replied Diego.

"Chad, bring your phone over to my desk," said Gina. Moments later Ashley had a screen open on her computer. Each camera was displayed on a network diagram. It took only six keystrokes to switch the cameras to cellular and only a few more to switch the inputs to the LA server running the AI program and the results to their office.

"I have the feed on my computer," called Ashley. "Have Diego give you his cell number and one from the marine watching the other loading dock and then tell them to stay off from their phones. I will monitor for hits on the container numbers.

If the target container is on camera five, I will dial Diego's cell. If it is on camera six, I'll dial the other. They don't need to answer, just tag the trucks at those locations when the phone rings."

"Were probably looking at ten or twelve hours before the loading is finished," said Diego.

"As long as you are there to take the calls, someone will be here monitoring and ready to call you," said Gina. "My guess is that any contraband containers will go out early and the general cargo later."

Chad watched in awe as the latest version of Team Walker picked up the slack. "The bad guys are good," he said to everyone in the room, "but you all are better."

"If we had your capabilities, we could crush the drug business in my country in months," said Acuna.

"Ramón, you know better than that," replied Gina. "It generates too much money and too many jobs. Our country just wants it under control until we have an economy that can replace it."

It took less than three hours before Diego called Gritt again. "We have tracking tags on all five containers that we're looking for. We did it with only four safety stops but we're going to run six more. Anyone watching us will have seen us inspect a hundred trucks before calling it a day. Nobody watching us will see a pattern. Then were heading home."

Gritt looked over at Pinky and Winston. "Are we ready to track five tags?"

"We already are," answered Winston. "One of us will be monitoring for 48 hours unless a target is still moving, then we'll stay on it. How often do you want updates?"

"Hourly, but you're going to have to call us with them," said Chad. "Ramón, Gina, and I are all headed south. If this is going to work at all, it's going to happen fast. We'll need to scoop up the leadership quickly or the group will be right back in business."

"Ashley, will you see if you can get us reservations to Zihua tomorrow morning?"

She nodded, "And what else, Boss?"

"You are the hacker in the group. See if you can get into the MEXAIR computer system and find past flight information. If it includes passenger lists that might help. Even if we track all five containers to where we expect they are going, we still do not have probable cause to search them. If we can build a tight case on this Ayala guy, maybe we can squeeze him hard enough to crack."

※

While they were waiting for their Alaska Airlines flight at LAX, Chad called Ma in China. He forwarded the enhanced picture of the Chinese drone, which Ma had instantly deleted. "That picture could only have been taken by one of your American Reaper drones," said Ma. "I have no way of explaining how I got it."

"Close, offered Chad. It was a Navy Triton drone, but both are basically the same platform." He heard the call for his flight. "I'm traveling. When I get to Mexico, I'll have a colleague in the Mexican navy draft a report confirming that their reconnaissance got a crystal-clear picture of the drone, identifying it as a Chinese military version of your export weapon. You can make up a story on how you got your hands on the report. Ma, there is no question that someone on your side of the pond is arming Mexican drug gangs. Whoever it is may be PLA. The arms are all military weapons, not export versions. We can now document that those weapons have been used to kill Americans. With what's going on in China right now, and the leadership's efforts to tone down the US-China conflict, your country doesn't need this. Your president is wining and dining American business executives begging for them to resume Chinese investment."

He'd dropped off the call with the agreement that Ma would take the Mexican report to General Ling who had already authorized a back-door investigation.

It was the middle of summer in Zihua. Tourism was minimal, and many of the tourist businesses had closed for the season. Most northerners didn't like the hundred degree temperatures. Working with Sonia and Thad, Ashley had managed to reserve one regular room in the same hotel where Thad and Sonia were staying, and two small condominiums for Ramón and Gina next door. A little separation might keep the bad guys from connecting the dots, at least for a while. The two Mexican members of the team were already in a cab headed downtown by the time Chad finally cleared customs.

Diego was waiting for him in the Mustang. "I've been doing some digging this afternoon on this Juan Ayala," said Diego as Chad slammed the door. "I've never met him, but he has a presence here. I've had to be careful, if he is one of the key characters in the group we're after, he will have a well-paid umbrella of local officials looking out for him."

"What have you been able to nail down?" asked Chad as they pulled onto the highway.

"Nothing hard, but about the same time that Mexican legal firm set up MEXAIR, they also handled the purchase of a small hotel over in Ixtapa as well as a medium sized warehouse just outside of the city. Both of those are within five miles of here. I think most of the local police are clean," he continued. "It would only take one question to one bad apple to tip Ayala or his associates about our investigation."

"So how do you close the loop on this scum ball?" asked Chad.

"I have a friend in the local police office whom I trust completely. His father was also an investigator working drug cartels years ago. Some thugs tried to gun down his sister and mother to send his father a message. They only wounded his sister, but his mother was killed. When his father didn't stop, they blew up his car. The son has participated in dozens of investigations that were never went anywhere. He's kept his head down, but still has copies of every one of the files. He needs a win. Mexico needs a win."

"Does he have anything on Ayala?" asked Chad as they sped past a National Guard checkpoint along the highway that wasn't operating when Chad and Olga were there earlier.

"He has a couple of files on Ayala. In one, two former employees of the drug operation that Maria Castillo's father ran fingered Ayala as the trigger man who enforced security for her father. Both of those people were found shot to death, which stopped the investigation. He also has a surveillance file on a warehouse where Ayala spends a lot of time. It was suspected that it was being used to repackage drug money and ship it out of the country. That investigation was terminated months ago," said Diego."

"What happened?" asked Chad.

"The lead sergeant on the investigation went out fishing one day with his two sons and never returned. A day later the lieutenant commanding the investigation ordered it dropped. He and his wife moved to Argentina and bought a huge house on a lake. *Oro no plomo.*"

"Sounds like he got the message when the sergeant disappeared," said Chad. "Mexican crime history is famous for that 'gold versus lead' offer.

"It is, but that warehouse may be the key to what we're looking for. He shared the file with me this morning. Among the trucks stopping regularly at that warehouse is one that arrives each week from the south. Each truck is carrying a container supposedly loaded with nitrogen fertilizer. It comes in one evening and leaves for Manzanillo the next morning. There is no reason for it to stop." Diego waited at a stop light to make a left turn which led to the main road into downtown Zihua.

"So maybe our suspicions of fertilizer shipments being important are accurate?" offered Chad.

"I have an idea on how we might close the loop," said Diego. "That odd ball incoming container from China, the one from Farm Supply Company, is consigned to the fertilizer company that Luis Cardenas owns. But the address for delivery is a small fishing resort this side of Acapulco."

Chad leaned back in his seat trying to connect the dots. "So?"

"The manifest lists the shipment as irrigation machinery. Now why would a fishing resort need irrigation equipment? If your friend Gina could explain that to her boss at the attorney general's office, then maybe there would be justifiable suspicion that the manifest is false, and the container contains contraband. It's headed south as we speak. Maybe we can get permission to search it." Diego turned up the hill toward Chad's hotel.

"How do we know what was on that manifest?" asked Chad.

"Your friends Pinky and Winston sent me a translation of the manifest when they identified the container and asked us to tag it."

"So again, our documentation came from a hacking operation that will not hold up in court." As the Mustang slowed, Chad's frustration was about to boil over.

"I anticipated that," said Diego as they stopped outside the lobby of the Del Mar Hotel. "So, we made copies of the manifest the drivers carried for every truck we did a safety search on. I have a copy of the original and the note on top where customs translated the information into Spanish."

"I don't know what the laws are here in Mexico," replied Chad. "Is that enough to get a judge to issue a search warrant?"

"I don't think we need one," said Diego. "The navy is in charge of security at Mexican ports now. There is a search on for Chinese made weapons coming into the country. If the attorney general and the navy agree that this is suspicious, I think they can authorize the inspection."

"Welcome back, Señor Gritt." Chad lifted his small suitcase from the backseat of the Mustang, stopping long enough to wipe the sweat dripping into his eyes.

"My friend Diego suggested that I come back and try some summer fishing. He didn't tell me that it would be hotter than hell. Still, Gustavo it is good to be back."

"The front desk will have a cold beer waiting," said the bellman as he headed across the lobby with the suitcase.

Chad turned back to Diego. "Pick someplace for dinner tonight, hopefully one with air conditioning. In the interim, I'm meeting with Thad and Sonia this afternoon. They're figuring out how to include Gina and Ramón without appearing too obvious.:"

"I'll pick you up for dinner about eight," yelled Diego as he drove away. "I'm bringing Elena. She wants to see you while you're here."

Chad walked up to the front desk where Lila already had his registration and key waiting. She wiped the sweat from a cold Pacifico beer and handed it to Chad. "The suite you stayed in this spring is occupied," she said. "I have you in a king room on the fourth floor."

"The suite was nice for Olga, but I'm here to spend some time fishing, so as long as I can get the room cool to sleep, I'm sure it will be fine. Is there any place where I can sit outside and drink the beer without melting?" he asked.

Chad turned to go just as an older couple started up the stairs wearing swimsuits.

"Señor Gritt, the American couple behind you have the top floor open air suite you and your lady had this spring. With the afternoon breeze it is the coolest accommodation on the property. But in a couple of hours, with the sun setting, the little patio and bar off from the lobby will also be comfortable."

The man behind Chad stopped, listening to the conversation, and then stepped to the counter. "My name's Walker, Thad Walker and the lady here is Sonia Ramirez. We're from Montana and without the ocean and the pool we would have melted a couple of days ago. We're on our way to the room to change and then have an afternoon bracer on the deck. You're welcome to join us if you'd like."

Chad extended his hand. "I'd be delighted to. I've got to get settled into my room. Would a half hour give you two enough time?"

"Perfect, said Sonia. "We also met two lovely Mexican nationals while on our way down for a swim who are also staying here. If you don't mind, we've also invited them to join us."

"Sounds delightful," said Chad. "I'll see you soon. Can I pick up some cold beer or anything?"

"My young friend," said Sonia, "Thad has been trying every local beer for days. We've got four or five of every six pack still in the refrigerator. You will find something you like."

CHAPTER 34

June 24, Zihuantanejo, Mexico

"Diego is onto something," said Gina. She smiled at the other three as Thad wandered back into the kitchen for another round of beers. "ANAM, our customs agency is a division of the finance department. They are tasked with controlling import and exports in the country and collecting fees. If they have the evidence you describe, that indicates document falsification, then they will generally refer it to the attorney general's office for investigation. If there is any reason for port security to question any action of ANAM in clearing a shipment, they too can refer it to the AG's office. If we in the AG's office agree that there is suspicious activity, we can authorize an immediate investigation."

Ramón drained his beer and leaned across the table. "And would such a request from the navy go to you?"

"It would, "said Gina, "and I would sign it off and encourage the navy to immediately conduct an investigation since the infraction, if any, occurred where they have security responsibility."

"How fast could such an approval get the ball moving?" asked Chad.

"What ball?" asked Thad as he placed five beers on the table."

"They were just following up on what Chad said a few minutes ago," replied Sonia. "I think Gina here is about to okay our first hard action since Team Walker was formed."

Gina looked over at Ramón and motioned for him to say something.

"Deputy Attorney General Gina Santos, as head of intelligence for the navy of the United Mexican States, my staff has uncovered what we believe is false documentation on a shipment just received in Mexico. Considering the ongoing investigation of illegal arms shipments to Mexico we request authority to track down that shipment and inspect it."

"Captain," replied Gina, "with the presentation of the evidence being discussed, I personally authorize you to conduct the inspection you propose. Please provide me the documentation in the next 24 hours and I will notify my office of my approval."

Chad pulled out his cell phone and called LA. "Pinky, can you tell me the location of the one container we are tracking from Farm Supply in Shandong?"

A moment later he clicked off the call. "The container in question overnighted somewhere near where we are. It was back on the road this afternoon, headed south. Pinky shows it in motion just north of Acapulco."

Ramón was on his phone to the navy search and rescue base at Lazaro Cardenas before Chad could put his back in his pocket. He ordered a helicopter to be flown to the Zihua airport. His next call was to Diego. "Lieutenant Cervantes, we are immediately following up on the lead you gave our friend Chad. I need you and at least two of your men, all armed. Bring me a sidearm and one of your new HK MP-5 assault rifles. My Barretta is in my office, so I will also need a marine issue Glock. Also, I don't have a uniform with me, so bring me a jumpsuit. We're going to see what's in that container headed for the fishing resort down toward Acapulco. Pick me up at my hotel in the next half hour. There will be a helicopter waiting at the airport. I think you are going to have to cancel your dinner with Chad. He's sitting right here."

He handed Chad the phone. Moments later Chad hung up as Ramón excused himself and headed to his condo. "I'm having dinner with a beautiful Italian girl tonight since her boyfriend just canceled on her with no notice."

The table erupted with laughter.

∽

The six-person navy helicopter was a version of the Eurocopter 350 found all over the world. It was airborne from Zihua international eighty minutes after Ramón's call. The flight down the coast took less than an hour.

"Make a pass directly by the buildings in that small resort," ordered Ramón. "Do not be obvious." The pilot didn't bother to slow as he raced just offshore. "I see the container," he said. "It's still on the trailer parked next to that warehouse below the resort. The truck has just pulled back onto the highway."

"It looks like they're about to open it," said Diego. "Four men just opened a door to that warehouse."

Acuna turned to the pilot. "Are you armed?"

"No sir, but there is an AR-15 with two clips above the port side door behind us. We've been carrying a rifle since that American helicopter was shot down.

"I want you to swing back north and land on the lawn next to the lodge. We'll be on a dead run from the moment you touch down and we don't know what we're getting into down there. I suggest you arm yourself as soon as you shut down."

"Diego, are you and your men ready?"

"We're ready."

The pilot tipped the helicopter into a tight turn and started to descend. Less than a minute later the skids touched down and Acuña, Cervantes and two other men raced toward the warehouse sixty yards downhill from a beautiful one-story lodge. The last marine positioned himself where he could cover both the front and rear entrances of the lodge.

Down the drive, the men who Diego had seen near the container stood, shocked, and then bolted for the warehouse. Ramón and one marine raced to the left side of the container, and Diego and the other marine to the right. As they passed the trailer, someone opened up with an automatic rifle from inside the gaping warehouse door, splattering the ground in front of the container. Diego's marines had been begging for some way to avenge the loss of two of their members for months. In seconds all three marines shredded the aluminum wall hiding the shooter who stumbled into the open before being shot down.

Ramón and Diego, covered by the other two marines, cautiously entered the building. They circled to the right and left, shocked by what they were seeing. What was missing were the other three men they'd seen from the air. Finally reaching the rear of the building they found an open door and outside of that a cement driveway descending to a dock and boat launch. A fishing panga was just starting away from the dock.

"Lieutenant," ordered Ramón, "send two of your men back to the helicopter. I want them to stop that boat. The pilot has loudspeakers wired into the intercom. If they even think the bad guys are going to shoot at them, they are authorized to use force," Ramón paused a moment while he looked around. "Have your man covering the building stay where he is, and after the helicopter lifts off, get your butt back here. I don't know what we just walked into, but it isn't a fishing operation or anything that uses irrigation machinery."

The roar of the helicopter over the warehouse drowned out any other sound, but only for seconds. While Ramón waited, he began taking pictures of the inside of the building. In the center was a large tractor and to one side a massive trailer. On both walls, work benches stretched over half the length of the building and where they ended, lockers and boxes of supplies were stacked almost to the ceiling. From the reinforced ceiling braces, three chain hoists dangled hooks just above head level as if they were preparing to lift something heavy.

"What in the hell is this?" asked Diego, trotting back into the building.

"I'm not sure," replied Ramón, "but my guess is that we are standing in the support facility for the drug running submarines." He pointed at several boxes with Chinese writing along one wall. "Let's open a couple of those crates first and then I'm really curious about what's in that Conex sitting outside."

The first two crates opened appeared to be spare parts for automobiles. The boxes were labeled in Chinese and English. All were marked BYD Auto Ltd. The third crate was more interesting. Inside were six small missiles, again all with Chinese labeling. "My God," said Diego, staring into the crate, "we've found their weapons warehouse."

"Only, I think, for the submarines. These are all hand fired weapons. But yes, these are the kind of weapons we're looking for. Let's open that container. I'll bet it's loaded with more of this stuff."

Instead, they found ten sections of shaped aluminum that when welded together formed a submarine. In the rear of the container were four large crates, all from the same vendor as the parts they'd found inside the warehouse, BYD Auto Ltd. A fifth box was from Lalong Marine Ltd of Shandong China. Ramón looked up both firms on his cell phone.

"BYD is China's largest manufacturer of hybrid automobiles and Lalong is a manufacturer of transmissions, drive shafts and propellers for the marine industry. This is a new submarine. How they can go at high speed and then submerge makes sense, because they run on gasoline using the engine in one of those crates, while charging batteries in another crate. When they need to submerge, they shut down the fuel powered motor. Both fueled and battery powered engines run through a transmission that drives the propellers."

"Someone put a lot of money into engineering this thing," said Diego.

"Wait here a minute while I call in what we've found. I'll ask our people in Acapulco to send enough troops to secure the entire facility." The last of his sentence was drowned out by the sound of the helicopter returning.

Ramón walked up toward the lodge where a marine sat bored on a rock retaining wall. His first call was to his boss in Acapulco, who's first question was whether there was room for a second helicopter. He was going to take custody of the submarine personally.

The second call was to Chad, who's first question was to find out if there were prisoners. While they talked, the helicopter made a long swing to the south, allowing it to land into the wind. "Hang on a minute," said Ramón. "Let me see what happened when we sent our helicopter after the three men who escaped by boat." He watched a couple of marines step from the helicopter, both smiling as they tossed six empty ammunition clips for their weapons from the floor of the aircraft. "So far, I don't think we have any prisoners, but we haven't entered the lodge yet," he said to Chad. "I'll call you back."

Inside the building they found a woman in her late twenties curled up on a leather couch overlooking the ocean, crying uncontrollably. "Tu' lo mataste! she screamed. "You killed him!"

Lying on the table in front of her was a cell phone. Ramón picked it up and scrolling recent calls, saw that the last number called was to a Juan Ayala.

"Who are you?" demanded Ramón.

"My name is Carmen Maria Lopez you pig," she replied. "You just killed Hector, my husband."

"Señora Lopez," said Ramón, "what was your maiden name?"

"Carmen Maria Ayala," she answered.

"What are you doing here?" asked Ramón.

"My father owns this lodge. My husband and I run it for him," she answered.

She ignored Ramón's questions about what he had found and how that fit into running a fishing lodge. He was especially curious about a photograph on the wall. It was of Maria Castillo and President Martinez sitting at an outside table overlooking the Pacific that the marine covering the rear of the house now rested his feet on.

"I'm sorry to do this at such a sad time in your life," said Ramón. "Carmen Maria Ayala Lopez, you are under arrest."

He turned to the marine standing just inside an ultra-modern kitchen and ordered him to keep an eye on the woman while he made a phone call, and then he stepped from the building and called Chad again. "We have one prisoner and four bodies," he started, "but I think our prisoner is the daughter of Juan Ayala. We have some serious leverage. The naval commander from Acapulco will be here soon. We'll take her there. Her husband just died, so I don't think she will be too cooperative right away, but time will tell."

He looked up as two Humvees rolled into the yard. The

commander he'd talked to in Acapulco was the first to step out of one of them. "It was a longer drive to the airport than to come directly here," he called as multiple armed men emerged from the vehicles. "Show me what you have, captain."

An hour later, Diego and his marines were back on the helicopter headed for Zihua. Ramón and the prisoner were in one of the Humvees on their way to Acapulco. A truck had been summoned to the lodge where it would reconnect to the trailer and Conex. Just offshore, a small navy inflatable from Acapulco was towing a ripped panga with two bodies back to the lodge.

In Zihua, Chad and Elena were sitting down to an early dinner at a second story restaurant in the middle of town. Thad, Gina, and Sonia were toasting their success with Pepsi Colas at the beach bar just below the hotel. With Diego on his way back, and with the team in LA researching Carmen Maria Ayala Lopez and the whereabouts of her father, it was going to be a long night.

"I called your friend, Olga," said Elena. "I told her that we were having dinner. She seemed a little jealous." Elena sipped her wine, a little curious about Chad drinking only a Pepsi.

Earlier that evening, Sonia had called Francesca who had gotten off from a plane with Maria Castillo. "We need to find Ayala, we're holding his daughter," was all she said. Francesca talked in code, indicating that there were people around, but code that indicated she'd gotten the message.

The search was coming together, but that day would be the last before it turned really dangerous. Everyone knew Ayala's reputation. The only thing worse than cornering him would be seizing his daughter and killing her husband.

Chad returned to his hotel room about midnight, after several hours of conversation with Thad and Sonia. It occurred to him that the three of them, if connected to the arrest of Carmen

Ayala Lopez, were sitting ducks, unarmed and except for a handful of Diego's marines, who were already stretched thin, without any support they could trust. He turned and raced back up the stairs and banged on the door of Thad and Sonia's suite, hoping they were still dressed.

Thad opened the door wearing the hotel's signature white cotton robe. "I was just thinking," said Chad, "that we have not kept Mat Chang's friend David in President Martinez's office up to date. He's the one who started all of this, looking for the source of Chinese weapons. Perhaps you should make a run over to Mexico City and brief him. And, while you're at it, see if you can get authorization for us to carry sidearms while we are here."

"Go get some sleep," replied Walker. "I called Mat Chang while you were at dinner and asked him to set up that meeting."

"Did you mention to Mat that if this blows up, we're very short of shooters?"

"I haven't had one of my investigations end up in a shootout since Viet Nam," replied Thad.

"That's a good thing since you won't use a weapon," offered Chad as he turned to leave. "But in the China conflict we could call on Navy Seals, and with the Iranian problem, we had the entire US military behind us." He knew as he headed back down the stairs, that he wouldn't sleep much that night.

CHAPTER 35

June 25, Mexico City, Mexico

Francesca handed her weapon to the security officer waiting for her and Maria Castillo outside the president's offices. She'd heard nothing about Ayala since the call two nights before. A guide escorted the two women to the executive suites.

As they waited, Francesca heard a familiar voice coming from another suite. She would have never noticed it, except that the conversation was in English. As she watched, a presidential advisor emerged from a closed door and close on his heels was Thad Walker. Maria looked up from her portfolio as the two men headed to the stairs.

"I don't know who the American is," said Maria, "but the other man is one of the president's international affairs advisors." Maria smiled. "Like you, he once worked for the American government, reportedly in espionage. Something went to hell and like you, he returned to his true homeland."

Francesca checked her watch. She had accompanied Maria

to two previous meetings with the Mexican president and both times, she had been on time, right to the second. This time they had already waited half an hour. It probably had something to do with her raised voice coming through the door.

Finally, her personal secretary opened the door, motioning for them to follow. Lupita sat behind a huge light-colored wooden desk; her face flushed as she glared at her computer.

"I'm sorry to keep you waiting." She smiled at Maria, but it lasted only seconds. "Have you seen the morning news?" she asked.

"No Madam President, but it appears you have and whatever you saw didn't make you very happy."

"All three networks are reporting that I have been discussing the use of American special forces with my counterpart in Washington DC. Supposedly, I was secretly recorded saying to him that if that is what it took to stop drugs crossing the border, I would look the other way. Can you imagine how that will infuriate our people? Hell, it's only been a couple of decades since the Mexican people finally felt truly liberated from our northern neighbors."

"You say that you were secretly recorded," commented Maria.

Lupita turned the monitor of her computer to where Maria and Francesca could watch. "I have made inquiries of the Americans, but only to see if they had any knowledge of how Chinese weapons are flooding into our country and why. But I have had no conversations like what is in this report."

She tapped a couple of keys on her computer and a reporter's broadcast started playing. The key part was when the reporter pointed to someone off camera and then a recording started. "Mr. President," it started, "my government is powerless to stop the drug trade running rampant in Mexico. It is now a threat not only to your people, but to the very survival of my presidency. I don't ever want American troops on Mexican soil again, but if that is what is needed to stop this scourge, then I will not order Mexican forces to engage yours."

"Wow," offered Maria, "that is quite a statement."

"The problem is, I never said that."

"I can understand your concerns," said Maria, "but the voice is yours, is it not?"

"Our own investigators have spent the last two hours digesting this recording. The voice modulation is almost identical to my voice, but I never said anything like this. If the president of the United States denies the conversation occurred, it will just inflame the situation. Even if he was planning the use of troops, he would deny it."

"Maybe, Madam President, we should discuss the mission the Castillo Foundation has undertaken in our prisons another time?"

"Nonsense. I will not be bullied, and I will not be intimidated by this obvious fake recording."

"May I offer a comment?" asked Francesca.

"Of course."

"While I was still doing security for the American Air Force, we had a class in the use of artificial intelligence and how it could be used to issue orders that might endanger base security. There must be dozens of AI platforms that can use samples of your voice to create this type of recording. Every speech you give provides samples."

"So how did your training teach you to handle this?"

"They taught us that if it just didn't seem right, and if we could not get a confirmation, to ignore it and do the job we were assigned as we were trained," offered Francesca.

"And that is exactly what I am going to do. "I've already issued a statement flatly labeling the recording as false. I just can't figure out why someone would want to do this."

Two hours later, Maria and Francesca arrived back at Castillo Corporate offices. "What happened to the president is really disgusting," said Francesca. "All that it can do is hurt her effectiveness. Even her supporters will have just a little less trust."

"You're right my friend," replied Maria. "Oh, I'm going to catch up on a bunch of office work early next week, so if you want to spend an extra day or two with your sister this weekend, I will not be traveling. I know it's been too long since you saw her."

❧

At the exact same time, an hour's drive away, Thad Walker and David Lopez parked their car and started a walk through the Aztec ruins of Teotihuacán. "I thought it better to discuss your request away from the office," said David. "With what just broke in the morning news, I don't want to risk someone misunderstanding your visit Mr. Walker. Interestingly, our navy has not yet reported what they found in that raid down by Acapulco to the president. Secrecy on any issue remains a problem for our government. I also understand the potential of this Carmen Ayala Lopez. If she is who you think she is, we may just have found a key to our search. But I agree with you that it also makes her father very dangerous and since we don't know who he works for, and how many men he commands. It is difficult to predict his next move."

"Our goal is to use her to rattle her father and get him to roll over," replied Thad. "If he is high enough up in whatever group we are searching for, to put his daughter in charge of the submarine facility, he knows everything we are trying to find."

"But until we can make the Chinese connection, we can't stop it," said David. "Your idea of sending the pictures our navy took at that warehouse to trusted colleagues in China makes sense. With our government in possession of the vary weapons China says could not be here, at least their denial will stop."

"David, I only know you through Mat Chang. We've both worked cases where one good lead opened the entire box of worms and other cases that just fizzled. My gut tells me this is the exact lead we've been looking for, but only if we can flip this Ayala guy. There are only seven of us working this in Mexico, four Americans and three Mexicans. Even if we are looking for a tiny cartel, they'll have dozens of soldiers. We're a little hung out here."

"I'm not going to take a request to arm Americans to the president, not with the uproar over this so-called recording. All I can promise is that if you are detained for carrying a weapon, I will do my best to get you deported rather than jailed. And I don't want to know where any such weapon came from."

"Okay, I've got it," said Walker. "But we may need the cavalry ready to ride in and save the day."

"You're already working with the one institution that our president completely trusts," said Lopez. "So far, the navy and marines have somehow stayed above the corruption. They deal with their traitors themselves. Some of the president's aids believe that's what happened to the two marines who disappeared in Zihua. Only a handful of us know they were on a mission. The navy will have to be your cavalry as you call it."

✧

An hour later, a CIA contact in Victoria, British Columbia forwarded a dozen pictures to Ma, who was expecting them after his earlier call from Chad. The pictures clearly showed who manufactured the weapons. The photos of the automotive parts implicated one of China's premier automotive companies. There was even a picture of the pieces of a submarine, propped up as they would look after assembly. "Ma, if the pictures do not get your government finding who is responsible for sending these weapons, my contacts in Mexican intelligence will have no choice but to believe that the Chinese government is responsible," offered Chad. "China appears to be betting its economy on building factories in Mexico, but those have only one targeted customer, the US. If my country has hard proof that China is undermining Mexico, you can bet that not a single thing built in one of those factories will cross the border."

Chad sat sipping strong black coffee at the tiny sidewalk café overlooking dozens of fishing pangas lining the beach in Zihua. The morning open air fish market was wrapping up. The shop was only steps away from the small Mexican marine corps' beachfront compound. Huge trees swayed in the mid-day breeze. Chad smiled, remembering Ma's warning about America threatening China. But what else would an intelligence operative of any country say after his not so subtle statement?

He looked up as Diego, flanked by two armed marines, stepped out of the way of a group of kids on bicycles before continuing down the brick walkway to where he was seated. "I'm going to have to miss lunch," said Diego. "Captain Acuna has decided to stay in Acapulco with the prisoner rather than move her to Pacific Fleet headquarters in Manzanillo. He's setting up a meeting down there, probably in three days. Before I leave, I want to establish a more obvious presence here. My Zihua troops will be down to six men while were gone." He paused, watching the overnight fishermen put away their gear and sales scales. "Maybe dinner tonight after I nail it down?"

"Call me my friend," replied Chad. "I came down to do some fishing, but I understand that duty comes first. If you can't make it, maybe you can give me Enzo's phone number. I'll charter the Porpoise myself, but it won't be as much fun."

He watched Diego and his troops walk away to continue their waterfront patrol. The short conversation had delivered the entire message that Diego might have offered at lunch. The navy was holding their prisoner, but Acuna was trying to set up a separate session for the critical people of Team Walker in Acapulco to finalize a strategy to flush out Ayala. The publicized offer to the family of Carmen Maria Ayala Lopez to come forward and work to clear her of suspicion was not working. Evidently, the thought that Ayala might just walk in and trade himself for his daughter was a pipedream. Ayala had evaded the police for decades.

After a flurry of activity, the investigation was back to a slog. Acuna was in Acapulco where both he and Diego would be headed in a couple of days. Walker was still in Mexico City and Gina Santos was headed there in a few hours. His morning briefing with the people in LA had tied the lodge to Ayala. That the same legal firm in Mexico City had created the corporation that owned it. A hotel in Ixtapa, a warehouse only miles from there, MEXAIR, and a fishing lodge used as a base for illegal drug shipments all owned by a corporation with so many interlocking pieces that positively identifying Ayala as the owner was impossible. The national police had been tasked with watching the warehouse which the operators described as a freight forwarding and customs preparation facility. Trucks with containers continued to stop there going both north and south but the federales reported nothing more suspicions. Without more to go on, they couldn't or perhaps shouldn't enter the facility.

So close and yet so far, he thought as he started back to his hotel. I could really use some good news about now. His phone rang. "Hi lover. I hope you are on the beach or doing something fun," said Olga.

Chad stopped his walk next to a life size bronze sculpture of a native Mexican woman carrying a basket, one of several sculptures along the walk. "I'm walking near the museum," he replied. "I wish you were here."

"That's nice to hear," she said, "because I'll be there in the morning. Your friend Mat at the agency asked me to accompany a high-level diplomat working on an international project to Mexico City. I'm TDY and already in Los Angeles waiting for a diplomatic flight. After I get the diplomat to the embassy, the pilots are going to drop me at Zihua."

"Get here fast," replied Chad, "because it looks like I'm headed to Acapulco for a couple of days later in the week."

"I can't wait," said Olga. "I barely had time to pack, but what do I need beyond a uniform, a nightgown, shorts and a swimsuit?"

"Nothing that I can think of," replied Chad as he continued his walk. "While I'm gone, it will give you a chance to catch up with old friends. Elena will be happy to see you, and even one of your old crew from Minot Air Force Base, Francesca Mateo will be here. She called a friend this morning to say she is flying in to visit her sister."

"All good," replied Olga, "but they won't scratch the same itch you can." There was a long pause before she added. "I would give a thousand dollars to see your face right now. See you," and she was gone.

Chad climbed the stairs toward his room, stopping at the pool. Only one lounge, under a huge umbrella was occupied. The middle of a Mexican summer was not a good time to fill a hotel. Sonia looked up from her laptop and waved. "I thought you had lunch plans," she called.

"Cancelled, duty and all for my friend," he said as he walked over, while she closed her laptop.

Sonia checked to make sure nobody was within listening range. "Thad is going to be in Mexico City three or four days, and with our new Mexican friends gone, this place is damned quiet. All I'm doing is monitoring what is going on in LA and passing it along."

"I may be the next one gone," he said. "But somehow my girlfriend Olga has engineered a trip down here, and Elena will be here. Even Francesca will be coming in for a few days. Except for Elena, it will be a 'ladies in intelligence' retreat. But both Thad and I will be back soon."

Francesca checked in later that afternoon, but a visit to see Sonia or Chad might blow her cover, so she took a cab straight to her sister's. With their new income, Mary had rented a luxurious home above the bay. Francesca's early morning call to Chad reported that the strange lights that had gotten two of Diego's marines killed meant that drug smuggling by submarine continued. Either the crafts were highly reliable, or the bad guys had already set up a new support base.

Chad took the call on his way to the airport where Olga's government flight was due. She and the Mexican diplomatic officer accompanying her headed straight to a gate next to the terminal where the diplomat waived credentials to a guard who opened the gate. Moments later the two young women approached the Mustang that Chad borrowed from Diego.

"Chad Gritt, this is my new friend Carlotta." Olga set a large briefcase next to the trunk and then motioned for Carlotta to drop her small duffle. "Carlotta is on the security team for President Martinez. One of the president's advisors loaned her to me to help me with customs here. She's on her way to some training in Los Angeles so we offered her a ride."

Carlotta extended her hand which Chad shook before she turned back for the gate. She turned to watch as Olga wrapped herself around Chad and started a kiss. It made her smile.

"God, it's good to see you," said Chad as he opened the

trunk of the convertible. He picked up Olga's duffle and then the briefcase. "What did you pack in that case, your rock collection?" he asked.

"No, just some things Thad Walker requested. He felt that the Americans working down here needed a little protection," she said. "He sends his best, along with the presents for you, Sonia, Francesca and, oh, and one for me."

Two thoughts flashed into Chad's mind. That explained the private flight and escort. Second, it telegraphed the level of approval of their efforts to find the source of the Chinese weapons. Both sides of the border must have approved a diplomatic visit as a cover to carry unregistered weapons into Mexico. "How long are you staying?" he asked.

"The diplomat from the state department and I cooked up some mission for her to work with her Mexican counterparts on the Chinese diplomatic efforts. She's just here as cover for my trip. But if your team does nail down a hard-Chinese connection, she's here to help the Mexican government strengthen their diplomatic message to China."

Chad pulled out of the small parking lot. "Does Mat Chang think this is going to end up in a shootout?" asked Chad.

"No, but Thad's call to him made it clear that this thing you're working on could get messy any time. I'm just a delivery girl who didn't need to be vetted by the agency," she answered.

Chad smiled at the stunning over-dressed woman sitting next to him. He'd never seen Olga in a business suit. It looked hot on the ninety-degree afternoon. "Just us two and maybe Sonia for dinner this evening," he said, "but we have time for a swim before."

Olga placed her hand over his riding on the floor shift lever. "After, not before," she said with a twinkle in her eye.

CHAPTER 36

June 29, Mexico City, Mexico

MARIA CASTILLO WAS summoned by Luis Cardenas the same afternoon that Francesca left. Slammed with work, she had begged off for a couple of days, which infuriated Cardenas. Now they were in the back room of the Italian restaurant where they usually met, waiting for both Ayala and Hao Sun. Uncomfortable with her former police officer driver knowing about the meeting, Maria had taken a cab.

"I don't know how big a problem we might have," said Cardenas as they waited. "All I know is that Juan called and said we needed to meet. He said something had gone wrong with transportation."

"While Francesca and I were with President Martinez the other day, there was an American I'd never seen meeting with that David Lopez guy in her offices. I wonder if it has anything to do with that."

"I don't know, but we're about to find out," said Luis. He pointed at Ayala and Hao being escorted to their private dining room.

"The fucking Navy," started Ayala before he ever sat down. The others just stared at him.

"The navy somehow got tipped off about the lodge. They raided it just as the shipment with the new submarine was being unloaded. They have crates of weapons and the submarine."

"I haven't heard of any such raid," said Cardenas. "They take great pride in announcing that type of victory, but there has been nothing in the press."

"I knew about it as it happened," said Juan. "My daughter called when she saw a navy helicopter land in front of the lodge. Her husband tried to defend the warehouse, but he was killed."

"I don't know about this warehouse you refer to, but I am so sorry for her loss," offered Maria. "How is she doing?"

"Remember the small lodge that I had you visit after your successful Acapulco trip?" asked Luis. "That's the place Juan is referring to. The big building by the water is the support facility for the submarines running up the Sea of Cortez. The woman who greeted you is Juan's daughter. She runs the lodge as a cover for the submarine operations."

Juan looked over at Maria and then at both Luis and Hao. "I'll answer your question. She is not doing well. The navy has her in custody and have quietly sent word that they might be willing to trade her for whoever is running the operation. She is now a widow but cannot grieve. Three of the mechanics made a run for it in a fishing boat, but they didn't get far. A helicopter intercepted them. Two of them were killed, the third was wounded but managed to slip over the side and eventually swim to shore. He contacted one of our security people and confirmed Carmen's story."

"With the exception of your daughter, is there anything there that can tie that facility directly to any of us?" asked Hao.

"No, nothing that I can think of," replied Ayala.

"Would your daughter ever betray you?" asked Luis.

"Never," answered Juan. "She was raised in our world. She knows to keep her mouth shut."

"So other than having to set up a new support facility and the loss of the materials that Hao sent us, there is no damage," said Luis. "Your daughter may serve a little time in jail until we can find someone high enough to get her released, but nothing has changed."

"Are you out of your fucking mind?" said Ayala.

The three others leaned back in their chairs, unsure how to respond.

"I don't want my daughter in jail. There are several places outside the country where she can start a new life. We need to get her out." Juan leaned down on the table, his head in his hands.

"My friend," said Luis, "we have had legal challenges in the past. With a little time, we have always found a judge or prosecutor or even a politician who, for enough money, fixes the problem. You need to be patient while our attorneys do some research."

He turned to Hao. "You need to get a new shipment on the way. The two submarines we now have will have to just keep operating until we get a third." Ayala paused as a waitress handed him the Pacifico he'd ordered on his way to the back room. "The hybrid gasoline and battery powered submarines have proven reliable, but still need servicing. We must come up with a short-term plan for that."

Luis turned to Maria. "And the plan to put you in the president's office is working. Hao's people did a masterful job with that recording of her inviting the Americans to invade. We have several more setbacks planned for President Martinez. She will not last a year, even if we must go with the assassination plan.

Once you're in office, there will be no further legal disruption of our operations. You can pardon Juan's daughter if she isn't free by then."

Juan looked up, slamming his hands on the table. "You aren't listening. I do not want my daughter in jail."

"Juan, this will be all right," said Hao. "Luis is right, for enough gold we can fix anything, and we have lots of gold. It will be difficult, but you must be patient."

Juan looked to Maria, hoping for some support. He could see the tears in her eyes. "Maria, you are so quiet. What would you do if your daughter was in a Mexican prison?"

"Juan, I have no children. I was once a little girl who watched her father being hauled away to a prison. I understand your hurt, your pain. It is not a lot different than what I saw in President Martinez's eyes when that false recording tore at her heart. If we can find no other way to get Carmen released, Lupita is the kind of woman who could be convinced to pardon her."

"Maria, I don't give a fuck how the president feels. She needs to go, and you will replace her," said Hao.

"Worst case," added Luis, "when we put Maria into the president's chair in a few months, she can pardon Carmen. You raised a strong daughter, Juan, she must remain strong. We will find a way to get a message to her that we will make this right."

"The one potential loose end I see," said Hao, "is this survivor of the attack on the warehouse. If the navy knows he exists, and they can find him, he can blow the whole operation. Juan, you must deal with him. He is the only witness against your daughter."

Ayala just sat with his head in his hands. He had no better plan right then, but the thought of Carmen locked in a cage felt like an elephant sitting on his chest. "We may need to discuss this further," he said. "I'll take care of the loose end. But I am telling you that you three better come up with a solid plan for Carmen's release, or I will."

"Juan," snapped Luis, "all the authorities can document is that Carmen is your daughter. I'll visit the attorneys this afternoon. Your former son-in-law was the person running the submarine facility. Your daughter is an innocent bystander, someone who found herself under arrest simply for loving her husband. I'll arrange for you and an attorney to visit her."

"All right," said Juan, "but if I don't see real progress to get her released in a week, I'll find another way." He looked over at Hao. "Your partners in China have most of our money. You need to get them moving on resupply. We will need spare parts for the submarines by air. It isn't a great option, but we can service the submarines on the northern end of their runs for a few months until we can find a suitable replacement for the facility the Navy found."

Juan picked up his cowboy hat from the middle of the table and turned for the door.

"I hope our partner, Juan, will not become another loose end," said Luis as he left.

Hao looked up at the ceiling. "My official Chinese colleagues are still sending us four trained military infiltrators every month. If Juan becomes a problem, we might need to have a couple of them eliminate the risk before we smuggle them across the border."

"Hao," said Luis, "I don't have a clue on how the transport and security is run. Without Juan, how will we stay in business?"

"Do not worry my friend. In my official duties I have made lots of contacts in Mexican business. One, Carlos Barrera, is reportedly the head of security for one of our rivals. He's already proven that he can be bought."

He looked over at Maria who had remained quiet for most of the meeting. "You look hungry, perhaps it's time to order lunch."

"That's a good idea," she responded. "It is also a good idea for you two to keep a close eye on Juan. He has four major lieutenants. You need to get close to at least one of them."

"Why can't you do that?" asked Luis. "You've known Juan since you were a child. You understand transportation. He would never question you. He would just think you were trying to help while he is so stressed by what happened to his daughter."

"Luis, if Juan does something rash, and I am tied to him in any way, your plan fails."

CHAPTER 37

July 10, Zihuantanejo, Mexico

THE PRESIDENTIAL AIDE, David Lopez somehow managed to keep the raid on the submarine base a secret, even from the president. He'd agreed with the navy that using the captive as bait to try to tie Juan Ayala to the cartel made sense. The overwhelming amount of circumstantial evidence against Ayala looked suspicious. The plan changed when the attorney general's office called him, curious about a petition from an attorney who requested to visit with a prisoner the AG didn't know about. They suspected the attorney had ties to the drug business, but the request was legal, and they couldn't refuse it.

Lopez managed to stall until Walker could travel from Zihua to the capital. David, Thad, and Ramón briefed the president and to say she was unhappy was an understatement. Between the president and the attorney general, a press conference was hastily thrown together where Ramón announced the seizure of the facility. He distributed pictures of the dismantled submarine and crates of Chinese weapons. Other photos included shroud covered bodies, and the inside of the facility. He'd concluded the event by announcing that the wife of one of the men killed by the marines was in custody. "She probably knows more about the operation than she has been willing to acknowledge," he said, "and that might be very important to dismantling the group running the operations. It also makes her a loose end for them, putting her life at risk."

A day later, 'retired businessman' Juan Ayala and his attorney visited the prisoner in Acapulco, escorted to Carmen's holding cell by Diego. A photo of her dressed in a yellow jumpsuit with PRISONERA on the back, made it into the press along with a story of how she had been prevented from attending the funeral of her husband. It took only days for Mexican folk songs singing her praises to hit the airwaves.

The raid was becoming a public relations fiasco, which was why Walker and Lopez now waited outside the president's office. A few hundred miles away, Diego was huddled with Mexican naval intelligence in Acapulco. The president had demanded that the AG hold Carmen in custody for the time being. Her attorney was advised that it might take months to bring her to trial, and until then, she would remain in custody, for her own protection. But Lopez knew that if the press continued to ramp up the pressure, she might be released on bail. So far Carmen had pleaded innocent, denying even knowing about any submarine at the 'lodge' even after the Mexican navy took her to a facility where they were assembling the seized craft.

Back in Zihua, Olga was now part of the team. Her TDY from the security detail at the Minot Air Force Base grated on base command, but her temporary assignment to the CIA had been signed by the secretary of the Air Force. Sonia mentored her on coordinating intel from LA and evidence seized in the raid while they continued the life of tourists. Olga and Gritt were like two lovebirds on vacation, even as both realized that the cartel they were hunting knew he was American military.

The weapons that Olga carried from the states had been distributed. The two women, Thad and Chad now carried snub nosed Glock 9mm pistols. While Francesca was escorting Maria Castillo, she was armed with the Barretta given to her by the police. But her permit didn't allow her to fly with it when she flew to see her sister.

After Olga's arrival, she and Chad spent as much time as possible away from the demands of the job. They were showering after an early morning swim when Chad's cell phone rang. He dashed naked from the tiled bathroom, returning a minute later. Olga handed him a towel to dry her back.

"I don't like the look on your face Mr. Gritt." She took the towel from his hands and began drying him.

"It was Diego. The Mexican technicians are almost finished assembling that submarine. They are confused by how the propulsion system and the guidance system are integrated. They called the Farragut Center in DC and asked for help. Since I'm already here, and my specialty is electronics, they suggested I might help."

Olga wrapped her body around Chad. "Does this mean you're leaving?"

"We have time for a light breakfast before the helicopter lands on the beach in front of the marine compound to pick me up," said Chad. "But," he wrapped his arms around Olga, "leaving is going to be a bitch and you can count on me rushing back."

"I thought the whole team was getting together for dinner," she said. "Thad and Diego were supposed to be home today. Francesca is due to visit her sister, Mary. I called Elena yesterday. She is anxious for Diego to get home. She and Mary invited us for dinner tomorrow. Only Ramón and Gina will be missing. They're stuck in Mexico City."

"Diego and Thad will be stuck for a few more days and it's probably better for a Mexican navy intelligence officer and a deputy Mexican attorney general not to be tied to us right now anyway," said Chad. "The dinner sounds like a great idea, but it'll be an all-girl affair. You, Sonia, Elena, Francesca, and Mary deserve to get away from this problem for a few hours. Everyone but Mary is directly involved, and my bet is that she's figured out that there is more to her sister's return than Francesca has divulged. Dinner will be a good opportunity to hand off that other Glock we have locked in the hotel room safe to Francesca."

A tear slid down Olga's cheek as she stared into Gritt's eyes. "Duty, duty, duty," she said. "It weighs so little except in moments like now." She walked into the bedroom and began studying the summer clothes she'd emptied into a drawer. The only time she went unarmed was when she wore the swimsuit she'd bought in LA. It would blow her cover if the clothes she wore to breakfast advertised she was carrying a weapon.

Fifteen minutes later she and Chad headed down the outdoor stairs and onto the winding beachfront walkway into town. Her embroidered yellow peasant blouse covered her holstered weapon. Chad carried a small backpack with shaving gear and a couple of changes in underwear. He carried his weapon in an ankle holster under baggy beach pants.

Unknown to either of them, in the penthouse of a nearby building, Luis Cardenas and Juan Ayala sat sipping coffee on the deck.

"It's been two weeks," started Juan, "and we are no closer to getting my daughter released. That attorney of yours has accomplished nothing."

"Juan, we discussed this with our partners. It might take a

little longer, but with the entire country now singing that stupid dirge about your daughter, the government will have to release her. She's becoming a folk hero."

"It was that bastard who commands the local marine compound. That's the guy who somehow figured out that something was wrong at the lodge," said Juan. "Carmen said he was one of the first men to question her. He was angry about the two marines who disappeared here."

"His name is Diego Cervantes. His father owns a lot of property up along the border. The dad's one of Hao's customers. He's building a factory by the border that one of Hao's contacts in China will be leasing." Luis poured more coffee from a silver pitcher into his cup.

"Maybe I'll have some of our guys up north grab the parents and hold them until Carmen is released," snarled Juan.

"He's a lowly lieutenant. If anything went wrong with grabbing his parents, it might just point directly at you my old friend," said Luis. "It might have been a mistake to visit your daughter. You are now exposed."

"Then maybe I will just have some of the local men grab him. Anyone familiar with what happened at the lodge will know that he is already part of this. He's a piss-ant lieutenant, not some admiral or something, but they would still trade him for my daughter," said Juan.

"He's a low-ranking shit, and nobody would care except the military," replied Luis. "Not enough leverage." He refilled Juan's half empty cup.

"Be patient," counseled Luis. "This Cardenas and his Italian girlfriend are well known and liked here in Zihua. I've had both Diego and this Elena watched. She's a doctor of some kind. One tipster who recognized him could bring a dozen marines down on your head. The American officer we observed in Manzanillo studying the damage to the ship our men shot up, is back here again, this time with his girlfriend. It's just their luck that their friend Diego is tied up in Acapulco. I'm told that the only reason that the American came back was to do some fishing with Diego. No, it is better to leave Diego alone and let our attorneys get your daughter out of jail."

"You didn't have to look into Carmen's eyes, Luis. You didn't see the hurt and fear I saw when I visited her. She should not be punished for what we are doing," snarled Juan. "Maybe I'll have to make Elena a widow before this Diego even asks to marry her."

Juan slipped on his denim jacket. "I need to get back to the Ixtapa warehouse. We have a fertilizer shipment coming in tonight. With our schedule disrupted, there's a huge amount of cash stored at the warehouse. I want to make sure that all of it is hidden in the fertilizer bags and on the way to China by tomorrow. The two cops watching the place are due to be replaced in the next few days. We don't know if their replacements will be as willing to look the other way."

Luis rose and clasped Juan on the shoulder. "You will figure this all out, my friend."

"Luis, I am not a patient man," said Juan. "That is what makes me valuable."

⁂

Along with two bottles of wine, Olga carried a large purse with what she needed for the evening. She had hidden a pistol, a clip-on holster, and three clips of ammunition in one of two boxes of chocolates for Francesca. Her own weapon was hidden in the pocket of the long jacket she wore. Francesca had sent word that she didn't want her sister to see any weapons.

The dinner invitation was for seven-thirty, when the patio of the small, rented house overlooking the harbor was a comfortable temperature. Olga and Sonia arrived to find Mary, Francesca, and Elena discussing how the town was changing. Elena had been driving Diego's convertible the night before when she was harassed at an intersection coming through town. Two men she didn't know called her by name and asked if she was interested in a real man for a change. They continued their verbal abuse at the next corner, laughing and waving beer bottles.

The same men followed her again tonight, until she pulled up next to the house, leaving only after she jumped from the car and screamed.

"That sucks," said Olga, as she handed Mary her chocolate box. "Is that normal here?" Olga crossed the room and handed Francesca her special box. Francesca smiled at her former Air Force boss and headed for her bedroom with the box and Olga and Sonia's coats.

"No, it's not," said Elena. "Sometimes a local guy or two will get drunk and get a little pushy, but these guys knew my name. If they know my name, they know who Diego is, and none of the local punks would pee in his pool."

"Now that is graphic," said Francesca returning to the group. "I have two large pitchers of margaritas in the fridge." She looked around the room. "Wine later with dinner if that's okay?"

Both Francesca and Olga took a couple of minutes to survey the area around the house before joining the others on the patio. "Observation is pretty ingrained in us," said Olga, "but we saw nothing to worry about in the neighborhood."

"I'm thankful you're here," said Elena, "but I will feel safer when Diego gets home. He called just before I left. He thinks he and Chad might come home tomorrow evening."

As Mary refreshed their margaritas, two men parked behind trees just over a hundred yards away studied the women with binoculars. They'd been watching since the marine's girlfriend had yelled at them. Their orders were to watch her, even make her a little uncomfortable, but not to force her to call for help. They'd been a little too aggressive, but neither would ever disclose it to Juan Ayala.

They watched the women as dinner was served. Finally, one of them plucked his cell phone from the dash of the truck and called Juan. "Hey boss, there is nothing going on with that woman you wanted followed. She's just eating dinner with four other women at a hillside house on the north side of the bay."

He listened for a full minute before adding, "one of the women is the girlfriend of that American officer. We checked with some neighbors, two of the women are renting the house. The last one might be a mother of that American woman. Man, four of them are hot, all but the grandmother and she ain't bad. But there is nothing going on other than eating and drinking, so Mateo and I want to know if we can head for home."

At the warehouse, Juan sat at a desk overlooking the loading dock. The fertilizer shipment was finally being reloaded on the trailer. Juan had been forced to hold the shipment for a day, until the cash from the latest submarine turnaround had arrived. The canvas bags from that shipment contained more than four and a half million in American cash. Three point two million of that along with more than eighteen million dollars from previous shipments was now buried in four canvas bags of nitrogen fertilizer. They would be in Manzanillo by morning where the container and an earlier one would sail with the Jai Mew the following night.

He made a mental note of the total he'd removed from the shipment over the previous six weeks. Two million dollars would go to pay his people. Four million would go to Luis to pay for supplies and shipping. He, Luis and Hao would split one and a half million. The remaining three hundred thousand dollars would go into his own emergency fund; after all he was taking most of the risks. Payment for the raw ingredients to make fentanyl would be deducted from the money on the way to China.

Juan stared at his phone. The slightest inkling of an idea crept into his mind. "No," he answered, "you and Mateo continue to observe. The guys will be finished loading here in the next hour, and I may need all of you for a new mission. Are you both armed?"

He waited for an answer before hanging up. Moments later he stood next to his foreman as the last bag of fertilizer was hoisted. "Paco," he snapped, "when you and the other guys get that load strapped down and the truck is on the way, I need to see all of you upstairs."

He punched in a number on his cell as he climbed the stairs. "Luis," he said, "remember that comment you made about that marine lieutenant not being enough leverage? I think I've got a solution for that."

On the other end, Cardenas listened, a little jitter in his stomach forming. "Juan, do not do anything rash."

"Getting my daughter on her way to some friends in Nicaragua isn't being rash my friend," replied Juan.

"Juan that place is a pit. The couple who rule it are old school communist dictators. Why in the hell would you send Carmen there? "Asked Luis.

"I have family friends there. For the right amount of payoff, anyone can live there like a king or queen. Besides, she would only be there long enough to get Maria into the presidency, then she will come home."

"Juan, please do not do anything foolish. We are so close to our goals," said Luis.

"My friend, when someone hands you the key to a lock you've wanted to open for a long time, you don't refuse it. I'll be in touch." Juan hung up just as the truck departed and the foreman started up the stairs.

"Paco, go down to the armory and pick up six of the Chinese assault rifles and two crates of ammunition and put them in the Suburban. Add about six of the anti-armor missiles. After you close the gate, issue the other men handguns and extra clips and bring them up here." He handed Paco a hand full of cash. "Here is an extra five thousand dollars for your men and for two men watching a house for me. You're all going to earn a little extra tonight." He handed Paco another envelope stuffed with cash. "This is to cover what might be a few days more if needed. Now get moving."

As Paco left, Juan packed the money he'd kept from the Chinese money shipment into a bag already containing just over a million dollars and slid it under his desk. He pocketed several thousand more dollars and called his bodyguard who was in town eating dinner. Then he sat down at his computer and typed a short letter, printed it, and then deleted the letter from his computer. He used a tissue to pick up the letter and place it in an envelope. He then placed that envelope in a second one.

Moments later, four smiling men made their way up the stairs. "Mi Amigos," started Juan, "you know what has happened to my daughter. Tonight, you are going to help me make that injustice right. In an hour you will surround a house on the hillside and then grab five women eating dinner there. Take the Suburban and the panel truck. Mateo and his partner are waiting in his pickup. You will take them to a compound not far from the village of San Antonio up in the mountains. Paco knows where it is. He and I spent a lot of time there when we were having some problems with the authorities years ago. Since then, I have used it only when I needed to get away, to plan and refresh my mind, but I keep emergency rations stored there just in case they might be needed. The old woman who watches it is my cousin, the widow of one of my soldiers in a different life. You can trust her."

He watched the smiles fade from the men as the seriousness of his request sunk in. "You will not use your cell phones, other than to call your families in the next five minutes to let them know you might be gone a while. Then turn them off. You will guard the women, but you will make them comfortable, and you will not harm them unless I order a change. Cover your faces."

He handed Paco an envelope, opening it so that the second envelope was visible. "You will leave this in the house where the women are having dinner. Make sure that you take the outside envelope out the door with you and then burn it so that there are no fingerprints. Each of you will take several pair of the nitrate gloves we use when handling the fertilizer with you. You must be very careful not to leave any evidence."

Paco looked down at his boss, his eyes questioning. "Juan, my old friend, how will this all end?"

"There will be a short negotiation Then the authorities will release my daughter and I will send her out of the country. You will ride up to the ridge above the compound and turn your phone on every morning at eight and every evening at eight. When I call you, you will bring the captives to the parking lot of the police station in Ixtapa at midnight and then go home."

Juan watched the faces of the men. All were worried. "It will not take all six of you to guard five women, so two may go home in the morning. Plan on rotating two men every other day. When this is all finished, there will be an additional ten thousand dollars for each of you." He handed Paco an address. "You will meet Mateo here and explain the mission to him. I want these women on the way to the mountains tonight."

As the two vehicles pulled away, he called Mateo, briefly

explaining the mission and putting Paco in charge. Outside the gate a black Suburban honked three times. Juan grabbed the bag of hundred-dollar bills from under his desk and headed downstairs, turning off the lights as he went. He knew that the police officers who were assigned to observe the building would be on their way home after they saw the workers leave. That courtesy was a bargain at $200 per day each.

He slid into the backseat of the black Suburban and slammed the door, his face beaming. "I need to be back in the capital by tomorrow morning," he said to the bodyguard at the wheel. "There is a thousand-dollar bonus in it for you."

CHAPTER 38

July 13, Zihuantanejo, Mexico

Olga and Sonia were discussing calling a cab. Two pitchers of margaritas and two bottles of wine had been a bit much. "Probably not necessary," said Elena, "at one in the morning, the town is empty. I'll get you two back to your hotel." Both women just stared before she added, "the drive is three miles at most. I'll keep it under ten miles an hour." The women at the outdoor table watched as Elena's face went blank. She pointed as two men wearing masks and carrying pistols rounded the side of the house. "What the fuck?"

Before anyone could react, two more men leaped over the short wall on the other side of the patio. One of them put a gun to Elena's forehead and ordered her to translate.

Elena stood, frozen.

The man issued a series of what could only be commands to Elena who quit holding her breath long enough to translate to Olga and Sonia. "We are their prisoners. If we do as ordered, none of us will be harmed. We are to gather our personal things for a trip. If we do not do as told, he will shoot one at a time until the others obey."

It was too dark on the patio for Paco to catch the looks that flashed from Francesca to Sonia and Olga. He did catch Sonia shaking her head. Paco moved behind her chair, ordering her to get up. Sonia's Spanish was good enough to be insulted by "get up old woman."

Francesca was the first on her feet, placing her hands on the table. She stared at Paco for several seconds before responding to him in Spanish. Of the five women, only Olga spoke no Spanish. "Why are you talking to this animal?" asked Olga.

"I told him that I wasn't afraid of him and that I was about to serve dessert to new friends," said Francesca. "I told him that I bought a couple of boxes of special chocolates. He told me to take them with us. He seems a little rattled, dangerous."

The women all rose and started into the house. Francesca picked up the box of chocolates that Olga brought for Mary as she, Sonia, and Olga walked into the bedroom. A fifth armed man stood between the bedroom door and the front door.

"We can take these guys," whispered Olga, "they are amateurs."

"Not now," replied Sonia, "one of us might get hurt in the crossfire, besides we don't know how many more are outside."

"Silencio," ordered the guard. "Mas ahora." He turned to Elena and continued talking.

"We are to leave our phones on the table. He wants us to hurry."

Olga and Sonia slipped on their jackets while Francesca grabbed a sweater. She placed Mary's chocolate box on top of hers and stepped into the living room. The leader pointed to the chocolates in Francesca's hands. She slipped the cover off the top box revealing rows of chocolate. The men from the patio began pushing them out the front door where a sixth man was talking on his phone. Moments later, a dark Chevy van pulled to a stop.

"Sube a la parte transera de la camioneta," ordered Paco.

"We're to get in the van," said Elena. She looked into the open rear area with no seats. Two of the guards stood several feet behind the van, nervously tipping their pistols up and down.

"Mas ahora," Paco ordered again, just before he and three of the guards climbed into an idling Suburban behind the van.

Olga was the first in, followed by Sonia and then Francesca. They sat against the passenger side of the truck as Mary and Elena found places on the other side. One of the two remaining guards climbed in behind the steering wheel as his partner slammed the rear door of the van and locked it. Moments later he slid into the passenger seat and turned pointing his pistol at the women.

"The other guards are following in the other truck," said Elena.

As the van began winding its way off the hillside, the only indication of the other vehicle was when one of the side mirrors caught a flash of its headlights rounding a corner.

"None of them speak English," whispered Francesca as the three armed women tucked their heads together. In the dark, she opened the bottom chocolate box and slipped a clip into the Glock and then pocketed it along with the spare clip. She carefully transferred several of the chocolates from Mary's box to the empty before popping one into her mouth and then passing the box on.

"Qué estás hacienda?" asked the man with the gun.

"Chocolate?" asked Francesca, handing the man the box. He took a candy before passing another to the driver and then handed the box back.

The guard spoke to Elena.

"He thinks it's good that we didn't create any problems," translated Elena who along with Mary had begun to shake, almost uncontrollably.

Sonia leaned across the van and placed a hand on each of the women. "It will be okay."

The three women behind the guard leaned together again. "So far they have gone out of their way to be kind," said Sonia. "Three of us against six of them doesn't seem fair, so I think we should let this play out a while. This may be the big break we have been looking for. Agree?"

The lights reflecting from the mirrors as the van turned out onto the highway gave just enough light for her to see the other two nod their heads. The van drove north for a half an hour before turning south again and then turned off from the highway onto a side road. Twenty minutes later it turned right again onto a rutted dirt road and then left onto a narrow path where branches and brush rubbed the side of the vehicle, finally coming to a stop.

They could hear the doors slamming from the vehicle that had followed them before the guard in the passenger seat slid out of the van, then the driver. Outside, several voices carried on a conversation before a woman's voice was added.

"They tried to throw off our sense of direction," whispered Sonia, "but I think we are no more than fifty miles from Zihua, up in the mountains."

"The Sierra Madre del Sur are really rugged, whispered Elena. There are hundreds of dirt tracks running deep into canyons. A lot of local bandits hide here."

Francesca leaned across the van. "Mary, Elena, you must be as quiet and agreeable as possible," she said. "But you must also be ready to do exactly as we say. Do you understand?"

Somehow the statement helped settle the two youngest

women, at least enough to get a nod from each. A key was inserted into the lock and the van door swung open.

The man who had been giving orders at the house pointed his pistol at Elena's face as he spoke.

"We are to follow Carlotta into the nearest house. She will show us where to sleep. The leader and three men will guard us, and the others will drive the trucks out of here. He warns us not to try to escape since the area is crawling with snakes."

Elena spoke to the man, waited for an answer and then translated. "I asked why we have been taken. He says we are to be traded for a prisoner. He says that his boss thinks the authorities will do anything to get five women released, especially the girlfriend of a marine officer and one of an American officer."

It was all that Elena could do to cover up her shock as everyone but Mary smiled.

The women followed a stooped grey-haired woman who walked with a handmade wooden cane across a dirt parking area and then into a single-story farmhouse. A crumbling shop area bordered the parking area on the right and another, smaller house on the left. Between the houses stood an outhouse that looked like it might collapse if you opened the door. Two of the guards took up positions outside of the house while the others unloaded what looked like weapons and several cases of beer from the Suburban. They carried the boxes into a smaller house.

They entered the living, dining, kitchen area of the 1940's Mexican farmhouse. Against one wall several cupboards surrounded a wooden counter and ceramic sink with a hand pump. The old woman pointed at a second room and then at Mary and Elena. Then she pointed at a third room and prodded the other women with her cane.

From the door she pointed at the last room and spoke to the women.

"The last room is Carlotta's," translated Francesca. "We are to stay out." Then she added in a stronger voice, "did you and Elena hear me?"

Mary nodded. "Yes, there are two bunk beds here. I think she wants us to get some sleep."

Francesca glanced around the room where she, Sonia and Olga stood. She turned to Sonia. "You take the bed on the left. Olga and I will double up on the right one. I suggest we wait for morning to see what we are dealing with and then plan."

Out in the parking area, they could hear car doors slam and then both vehicles drive away.

"We are without transportation," said Olga. "But the odds just got better; it's now four to three."

"Do not ignore the woman," said Sonia. "Over the years, I've come in contact with several like her. My guess is that she's the widow of a soldier and completely dependent on whoever is running this show. Count on five to three. Maybe we'll be pleasantly surprised. But I'll bet she knows where all the skeletons are buried." She smiled at the other two women who were looking for a place to hide their weapons. "I'm a little sleepy, but I can take the first watch. I think one of us should stay awake; maybe in two-hour shifts." She looked at her watch, surprised that they had been eating and drinking peacefully only two hours before.

Four hours later she was asleep when the first rooster began to crow.

∽

None of the other homeowners near Mary and Francesca's house noticed anything wrong, or at least decided to mind their own business. Diego's mustang was still parked, and the front door stood wide open. The general manager of the hotel where Mary worked was furious as he drove to Mary's house and parked.

Mary was supposed to relieve the night desk clerk hours earlier, but she hadn't even called.

Knocking on the wall next to the door, then calling, and getting no answer, he walked into the house. Pots and pans as well as empty bottles covered the counter next to the stove. On the patio he found five sets of dirty dishes and partially empty wine glasses. It looked like some alien craft had sucked whoever was having dinner into thin air.

A little nervous, he turned back for the house. On the dinner table was an envelope with the word EMERGENCIA written on the front. It was balanced on five cell phones. He picked up the envelope and slid the one page note out. Within seconds of reading it, he was on his phone and soon the house was crawling with local and federal police.

Neighbors reported that Francesca and Mary were the renters. It took almost an hour for the supervising detective to reach anyone who could tie the women to the cell phones. It would have been easier to simply make calls from them, but the batteries had been removed.

Recognizing Elena's name, the detective called the marine corps compound. After explaining the scene to Diego, the detective held the phone away from his ear for a full minute as rage exploded on the other end of the phone. After calming him enough to continue a conversation, he was shocked when the only documentation that Diego had requested was a copy of the letter. The detective took a picture with his phone and sent it before giving Diego his direct phone number.

In Acapulco, Diego trotted from the office where he was working to the building where the navy was assembling the submarine. By the time he found Chad, he had calmed down. "My friend, I need to go home right now. Elena has been kidnapped, mierda, mierda, mierda."

Chad stood silently for a full minute before asking "where, when?"

"Apparently last night," replied Diego. "She apparently was having dinner with Mary."

"Fuck, fuck, fuck. Olga, Sonia, Francesca and Elena were all supposed to be having dinner together last night. I tried to call Olga just an hour ago and got no answer."

Diego shook his head. "Let me translate the note that was left behind." He opened his phone to the picture sent him only minutes before and enlarged the note one section at a time and then translated.

Date July 13. The five women taken from this house are being held until Carmen Maria Ayala Lopez is released from custody and is safely out of Mexico. Do not try to find them.

I will call the office of the attorney general in the capital at ten tomorrow morning to give them specific instructions on making the exchange. The phone I will use will be untraceable and I will be traveling by car, so you will not be able to track me.

Carmen is a valuable part of our operations, and the entire organization is committed to her release. You know how well armed we are, and her guards have been ordered to kill all the hostages if you try to rescue them."

"Diego," said Chad, "you find us a ride back to Zihua. I'm going to call Thad, Ramón and Gina."

An hour later, the three team members already in Mexico City were huddled in David Lopez's office. In the corner, the president of Mexico sat listening.

"Sonia, Francesca, and Olga all know that the US will not negotiate with the kidnappers," said Thad. "The odds are that they will be killed the moment Carmen Lopez is released."

"Maybe, maybe not," said Gina. "In Mexico, paying kidnappers often gets people released. But in this case, we have been working for months to nail down this gang, and still have only one hard suspect: Carmen. This is probably Ayala, but we have no proof."

"Worse," offered Ramón, "except for his visit to his daughter, we have no idea of how to find him. He is like a ghost. The man who tried to tail him, lost him within minutes."

Thad turned to Ramón. "When you talked to the local police, did they have anything hard, you know anything that might be a solid lead to find them?"

"The local police are waiting for the federal police to bring in a forensics team," said Ramón. "There was nothing obvious. No neighbor reports. No cameras." He paused a moment,

"at least there is no blood or indication of any struggle."

Thad looked over at Mexico's president who sat quietly, taking notes. He looked up at Ramón. "Did the local authorities find any weapons at that house?"

The president looked up at David, an unspoken question in her eyes.

"Madam President, I looked the other way when the team decided to arm themselves."

Ramón didn't wait for her response before offering, "there is no report of unregistered weapons at the crime scene."

"Gritt told me that at least Sonia and Olga were armed, and Olga was carrying a pistol for Francesca the evening they disappeared. They may be armed, but we have no reports of any shootout. Or maybe the kidnappers found the weapons. That would put the women in greater danger." Thad chanced a glance at the president, noting a subtle nod of her head.

"So, for now," said Gina Santos, "we need to let this play out a bit." She turned to Lupita. "Madam President, I would appreciate it if you would call the AG and direct him to allow me to be the only go-between for now. We've been working this for months and the team that David put together is our best chance of getting the hostages back without losing the one thread we have to the group responsible for so much misery."

"Before you go, I have a question," said Lupita.

"Ask anything, you initiated this effort," replied Thad, "and the team is made up of trusted Mexican officials and guests in your country."

"You used the name, Francesca a few minutes ago. Would that be the same Francesca that travels with Maria Castillo?"

Gina was on her feet and headed to the door. She turned and smiled. "Yes, Madam President."

"Is Maria a suspect in all of this?"

"Not necessarily," said Gina, "but there are several things about her and her operations that are suspicious. If she's involved, we can't tell you how. But key to the movement of drugs and money and even weapons is a sophisticated transportation system, and the one she runs seems to have connections everywhere we look."

"I like Maria," said the president. She has done a lot for this country in a short period of time. I'd hate to think she is somehow involved."

"It's possible," said Thad, "that the bad guys see the same organizational skills you see in her. They may be using her and her company and she in turn is using the newfound wealth to do good things."

The president looked at Gina. "You had better get over to the AG's office before the morning call. I'll call him and make it clear that you are running point on this."

As Gina closed the door, Lupita turned back to the others. "The next call I'm going to make is to Maria Castillo. I want to see what she says when I reveal her bodyguard has been kidnapped."

Thad leaned forward in his chair. "If you would, Madam President, "please make the message clear that her sister and some friends were kidnapped and that it appears that Francesca just happened to be there. If Maria Castillo is involved in this, we don't want to tip off the bad guys that Francesca is working with us."

The president rose and smiled at Thad. "All that young woman has done so far is to try to help Mexico, both through her work with you and with Maria. I don't want her to die for that."

※

The call came into the AG's office almost fifteen minutes late. The receptionist transferred it to Gina's office where she and the attorney general waited.

"Who am I speaking with?" asked Gina in Spanish.

"That is not important. I assume that the AG has passed this on to you so that no matter what happens, it will not stick to him."

"Perhaps. Anyway, I have been asked to resolve this matter," said Gina.

"Do not mistake this call. There will be only one resolution and that will be the release of Carmen Maria Lopez from custody and her transport out of the country."

"I am not arguing with you, Señor," said Gina, "only trying to resolve this without bloodshed."

"Bueno," answered the caller. "Now write this down. The day after tomorrow at ten in the morning, a small, chartered jet will land at the airport in Acapulco. You will have no more than two unarmed men transport Carmen to meet that plane. They will stay at least one hundred meters away as Carmen walks to the plane and closes the door. Then the plane will depart to the south. I will have others observing. When it lands and Carmen uses the phone on the plane to report she is safely out of the country, I will call my men."

"What will you tell your men when you call them?" asked Gina.

"Do not trifle with me, just get her there and on the plane. If there is any effort to stop the plane or to follow it while it is in the air, I will not make the call. When I hear Carmen is safely back on the ground, I will order my men to release the women."

"Where and when will you release them?" asked Gina.

"They will be released where and when I choose. I assume that there are others in the room with you, so let me be clear, it will be someplace where my men can drive away without risking arrest. The release location will depend on observers assuring that there is no police or military presence."

"How can we be sure that the hostages will be released?" asked Gina, knowing that a team in the next room was working to trace the call.

"You don't, yet you have no choice. If Carmen is not at the airport and on her way out of the country by ten-thirty that morning, one hostage will be maimed, not killed. Another will follow every hour until you comply." There was a slight pause. "Now I am hanging up and this phone will be destroyed. If you do not comply, I will call you back on a new phone at eight-thirty tomorrow night and you can tell me where to send the body parts we remove."

"Wait," said Gina, "will you be on the plane?"

"No, I will be somewhere dreaming up something even uglier than we have been discussing if you mess with me." The line went dead.

Gina and the AG sat looking at each other for several seconds before a man tapped on the door and entered. "It appears to be a disposable phone, and it registered off from two different cell towers here in the capital," he said. "We will begin a camera search to see if we can identify the vehicle."

"Go ahead," said Gina, "but I think you will find that the towers align along one busy road, so you would have to look at hundreds of cars and pick one that somehow stood out."

As the man left, she looked up at the AG and shook her head. "It could be worse. I'm surprised that he gave us almost two days. My guess is that he hasn't made arrangements where he's sending her."

"I'll have every officer in the country trying to find these women," he said.

"Don't. We know some are compromised. Let our small team try to resolve this, sir. But I do have one request. We suspect that if this is Ayala, he will probably use a plane from a small air charter service we think he owns. If you can have a couple of completely trusted officers watch that location, and then follow Ayala if he shows up there, we can pick him up after the hostage crisis is over."

"With seven of your 'so-called team' on the ground here in Mexico, why not use one or two of those people?" asked the AG.

"Well, two appear to be hostages, and two are in Zihua right now looking for any leads. Our oldest member has been seen going in and out of David Lopez's office, so he may be compromised. That leaves Captain Ramón Acuna, the naval officer who will have to coordinate any rescue attempt from here in the city and me. Besides, I doubt that Ayala will be dumb enough to go to that airport. I'm sure that there is already a letter directing the flight at that location, and that payment was made in cash."

"You seem pretty damned sure of yourself Ms. Gina Santos," said the AG.

"This is still new to you, sir. I've been tracking drug kingpins for a decade. They aren't dumb and they have well-groomed organizations. Violence is part of that grooming."

As the man left her office, Gina dialed Thad Walker's number, to brief him on the call. "Any ideas on where Ayala might be sending his daughter?" she asked.

"No, but I called the team in LA and asked them to spend no more than a couple of hours figuring out where she might be granted asylum. Like you, I assume that this is Ayala and if it is, the location must be within range of one of the planes operated by his flying service."

Gina could hear Thad tapping his fingers on the back of the phone. "Maybe it's time for me to call the Chinese again," he added. "None of our people have fully disclosed what the Mexican navy found in that container. Chad has been in contact with his old nemesis, Ma Mingze and I reached out to a very old acquaintance earlier, Ma's boss, General Ling. They should be able to trace the serial numbers of the weapons found in that warehouse. There can't be many places in China with the expertise to build an inexpensive submarine and equip it with hybrid propulsion, GPS navigation, and internal air compressors to recharge diving tanks."

"I've been thinking somewhat along the same lines," said Gina. "Here in Mexico, we are probably looking for six to ten principals. The Chinese may have just as many, but only a couple of them are connected to the drug cartel we are trying to stop. If they can identify one Chinese national illegally operating here in Mexico, we might be able to leverage him into disclosing his local partners, or at least into telling us how to find Ayala."

CHAPTER 39

July 14, Sierra Madre del Sur Mountains, Mexico

THE THREE OLDER hostages had been awake when the leader of the kidnappers fired up an old Yamaha dirt bike and rode it out of the yard. Olga stood at the front windows watching as he turned the bike onto a narrow trail at the base of a small mountain next to the farmhouse.

Behind her she could hear a heated argument between Carlotta and Francesca. "Move away from the windows," called Francesca. "Carlotta worries that spying on any of the men outside will just give them an excuse to turn us into playthings."

"Whose side is she really on?" asked Olga as she turned away to watch Mary and Elena come into the room.

"Her roots with the leaders of this group go back decades. One of the guards is her nephew," replied Francesca. "She's a loyal soldier, but one that is really disturbed by taking women hostages. She's especially worried that some of us are Americans. Years ago, her husband was killed in a shootout with Mexican marines aided by American DEA agents."

Olga checked her watch. It was ten minutes to eight. "I think the leader of the guards just left here to find higher ground. I watched him fumbling with his cell phone. My guess is that he needs to check in at eight and down in this canyon, he has no coverage. Whatever is going on, I think will be resolved within 48 hours or they will want us dead."

"Agreed," said Francesca. "Whoever is behind this threw it together. If it drags on, we become a liability."

"One more piece in the puzzle," offered Sonia from the kitchen where she and Carlotta were preparing a breakfast of tortillas and eggs. "It's good to know that one or two of us now have a ride out of here after we take care of the guards." She looked over at Mary and Elena who sat at the table gasping. Sonia placed her finger over her lips.

※

"Luis," snapped Maria Castillo, "what in the hell is Ayala doing? I see a morning news report about some kidnapping in Zihua and then the president calls me to tell me that Francesca, the woman you helped me hire as a bodyguard is one of five women seized."

"All I know is what the news tells us," said Luis. "I have no idea who is behind this kidnapping."

"Do not play the fool with me, Luis. The kidnappers only demand is the release of Carmen Ayala Lopez." Maria began tapping on the keyboard in front of her, looking for anything new on the situation. "I will not be part of this."

"I will call Juan and tell him that he must release this Francesca woman," said Luis.

"She will never leave without her sister. If Francesca gets her hands on a gun, people will die. I doubt that the punks who work for Juan in the Zihua area have any idea who they are dealing with. These are not his hardened soldiers from along the border."

"I will make the call right now," said Luis. "I will tell Juan that he must find an excuse to release the two sisters. Hell, the girlfriend of a Mexican marine officer and of an American naval officer should be leverage enough to get Carmen released," said Luis. "A contact in the president's office told me that the older woman taken is somehow connected to an American friend of David Lopez, so she also has trading value."

"So, you knew about this."

"No, but in my last conversation with Juan, he indicated that he thought he'd found the key to getting Carmen out of the country. When I saw the morning news, I figured it out." Luis paused a moment before adding, "your Francesca and her sister may end up disposable to keep our plan alive."

"Luis, I grew up in the drug world. I understand the need to protect ourselves, but killing two innocent young women is more than I can accept. I suspect that holding another older woman with connections to the president's office may also be a mistake. Maybe it's time to find a replacement for Juan instead. If not, maybe it's time to take our winnings and go home. Call."

⁂

The guards ran frantically to their small house, emerging moments later, carrying weapons that few armies owned. They took positions around the parking area as the van rolled back into the yard. The guard leader met the van just as two armed men emerged from the rear, along with the driver and another guard riding shotgun. Like the other guards, they all wore face coverings. The leader and driver spent more than ten minutes discussing something before the leader headed toward the house.

Opening the door, he motioned for Carlotta and her hostage guests to follow him outside. He ordered Elena to translate.

"I am told that two of you were born here in Mexico," he said. "Which two?"

Francesca and Mary cautiously held up their hands.

"For our purposes you two have no value. You are to be released. Gather your belongings and meet me at the van. Now, please go back inside."

"I don't like this," said Olga as she and Francesca retreated to their bedroom. "Why would they release you less than a day after bringing us here?"

"I don't know," said Francesca, "but assuming we make it down the mountain without ending up with a bullet in the brain, we can get help. I know generally where we are, and I will pay attention on the drive out of here. By now, Chad and Diego will be looking for us. It won't take them long to round up what you Americans call a posse."

The women turned as Carlotta called to them, directing Francesca and Mary to hurry."

"I hid my weapon under a loose board under the bed," added Francesca as she turned toward the door, carrying her coat.

Sonia, Elena and Olga watched Mary and Francesca walk to the van where a guard covered their heads with pillowcases and then roughly pushed them into the back of the van, slamming and locking the door. He then joined the driver and the van turned for the narrow-rutted path out of the compound.

The three stood at the windows for several minutes after the van left. "Not good," mumbled Sonia as she watched. "We have one less shooter and they added two more guards."

She turned to Elena. "If you haven't figured it out yet, Olga, Francesca and I are all here courtesy of the US government to help Mexico. Francesca left her pistol just now. Can you shoot?"

Elena's eyes turned glassy, and her lips quivered before she managed, "I hate guns."

"Then," said Sonia, "if shooting starts here, your job will be to point Francesca's gun at Carlotta to keep her out of the fight."

"I don't know if I can do that," said Elena.

"Then either Olga or I will have to shoot her right away to cover our backs." She watched Elena take a deep breath before quietly mouthing, I can do it.

※

The van had jostled the two women in the back, leaving each of them with bruises and Mary with a small cut on her chin. Both were relieved when the trip ended with the van sliding to a stop on a dirt road just off from a smooth highway. The back door opened, and a man's voice ordered them out; helping them struggle to their feet. He ordered them to forget everything they had seen or heard. "Do not try to be heroes," he ordered, reminding them that they knew where the sisters lived. "Thank the saints above for your freedom. If anyone tries to rescue the other three women, all will die."

One at a time he led them to a bench beside the road, ordering them to leave their head covering in place. Both followed his orders and left the pillowcases on until they could no longer hear the van racing back toward the highway.

Francesca was the first to tug hers off. As Mary tugged at hers, Francesca looked down at her watch. The ride from the time they left the farmhouse to when they were released had taken exactly one hour and twenty-three minutes. She was guessing, but the first third of that time had been on rough dirt roads, with the rest at highway speeds. At sixty miles an hour, that meant they were almost exactly an hour from the turnoff onto the dirt track.

"Where are we?" wondered Mary.

"My guess is, not far from home," replied Francesca. Across

the road, out in a coconut plantation, they could hear voices. "Let's go get some help."

Twenty minutes later four police cars and two with markings of the marine corps were parked among the towering coconut trees just out of La Salitrera, a tiny village just north of Zihuantanejo.

While Mary went with the federal police who were anxious to get her statement, Francesca rode between Chad and Diego in a khaki-colored truck with two more marines in the back seat. She too would have been with the federales except that the marines were better armed, and Diego was more forceful.

"The guards at that farmhouse are very well armed," said Francesca. "They have assault rifles as well as handguns. I saw handheld rocket launchers and if these are the same people we've been hunting, they probably have surface to air missiles. I counted six guards total."

"You say there is only one track in and out of that compound?" asked Chad as he took notes on his cell phone.

"One track that can accommodate vehicles, but there is a dirt track to one side of the parking area that goes up the side of a small mountain. The buildings can be approached from that direction, and I doubt that the guards will be watching. They seem focused on the main track. My guess is that they are all locals and not well trained."

"Could you identify the compound from the air?" asked Diego.

"I think so," she replied, "It's northeast of where we were dropped off, about an hour on a highway and then east on a rough dirt road maybe five miles. There are two houses, one a little larger than the other and off to one side some shops. Several rusting vehicles are parked in front of the house, probably to provide cover if there is an attack."

"Must be somewhere off from Highway 134," said Diego.

Chad looked over at Diego sitting behind the driver. "We have about six hours of light left. We're only an hour from the Zihua airport. Can you get a helicopter there quickly?"

"Probably," replied Diego, "but the only helicopters in the area are military, so it would tip off the bad guys. They probably have watchers posted, especially after releasing two hostages. We'd be better off with a small plane, up high, and binoculars. I know a private pilot with a Cessna, let me make a call." He paused a few seconds before adding, "from the air we could coordinate a rescue."

"Better have your men get ready to assault this place; find a couple of unmarked trucks and head up that highway. But get a helicopter on standby. Maybe the terrain will let us get to the upper end of the trail Francesca described. It will be better if we can approach from both sides of the compound. If it looks good, the helicopter can meet us when we land the Cessna. I'll need some body armor and a rifle," he added.

"What about me?" asked Francesca. "If I can get to the compound quietly, I might be able to get into the house. With all their firepower, it might be helpful to have help from inside the house."

"That might work, especially if we go in at night," said Chad. "Did you see any night-vision equipment?"

"No," replied Francesca.

"Okay," offered Diego, "we do a high-altitude search first. Until we know whether we can access that trail up the mountain, we won't know enough to develop a plan."

"Can we trust your pilot friend?" asked Chad.

"I do," replied Diego. "He used to fly for Aeromexico before it shut down, and before that, the navy. Now he runs a guide service for gringo fishermen including flying them to several mountain lakes for great bass fishing. He and his wife sold an oceanfront house for a bundle to an investment group several years ago. He doesn't need drug money." Diego leaned into the front seat and ordered the driver to the airport.

He called the marine compound and directed them to be at the airport with three pairs of binoculars. A call to Ramón Acuna assured him that the navy helicopter from Manzanillo would be standing by if needed.

Finally, he called the man with the Cessna.

An hour later the six-passenger high wing plane was airborne and climbing.

"I'm pleased you accepted my offer to help," said the pilot looking at Diego in the co-pilots seat. "I called as soon as I heard about Elena. All my customers are from the states. This kind of thing hurts business. Besides, this Italian girl is finally making an honest man of you, my friend."

"I should have told you two," said Diego, "that our pilot speaks English. It's the international language of air traffic control."

From five thousand feet up, Highway 134 looked like a black ribbon climbing into the hills to the northeast of Zihua. From the moment they crossed the intersection of 134 and the coast highway, the pilot set a timer on the panel and pegged the airspeed at 110 knots. The timer went off twenty-five minutes later and the three passengers began searching the highway below for a dirt road exiting to the right, finding three within a few minutes.

"From the pavement, we drove approximately thirty minutes," said Francesca. "The first half of the track was smooth, and the truck was going about twenty miles an hour. Then we turned left onto a rough trail with brush rubbing the sides of the vehicle. We went over a ridge, then down across a rushing stream, and then over a second ridge before we stopped. They couldn't have been driving faster than ten miles an hour on that leg."

The pilot looked over the seat at Francesca, a huge smile on his face.

"I trained in base security while serving in the American Air Force," offered Francesca.

Chad was surprised by the labyrinth of dirt tracks snaking back into the mountains. They followed each track for ten minutes before backtracking to pick up the next side road. They were following the third when Diego spotted an abandoned ranch along a small stream to his right.

"That might be it," he said into the intercom. "Look to the right just in front of the plane."

"That's it," said Francesca. "The buildings are just right and there are old trucks parked in front of the bigger house."

"The path into that place runs through the trees and even most of the abandoned fields are grown up," said Diego. "Let's fly another few miles and then backtrack. I want to look for that narrow trail up the mountain."

"Why are so many of the small mountain tops clear of trees?" asked Chad who couldn't see the farmhouse from behind the pilot.

"The ranchers took the land that was not good for growing food crops," answered the pilot. "They cleared the brush and trees to open up pastureland. The cattle prefer the ridge tops where there's a breeze and fewer biting flies. Over a few decades they grazed on all the small shrubs and trees which left nothing on top to reseed the high pastures. The lower pastures have revegetated." The pilot reached up and entered a waypoint on his GPS system, marking the latitude and longitude of the ranch.

The plane flew several more minutes to disguise their

surveillance before reversing course. "I don't see the small track going up that mountain," said Diego, "but the hill is exactly where the guard was riding a dirt bike, and the top of the hill is all grass."

"I think I see where it leaves the compound," said Francesca. "And up the hill, where the trees end, there is a narrow path through the grass. Someone's been up there recently. That's the place. Let's head back to the airport."

"One short detour," offered the pilot. "One of my favorite aviation sports is flour bombing."

"What the hell is flour bombing?" asked Chad.

"You're about to find out." The pilot turned directly back to Highway 134 and pulled the power. "Mr. Gritt, under your seat you will find a small cotton shopping bag with a large zip-lock of white paint inside. Hand it to Diego."

Diego turned, staring at the pilot.

"In about eight minutes I'm going to pick out a gap in the traffic on the highway and drop down as low and slow as I can past the track that runs to the compound. Diego, you're going to open the window and toss that bag down on the highway. It'll mark the side road you will take when you come back to rescue Elena. And don't hit the landing gear when you toss it, or I'll have you out at the airport for hours cleaning paint off the airplane." The man began to laugh. "Some American fishermen who come down every year have a saying that seems appropriate. "We're having fun now."

CHAPTER 40

July 15, Sierra Madre Del Sur Mountains near Zihuatanejo

CHAD GLANCED DOWN at his watch. "It's ten after three" he said to Diego. "Your men should be waiting by now. "It's time to go."

"Give it another ten minutes," said Diego, buckling up his bulletproof vest. "I told them to wait where the trail to the compound turns off from the dirt road. We can't reach them from here and I don't want to risk the guards hearing the helicopter until they are within minutes of their assault positions."

Chad turned back to helping Francesca adjust the men's vest to fit her. "The two pilots, the gunner and we three make six going in on the helo," he said. "That means we have room for the three hostages coming out plus one empty seat. I would love to do this without firing a shot. Your sergeant and the other marines in the trucks can bottle up the bad guys until the federales get there to make arrests."

"That depends on whether I can get into the house without

being seen and get the girls out the back and over to the helicopter," said Francesca.

"First, we have to get to the farmhouse," said Chad, handing Francesca some night vision goggles. "You said the kidnappers have a helper watching from inside the building. Even if they tie her up, there's a risk of her somehow alerting the guards that we are on the trail up the hill."

"Then we take her with us," said Francesca. "She's been kind to us even though our arrival was a surprise. I'd hate to see her killed."

"Time to saddle up," said Diego. "I can reach my guys on the tactical radios from fifteen miles out."

The helicopter pilots entered the GPS location that the Cessna pilot had given them on their own GPS and then started the engines. "God, I hate these things," said Francesca. "It's a miracle of engineering that they don't shake themselves apart."

They were airborne about twenty minutes when Diego pulled the handheld radio from his belt and called. He reached into the cockpit giving the pilots a thumbs up as they approached the mountaintop under a half-moon, slipping the helicopter sideways to avoid looking directly into the moon with their night vision goggles. The pilot positioned the open door where his gunner could cover what they hoped would be the upper end of the trail before setting down. He allowed the craft to go to idle for a few minutes before shutting down the engines. Diego handed both the pilot and the gunner a radio, then Chad, Francesca and he started down the mountain.

It took thirty minutes to reach where the trail opened into the back of the parking area at the compound. Diego stopped twice to communicate with his men who were observing three guards patrolling the parking area in front of the farmhouse.

"They aren't expecting company," whispered Chad as they waited behind the outhouse.

"But the one across the parking area sitting on that old tractor turns occasionally to observe the house," said Diego. "Is there a door in the back of the house?"

"No door, just a big window that Carlotta leaves open to get fresh air in her room. I don't know if any of the other windows will even open," said Francesca. "It looks a little risky for us to try and slip past that man on the tractor and into the house through the front door, and trying to get in through Carlotta's room could be a disaster. She keeps a shotgun next to her bed."

"We may have to assault this place after all," said Diego. "There are only three outside and the other three are probably asleep."

"I have an idea," said Francesca. She pulled the bottom of her blouse from her jeans, then motioned to Diego to give her his knife. She cut six inches off from the bottom of her blouse and then gave it back to him.

"The outhouse is the only bathroom, and the night I spent here, two of us had to come out in the dark and use it. We were as quiet as possible, but both times the guard on the tractor saw us either coming or going. He just waived."

She began watching the guard intensely. "When he looks the other way for a few minutes, I'm going to slip into the outhouse and when I leave, I'll bang the door. From across the parking area, I hope that he will mistake me for one of the other girls as I walk directly back to the farmhouse and inside." She paused before adding, "be ready to kill that son of a bitch if it looks like he is becoming a risk."

A moment later, she wrapped the torn cloth over her hair and slipped into the tiny building. Emerging a minute later, she deliberately let the door bang and when the guard looked over, she waved feebly as she made a beeline for the farmhouse. A moment later she was inside, and the guard turned away.

Francesca found Sonia asleep in her room. She leaned down and whispered, "the cavalry has arrived. It's time to go."

Sonia didn't move, but her eyes opened, and she stared up into Francesca's face. She smiled. "What do you want me to do?" she asked.

"Arm yourself and then slip into Carlotta's room and make sure that she stays quiet. If you must, knock her out, but we'd like to take her with us. Maybe that will get her cooperation. She has a nephew outside. If this turns into a firefight, the marines watching this place are not in the mood to take prisoners." Francesca turned toward the door. "I'll wake the other girls. We need to leave through that window in Carlotta's room. We have help outside, and a helicopter waiting at the top of the mountain."

It took ten minutes before Diego saw the first legs sliding out the window in the back of the house. "You watch the guy on the tractor, I'm going to help get the women out of there."

Moving silently in the dark, he slipped up behind the first woman on the ground and wrapped his hand over her mouth before whispering "I love you," to Elena. She turned and threw herself into his arms. "Later," he said, "we need to get on the trail before anyone notices you are missing."

Sonia was the next one out, followed by Mary and then Carlotta, her hands bound behind her, a rag tied in her mouth. Moments later, Mary and Francesca slipped out the open window. Diego signaled for them to lean closer. "Chad is behind the outhouse watching the guard across the driveway. Stay behind the corner of the house until he signals it's clear and then walk one at a time as quietly as possible past him, and then up the trail. If he signals you to stop, freeze until he indicates it's okay to move.

After a couple of hundred meters, you'll get to a small creek. Wait there."

A minute later, only Carlotta, Francesca and Diego were behind the house. "Do not force my marines on the other side of the parking area to open fire," whispered Diego in Carlotta's ear. "I'm going to carry you to the trail. Hold onto your cane, you're going to need it."

He waited until Chad signaled and then swept the frail woman into his arms and started across the opening to the outhouse. He was halfway there when Chad held up his hand. Diego froze with only a small bush in front of him. He slowly turned his head to look over at the guard, just as a second guard walked up to the tractor. The man on the tractor jumped down and moments later lit a cigarette as his replacement climbed onto the tractor seat. Then the first guard disappeared in the direction of the house. Diego looked back at Chad who was motioning for him to hurry.

Ten minutes later all seven people were huddled under the heavy canopy of trees. "Do you think that Carlotta, here will help us find Ayala or whoever is running this shit show?" asked Chad as Francesca helped the old woman start up the hill.

"She didn't know we were coming," said Francesca, "but her life has been tied to whoever is running this show. No, I doubt that she will talk, but I got the impression, she was weary of her life alone in that old house."

"Damn," said Chad, "we got all of you out of there, but we're no closer to tracking down Ayala then we were before. We're going to have to move faster than Carlotta can walk."

"Then you and Diego are going to have to take turns carrying her," said Francesca. "That old woman may never tell us exactly how to nail the ringleaders, but she knows a lot. Maybe a good interrogator can piece together what we need."

"Did you leave the present we made in the house?" asked Chad.

"I set the timer for forty-five minutes. It won't make much of a boom when it goes off."

"Diego and I agreed, we don't want a boom. We just want a fire. Hopefully it will distract the guards and keep them busy until we get to the helicopter. Please tell Carlotta that I'm going to carry her a while," added Chad.

The small group was just breaking out of the trees when the radio on Diego's hip sounded. "They discovered the fire a few minutes ago," he translated. The guards appear to have extinguished it quickly; they know the women are missing. One of the men is pulling that dirt bike out of the shed. Do we want them to shoot him?"

Chad paused and lowered Carlotta to the ground. He and Diego had traded off carrying her. In the eighty-degree heat, it left them both drenched in sweat. "No," he replied. "But I have an idea."

He turned to Sonia and Francesca, "the helicopter is only a quarter mile further up the hill. Get everyone on board and strapped in. Diego and I will be along soon."

He watched the five women continue up through the faint trail beaten into the grass at the top of the hill before turning to Diego. "Call your watchers. If the guy on the dirt bike heads for the road, have them grab him, but I think he'll be coming this way. Call the chopper pilots and have them prepare to get the hell out of here the minute they see us on the trail."

"What do you have in mind?" asked Diego.

"I'm betting that the guy on that bike is the guard leader and that the minute he sees the women missing he'll start a search. I'm also betting that he uses that bike to search up this trail. We'll grab him when he gets here. Even if he won't talk, he'll be carrying the phone he uses to check in. The call log might lead us to Ayala."

"How will we stop him without shooting?" asked Diego.

"I once watched a dirt bike racer stray off the course," answered Chad. "He ran into some brush and a stick rammed through the spokes of the bike. Both bike and rider went end over end. Come on."

He and Diego walked back down the hill a hundred yards to where the trail broke out of the trees. Chad searched until he found a long, strong tree limb and then he began breaking the smaller branches from the limb, leaving a six-foot pole. "This through the front wheel spokes should do the job," said Gritt. A voice on Diego's radio reported that the rider was headed up the hill.

"If the guy survives the crash, we can take him with us," added Chad.

"The helicopter can only carry ten people," said Diego. "In the Mexican navy the pilots are obsessed with following regulations."

"Who's counting?" replied Chad as the sound of the motorcycle began to echo up the hill.

Diego picked up another tree limb and began stripping away the smaller branches. "If one is good, two is better," he said as he crouched down into the tall grass on the opposite side of the trail from Chad.

They used their night vision goggles to study the rider who came around a curve well below where they hid. The rider gunned the machine heading for the top. Both sticks slammed into the front wheel of the bike, sending it cartwheeling, the rider launching over the handlebars and tumbling before coming to a stop. He didn't move.

Diego and Chad, weapons in hand, jogged up to where the

rider lay motionless. "I know this man," said Diego, "his name is Paco, and he works for the freight transfer station near where Highway 134 and the Coast Highway come together. He has a wife and five kids."

Chad slipped his fingers against the man's neck. "He's alive, with a strong heartbeat. Let's pick him up and take him with us." He felt through the man's pockets, handing a cell phone to Diego. "I don't know how serious kidnapping charges are in Mexico, but in the states, they might be enough to make a man talk. Unless he cooperated, a man of this age would never see his family again, except from behind the bars of a prison." Chad tugged at the rifle that somehow was still clinging to the kidnapper's shoulder, finally freeing it. He pulled the clip and tossed the rifle into the trail. "Call the chopper and tell them to wind it up. Then call your guys down below. Make sure they keep the rest of these guys under wraps until we call. It may work out better if whoever is calling the shots on this, doesn't know that there's been a rescue."

He and Diego each threw an arm of the unconscious man over a shoulder and launched themselves up the trail. It took ten minutes to carry the dead weight of Paco to the helicopter. Both Diego and Chad were screaming to go at the top of their lungs as they approached. They didn't want to debate a pilot who might be a stickler for regulations over whether the craft could carry eleven people.

"Have the helicopter land at the navy compound in Manzanillo. We don't want any watchers in Zihua to report the rescue," offered Chad as he leaned across the seat and grasped Olga's hand.

"We would have been out of that place in the morning," she said. "Sonia and I had a plan. But, getting rescued is a lot more romantic."

CHAPTER 41

July 16, Manzanillo, Mexico

"It's going to drive Ayala nuts when his daughter doesn't make it to the Acapulco airport," said Sonia. She and Thad were sitting in a quiet office.

"We're counting on that," replied Thad who had just arrived at the Manzanillo navy compound. Chad's plan should work. The last two calls that Paco guy made, both from the mountain above the farmhouse, were to a burner phone. We have the number. When his men don't check in this morning and his daughter doesn't meet the plane this afternoon, our guess is that he will use that phone to try to figure out what went wrong. I have Pinky and that DEA hacker Ashley waiting to track any calls."

"Are the Mexican phone companies cooperating?" asked Sonia. "That's not what I've seen in the past."

"We didn't ask them," replied Thad. "The LA team is hacking them. Normally a guy with the experience of Ayala would never stay on the line long enough to trace a call, but he's on a burner and he should be desperate. We got this Paco guy talking long enough to get a good voice print on him. Ayala won't know that he's talking to Diego through an AI voice translator."

"This all assumes that we are right, and Ayala is behind all of this," replied Sonia.

"If it's not him, we will still be able to track whoever is calling the shots, at least to the cell tower carrying his signal. Diego may have to wing it, you know, bait a trap. The Mexican navy's press release that this Carmen girl was rescued on her way to the airport should get Ayala moving. He doesn't know who is holding her. Paco's phone will explain that a couple of Paco's men were pulled off the rescue and that Carmen is being moved to the farmhouse where you were held." Thad leaned across the table and kissed Sonia on the cheek. "We're getting too old for this. I just found you after waiting most of my life. I knew you'd be okay, but I still worried."

She reached out and brushed his cheek with her fingertips.

In the next room, Chad and Diego sat with one of the marines who had been watching the farmhouse. "When the leader, this Paco guy, didn't come back down the mountain," translated Diego, "the remaining five kidnappers panicked and started to walk out to the highway. They were surrounded and disarmed before they had walked five minutes. Three of my men stayed at the farmhouse while the rest escorted the prisoners here."

"Smart," replied Chad. "But we can't communicate the plan to the guys at that farmhouse. If my idea works, Ayala or whoever is running this op should be on his way there by tomorrow morning, probably with a small army."

"Once we see that he has taken the bait, you and I and our own small army will be on our way back there. From here, it's just an hour by helicopter. The men who escorted the prisoners will grab some food and a little sleep and then position themselves to reinforce us if needed." Diego yawned. "Speaking of sleep, I better grab a little myself. Once Paco's phone rings, things could get busy."

"Makes sense. Sonia speaks fluent Spanish," said Chad. "She and I are going to take another crack at that Paco guy and then grab some rack time ourselves."

"I think you are wasting your time," offered Diego as he headed for the rooms that the local commander had made available to them. "But if the head is Ayala, and we get him in custody where he can't direct retribution, a guy like Paco might begin thinking about his family." He paused a minute. "I know Sonia and Olga are here, but where are the other women?"

"Francesca is on her way back to Mexico City. Mary and Elena are being escorted to a safe house."

"So now we wait. That's always the hardest part," said Diego.

Chad tapped on the door where Walker and Sonia were chatting." Diego thinks we're wasting our time, but let's take a crack at this Paco guy anyway. If he'll give up the brains behind this operation, it might save us some time."

"Agreed," said Sonia, "but Diego's probably right. Still, we might get something that helps. Knowing how far away the big boss is, or how many guards he travels with would help."

Less than fifteen minutes later, Chad and Sonia retreated. Paco had been defiant, talking in riddles. "Hypothetically, a 'leader' who would take such a risk to save a minor character like Carmen, would do anything to save the man who ran the local operation, the man who had recruited more than thirty employees. So, if you are right about me, I have nothing to worry about, and if you are wrong, I shouldn't even be here." Paco implied that the real hard cases might be 'working' along the border, which meant that it might take a day to move them south. "Besides," added Paco, "I was offered a job to make sure that the women in the farmhouse were not harmed. It was all set up by phone, and I succeeded."

§

It surprised Francesca when Maria Castillo was waiting at baggage claim for her. Castillo almost lifted Francesca off her feet with a hug. "Our driver, Paco, is waiting with the Cadillac," said Maria. "You must tell me all about this terrible experience on the drive to your apartment."

The two women made small talk as they waited for the suitcase that Francesca had quickly packed. Just being back in the house where she was abducted left her shaking before leaving for the Zihua airport. Hearing the name Paco again, unsettled her. "I just can't seem to get away from men named Paco," she said to Maria, going on to explain more about the abduction. "I didn't know that Paco was such a common name."

"I'm just happy that I was able to help get you and your sister released," replied Maria. She was too busy trying to corral her long hair on a windy day to see the look on Francesca's face. "You were out of that awful place in less than a day. I thought you might fly back last night, but I suppose it was important to make sure your sister was all right."

They stopped at Francesca's apartment just long enough for her to drop her bag, change clothes, and retrieve her pistol from the small safe in her closet.

"I canceled my morning appointments to give us a little time to talk," said Maria. "I'm having a light lunch delivered."

The two women settled into the overstuffed chairs near the window of Maria's office. "We talked about my abduction on the drive," said Francesca. "I need to fill in a couple of more blanks on that." She waited for Maria to turn her attention away from a bowl of soup before continuing. "Mary and I couldn't avoid the authorities after we were released on the side of a dirt road just north of Zihua. We were questioned separately, but I suspect the questions were the same. One question was asked over and over. The captives included the older girlfriend of an American diplomat, the girlfriends of both a Mexican and American naval officer, and two Mexican women, one a simple bodyguard and the other a hotel employee. Who would think those last two were important enough to force their release. I admit, I've been asking myself the same question."

Maria looked away before saying, "maybe you really weren't that important in whatever plan the kidnappers had."

"But the kidnapping happened in our house," said Francesca. "Obviously, they were watching it. If we didn't matter, why take us in the first place?" She waited a few seconds, watching Maria before adding, "and on the drive, you said you were happy that you were somehow involved in getting us released. Maria, the authorities let it slip that they knew who was behind all of this and were tracking him as well as people he seemed close to." Francesca turned to look directly into Maria's eyes.

"While I was in the American military, I was involved in a couple of drug operations where we knew less than the authorities seem to know about the kidnapping. I watched the bad guy's operations collapse like a house of cards. People with little involvement, people who could have helped bring down the operation but didn't, got caught up in it. Some will be in jail for decades. If you are involved in any way, we need to think through how to insulate you, my friend. If I can help in any way, it is the least I can do for what you 'may' have done for my sister and me. If any of the three women left behind are harmed in any way, there will be hell to pay."

Maria finally turned to face Francesca. "All I did was make a phone call."

"You're smarter than that," replied Francesca. "You knew who to call. Your name came up repeatedly in my interrogation. Both men who questioned me were clear that they hoped you weren't involved because of the good you are doing, but you're on their radar."

"Francesca," offered Maria with a smile, "perhaps you should go have a drink or two and then head home for a little rest. That will give me some time to figure out how a couple of phone calls from me worked miracles. I'm planning a new trip, so we should get back together this evening. I'll buy dinner."

Maria rose, signaling that the conversation was ending. "I'll have Paco drive you home, but this evening, it will just be you and me."

Francesca began to laugh. "I wasn't kidding when I said I was a through with men named Paco. I'll walk home. I can use an hour alone." She stood facing Maria, "you are more like the older sister that I never had than an employer. I have a sixth sense about trouble. If there is anything we need to worry about, unless it is blatantly against the law, let me help you get ahead of it. Even if there is nothing, if the authorities think there is, and if there is any connection to criminals, my job protecting you just became more complex and important." Francesca headed to the door.

Minutes later, Maria's phone rang. She recognized the fake name on the display and didn't answer. When the same caller persisted for ten minutes she gave in. "Hao, you never call me directly. Why now?"

"Our friend Luis called me this morning. It appears that Juan has gone off the deep end. He might be behind that kidnapping that's all over the news. If the authorities connect him, there is a risk. He might throw all of us under the bus."

"Hao, I have nothing to do with any of that. But Juan was a loyal soldier for my father. He's not the kind of man that would ever betray us. I think he would fall on his sword first. Besides, I'm just the woman who arranges for trucks to move from A to B and use the profits to do great things for the Mexican people. "

"Maria, perhaps it would be better for all if one of my associates helped Juan fall on that sword," said Hao.

"I can't even be part of thinking like that. But I know he has loyal followers, especially his daughter. They might be more dangerous than the authorities."

"You haven't heard," said Hao, "the navy just announced that his daughter has been rescued while they were preparing to release her for a plane out of the country. I'm betting that plane was arranged by Juan."

"So now there is no reason to hold the hostages," replied Maria. "The authorities will not want to press this, to show how inept they are. Hopefully this is all over for now."

"Maria, the men I work with, my countrymen, are betting their fortunes, even their lives on the plan succeeding. The dozen men under my command along the border, the men who feed intelligence to Juan's soldiers are risking their lives. Juan must control himself. None of us is so important that they can risk the entire plan. All of us are expendable."

"Does that include me?" asked Maria.

"No," answered Hao after several seconds. "The entire plan depends on replacing the current Mexican president with a new one, someone with a vision of a Mexico truly independent of American influence and welcoming of China's support. You must become president of Mexico. Success here will lead to change in China."

Maria sat staring at her phone until Hao asked if she was still there. "My friend, Hao," she finally continued, "I became involved to make Mexico a better place for our people. Assuming I become president, even I will not trade domination by the United States for dominance by China." She paused before adding, "You need to talk to Juan."

"My colleagues and I only want China to take its rightful place as a world leader. Part of that requires that the Americans find themselves in such turmoil that they can't hold us down. Fentanyl is part of that, and cartel soldiers in the states are part of that. When things heat up, the hundreds of Chinese soldiers now in the states will help ratchet up the conflict. Mexico helping us will make us eternally grateful." He didn't wait for an answer. He just terminated the call.

※

An hour later, Thad Walker sat in a hotel room next to the naval compound in Manzanillo, studying a transcript of a call forwarded by Pinky and Ashley. "As you can see, they did discuss the kidnapping. Winston Wang is convinced that the caller has a Chinese accent, even though his English was almost flawless. The caller surprised the Mexican man with news of this Carmen's rescue. He virtually demanded that the kidnapping be resolved immediately and without further publicity. The only name used was Maria. He said that this whole affair was disturbing someone named Maria."

Thad looked over at Sonia, sleeping on the queen-sized bed next to where he sat. "If that is accurate, then what we thought was a simple business arrangement for selling drugs and weapons is something more. What if, instead of just being vendors and money launderers for the Mexican group, the entire operation is being run by the Chinese? What is their end game? Before she flew back to the capital, Francesca was trying to figure out why she and Mary had been released. She works for Maria Castillo."

"We're looking at that now," said Pinky. "So far we see no connection, but maybe we should set up monitoring on her phone."

"For now, we'll follow US rules. If there isn't enough evidence to get a judge to sign off on a wiretap, we'll hold off. But it wouldn't hurt to leave a coded message for Francesca. She might have enough to make a tap okay. She could at least give you a phone number so that you can plan."

"Thad, hold a second," said Pinky. "Winston and Ashley are waving at me." A full minute later she was back. "The caller we are monitoring has just dialed Paco's phone, the one Diego is carrying. We're holding the connection long enough to engage the AI voice on Diego's end." She paused again. "Diego and the caller are now talking. Gotta go. Tracing calls remotely is a bitch."

Thad crossed the room and sat down next to Sonia. He stroked her hair with the back of his hand. "Hey, you," he said, "time to wake up. Diego is talking to that phone we think might be Ayala's. We should get back to the base."

"Give me a second to brush my teeth for the first time in two days," she said. She reached up and squeezed Thad's hand. "Let's wrap this up so that we can spend a little time on the beach."

Ten minutes later Thad and Sonia walked into a small conference room where Diego sat beaming. "Thank God, your Pinky texted me about the earlier conversation," he said. "It prepared me for the call; you know, no names and little detail. I think it was Ayala, but there is no way to be sure. I think I convinced whoever was on the other end that I will be holding this Carmen woman at the ranch along with the other hostages, and I am awaiting his orders. I told him that my guys had stumbled onto her and two guards while they were having lunch and ambushed them in the parking lot. They left the guards alive but out cold and were rushing her to the ranch house. I expect her within a couple of hours."

"That might not be a good thing," said Sonia. "Once this Carmen meets the hostages, they become big liabilities."

Diego smiled even broader. "Yeah, that's what the caller said. It sounded like he doesn't dare kill them, but he doesn't want them and Carmen together. I told him that we would hold Carmen in the smaller house and that seemed to satisfy him."

"You're good," offered Thad.

A moment later, Chad and Olga joined them. "The troops in LA have been busy," said Chad. They traced the cell phone to a tower in Puerto Peñasco, right up along the border. It took a few minutes for them to plot out the maximum range from the tower. I think the call came from that same warehouse we watched from the drone, the one where the Chinese attack drone is stored."

"While Chad was talking to them," said Olga, "Winston called me to tell me that a light jet just about to land in Acapulco diverted, and that the new course would take it straight to Puerto Peñasco. It came from the same air service in Mexico City that we think belongs to this Ayala guy. If we're right, he's wasting no time. Winston will monitor flight tracking and keep us posted. Odds are that he's headed down here."

"That's what I heard as well," said Diego. "Ayala, or whoever I was talking to, told me that Carmen would be 'picked up' sometime tonight and would be out of the country tomorrow. I was to release the hostages when she crossed the southern border."

"I can pull five men and get them on the way up Highway 134 within an hour," said Diego.

"Get them started," said Chad, "but have them find some

place to hide their vehicle near where the dirt road leaves the highway. We want them in position to box in the bad guys if they get past us at the ranch."

"What if this is all a ruse?" offered Olga. "What if they change the plan?"

"Make sure your troops have a sat phone so we can stay in touch," said Walker. He turned to Diego. "How many more men can you get for a helicopter trip to the ranch?"

"Unless we want to include people from here in Manzanillo, all I have are the three already at the ranch, plus the five we just discussed."

"We don't have time to vet new people. So, it will be those three, plus you, me, and Chad," said Thad. "If they really do come with an army, we're going to be outmanned."

"You aren't leaving Olga and I behind," said Sonia. "Plus, we have another advantage. When they kidnapped us, they took a small arsenal with them. They carried at least a dozen rockets into the house where they slept. We have real firepower."

"Perhaps we should wait where they are going to land the jet," said Olga. "We could catch them just leaving the plane."

"That's good," said Thad, "but we don't know where they'll land. It sounds risky to land in at the big airports in Puerto Cárdenas, Manzanillo, or Zihua. Wherever they land, they'll be meeting more of their own shooters. Besides, just getting out of a plane is not illegal."

Diego stood and walked over to a map of southern Mexico on the conference room wall. It displayed the coastline out to three hundred miles and inland just over a hundred miles. "There's a small airport, Santa Barbara Regional in Altamirano an hour up Highway 134 from the dirt road. It's big enough to handle a small jet. There is no scheduled service or a control tower, usually nobody there at all. That's where I would land if it were me. You could stage fifty shooters there without attracting much attention."

"They won't take fifty shooters," said Sonia. "They think this is just a quick pick up from friendly faces. Cartel leaders don't like to be known directly by too many of their own men. They won't be bringing many men south with them. Remember, I'm a pilot with a small jet. They won't want to stop to refuel after they rescue Carmen, so they will have the inside of that jet loaded with jugs of jet fuel. While they pick her up, the pilots will be refueling. From the airstrip, they'll take a couple of vehicles; five or six bodyguards, and another vehicle to get the men already there and the hostages out after Carmen is out of the country."

"So, do we focus on this small airport?" asked Olga.

"No," said Chad. "We might be wrong about where they're heading. And like Thad said earlier, just getting off from a plane isn't illegal."

"So, we arrange a welcome for them at the ranch," said Thad. "We'll need sat phone communications as well. Winston is going to put in a long night monitoring Mexican airspace. We will want to know where and when they land." He walked over to the map Diego was studying. "If they land in Altamirano, we will have two hours to prepare."

CHAPTER 42

July 18, Sierra Madre del Sur, Mexico

"My guys watching the highway report three vehicles turning onto the dirt road. Two Chevy Suburbans and a van," said Diego.

"Damn," replied Thad. "Hand me the sat phone." It took several minutes to reach Winston in LA.

"Boss," said Winston, "I was about to call you. That light jet that we are tracking left Puerto Peñasco an hour ago. It's probably an hour north of you. The pilot turned off his squawk code within minutes of getting airborne. I can't track him, but his initial course was southeast."

Thad leaned against the doorway of the farmhouse, pondering. "Did any other aircraft depart Puerto Peñasco recently?"

"Yeah," replied Winston. "Another light jet left within fifteen minutes of the arrival of the Acapulco plane." He paused for several seconds. "I didn't think it was important."

Thad hung up and handed the phone back to Diego. "Have your guys on the highway mount up and follow those three vehicles. Tell them to stay well behind and watch out for an ambush." Thad turned to the rest of the team. "They used a second plane. The bad guys are already on the dirt road. We've got thirty minutes to be ready. The first plane didn't need to carry extra fuel, so they might have four or five shooters from the north as well as at least three locals who are driving."

"Looks like about eight against eight," said Olga. "We have a strong defensive position."

Diego looked over at her, a scowl on his face. "We have the advantage if they come through the front door. But if they spread out and come in through the forest…"

"You're the infantry officer here," said Chad. "What's your plan?"

"I think we should try to trap them between us and my guys coming in behind them. We need to throw up a roadblock this side of the hairpin turn a hundred meters from the parking area. It's in part of the old pasture with some open areas on the side but trees along the road. We'll challenge them to stop." Diego sighed. "That should catch them off guard. Maybe we won't have to fire a shot."

"What do we use for a barricade?" asked Chad.

"None of the old trucks in front of this building run," translated Diego after questioning one of his marines. "But the pickup my guys drove in will work."

"You set it up," said Thad. "If they only take a half hour from the highway, we'll still have a little light left. If it takes longer, it'll be dark."

Fifteen minutes later the four Americans stood behind a green pickup which had been loaded with firewood as a shield. The marines had stacked everything solid they could find from the old shops in front of the truck. Diego and a marine were in the pasture to the left and the other two marines to the right.

They could hear the vehicles splashing though the creek at the bottom of the hill.

The lights of the first Suburban flashed through the trees and then directly on the barricade. The brake lights from the first vehicle stopped the second only yards behind.

Sonia walked to the side of the pickup just as the front door of the first Suburban began to open. "Stop, throw out your weapons. You are surrounded!"

The speed of doors opening in the Suburban barely gave her time to dive behind the pickup before the first burst of automatic rifle fire slammed into the barricade. That was a mistake. Both Chad and Olga unleashed Chinese made rockets at the truck, which exploded.

To the right and left, Mexican marines who had been dreaming about revenge for weeks raked the second Suburban with rifle fire. Doors opened on both sides and men carrying assault rifles stumbled out just far enough to lose the protection of the doors. Four men collapsed; their bodies ripped by dozens of bullets.

Downhill, they heard the van gunning its engine and then splashing back through the stream. They could hear it shifting gears repeatedly as it tried to turn around.

Diego stood and keyed the military radio on his belt and snapped an order. Moments later they saw headlights snap on and shine across the small gorge and then heard three or four shots. The people behind the pickup carefully walked toward the smoking wreckage of the first vehicle just as Diego reached it. All four tires of the Suburban were still inflated, but above them was a mass of shredded metal, glass and men.

"I told my guys following not to shoot up the van. We may need it to get out of here," he said. Moments later a rushed message crackled from the radio. "They have two men in custody and the van. I told them to come on up here."

While three of Diego's marines pulled on night vision goggles in the failing light and took up positions on either side of the road, Diego and the four Americans walked carefully up to the second Suburban. The driver was slumped over the steering wheel and two men lay on each side; their bodies soaked in blood. Diego and Chad walked to the open back door and pointed their rifles inside.

The dome light revealed one more person, an elderly man clutching his stomach, fighting to keep his intestines from spilling out from where a bullet had sliced across him. The man looked up at Diego and scowled. "Dónde está mi hija?" he managed. When Diego didn't answer, he turned toward Chad. "I recognize you. This is not your fight." The man took several deep breaths, exhaling raggedly. "Where is my daughter?"

"Senior Ayala, she is in Acapulco and safe in prison. I will tell her you died loving her."

Diego and Chad watched as a smile somehow crossed Ayala's face before it went blank. He then slumped forward.

"Damn," said Thad as he shined a flashlight into the back of the vehicle. "We really needed him alive. Even if he never talked, we could have let it slip that he was singing like a canary. That might have gotten the others at the top of this enterprise to panic or better yet, offer to help us finish cleaning this up for some leniency."

Sonia and Olga worked their way around from where the rockets had destroyed the first Suburban and joined the men. "As of right now, we are the only people on earth who know Ayala is dead. We need to keep it that way."

Thad looked up at Sonia who still carried a Glock in her right hand. "I don't know if you surprise me my dear but considering what just happened and how this could have gone all wrong, you're way ahead of the rest of us."

"Thad, I chased drug lords in the US and Mexico for decades and this is the first one I've ever seen actually taken down. I feel terrible about him and his family, but for me, this feels really good."

Diego looked over at her and smiled. "For my men and me too." Then he turned to Thad Walker. "Where is your weapon?"

"We should have warned you," said Chad. "Thad Walker could never point a weapon at anyone and pull the trigger. Maybe someday he will tell you why, but I've known him for years and have only heard rumors."

"Let's get this mess off the road," said Sonia. "We can leave the bodies in the small house for now while we figure out how to leverage this."

The group started dismantling the materials in front of the pickup. They were lucky. Only a handful of bullets made it to the truck. Diego jumped into the front seat and turned the key as Thad raised the hood and shined his flashlight onto the engine. The truck started instantly and there were no obvious leaks. Diego drove it off the road and then backed it toward the smoking wreckage of the first Suburban, its cab ripped open, and the doors twisted toward the roadway.

A marine jumped into the back of the truck, tossing firewood to the sides until he reached the heavy toolbox behind the cab. Moments later he jumped down and hooked a tow strap to the wreck and then to the truck and signaled for Diego to pull the derelict out of the way. Behind that wreck, someone got the second Suburban running and drove it into the overgrown pasture.

Diego dropped from the cab and began directing his men to load the bodies into the bed of the truck. One of his men motioned for him. The man pointed down at a body from the first vehicle. Behind him, the four Americans were engaged in a boisterous conversation. Finally, Chad walked over and tapped Diego on the shoulder.

"Before you say anything," responded Diego, look at that body. That man does not look Mexican to me. We have a small community of Chinese expats living in Mexico, and my guess is that he's one of them. We searched the bodies, and none of them have any ID."

Chad stared down at the body. The man was of Asian descent, but maybe that meant nothing. "Sonia's idea is to let the press know that we have Ayala in custody and imply that in return for leniency for his daughter, he has become helpful."

Diego turned and smiled, "makes sense to me. You guys have a plan for..." he froze, and his smile faded. "Keeping Ayala's demise, a secret will be critical. What are the pilots of those two jets sitting only an hour from here going to say? Maybe we should grab them as well. What will they say when neither he nor his daughter show up?"

Chad paused for a second before answering, "they will probably say exactly what we want them to say, that Ayala went to pick up his daughter and never came back. We will announce that since the pilots really hadn't done anything illegal, we decided to let them leave."

"You know that there is probably a satchel full of cash on one of those planes," said Sonia. "Ayala wouldn't send his daughter out of the country without enough money to pay off the authorities wherever she was headed."

"Sounds like an opportunity for the Mexican AG's office to score some points," said Thad. "We'll use the sat phone to call Gina Santos and tell her we have Ayala, and tip her that She needs to meet the two planes wherever they land and retrieve what we expect is a pile of cash."

"Won't Gina be a little pissed if we mislead her about Ayala?" asked Chad.

"Who knows when a wounded man might die," said Thad.

"We'll make it up to Gina when we can wrap up the whole gang. Hell, this is a Mexican op so the Mexican Team Walker colleagues will get all the credit."

"Then let's do this right," said Sonia. She turned to Diego. "I've got a package of wet wipes in my bag in the ranch house. Let's clean up the blood on Ayala's face and get a picture of you talking to him in the back of the Suburban. We will do a close-up photo from an angle that hides his eyes. We'll send it to Gina when we get back to Zihua along with ideas for a press release. The press statement will look stronger if we have a picture of Ayala with Diego."

"I'll have the helicopter pick Sonia up and then drop her on the beach in front of your hotel. We'll make a big deal of her release," said Diego.

Thad nodded. "We'll give the Marines a pile of thanks for rescuing us," said Sonia. "It will look better to the press if you can arrange obvious security at the hotel. When you are comfortable with the security here, you and some of your men should come back to town. I suspect that you will get a hero's welcome. It will give us another chance to talk about how the navy has moved Ayala to an undisclosed location to protect him."

It took several minutes to clean Ayala up for the cell phone picture. When finished they slid his body out of the Suburban and carried it to the pickup.

"Just a second," said Olga as she jogged up to the truck. She rummaged through Ayala's pockets, finally handing his cell phone to Sonia. "That Paco's phone turned out to be gold. This one must be platinum. While we wait for the helicopter, we can scroll through it and jot down phone numbers. Maybe there are messages."

Sonia began tapping on the phone. "It's locked," she said.

"That's why getting it now is important," said Olga. "I'll

bet he uses fingerprint security, and we have all ten fingers right here." The phone opened, but only the directory. Messages were encrypted.

※

Thad, Sonia, Chad and Olga sat on the deck of the suite at the top of their hotel. On the beach below were two local police officers, and in the hotel lobby two federal officers sat monitoring everyone coming and going. Less than an hour before, the navy helicopter had deposited the four on the beach, creating quite a stir.

Two detectives from the federales and two officers from the local police had been waiting. The group had been given a few minutes to make phone calls before they were ushered into the empty restaurant at the bottom of the stairs. Their interrogation lasted only ten minutes, since the kidnappers had either been captured or killed and all the women were safe. One of the local officers had pressed for more information on the ringleader. He'd left with a scowl on his face and a suggestion that he contact naval intelligence for more information.

With the police visit over, the four Americans and Elena had been swarmed by more than thirty reporters and camera men, some from as far away as Los Angeles. The hotel had cleared the pavilion next to the pool for the improvised press conference. As the reporters and camera men prepared, the hotel set up a small bar and kept champagne flowing throughout the conference. The five chose Sonia as their spokesperson since she could answer questions in both English and Spanish.

"I don't think any of the marines involved in the rescue were hurt," she said. "But several of the kidnappers and a handful of guards for the man she believed responsible had been killed. The Ayala guy had been brave but had surrendered inside a vehicle when four rifles were pointed at him. There was no place to go," she added. "He'd inquired about his daughter and was relieved to learn that she had been recaptured and was back in prison. But she is now an accessory to kidnapping and is facing decades in prison," added Sonia.

"Where is this Ayala guy now?" asked an American reporter.

"He's being held by the navy in a secure location," said Sonia. "He's agreed to cooperate in return for leniency for his daughter. We know there are several other leaders of this gang, and the authorities suspect that he won't live very long if he isn't hidden."

A request from Thad to the hotel manager ended the conference. But not before the mayor had offered, "We here in Zihua take the safety of our visitors very seriously. I credit the navy for their quick response. As thanks for the safe return of our guests, the restaurants and bars of the city are making the first drink free for every American visitor for the rest of the evening."

Elena excused herself at the end of the press conference, after answering a handful of questions about her hero boyfriend. Carefully coached by Sonia during the helicopter ride, she maintained her calm, but the ordeal had taken a toll. She would spend the night in the home she shared with Diego, guarded by two marines and two local policemen, who had arrived uncharacteristically carrying handguns.

"God, I hate publicity," said Walker as he popped the cork from another bottle of champagne and began filling glasses. He turned to Sonia and smiled. "Your explanation that I had been invited to observe the rescue so that I could report to friends in Washington DC seems a little flimsy. I hope it holds up. There are now pictures of all of us."

Olga glanced at her watch. "One more glass of bubbly and then we better get on the phone. The video feed from that press conference will be all over the world by now."

"What is Diego doing with Ayala's cell phone?" asked Olga. "It opened, but with encryption, there has to be more there."

"The helicopter pilots took it to Manzanillo. Ramón is flying into Manzanillo tonight and will hand carry it to LA," said Chad. "Pinky, Winston, and Ashley will meet him and set up surveillance on the numbers that seem critical. It will take longer to read the messages. It helps that he's old school and kept his directory by name. The one name that popped out to me is a number for a Maria. There was also a number for someone named Hao. That may be their Chinese contact from that transcript that Pinky sent down."

"Chad, it's probably time for you to reach out to your Chinese contact, Ma again. Give him a complete rundown on the weapons that have been seized and ask him if the name Hao rings a bell. Our speculation that the whole show might be run by the Chinese, is in direct conflict with their government's pronouncements."

"While he makes that call," said Olga, "Sonia and I will call Francesca."

"And I will call both David Lopez and Gina Santos," said Thad.

"Let's make sure that we have our story straight for those last two calls," said Chad. "For now, even though they're part of the team, all they need to know about Ayala is that we have him in custody and that he's given us enough to start looking for a Hao and a Maria. There were several calls to an L.C., but we don't have a name."

"Let's get back together in an hour," offered Sonia. "I suggest we have dinner downstairs tonight, just to show off the security surrounding us."

Maria drove herself to Francesca's apartment and then the two headed to the Italian restaurant where she, Hao, Luis and Juan usually met. The owner met them at the back door and ushered them into the same small dining room in the back before leaving with an order for a bottle of cream tequila, a drink usually only served during the holiday season.

"Our donations have increased dramatically after word got out that one of my most valued colleagues was part of the kidnapping," said Maria. "That will help fund our next project. I'm planning a trip to Oaxaca. That's where a group of students disappeared several years ago. The president believes that they died by order of a cartel but that the triggermen were local police. I want to fund a reward for solid proof of what happened to those kids. The government is dragging their feet on this case."

"Two things come to mind, Maria. "First, your communications with the president are the kind of public relations that might offset any negatives coming from what we discussed this afternoon. Second, Oaxaca is the most dangerous place we have traveled. We need to plan this carefully."

The restaurant owner tapped on the door and then carried an almost frozen bottle of cream tequila to their table along with two small snifters. He left quickly after Maria ordered for both of them.

"Have you ever tried this?" Maria asked. "It's more a desert than a liquor, and normally only for special occasions, like Christmas. Getting you and your sister released is a special occasion."

Before Francesca could answer, her phone rang. "I'm just sitting down to dinner with Maria Castillo," answered Francesca, recognizing Sonia's phone number. "Where are you calling from, and are you free?"

She touched mute on her phone before looking up at Maria.

"It is Sonia Ramirez, one of the women I was kidnapped with." She watched the color drain from Maria's face before going back to her call.

The next five minutes were all, 'that's great, tell me more, who was involved,' before Francesca terminated the call. "They are all safe," said Francesca. "The marines figured out where they were being held and raided the place. After my friends were freed, but before they could be transported, a group of men drove right up to where the marines were securing the kidnappers. There was a firefight, and a bunch of the bad guys were killed. Evidently the leader, some guy by the name of Ayala was captured. He was trying to get his daughter released from custody in Acapulco. Sonia says that since they took custody of this Ayala guy, they have secured several names for further investigation. She's just happy to be back in Zihua with her friends and on her way to dinner."

"What names?" asked Maria, sipping her drink.

"Sonia isn't part of the investigation, just a woman in the wrong place at the wrong time," answered Francesca. "But she remembered the names Maria and an odd name, Hao or something like that. Evidently there was a quick press conference with more information, but my friend just wants a quiet dinner and then some time at the pool. She's still so wound up that it will be a while before she can sleep."

The rest of dinner was very quiet. The conversation about Oaxaca was replaced by more conversation about Francesca's kidnapping. "Francesca my friend," offered Maria after an hour, "let's pick this up tomorrow morning. But before I take you home, I need to tell you that I know a man by the name of Ayala. It is not a common last name. I have nothing to do with anything like kidnapping or shootouts with the authorities. You mentioned getting ahead of a problem earlier today. I need to see if the Ayala I know is the same Ayala who kidnapped you and your friends."

"I told you that both me and my sister owe you one, Maria. Maybe this is nothing, but if it is, let me help."

※

Ma answered every call on the phone ringing in the drawer next to his bed. Usually, the calls were from his boss, General Ling, or another of the human intelligence officers of Peoples Liberation Army, PLA-2. The caller ID for this call was blocked, but then most call on this phone were blocked. He'd talked to Chad Gritt only a week or two before, so he was surprised by his voice.

"Our investigation of the weapons and the manufacture of that submarine is still ongoing," said Ma after Chad identified himself. "I don't have much more on any of that yet."

"Well, I have a little more for you," said Chad. "I was just involved in a shootout with some cartel people in Mexico. We found an additional cache of weapons. I will text you some serial numbers, but the interesting thing is that they appear to have inventory stickers from the Chinese army on the carrying cases. We also picked up one of the heads of the group running fentanyl from Mexico to the states. We got a name from him, Hao. My people tell me that is a common first name in China, but you may be able to cross reference the name to known intelligence officers or even businesspeople known to be involved in Mexico."

"The inventory numbers should be a good lead," said Ma. "The name, maybe. My government's official position has not changed. We are trying to ratchet down tensions with the US. Your administration has committed to the same. I know nothing more now, Chad."

"If I am right about this group in Mexico, then the actions

of some Chinese citizens are not consistent with that official position. One of the men killed in the shootout appears to be Chinese. This Mexican group has tons of money and a lot of it is flowing to your country," said Chad. "There are indications that the whole operation may be Chinese controlled."

"I will take what you send me to General Ling," answered Ma, "I know he is concerned."

There was a long pause before Ma added, "not all of the people in positions of authority in my country agree with the new official policies."

"And, Ma, in your line of work, you know that sometimes the official policy and the operating policy of a government are not the same," said Chad. "It may surprise some in your country, but America's reassessment of the relationship between our two nations is still open to review. What we've found here in Mexico is not good for a positive relationship. As we dig deeper, that might be an understatement."

"Both of us are simple public servants," said Ma. "You do no good trying to scare me."

"I am not trying to scare anyone. I am just stating the facts as I see them." Chad waited a minute and when Ma offered nothing more, he hung up.

CHAPTER 43

July 20, Mexico City, Mexico

Maria tried to shake off her feeling of dread. She buried herself in work for a day but found she couldn't concentrate. Her frantic call to Luis Cardenas the next morning triggered a call to Hao. "Maybe you were right after all," said Luis. "By now I'm sure you've seen the news. The women Juan kidnapped were recovered by the Marines. Several of Juans men were killed in a shootout. If the reports can be trusted, Juan is in custody and is cooperating with the government."

"I warned you," said Hao. "His daughter is his Achilles' heel. Most of what you have heard, I have confirmed. I had one of my own men travel from Puerto Peñasco with Juan when I learned what he was doing. I wanted a trusted voice to confirm that all was well."

"What did your man tell you?" asked Luis. "Or was he there to make sure that Juan didn't survive if everything went to hell?"

"I haven't heard from him. I assume that he was one of those killed in the shootout."

"So, what do we do next?" asked Luis.

"You and I and Maria are all fairly insulated from Juan. Anything he says will be just the words of a kidnapper. His second in command in the north can take over logistics, but he's not a leader like Juan. What Juan does for our mission is critical. For now, both my intelligence people and Juan's logistical people will report to me."

"Remember my warning," replied Luis. "Juan's people are very loyal to him. Monitor their response to his capture carefully. If he dies, we may have to replace all of them."

"We will discuss it more," said Hao, "perhaps we can buy their loyalty. But the most critical piece for my group is the change in Mexican leadership. We must keep Maria on board."

"She's rattled. Juan's kidnapping actions hit close to home for her. Still, her embrace of her philanthropic role has become her identity. We just need to keep pumping money into her projects. When the public demands she step up, she will."

"We may have to increase our efforts to see regime change," said Hao. My people are working on a new disinformation campaign. Having Maria in office would be a nice insurance policy for all of us. I think it would be best if I went up to the border myself to ensure that shipping schedules are maintained. My men providing intelligence on what other cartels are doing and on the American efforts to protect the border are all ex-military. If this starts to spin out of control, we can count on their help."

Hao was on his computer and then turned his attention back to Luis. "Could you track down that Paco guy who coordinates shipment for Juan? Promote him, but make sure he understands that the choice is lead or gold. We need to keep our submarines on schedule. I just asked one of my Chinese partners when the replacement sub would be available. I expect to have an answer in a day or two."

"I'm going down to Zihua tomorrow. I hope that Paco wasn't among those killed in the shootout," said Luis. "If not, I'll find him."

⚜

The Los Angeles offices of Team Walker were deathly silent as the translation program finished running a transcript of an intercepted conversation between two phone numbers taken from Ayala's phone. From the first few words the members of Team Walker understood the importance of the message. The caller's phone had been traced to a cell tower in Mexico City. The other phone's signal had bounced across two cell towers near Manzanillo.

The team now knew the general location of two more of the people running what they now called the 'pharmacy.' Pinky had come up with that name only a day before as they set up remote monitoring of five phone numbers, four of which had a Mexican country code, and the fifth was a number out of China. Winston dialed that one, just to see who answered. The unanswered call went to a voicemail that simply commanded "call back."

Winston then contacted CIA headquarters looking for help connecting the number to a person. The agency maintained phone directories hacked from telecom companies all over the world. Turns out it was registered to a grocery store clerk who had died a year before. The number included a prefix for Shandong Province which didn't help in a province with over one hundred million people.

As the final translation of the call appeared on their computer screens, the silence turned to cheers. "While at the DEA I never saw a more damning translation," said Ashley.

"Agreed," said Pinky. "Let's get this to Walker and Gritt right away."

"I just hope that their Mexican allies can capitalize on this," offered Winston. "The way things were in Mexico until recently, there was little interest in taking down the bad guys."

"But this statement specifically targets the president of Mexico," said Ashley.

∽

Ramón's private jet was already on its way back to Mexico City when the pilots were diverted to Zihua. The only thing they were told was that they could expect to be on the ground only long enough to add fuel and for a new passenger to come aboard. Even Ramón was surprised when two people, Thad Walker and Sonia Ramirez were escorted to the waiting plane by two marines.

Two hours later, Ramón, Thad and Sonia sat around a small conference table in the president's office. David Lopez watched his boss's face as she first read the English version of the intercepted call and then the Spanish version. He watched her initial fury slowly turn to sadness.

"This must refer to Maria Castillo. I consider her a hero of the nation and a personal friend."

"Madam President," said Thad, "there is nothing in this message that specifically accuses Maria of being part of a plot to push you out of office. All that it says is that some people we don't like would like to see her in your chair."

"But we have a plan to figure out her involvement," said David Lopez. "We'd like for you to call her directly and ask her to meet with you this afternoon. Suggest that she bring her own security along because there are rumors that she might be in danger."

The president picked up her phone and directed her assistant to find Maria. "I don't understand why bringing Francesca is important."

"If Maria knows anything, she also knows that people in the drug business will do anything to stamp out risk. We aren't lying when we say she is at risk," said Ramón. "What Maria doesn't know is that Francesca has been working with us all along. She was the one who identified where the kidnappers had taken the women. Francesca called Thad yesterday to tell him that Maria was shaken when she heard Ayala's name."

The president's phone rang. "Maria, my dear, I have just been briefed on a report that you may be on a hit list. I want to make sure that you are fully briefed along with your security people. If necessary, the government can offer more security, but my bet is that this is much ado about nothing. Still, if you can come by my office in the next couple of hours, it makes sense to be a little overly cautious."

The call went on for a few more minutes before she hung up. "Maria is on her way. Who else should be involved in this?"

"Madam President," started David, "you tasked me with figuring out who was behind the flow of Chinese arms into our country. Three of the people from the group I recruited are here now. That is all you need until we know more."

The president smiled. "This has interrupted my lunch, Are any of the rest of you hungry? We have an hour or so, and I know that until after we talk to Maria, I won't get any work done."

The power of walking into the president's office anywhere in the world influences even powerful people. Maria and Francesca being ushered through the executive suites and then into the large conference room where the president waited with five other people was a great example of that. "Please sit," said the president. "Allow me to introduce the others here. Each of them has been working on a project at my request for months. That project has expanded to include you and Francesca here."

Listening to the names, Maria slid into a chair next to the

president with Francesca sitting next to Sonia. "Before we start our discussion, Mr. Walker here has a transcript that he would like to share with you and Francesca."

Thad handed the transcript to each of the women, then he sat down. It was a full five minutes later, when both looked over at him. Thad turned to Francesca, ignoring Maria.

"Francesca," he said, "it's nice to see you again. "This transcript came from an intercept of phone numbers that our colleagues Olga and Sonia here took from this Ayala fellow. Their rescue is largely because of your help finding the ranch house where you and your sister were held. As you can see, the Mexican marines' quick response not only led to the release of the other hostages, but to a door that lays bare the workings of the cartel we've been tracking."

Turning to Maria, Thad continued, "before you is an exact transcript of a call from early today. With the help of authorities on both sides of the border, we were tracking two phone numbers, one from this Hao guy, and the other from someone that Ayala only refers to as LC. We are told that you know them both. We know that they are kingpins in fentanyl shipments to the US and are responsible for killing Mexican citizens with weapons supplied by Hao. The transcript makes clear that this is not only a commercial enterprise, but one with the goal of seeing President Martinez removed from office and you as her replacement. Who is this L.C.?"

Maria turned her ashen face toward Francesca. "Are you a spy for these people?"

"No, I am exactly what I said I was when we first met. I am your first line of security, and with what we know now, more important to you than ever. Your never disclosed your connection with these thugs in our conversations. But you tacitly told me that you might be in trouble just a day or two ago. We discussed how to keep this from ruining everything, and that begins with you answering Mr. Walker's question."

"I am not part of any cartel," said Maria. "I have nothing to do with any violence."

The room remained silent for several minutes before she continued. "L.C. is Luis Cardenas he owns pharmaceutical plants here in Mexico. He is a good customer of mine."

"And this Hao guy?" asked Sonia.

"He's a businessman from China. He has helped many Chinese organizations make investments in Mexico. Many of those are good customers of Castillo Transportation."

"Did you know that they were in the drug trade?"

Maria looked straight at the president for several seconds before responding. "I suspected it. Juan Ayala once worked for my father who I'm sure you know was in the business. He introduced me to them. But my company does only what we are chartered to do, move freight."

"Whose idea was it for you to rapidly expand the freight company and use the profits to build the Castillo Foundation?" asked Thad.

Maria leaned back in her chair. "It was mine, but Hao and Luis thought it was a great idea and have helped financially. Hao has been especially helpful. From the beginning, he has referred to me as the Mexican Robin Hood."

"Maria," said David Lopez, "are you part of a plot to see President Martinez out of office? Have you been part of the disinformation campaign that has disparaged her?"

"Juan Ayala was the first person that I talked to when this all started. He said that Mexico would be better off without close ties, especially legal ties, to the US. He said that China was interested in becoming Mexico's closest ally and with what happened to my family after Mexico and the US teamed up to destroy my father, that seemed reasonable. I wasn't part of a plot but was asked to prepare myself should the country need a new president."

She turned to Lupita. "As I began to work with you and saw how similar our visions for the country were, that thought faded. I love what I am doing and would rather be Madam Robin Hood than hold any office. You don't have to believe me, but that is the truth."

"Maria," said Francesca, "I believe you, but you have been running with a pack of wolves. Some maybe even foreign spies. That group is about to be dismantled. It is going to be very dangerous and even though you have pulled away lately, you were part of the pack. The only chance you have of surviving this is for the pack to all be imprisoned or killed off."

Thad leaned forward so close to Maria's face that she pulled away. "There isn't a person on the North American Continent who can intervene to crush the Chinese arm of this group. The Chinese criminals usually just make opponents disappear. But if we dismantle this group correctly and publicly, we might be able to force the Chinese government to clean up their own mess. We are already talking to them."

"Do you believe that my government is about to destroy the drug ring that has been your benefactor?" asked the president.

Maria shook her head yes. "I know that the whole effort includes only a handful of leaders. You already know who most of them are."

"I do not want you destroyed along with them. You probably know enough to help make this quick and painful only for the leadership. Your future is in your hands."

"Juan is the key person. He knows everything."

"And beyond Juan, who has the best understanding of how this whole thing is run?" asked Ramón.

"That would be Luis. I would say Hao Sun, but he is very difficult to pin down on anything," answered Maria.

Thad made a big show of using his cell phone. "Chad, call your friend Ma Mingze and tell him we have a last name. The Chinese contact here is Hao Sun." Thad hung up.

"Now Maria, we are going to discuss how to help your friend Luis Cardenas come over from the dark side," said Thad.

"What about Juan?" she asked.

"This will be new news to everyone in this room except for Sonia here and myself," said Thad. "He was wounded in the shootout. But before he died, he asked about his daughter. He was thinking of her. When this is all done, you should probably be the one to tell her."

"Now, let's discuss Cardenas," said Ramón.

"I tried his office before we drove over here," said Maria, "He's driving to Zihua. He hates planes."

∞

"What are you doing here?" asked Luis as his bodyguard ushered Maria and Francesca into his luxurious townhome overlooking Zihuatanejo Bay.

"We need to talk, just the two of us," Maria replied. "Perhaps over a glass of wine out on your deck." She turned to Francesca and the other bodyguard and smiled. "You two will excuse us for a while." She headed to the open glass doors overlooking the bay.

"Alright, Maria," replied Luis, following her. "But in the next hour, I need to complete a task that you do not need to know about." He called to his maid and asked for wine and two glasses.

He walked to the railing and stared out toward the lighthouse at the entrance to the bay, waiting for the wine to arrive before he seated himself next to Maria. "Now what is so important that you would fly over here just to talk?"

"Before we talk, I have something for you to read," she answered, handing Luis the intercepted transcript. She watched the color drain from his face."

"Outside this building there are more than ten marines and their officer right now," she said. "With them are representatives of the attorney general's office. I was challenged with this document in President Martinez's office earlier today. We are both about to be arrested, and charged not only with drug offenses, but also in the murder of security people, accessories to kidnapping, and worse, with insurrection."

"Maria, how did the authorities obtain this? Is it even real?" he asked.

"Luis, you know it's real. You were part of this conversation that implicates all of us. As to how it was obtained, I have no clue."

"The telecom authorities everywhere we operate are paid handsomely to refuse to tap our phones without first notifying us. This must have been obtained illegally. We have the best attorneys in Mexico on retainer," said Luis.

"Did I forget to mention that along with the others outside, there are American authorities and in their possession an extradition document signed by the president, one that they can execute tonight?" Maria took a deep breath. "I have done nothing illegal, but I am tied to you. My only role was to become famous as the Mexican Robin Hood. I suspect that I might get a short sentence in an American VIP prison. But tomorrow morning the authorities will be raiding your companies and documenting manufacture of fentanyl that is being shipped across the border. You will probably never get out of an American prison, but if you do, you will be extradited back here without the kind of money that bigshot attorneys would demand to help you."

Luis began to relax. "Yet you are allowed to come into my

home, along with your bodyguard by these same authorities. Why are you really here?"

"The president has asked me to make clear to you that she would prefer to finish this affair by demonstrating to the Americans that she is willing to crack down on the pills crossing the border and killing Americans. She would prefer to gather up what Juan calls his Mexican soldiers and reward them for giving up this life. But what she really wants is to nail down the Chinese connection committed to her demise and then confront that government for interfering in our government."

Luis looked out to the head of the bay where a light blinked three times. Maria, seeing the same thing, reached across the table and grasped Luis' hand. "You do not need to worry about the submarine tonight, my friend. Within a few minutes, it will either be under the command of the Mexican navy or at the bottom of the sea."

Luis turned to stare at her.

"That was going to happen tonight even before the phone tap. I was briefed on the government airplane that flew me from the capital," said Maria. "Killing those marines just reinforced their commitment to stopping that submarine. They got help tracking it from the Americans."

Luis poured a full glass of wine and drank it before pouring another glass for himself and one for Maria. "So, they have asked you to come here and make a deal with me?"

"No, that may be possible, but it will depend on what more you have to offer and how willing you are to help dismantle what you, Juan and Hao have built. If that is of interest to you, there are four people waiting downstairs who can coordinate a deal."

"Why not just have my guard seize you and hold you hostage until I can arrange to get out of the country?" asked Luis, smiling as if he didn't really mean what he was saying.

"Well, for one reason, by now, I'm sure that Francesca has disarmed your man and pushed him out the door to where the marines are waiting."

Luis casually looked back to the living room where Francesca sat alone, waving at him.

"I'll have the maid bring another bottle of wine and three more glasses," said Luis. "Call the people waiting downstairs."

"I'd be really nice to your new maid," replied Francesca, "when the authorities picked up your housekeeper this morning, she was one of the federal detectives that took her into custody."

Maria pulled out her phone and called. Before the wine arrived, there was a knock at the door and Francesca ushered Gina Santos from the AG's office and David Lopez from the president's office into the apartment. A moment later she opened the door again for Chad who strode across the room before announcing, Lieutenant Diego Cervantes should be arriving soon."

The three newcomers extended their hand to Luis before seating themselves. "We do not need to make this uncomfortable," said Gina. They were interrupted by the sound of a helicopter looping over the bay before landing on the darkened beach below the building.

"That would be Diego," she added.

They waited for Diego to make it up the elevator. "My apologies, but I have come straight from the ranch and have not had the opportunity to shower or shave for several days," said Diego, taking the last chair at the table.

Gina looked at Luis. "Tell us about this Hao Sun character, how he is involved, and where he is. Make sure that you include all the goodies that would lead me to go easy on you."

"Two things," said Luis. "First, Maria here was not involved in the drug business in any way. We made sure she got lucrative freight contracts, but her only role was to be prepared to step in when Hao maneuvered the current president out of office. Second, there is literally billions of dollars in Chinese owned banks that could be used to continue Maria's work to make Mexico a better place."

Gina picked up her wine glass and held it out over the table, where everyone but Diego, who was in uniform, held up a glass. "Now that is a very good start to this discussion."

"Before we get into the nitty gritty part of the discussion," said Chad, "where is Hao right now?"

"I believe he is at the intelligence office up near the border," replied Luis.

"Would that be the same warehouse building an hour out of Puerto Peñasco, the one where the Chinese attack drone is hidden?" asked Chad.

"As I said," offered Maria, "the wiretap is just part of what they know."

Luis nodded. "Hao has seven or eight Chinese nationals there with him. They coordinate intelligence on the other cartels and on what the American and Mexican border authorities are doing. He told me that all of them are former military and well trained."

"We got that from the intercepted phone call," said David Lopez. "Are they also responsible for the misinformation campaign?"

"I don't think so. Hao has mentioned that there are some Chinese students in Mexican universities that he can call on."

"If we wanted to meet with Juan's soldiers, to give them the choice of prison or a new life, who should we be talking to?" asked Gina.

"Probably Juan's right arm here in the south, a man called Paco," replied Luis, "but I've been trying to reach him all afternoon. He may have been killed in that shootout where you captured Juan."

"He's downstairs handcuffed to the strut of the helicopter," replied Diego, "I shared the small part of the transcript where you and Hao discussed possibly having to replace all of Juan's people. He interpreted that as a death threat. He has offered to help."

"I'd like to suggest that we postpone much of the minutia of this conversation until later," said Chad. "I've tangled with the Chinese before and keeping the lid on even what is happening here tonight will be impossible. If this Hao doesn't run the moment he is informed, his government is going to pin a target on his back. We need him in custody right away. Let's focus on how to make that happen."

CHAPTER 44

July 22, Puerto Peñasco, Mexico

There was barely room in the navy operations center for Pinky and Winston. The navy drone operator maneuvered the Triton high altitude drone above Hao's warehouse on the north end of the Sea of Cortez. The drone had arrived just in time to watch a group of men back a tractor-trailer into a channel off from the sea and recover a small submarine. The transport to the warehouse, along with other detail had been relayed to a Mexican CASA 295 transport on the way north. A second CASA coming from the gulf side of Mexico would rendezvous with the one from Manzanillo only minutes before they landed at the Puerto Peñasco airport.

The two transports touched down and within five minutes, thirty combat ready marines lined up in time to watch an American C-130 transport land and discharge three Humvees before departing to the north. Twenty marines loaded their gear along with captured Chinese rockets into the Humvees and departed the airport. Ten minutes behind them, two helicopters that had flown from bases on the Pacific across the Baja Peninsula touched down and began refueling from dozens of jugs carried in the Mexican transports. To the east, the first tiny traces of morning began to erase the dark.

Diego checked his cell phone, 'no signal available.' Ashley had taken the local cell phones off the air. Diego nodded at Chad. "She's really good," he observed.

Ten minutes later the last of the marines were airborne for the short flight to the warehouse complex. Exactly forty minutes after the first transport had touched down, the cell phones miraculously began working again.

The helicopters buzzed the Humvees only moments before they spread out across a large parking area and began to discharge the marines who took cover behind piles of supplies and parked vehicles. The helicopters landed behind the complex which included the main warehouse, a second small office building and what looked from the air like two small dormitories. Ten of the marines raced for cover as the pilots moved the helicopters toward a small hill a mile away. Diego called the number for Hao that had been recovered from Ayala's cell phone. "Hao Sun, my name is Diego Cervantes, and I am the commander of the marines that have your compound surrounded. If you and those with you open the front doors to the warehouse and surrender yourselves, there will be no bloodshed."

The answer was a burst of rifle fire from a half dozen windows on the sides of the warehouse. The marines returned fire. Additional fire erupted from the dormitories.

"Damn," said Diego," I'd hoped this might go easy." He looked over at Chad who was pointing out fire from the dorm windows. The four marines with Chad were returning fire, shredding the areas around four windows. There was no fire from the other two buildings.

Diego keyed his radio. "You are cleared to use the heavy weapons," he ordered.

The warehouse windows disintegrated as Chinese rockets ripped into the building. Two more rockets slashed through the warehouse's front doors and ignited some kind of fuel inside. The explosion blew the doors off the front of the building. From inside the firing stopped for several seconds before starting again, but only from two windows.

A rocket slashed out of the gaping warehouse door and destroyed one of the Humvees, killing the two marines hiding behind it. That rocket was answered by four more from the marines. Moments later three thirty caliber light machine guns began pouring fire into the warehouse.

To the right of the warehouse, one of the dormitories was on fire after two rockets blew through the light walls and ignited something inside.

To the rear of the warehouse, a garage sized door flew open, and a small pickup truck raced toward a well-worn dirt track. Fire from two men in the bed of the pickup raked the ground near where Diego and four marines fired into the building.

Diego watched one of his men slump forward only feet away, blood pouring from under his helmet. He was so focused on the wounded man that he missed the other three marines ripping the racing truck with bullets, leaving it half buried in a sand berm where it flipped after the driver died. Three other Chinese men died in that truck. A fifth lay bleeding where he'd been thrown as the truck flipped. He was in obvious pain, but since none of the marines spoke Mandarin, all they could do is carry him to the triage area and secure his hands and feet. Unlike the others, this man wore slacks and a tailored white shirt.

The firefight was over in less than five minutes. Upon entering the warehouse, the marines found eight dead men and two badly wounded. All but two were Chinese. Perhaps Paco's call to his northern counterpart suggesting that he move his people away from the warehouse only a couple of hours before had worked. Paco told his northern counterpart that he suspected that the Chinese might have something to do with Juan's death, and that he no longer trusted them.

Diego led two of his men into the burning dormitory. They found four more dead and two wounded. In the upper room, overlooking the Sea of Cortez they found a man who didn't match the picture of Hao that Francesca had taken. He was still holding Hao's cell phone. He'd been hit at least three times before collapsing on one of the bunks, a partially made call on the phone in his hand, an empty assault rifle on the ground next to the window. Diego carried his body from the burning building and laid him next to where a medic was treating the wounded.

Diego was helping search the second dorm when his cell phone rang. "Diego, I'm in the office building," said Chad. "This place looks like a showcase for high tech. There are five computers and a bank of monitors and at least two radio systems. All of this is in Chinese so I'm not going to touch anything. I don't want to trigger any self-destruct programming. But my bet is that there is a complete record of everything that has happened up here. We'll need to get some help, people with a lot more knowledge on this stuff than me. Maybe call in Pinky and her team from LA."

"Let me tell you what we just found in the second dorm," replied Diego. "There are five Chinese men in a small bedroom in the back of the building. One of them just asked me what all the shooting was about. He wanted to know if we were there to lead him across the border. These guys all look military. We're securing them now and I will leave two of my men here to guard them."

Six hours later the warehouse complex looked like a small city. Leadership from the local police, the federales, the navy and a half dozen other agencies had descended on the facility. At Chad's request a private plane would drop Pinky, Ashley, and Winston at the closest airport late that night. Gina Santos was sending data experts from the attorney general's office to work with them. Until they arrived, Diego had placed two of his marines at the office entrance and was not allowing anyone inside.

"I don't get it," said Chad as he and Diego wrapped up briefing the Mexican authorities who had descended on them after the shooting stopped.

"Don't get what?" asked Diego.

"The phone intercepts indicated that Hao would be here. We got his cell phone. He'd passed it to someone else." Chad leaned against one of the Humvees as one of the helicopters lifted off carrying wounded to the hospital. "We knew he was here. His voice was traced to a cell tower in Puerto Peñasco. Where the hell did he go?"

"Was he tipped off that we were on the way? added Diego. Maybe the injured man we pulled from the truck wreck can give us some answers."

"He's scheduled to go out on the next helicopter lift," said Chad. "I'll take care of that."

Chad walked over to where the marine medic was trying to keep the last two wounded men comfortable. "Do you speak English?" he asked.

The medic nodded his head. "How badly hurt is the man from that truck wreck?" asked Chad.

"Broken arm, shoulder, but I don't believe he has any internal injuries."

"Good, I want you to give him whatever it takes to make him comfortable and then move him up to that office building. He's not to be evacuated until either Diego or I approve it. Make sure he is well guarded. We'll have an interpreter here by morning so we can get some answers."

Chad looked up as an argument broke out between the top federal policeman on site and the navy commander who had coordinated the helicopters from a base on the Pacific. Walking back to where Diego sat on the front fender of a Humvee, he watched him smile.

"Now the battle really begins," said Diego. "Who is going to get credit for this raid and who will have custody of the prisoners?"

"With the exception of the office and the one wounded man who might give us some answers, I don't give a damn," replied Chad. "You and the navy people who put this together should get credit, but maybe it's best if your picture isn't all over the television."

The next couple of hours was spent documenting the scene. Like the warehouse near Acapulco, this one was set up to service the submarines carrying drugs from southern Mexico. But it was also some kind of information center and the hanger for not one, but two Chinese-made recon and attack drones, including crates of rockets for the drones.

"If someone tipped off Hao," offered Chad, "he didn't spread the word. If these guys had been ready for us, this could have been a bloodbath."

Diego pointed to one of his Humvees just pulling into the parking area. "Maybe your people from LA can help sort this out."

The two men walked over to where Ashley, Pinky and Winston emerged from the vehicle. "Thank you all for coming," said Chad. "I'm sure you're damned tired, but before you get any rest, we need help trying to find where the mastermind of this whole operation is." He turned to Ashley. "You traced Hao's cell phone here, and we know it was him on the recorded conversation. But he was gone when we hit this place."

The three techies stood staring at the carnage around them. Vehicles and buildings were blasted apart. One building had burned to the ground. Emergency lighting that had been set up across the entire complex revealed pools of dried blood. Finally, Pinky responded. "When you just sit in a nice office and mine data, what you guys in the field do seems romantic, you know, exciting. We're always jealous of how much fun you guys are having. But I for one, will never think that way again." She physically shivered before asking, "what can we do?"

"First, we need Winston to interview a wounded Chinese man. We need to know if Hao was tipped off and where he is now."

Ten minutes later, Winston came out of the offices where the wounded man had been moved. "That man ran the data center for Hao. He didn't think Hao had been tipped off. Evidently there is a huge stash of US dollars somewhere and Hao headed back south to make sure that some guy named Paco was getting it packed to be shipped out of the country. He accidently forgot his cell phone when he left."

"How is he traveling?" asked Diego.

"That man says one of Hao's partners owns a flying service. He flew out of Puerto Peñasco late yesterday. Now all the wounded man wants is a doctor and to go home to Shandong. I need to call Gina Santos in the capital. I suspect that wounded Chinese man isn't going home for a long time."

Chad made a call on his cell phone. A sleepy voice answered. He listened for the first few minutes of the call. "Thad, this went like clockwork. The bad guys put up a fight, and Diego's men killed about sixteen, most of them Chinese. He lost three of his marines, but that's not why I called. That Paco guy we are holding evidently is the key processor for smuggling money out of the country. We believe that Hao is on his way back your direction to make sure that a large stash of cash gets out of the country. We don't believe that he knows about the raid yet." Chad paused a moment. "Winston is transcribing all the phone numbers in a cell phone we found here. I'm going to send the phone numbers from China to Ma. This looks like a Chinese operation. Maybe he can help clean up this mess on his end."

"I'll take a run at this Paco guy," offered Walker. "He is being held in the stockade in Manzanillo."

CHAPTER 45

July 24, Manzanillo, Mexico

THAD, OLGA AND Sonia arrived in Manzanillo by police escort. The federal officers were blocked at the navy base gate by military policemen on the orders of Captain Ramón Acuña who welcomed the three. Five minutes later they were in a conference room where a shackled Paco sat, his head covered with a cloth bag.

"Before we start our conversation with this man who, depending on his answers this evening, may spend the rest of his life in jail, I thought we should watch the president's press conference. She is furious over what we found up north."

Thad pointed at Paco. "Maybe we should let our guest see how much trouble he's in."

Acuna motioned for one of the military policemen in the back of the room to remove the bag while Acuna switched on the sixty-inch screen on the front wall.

They missed the first few words of President Martinez's speech, but only a few. "At a facility just outside of Puerto

Peñasco," she said. "There, our marines fought their way into a compound primarily staffed by Chinese nationals. About twenty died in the firefight, including three marine corps sons and four other Mexican citizens who were working for the Chinese. Inside the facility our authorities found a sophisticated intelligence operation that not only tracked what the Americans are doing to protect their border, but massive files on the Mexican government that on the surface have nothing to do with smuggling."

President Martinez paused to sip from a plastic water bottle before continuing. "This operation was smuggling not only drugs across our northern border, but also Chinese nationals, all young men of military age. At the compound, most of those killed were foreigners of the same age, trained to use sophisticated Chinese manufactured weapons, the same kind of weapons used not long ago to destroy one of our navy ships and shoot down an American helicopter that came to their aid."

"She's using the water sips to control her fury," offered Sonia.

"Records found indicate that more than two hundred Mexican nationals are involved in what they probably thought was a simple smuggling operation. We have their names, and in the last few days, several have died fighting for a foreign power that we now believe is trying to overthrow this government. Between the seizure of the warehouse near Acapulco and the one taken last night, our navy has seized more than four tons of sophisticated weaponry sent illegally into our country by the Chinese."

She stopped to point at a man in the back of the room, and the camera's swung to focus on him. "This man, Ambassador Yuze Zhang of The Peoples Republic of China, was nice enough to rush from his home for a morning briefing on what we found. Unfortunately, he didn't arrive before this press conference started. So, he is learning about all of this at the same time as the people of

Mexico. Mr. Ambassador, you have seen enough to recognize how serious this is. I expect a full report from you and your country's leadership. Our future relationship, if any, with your nation will depend on what we hear. You have five days to fulfill this request before we break off all diplomatic relations and move to begin seizing Chinese-owned assets in Mexico. We justify that move by pointing out that it may be impossible to sort out legitimate investments from those that are part of this plot. One of your country's investment advisors, a Mr. Hao Sun appears to be the Mexican coordinator of this enterprise, an operation that my advisors tell me must include a significant group of influential Chinese citizens or the government of China itself."

President Martinez sipped more water before closing. "I will assure the people of Mexico that we will keep you posted on this plot as new information becomes available. Let me close with this message to those Mexican citizens who were part of this enterprise, people working for Hao directly or his Mexican partner, a Juan Ayala, who was killed last week in an operation to free several kidnapped women. If you come forward and volunteer help in cleaning up this mess, the government of Mexico will be grateful. I suspect that will be important to your future and that of your families. Thank you."

Walker looked over at Ramón. "Let's begin our discussion with Paco here by unshackling him and bringing him some black coffee since I doubt that he has been sleeping well. Captain Acuna, we don't want to disrupt your conversations with the prisoner, especially now that we know his crimes may include insurrection, but if you would interpret for me, there are two questions that we need answered immediately."

Ramón took a seat where he could whisper in Paco's ear, leaving Thad speaking loud enough to be heard from the far side of the huge table.

"We were told by a Chinese national wounded and captured last night that Hao is probably down here somewhere assuring that a large supply of American cash is being spirited out of Mexico. I'm sure that you, like most of the two hundred Mexican citizens that the President referred to were duped, that you did not know that you were a plot to take over Mexico. The authorities would appreciate knowing where they might find this Hao guy. I'm sure you know how important it is for you to help them."

The interrogation of Paco began slowly. Acuna's clear comparison, life in prison, or consideration before the courts, or maybe even a presidential pardon, got Paco talking.

Three hours later, Acuna and the Americans huddled outside the building. "You need to seize that warehouse down by Ixtapa and go through it thoroughly. If Paco is telling the truth, it is the primary packaging point for illegal cash moving to Chinese banks. You need to figure out if that nitrogen fertilizer plant is part of this, or only a supplier who is being used by the cartel."

"There are four of Diego's marines still in Zihua," replied Acuna. "They will take that facility this afternoon. But for now, we need to look at that Chinese ship, the Jai Mew. It's only a mile from here. If she is docked in Mexico, she is under the authority of the harbormaster."

Fifteen minutes later, Acuna and the four Americans stood watching as the ship, already out in the harbor, turned for the open ocean and picked up speed. On the dock, some Mexican longshoremen stood arguing with several Chinese men.

"Our guys are furious that the Chinese are doing work that their labor contract says is reserved for the local union," said Acuna. "They rushed down here when the harbormaster called telling them that some Chinese guys were helping the Jai Mew get under way. They left more than twenty empty containers on the dock in their haste to depart."

"Can you stop that ship?" asked Olga.

"No, we can use airpower to sink her, but we have no way to stop her," said Ramón.

The four headed back to the green Ford parked behind a huge stack of containers.

Thad's phone rang as they were getting into the car. "Thad, it's Gritt. I just got a call from Ma in China. I called him last night with the Chinese phone numbers we recovered from Hao's phone. He was already researching the name Hao."

"We still don't know where Hao is," said Thad. "We just tried to stop a Chinese ship from departing Manzanillo. We think it is carrying a pile of illegal dollars."

"That would be the Jai Mew," said Chad. "You can quit looking for Hao. He's aboard that ship. It appears that this Hao guy is a PLA-3 intelligence officer who went off the reservation. He was ordered back to China by Ma's boss; your old friend General Ling. Ma found the owner of the Jai Mew and the ship was ordered to take Hao on board and to get out of Mexico immediately."

"So, now what do we do to wrap up this mess?" said Thad.

"Ma wants this cleaned up as quietly as possible. It will be a Chinese-American-Mexican operation."

"What the hell does that mean?" asked Thad.

"The Jai Mew will pass the Hawaiian Islands in about four days," said Chad. The Chinese authorities would like American help putting four investigators aboard the ship when it passes. That will give them four or five days alone with Hao to get the rest of the story."

Thad covered his phone to brief the others in the car. He watched Ramón turn red.

"I don't think that is going to satisfy the Mexican government," said Thad. "I'm with Ramón now and they are looking for a pound of flesh."

"Ma made it clear that they will deal with their side of this mess," said Chad. "Ask Ramón if instead of a pound of flesh, the Mexican government will be satisfied with literally tons of US dollars and an invitation for their diplomats to monitor the trials of those Chinese responsible for all of this."

He paused. "They will also be invited to view his body before it's cremated. Mai read me a press release from the People's Liberation Army. It reports that one of their affairs, a Hao Sun has disappeared on a diplomatic trip to Latin America."

"What do you mean, tons of dollars?" asked Walker.

"Apparently the ship's owner was forcefully interrogated yesterday. He divulged that a Chinese bank was created just to open a Mexican subsidiary. There are literally billions of dollars held there for the Mexican partners. There are billions more stashed which were going to be used to not only screw with the Mexican government, but to influence the Chinese government. Ma says that his boss, General Ling watched the Mexican president's news conference live, and while he will not make the final decision, he believes that China will make President Martinez an offer to move the entire amount into a trust for the benefit of Mexico. He also suggests that the story be sanitized so that both the Mexican and the Chinese government can save face. He requested that you ask the Mexican government for their help in containing this. He implied that there was, perhaps as much as ten million dollars stashed in a safe house in Mexico that could be used to keep the Mexicans working for this group quiet." There was a pause. "Hey, Thad, I've got to go, the plane is waiting for me. Tell Olga that I will see her tonight."

Thad smiled at Acuna who was still furious. "Perhaps the plane that brought you here from the capital is still available. As incredible as it seems, the Chinese government has asked for America's help cleaning his up. I believe that I was just authorized to discuss an offer that Mexico should consider. You and I should go discuss it with your government in person."

He turned to Sonia and Olga in the back seat. "I'll try to make it back by this evening. Chad and Diego will be home. See if you can set up a private dinner for the six of us this evening. It's time to celebrate. The next week of our vacation will be courtesy of the Chinese government. They don't know that yet, but I'm sure after the last 24 hours they recognize that we all need some time away. Oh, and call Pinky, Winston, and Ashley and tell them to pick a hotel there in Puerto Peñasco and to take a week off on us.

CHAPTER 46

July 30, Mexico City, Mexico

THE PRESS CONFERENCE began a little after eleven. President Martinez stood at a podium on a stage hastily erected in front of the grand pyramid at the Aztec ruins of Teotihuacan just outside the city. On stage with her was the Ambassador Yuze Zhang from China along with the attorney general and the commander of naval intelligence of Mexico. Seated just below the stage were Diego, Ramón, and Gina and just to their right, Francesca and Maria Castillo.

The first fifteen minutes of the speech were dedicated to a complete, yet sanitized summary of the events of the last week. "I want to take a minute to ask three dedicated Mexican patriots to stand and be recognized," said the president. Lieutenant Diego Cervantes of the marine corps, Deputy Attorney General Gina Santos and Captain Ramón Acuna of Naval Intelligence, we the people of Mexico want to thank you for leading a small task force that destroyed this cancer in our country. The Chinese government is also pleased that you help root out a rot in that country and after this meeting, the ambassador would like to meet each of you to express his county's gratitude."

"Now to the primary reason for this conference. Maria Castillo, will you please join me on the stage."

Maria hadn't talked to Martinez since the plot had first been discovered. Her nervousness showed in her shaking legs as she mounted the stairs.

"Mexico does not know that Maria was one of the first people to discover the plot against our country. Her perception was that all was not right. Maria helped Gina, Diego and Ramón. We all know her for her good deeds in Mexico. And in my personal conversations with her, only financial constraints hold her back from doing even more. With that said, I would like to announce that the Chinese government has recovered just over fifty billion US dollars that the leaders of this operation and their Mexican allies took from our economy. They are placing it in an investment account with the proceeds to be used to make Mexico a better place for its citizens." She turned to Maria. "If you would accept, and dedicate your life to helping Mexico, I would like to designate the Castillo Foundation as the recipient of that largess. That would amount to about twenty-seven billion pesos a year for your work."

At the same time, Olga and Chad were just sitting down for a late breakfast with Thad and Sonia. All four had finished their morning swim, rinsed, and given themselves an hour in beach chairs to dry a bit. The waitress in the Del Sur beachfront restaurant had just delivered four mimosas to the table.

"A toast," offered Sonia, "to the four of us and the dozen other people who helped unravel this case. I'm told that China has committed to crack down on fentanyl shipments, and that the US government has greased a path to citizenship for Francesca's sister. But more than either of those things, I toast to four days of doing nothing in a beautiful place." She reached over and squeezed Walker's hand and watched as Olga ran her fingers down the side of Chad's face.

Read the next book in the Team Walker Series,

THE DIAMOND:

First Contact

AUTHOR'S NOTES AND ACKNOWLEDGEMENTS

This book began as historical research for my earlier novel, TWO CIVIL WARS. That story's origin came from doing political research for a client more than three decades ago. I was surprised to find that during the Mexican Civil War (1858-1861) and America's War Between the States (1861-1865), Abraham Lincoln tipped the scales in favor of Benito Juarez and his battle against Mexico's large landowners, the Catholic Church and

European meddling in Mexican affairs. Without Lincoln's help, Mexico's Civil War might have been even longer and bloodier, but it might also have forced a compromise settlement that many feel eludes Mexico today.

That got me interested in how the Mexican people view Lincoln's actions. I was shocked to find that almost no one I knew in Mexico was aware that Lincoln had provided the weapons that allowed Juarez to field a modern army. When asking about it, I repeatedly heard that the Juarez legacy was one of fierce Mexican independence. It appears that Mexican history ignores the involvement of other nations, choosing to focus on the will of the Mexican people. Bad or good, that seems to be how the people of Mexico view themselves. That spiked my curiosity on China's current massive interest in Mexico. From banking and manufacturing to the drug trade, where much of the inventory comes from China including ninety percent of the fentanyl and weapons for the gangs. In conversations with Mexican friends, many feel that Mexico has little to worry about; even the illegal activity is firmly in control of Mexican gangs. But not all Mexicans feel that. Some are worried. Are the cartels dictating to the Chinese, or is it the other way around?

Carmen and I love Mexico. We travel there every winter to take a break from Alaska's cold winters. Over the last several trips I've continued my research and had many rich conversations. Like in history, Mexico's citizens don't see the Chinese meddling or don't talk about it. This book started long before the election of Mexico's first female president. Mexico has a long tradition of supporting intellectuals and leftist politics. It's part of the culture, and is consistent with Benito Juarez's teachings about unconstrained democracy and caring as a roadmap to peace. But like what happened in the 1850s when Mexico found itself at odds with the monarchies of Europe, China is not a democracy.

And China uses their financial muscle to get what the Chinese Communist Party (CCP) wants.

My first acknowledgement for this book, goes to the resilient, rebellious, strong people of Mexico. As always, my appreciation goes to Carmen for her unwavering support and work on the parts of my writing career that I'm not good at. I also acknowledge my publicist, BTS Designs for introducing me to many of the extraordinary writers who I've learned from and for their tireless energy in promoting the books of Rodger Carlyle. The fans who have generously given their time as Advanced Reader Copy readers made this book much better than if it was my work alone. As always, thank you to Damon Freeman and his talented team at Damonza who do incredible work on my book covers and interior design. But my greatest appreciation is to you, the readers who make this all possible.

www.rodgercarlyle.com
Goodreads author Rodger Carlyle
Amazon author Rodger Carlyle